COLLECTED PLAYS FOR TELEVISION

By the same author

THE PARTY

COMEDIANS

OCCUPATIONS

FATHERLAND

REAL DREAMS

This volume contains only original single plays. Other works for television by Trevor Griffiths include:

BILL BRAND

SONS AND LOVERS

THE LAST PLACE ON EARTH

Trevor Griffiths

Collected Plays For Television

All Good Men

Absolute Beginners

Through the Night

Such Impossibilities

Country: 'A Tory Story'

Oi for England

With an Introduction by
Edward Braun

ff
faber and faber
LONDON · BOSTON

First published in 1988
by Faber and Faber Limited
3 Queen Square London WC1N 3AU

Photoset by Parker Typesetting Service Leicester
Printed in Great Britain by
Cox and Wyman Ltd Reading Berkshire

British Library Cataloguing in Publication Data

Griffiths, Trevor, *1935–*
TV plays.
Vol. 1
I. Title
822'.914

ISBN 0-571-15168-X

CONTENTS

INTRODUCTION

Edward Braun

Early in 1972 Trevor Griffiths at the age of thirty-seven was gaining increasing recognition in the theatre. *Occupations*, his play about Gramsci and the Turin factories occupation of 1920, had recently provoked much attention and debate when Buzz Goodbody had directed it for the RSC at The Place. *Sam, Sam*, completed a year before *Occupations* in 1969, had just opened at the Open Space Theatre, directed by Charles Marowitz. In the previous three years there had been seven productions of his plays and Kenneth Tynan, Literary Manager at the National Theatre, had commissioned a new work from him. Yet even at this stage of his career Griffiths's preference was clear, as he stated in an interview:

> . . . I'm very pessimistic about theatre. I don't see it as in any way a major form of communicating descriptions or analyses or modifying attitudes. The way I feel about theatre is, I think, the way Russell felt about philosophy. When he was finally challenged to justify spending a lifetime doing philosophy, he said, 'Well it's no fucking use, but it's tremendous fun, it gives me the greatest pleasure.' . . . It's in television that I think, as a political writer, I want to be, because very large numbers of people, who are not accessible any other way, *are* accessible in television.[1]

Sixteen years on, Griffiths has remained true to this conviction. By 1988 he had still completed only five full-length plays for the theatre (three of them revived repeatedly) compared with a transmitted television output of four series (a total of thirty-nine episodes), five single plays and a number of adaptations. To these can be added two radio plays, two films and three as yet unmade screenplays.[2]

Unlike the majority of young writers who are recruited by television from the theatre, Griffiths worked initially in television, joining BBC Leeds in 1965 as a Further Education Officer after eight years spent teaching. As well as gaining a wide understanding of the structures of control in broadcasting, he began to write for the theatre, radio and television. In 1971-2, his final year at the BBC, he wrote fifteen half-hour parts for the Granada Television series, *Adam Smith*, using the pseudonym 'Ben Rae' to evade the BBC rule forbidding work for a rival company. *Adam Smith* was instructive for Griffiths in demonstrating the constraints under which the television writer is forced to operate:

> . . . I had no automatic right of entry into the production process and I found that many ideological insertions were being made from producers, directors and actors. So that I felt like somebody making wallpaper. I hated that but it taught me a very important lesson, which is that television is very powerful, not just as a medium of communications but as an institution, an establishment, a set of practices and relationships. I learnt that that power had to be tackled if a writer was going to do anything.[3]

In tackling that power, Griffiths was soon to grasp a further truth: namely, that as a consequence of their very size and complexity television systems possess an inherent 'leakiness', there to be exploited 'so as to speak intimately and openly, with whatever seriousness and relevance one can generate, to (though it must in time be *with*) the many millions of cohabitants of one's society who share part of a language, part of a culture, part of a history, with oneself . . .'

Just such an opportunity had presented itself soon after the original Manchester Stables Theatre production of *Occupations* in October 1970 when Griffiths was invited to contribute a play to the projected BBC series *The Edwardians*. Anticipating yet another exercise in lavish nostalgia in the manner of *The Forsyte Saga*, *Edward VII* and the newly launched *Upstairs, Downstairs*, he chose as a corrective to the series the figure of the labour leader, Tom Mann, and his leadership of the triumphant Liverpool dock strike of 1911. In the same way that, implicitly, *Occupations* had been as much concerned with the questions of revolutionary leadership thrown up by the events of 1968 as with the role of the Comintern in Italy and elsewhere in the 1920s, so *Such Impossibilities* now addressed itself equally to the mood of industrial militancy in Britain in the early 1970s. As Griffiths was completing the script in January 1972 the National Union of Mineworkers rejected a Coal Board pay offer and began a strike that lasted for almost two months. It was the first major test of the new Industrial Relations Act, and thanks to brilliant organization and the solidarity of other unions, the miners' action forced an inquiry that led to a pay award three times the size of the original Coal Board offer. It was the first major test of the new repressive Industrial Relations Act and the outcome was a humiliating defeat for Edward Heath and the Tory Government from which they never recovered. At that time, the play's concluding quotation from Tom Mann seemed not so very distant from the current industrial reality: 'Political and industrial action must at all times be inspired by revolutionary principles. That is, the aim must ever be to change from capitalism to socialism as speedily as possible. Anything less than this means continued domination by the capitalist class.' (p.232.)

With its vivid portrayal of the central figure and the rapid unfolding of the strike's drama against the Liverpool background, *Such Impossibilities* gives promise of compelling television. However, there are no more than fleeting intimations of Tom Mann the *private* individual (as in the final scene with his wife, Ellen) and none of the uncomfortable contradictions found in *Occupations* and all the later works. Nevertheless, the text does succeed in achieving Griffiths' main objective: 'to restore, however tinily, an important but suppressed area of our collective history, to enlarge our "usable past" and connect it with a lived present, and to celebrate a victory.' (p.181.)

Unfortunately this objective was denied the chance of realization. Having accepted Griffiths' detailed outline, the producer Mark Shivas had misgivings over the completed script and wanted to discuss alterations. Griffiths refused and Shivas rejected the text altogether, claiming that the already overstretched series budget could not cover the large cast and extensive use of filmed locations that it demanded. Griffiths remained suspicious of Shivas's motives, arguing:

> ... it's at least as likely that the play offered too brutal and too overtly political a contrast with the remainder of the series, which included ... pieces on E. Nesbit, the Countess of Warwick, Marie Lloyd, Baden-Powell, Conan Doyle, Horatio Bottomley, Rolls-Royce and Lloyd George. Tom Mann might well have roughed up the series a bit, but it's arguable he might also have done something towards redressing its balance. (p.181.)

Shivas has since argued that Griffiths was wrong to write off *The Edwardians* as politically innocuous,[4] but without question nothing else in the series grasped the opportunity 'to connect with a lived present' as *Such Impossibilities* did.

When Griffiths was commissioned by Kenneth Tynan in 1971 to write a play for the National Theatre his intention was to base it on the Kronstadt Rising of the Red Fleet in 1921. What finally emerged was *The Party*, set in London in 1968 against the background of the May events in Paris. John Dexter's production, with Lord Olivier in the role of the veteran Trotskyite, John Tagg, eventually had its première at the Old Vic in December 1973. In the original version (rewritten by Griffiths for a touring production directed by David Hare in 1974) the play was unwieldy in structure, extravagantly designed by John Napier, and overloaded with a range of merely emblematic minor characters. Even so, like *Occupations*, it demonstrated the dramatic power of complex political debate in which one side is pitted against the other with equal conviction, challenging the spectators to form their own synthesis from the dialectic presented. Reviewing the production in *The Guardian*, Michael Billington wrote: 'In the modern theatre we have lost the simple art of listening; and if Griffiths does nothing else, he at least obliges his audience to concentrate with the same intensity you find in the Festival Hall.'[5] The dialectical form of *The Party* had been adumbrated by Griffiths both in *Sam, Sam* (1969), in the characters of the two brothers, and in *Occupations*, with Gramsci, the passionate advocate of comradely love, forced by the failure of the Italian factory occupations in 1920 to concede the necessity for ruthless organization exemplified by the Comintern agent, Kabak. The danger with both these plays is that the audience may see the two characters as representing an either/or choice, whereas in *The Party* the clear invitation is to pursue the argument further in one's own mind. Here, as elsewhere, Griffiths refuses to fake a conclusion that would not stand scrutiny in the harsh light of political reality beyond the theatre.

This has remained a fundamental principle of his work. As he said in an interview in 1976: 'I'll probably never complete a play in the formal sense. It has to be open at the end; people have to make choices, because if you're not making choices, you're not actually living.'[6] In the summer of 1973 Griffiths was suddenly invited by Ann Scott, the script editor of BBC's *Play for Today*, to write a 75-minute play to replace another that she had commissioned for the series but then rejected. The production budget was extremely limited, permitting no more than a multi-room studio set, no filmed inserts, and a maximum of five characters. Furthermore, the script had to be delivered in six weeks. Even so, Griffiths found the offer irresistible; the opportunity of a platform to speak to the large audience regularly commanded by *Play for Today* overruled any reservations that he might have had about writing to order. Also, having recently read the reissued and updated edition of Ralph Miliband's *Parliamentary Socialism*, he was already contemplating a dramatic treatment of the theme of traditional Labourism.

What followed went far beyond the common experience of the tyranny of television schedules. In January 1974 Britain was in deep crisis. For three months the National Union of Mineworkers had sustained a ban on overtime in pursuit of a pay claim that would destroy the Conservative Government's incomes policy. The Prime Minister, Edward Heath, was forced to introduce legislation restricting the supply of electricity to industry to only three days a week, and among other emergency measures television was required to observe a daily 10.30 p.m. curfew. In consequence, the text of *All Good Men* had to be cut from 75 minutes (roughly the published version) to 63 minutes, losing the greater part of the opening scene. The sacrifice was considerable, but it was more than outweighed by the added relevance to current political and industrial events that the play's central conflict now acquired.

In the winter of 1973–4 the TUC leadership, while not actually opposing the miners, pursued its customary policy of conciliation with the Government. It distanced itself from what many miners clearly wanted: not merely a dispute about wages but a confrontation that would immobilize the country and bring down the Government. Within the NUM itself a member of the Executive attacked 'communists within the Union who are making an open attempt to wreck democracy',[7] and there was open conflict between the Union's right-wing president, Joe Gormley, and the communist vice-president, Mick McGahey. While McGahey maintained publicly that the miners' action was a wages struggle and not politically motivated, there was little doubt as to his real objectives – and with good reason. At that time the industrial climate in Britain remained one of organized militancy. The miners' strike of 1972 had been just one of a series of major victories for organized labour since the Heath Government had come to power in 1970. Some years later Raymond Williams recalled:

The whole series of battles up to the climax of the miners' strike of 1973–4 was a return to real class politics. The re-emergence of genuine socialist militancy on a massive scale under a Conservative Government seemed to me to confirm my assessment of the Labour Party: once its manipulation of class forces to avoid any actual class *battles* no longer held, the situation became much more dynamic and explosive.[8]

So what of the Labour Party in January 1974? While the leadership remained predominantly right-wing and concerned only with the humane management of capitalism, the Party's rank-and-file was organizing itself and moving decisively to the Left. In the policy document *Labour's Programme for Britain*, adopted by the 1973 Annual Conference the Party's proclaimed aim was 'to bring about a fundamental and irreversible shift in the balance of power and wealth in favour of working people and their families'. Whether Labour in goverment would honour that pledge was another question. It was a question to be answered soon enough: the miners voted overwhelmingly for all-out strike and Heath was forced to call an election. On 28 February the Tories were defeated and Labour returned, albeit with no overall majority – the miners had brought down the Government and Labour was to remain in power until 1979, when Margaret Thatcher became Prime Minister. It was around 1973 that the bitter conflict that still divides Left and Right in the British Labour movement had its beginnings, though its real roots extend back much further. It is this conflict, between parliamentary Labourism and radical extra-parliamentary socialism that is central to the conflict of individuals in *All Good Men*.

The conflict between 'Lord Waite' and his left-wing graduate son, William, is as much about the pursuit of socialism in the 1970s as it is about the TUC's betrayal of the General Strike in 1926 and Labour's record in office since it first gained power in 1924. In the production the parallels were cunningly emphasized in Bill Fraser's portrayal of Edward Waite, his impatient rhetoric a shade too well practised to be entirely convincing and subtly undercut by inflexions and mannerisms suggestive of figures in the Labour establishment, and in particular the tellingly deployed pipe of the party leader, Harold Wilson.

Already in the theatre with both *Occupations* and *The Party* Griffiths had demonstrated his confidence in the capacity of sophisticated ideological debate for holding an audience. Now he did the same with the birthday party confrontation of *All Good Men*, while taking care to invest the situation with a more personal dramatic tension. Firstly, we have seen Edward Waite a few days earlier suffer a mild heart attack, so we are aware he may now be in danger of collapse; secondly, William is no chance left-wing adversary, but his own son, and a reflection of the young working-class idealist that perhaps he himself once was. Much of William's resentment towards his father springs from the fact that he has been given the chances Waite never had: early in his life, the family had moved from a dingy little house in his Beswick constituency in Manchester to suburban Didsbury – 'four bedrooms, attics, cellars, gardens, playschools, parks . . .' – and later to his present sequestered property in Surrey, where the worst problem is the squirrels attacking the yew trees. William is objecting both to his own and to his father's deracination, and by analogy to the Labour Party leadership's loss of touch with true working-class origins and aspirations.

At the play's conclusion the shot of Waite in his baronet's robes, washed out like a pallid waxwork, seems an image of the shabby pragmatism of Labour in office; yet the alternative offered by William of high-minded revolutionary zeal has about it a dogmatic certitude that is no closer to working-class humanity, and in any case is compromised by his dubious alliance with the television presenter, Massingham. Through Massingham, with his claim to be 'simply the film camera, the tape-recorder, the lighting man . . .', Griffiths contrives to expose the subterfuges of documentary television, indicating that it is no less slanted, manipulative, selective than the most 'unfair' drama. Here, as in his other 'history' plays and films (which in a sense describes nearly all of them), Griffiths shows that there is little separating the work of the historian from the work of the dramatist.* The only real difference is that dramatists tend to be more frank about their intentions, and the audience is allowed more space to exercise its judgement.

The critic John Bull writes:

> One of the obvious attractions of television for Griffiths is the potential that it affords for a more pressing version of the dialectic. Unlike theatre, television can be easily utilized to present a multiplicity of viewpoints, so that a viewer is not looking in on the total event but is able to become involved to some extent with the experience and analysis of a number of differing characters. On stage, the writer, and indeed the actor and director, has at his disposal any number of ways of focusing on the individual – the power of rhetoric, the use of soliloquy, techniques of blocking, lighting effects, and so on – but no way of *enforcing* it in the way that film or television can. This is not just to speak of talking heads. Rather, it is its ability to present events from differing perspectives that is important.[9]

What more literal way of doing this is there than with a three-camera set-up in a television studio? *All Good Men* on the screen supports the argument. Given that the available resources were minimal, the director Michael Lindsay Hogg was content to work largely well within the prescribed limitations of studio production, relying on deeply concentrated performances by Bill Fraser, Jack Shepherd and Frances de la Tour as Maria, plus numerous significant reaction shots. Even the lengthy rhetoric becomes plausible, given that Waite has clearly held forth in similar terms to larger gatherings and William has evidently rehearsed what he intended

*Griffiths's original title for *All Good Men* was *History*.

to confront his father with. As Waite says to Massingham, 'It's been *created* in your honour.'

The language of the metaphors remains mostly verbal: the implicit parallel between the squirrels' gnawing the trees to death and Waite's gradual erosion through compromise; the reiterated (over-reiterated perhaps) reference to the fate of the North American Indians, betrayed, like the British working class, by their own people. The two conspicuous *visual* metaphors are the closing waxwork image of the robed Lord Waite and the rapid succession of jerky close-ups and echoing voice-overs from the past when accumulated guilt, triggered by his acceptance of a peerage, seems to bring on his heart attack. In this last instance alone, the production seemed to stretch the form to its breaking point, risking confusion for the viewer.

With little or no advance publicity, *All Good Men* drew an audience of about 5 million, which was small for *Play for Today*, though apparently the reaction index was highly favourable. One of the few critics to take notice was Dennis Potter, at that time television critic for the *New Statesman*. A dramatist totally different in style from Griffiths, Potter wrote:

> I prefer to see plays in which the 'ideas' are not exposed on the surface like basking sharks (or, in some cases, stranded cod) but arise with the insistence of discovery out of the fumbled yearnings, uncertain liaisons and perilous stratagems we usually make out of life ... But *All Good Men* almost overcomes its self-imposed schema. Griffiths clothed the debate with some of the sharpest, most telling and intelligent speeches ever heard on television.[10]

Griffiths himself has said: 'I like that play and I loved that production. I loved its stillness. It moved against the time of television and all these conventional prescriptions that you get about what television can handle and what it can't.'[11]

No less of a challenge was posed by Griffiths's next work, *Absolute Beginners*, described by him later as 'a play that is as dense and as difficult as anything that I've written'.[12] Presumably influenced by what had gone before in the series, the television critic of *Time Out* offered this advice: 'Do not be tempted to watch this Griffiths play, despite the fact that his last offering, about working-class betrayal during the General Strike by a Labour Life Peer to be, was a powerful political play. This is about Lenin, but in the nostalgic *Fall of Eagles* series. There are better things on BBC2.'[13]

While it is true that *Fall of Eagles* as a whole was little more than costume drama, a nostalgic grand tour in thirteen parts of the declining years of Europe's remaining autocratic dynasties, the episode that Griffiths was asked to contribute was seen in a very different light by Stuart Burge, who had become the series producer part-way through. 'I needed a demonstration somewhere in the series of what was happening in the undergrowth, in the revolutionary world', he recalled.[14] Griffiths leapt at the offer:

> Here was the opportunity to write a play about a very serious event in socialist and revolutionary history pretty well unimpeded, with a fair amount of resource, and – most important – lodged in a series which was going to be contemptibly popular. I mean, whatever Stuart did at this late stage, this was a series with one sugar-coating after another, and I sensed that to put a bitter pill inside that sugar-coating would actually get it swallowed, and tasted and used quite extensively.[15]

The outcome surpassed all expectations: as Griffiths gleefully recounts, *Fall of Eagles* was repeated twice by BBC and was sold to fifty-four countries, making it one of the half-dozen most popular series ever made by the Corporation, surpassing even the legendary *Forsyte Saga* (1967). The conflict presented to this mass audience offered no clear judgement or easy solution. Adhering closely to the recorded events of 1903 at the London Congress of the Russian

Social Democratic Party Congress, Griffiths contrasts the advocacy by Martov and Zasulich of a revolution determined by the ideals of human brotherhood with Lenin's ruthless insistence on a selfless vanguard leadership. This dichotomy is crystallized in the dispute over the reported conduct of Bauman. For Lenin, Bauman's value as an agent overrides all questions of personal morality. For Martov the two questions are indivisible:

> MARTOV: (*losing control*) You can't separate private from public like that, can't you see it, man? We are what we *do* . . . you, me, Bauman, all of us. Party morality is more than just loyalty to the party . . . it's the highest level of ethical consciousness yet afforded to the human species . . .
>
> LENIN: Metaphysics, Julius. Another time, perhaps, we may speculate. Just now we're trying to make the revolution *possible*. (*Silence.* MARTOV *disturbed, thrown, shivering a little, unused to being in conflict with* LENIN.) (pp.102 – 3.)

Yet it is essential to Griffiths' purpose that the action presents not simply the contrast *between* a 'hard' Lenin and a 'soft' Martov, but equally that the conflict should be seen *within* the individual. Political will needs to be reconciled with human instinct. His problem was that, apart from Lunacharsky's *Revolutionary Silhouettes* and Krupskaya's own memoirs of Lenin (written in the later hagiographic phase of Soviet history), there are few eye-witness accounts of the revolutionary leaders as *people*. As Griffiths puts it: 'None of them said much about Lenin's gut.'[16] So it was a matter of taking what scraps of anecdotal detail there were (such as Gorky's recollection of Lenin's wariness of the 'softening effect' of music) and fashioning them into dramatic incidents that served the play's argument.

Lenin's refusal to entertain the complaint against Bauman is one example; another is his delirious resistance to the agony of shingles, suggesting his determination to suppress all human frailty. Similarly, our first sight of him in the play is as he completes fifty press-ups before breakfast. Conversely, when first we see Martov, he is in impassioned debate with anarchists in a pub by the British Museum, and he is 'thin, smallish, bearded, untidy; papers and pamphlets bulge from his person'. Lenin, by contrast, is seen at this point against the background of the British Museum; 'He carries a roll of galleys under his left arm; stares sombrely at the entrance of the pub across the way.' In other words, Martov, for all his closeness to Lenin, is an émigré, 'dilettante, intellectual, unreliable'. He epitomizes the weaknesses that Lenin seeks to purge from the party organization. Similarly Georges Plekhanov is first encountered in his home in Geneva; his study is 'large, expensive, tastefully and expensively got out. Double doors join the next room. A view of mountains from the window. The room is full of books and "objects".' It is evident that he belongs to the theoretical past of Russian Marxism, but not to its revolutionary, activist future. The key contrasting image of Lenin is at the London Congress: at the crucial stage of the debate he is seen backed by an impassive circle of 'hard men'.

Yet the character is far from monolithic: As well as the attack of shingles there are moments of intimacy with Krupskaya, when she feeds him bread and milk on his sickbed, tentatively offers herself at night, and quietly defies him to console Zasulich. Then there is the final ironic impression after the awkward farewells have been exchanged by the conference delegates over Karl Marx's grave in Highgate: Lenin and Krupskaya 'turn, walk off towards the gate, two simple bourgeois on a Sunday morning stroll' – cutting abruptly to Tsar Nicholas shooting crows in the park at Tsarkoe Selo to the ominous opening bars of Shostakovich's Fourth Symphony. What comes across is perhaps more predetermined than Griffiths intends because one cannot help superimposing on the action what one knows of subsequent historical events. Also, the text suffered in clarity through being cut to fit a fifty-minute slot compared with the eighty plus of Griffiths's original version.* In particular, some depth

*The version published here is somewhere between the two.

is lost from the relationship between Krupskaya and Zasulich, from the portrayal of Bauman (and the justification for Lenin's retention of him), and above all from the depiction of Tsarist absolutism in the opening scenes, designed to motivate Lenin's ruthless aim of 'a party built like a fist, like a brain balled'.

Deprived of this early view of the barbarism and total lack of scruple in Nicholas's police state, the viewer is in danger of concluding that the London Congress was where Russian Communism lost its soul and set itself on the course that led to the terror of the 1930s. Nothing could be further from Griffiths's intentions: what he was seeking to pose was the classic dilemma of ends and means in terms of human as well as political behaviour.

Nor did he consent to compromise with the conventional demands of a popular series: there is no simplification of the inter-factional debate within the ranks of the Social Democrats, and indeed the viewer is as hard put as Martov himself to keep pace with Lenin's manoeuvres in the final stages. However, the broad lines of conflict are clear enough, and the personal tragedy of the courageous Zasulich deeply moving at the end. In an interview with *Theatre Quarterly* in 1976, Griffiths said:

> In TV one is up against the notion that the audience is soft-headed, that the material must be pre-digested and so on. I contest and contend that the whole time, and I won't have any script editors working on my work finding knotty and difficult bits, and cutting them off, and getting the thing down until it's a story and nothing else.[17]

Without doubt, *Absolute Beginners* suffered no such simplification, even though, due to time pressures, Griffiths himself had no part in the final edit. If anything, the cuts in the script make it *more* difficult to assimilate.

Far more serious damage was inflicted on *Occupations*, when it was transmitted by Granada in September 1974 and the two-hour theatre text was pruned to achieve a running time of 78 minutes. Griffiths was prepared to make the sacrifice in order to reach a wider audience but in this case much of the play's power and meaning were diminished, particularly in the scenes where the theatre auditorium becomes the factory in which Gramsci addresses the Turin workers.

In addition to having three plays produced on television in 1974, Griffiths completed the writing of two more: the first, *Comedians*, was staged by Richard Eyre at the Nottingham Playhouse on 20 February 1975, transferring subsequently to the National Theatre at the Old Vic, and the following year to Wyndham's Theatre;* the second was another television play, *Through the Night*, which had to wait a year before it was transmitted on BBC1.

Originally, *Through the Night* arose out of a commission from Granada for a play based on an experimental prison in Sheffield. Griffiths's interest in this subject was overtaken by his reaction to a diary that his wife, Jan, a social worker, had kept when she was admitted to hospital for a biopsy on a lump in her breast, and came round to discover that the breast had been removed. Out of this recorded experience and Griffiths's own reaction of 'anger and fear' there emerged a rapidly written script, originally called *Maiming of Parts*, and submitted to Granada as *Through the Night*. Granada's response was swift: the play's focus was hard to locate, it would cost a lot, and they didn't want to do it. Incensed by this reaction, Griffiths sent the text to Ann Scott, the script editor of *All Good Men*. Deeply disturbed personally by it, she was eventually persuaded by a doctor friend that the horror of the subject was not to be ducked. Similarly, Michael Lindsay-Hogg needed to overcome his physical aversion to the content before he could agree to direct. There were further obstacles to be met: in particular, Griffiths recalls pressure from above to cast a star in the role of the cancer

*A television version of *Comedians*, also directed by Richard Eyre, was shown on BBC1 in October 1979.

victim in order that the audience might have the reassurance that she would not die. Also Griffiths and Lindsay-Hogg decided to resist the then customary mix of film and studio video. As Griffiths explained in a letter:

> The play was originally accepted as a studio-based play, and costed and budgeted and scheduled internally accordingly. Approximately 20 minutes' worth of film effort comes with that package, if the text demands it. MLH initially wanted to do the whole piece on film, in real locations, but the BBC turned that down for internal budgetary reasons. MLH, a great purist, swung to the other pole and asked whether we could do it all in the studio ... I think MLH's reasons for urging all-studio were principally aesthetic – he hates the film/video mix – but undoubtedly he was also seeking to maximize control over the environment. There was also, I'm sure, the challenge of trying to create high realism in extremely artificial surroundings.
>
> For me, the attraction of all-studio was the coherence it afforded of tone, texture, and argument. *Through the Night*, on film, mixing actors and reals, actual exteriors with dressed interiors, and all the rest, might well have lost its fictive purchase on the imagination of its audience; and on film and tape, might well have seemed dishonest. A further important benefit was the extra rehearsal time we gained, since filming usually takes place *during* the rehearsal period and has to be scooped from it. In the event, I liked the result and thought it vindicated the choice we made, though there were things we clearly didn't manage (e.g. the grottiness of the hospital).[18]

A valuable by-product of this decision was the comparison that the visual style prompted with the familiar appearance of television hospital series such as *Emergency Ward Ten*, *General Hospital* and *Angels*. As Griffiths has said: 'The plays which get deepest are plays which are aware of their own conventions, and which somehow or other manage to spring the unexpected within these conventions.'[19] While *Through the Night* has nothing like the conscious scheme of visual and genre references that *Country* was later to exploit, it leaves the viewer in no doubt as to the ironic contrasts with the more reassuring portrayals of hospital life. As Peter Lennon observed in the *Sunday Times*:

> There was an interesting contrast here with the hospital series *Angels* (BBC1), which in the relatively inessential details of hospital routine is authentic enough. But the nurses in *Angels* consider that they are rising adequately to the final crisis in a man's life by giving his hand an encouraging squeeze to help him to oblivion.[20]

The contrast is pointed by something Dr Pearce says to Christine in his room about the surgeon's remoteness from his patients:

> Mr Staunton's a good man. He is just . . . not used, not equipped to deal with you as a person. The gap is too great. (*Pause.*) And there's something else. The reason he can't speak to you, look at you, after the operation is that for him you represent a failure, even when the operation is a success. Because each time we use surgery, we fail, medicine fails, the system fails, and he knows it, and he bears the guilt. (pp.173 – 4.)

In essence, the same point has already been signalled to the viewer by the uneasy detachment of the surgeon and his entourage during the ward round, their muttered exchanges and medical terminology incomprehensible to Christine. The nurses' nursery talk to the patients ('We're going to take you for a nice wee ride down to the theatre') serves to preserve the same defensive distance. The extreme of impersonality is conveyed by the pathologist, Mount, who falls with voracity on his fifty grams of tissue. Griffiths wished to go much further by including the horrific image of the amputated breast dumped casually into a waste bin, but this was resisted in production. The point he is making is that the medical profession allows the necessary scientific detachment of its treatment of the patient's *parts* to extend to its care of the whole individual, leaving him or her adrift in ignorance and fear. Quoting Hippocrates, Pearce says to Christine:

> 'For whoever does not reach the capacity of the common people and fails to make them listen to him, misses his mark.' Well, we're all missing the mark, Mrs Potts. And we need to be told. Not just doctors and nurses, but administrators and office men and boards of management and civil servants and politicians and the whole dank crew that sail this miserable ship through the night. (p.174.)

Thus the play's broader political implications are indicated, and the continuity with Griffiths's other work emerges: as Gramsci says in *Occupations*, 'The army not only can, but *must* be loved.'

In the course of production the script was extensively revised, particularly in response to solicited medical opinion. As Griffiths said, the scene between Christine and Pearce (pp.171 – 5) 'bears all the torsions of organized BBC advice'. Specifically, he was confronted with the moral obligation of ensuring that the play did not deter women from referring lumps in their breast to their doctors, advice he could hardly ignore, but not relevant to the main argument about the way patients are treated when they are in hospital.

Immediately following the screening on BBC1 on 2 December 1975, watched by an estimated audience of over 11 million people, the Corporation duty officer logged close to a hundred phone calls, the producer's office and the *Radio Times* received many letters, and Griffiths personally some 180. Marjorie Proops in the *Sunday People* opened her columns to readers with experience of mastectomy treatment and received over 1,800 letters in ten days. Thus the play loosened the taboo on the most feared of diseases – though not for the *Observer* critic who wrote, 'I found this week's episode of *The*

Nearly Man by Arthur Hopcraft sufficient excuse for not watching *Through the Night* (BBC1), a Trevor Griffiths play about breast cancer which I lacked the nerve to face.'[21]

As Griffiths says, *Through the Night* is, without question, his best-known piece. He also regarded it in 1979 as the high point so far of his collaboration with Michael Lindsay-Hogg. One can see why: the studio settings yielded nothing in authenticity while, time and again, the camera and lighting made telling comments within the naturalistic context, frequently adopting (again in contrast to conventional hospital drama practice) the patient's viewpoint. There was the opening examination in out-patients, with Mrs Potts uncovered and in distant isolation beyond the backs of the doctors in close-up; there was the arrival and departure of friends and relatives at visiting time through a sequence of glass doors and past the ward sister's office that kept the inmates well segregated from the outside world; there was the corridor ceiling seen by Christine from the trolley through advancing sedation on her 'wee ride' to the operating theatre. None of the shots was technically obtrusive but all of them underscored rather than merely registered the experience. The acting throughout, with Alison Steadman as Christine and Jack Shepherd as Dr Pearce, served only to bear out Griffiths's contention that naturalism is the form most accessible to the television audience, and hence presents least obstacles to the full assimilation of a complex argument. Between Alison Steadman and Thelma Whiteley as the decent but remote house surgeon, Dr Seal, a wealth of meaning was conveyed even by the following simple dialogue:

SEAL: How long ago was it we saw you?
CHRISTINE: Just coming up to three weeks, doctor.
SEAL: Yes. (*Still feeling* CHRISTINE*'s breast*) Still no pain?
CHRISTINE: No.
SEAL: Good. Yes. Good. (*She feels again under the armpit.*) Is it about the same size would you say?
CHRISTINE: No. I think it's a bit bigger. (p.142.)

Only in the nocturnal scene between Christine and Pearce did the weight of the rhetoric seem to put strain on the context, for all Jack Shepherd's skill in making intricate concepts sound like newly coined thoughts. Here, 'the torsions of organized BBC advice' seemed actually to be contorting the natural speech rhythms and demanding the impossible of Shepherd; yet still he managed to retrieve credibility with the concluding line 'Do you know something? My mother's proud of me. (*He laughs drily*.) Wow . . .'

Nearly six years were to elapse before Griffiths's next single play was seen on television, but during that time he completed two major serials. The first was *Bill Brand*, transmitted in eleven episodes by Thames Television between June and August 1976. Tracing the first year in the parliamentary career of a newly elected left-wing MP, this major project extended the debate initiated in *All Good Men* between parliamentary Labourism and radical socialism. As Griffiths put it:

> What I was trying to say throughout the series was that the traditions of the labour movement were inadequate to take the struggle further, and that we had to discover new traditions or revive even older ones. And that we had to seek connective tissue between electoral party politics, which still has a mystifying mass appeal, and extra-parliamentary socialist activity.[22]

When the series was already in production in late 1975 Granada screened *The Nearly Man*, a series by Arthur Hopcraft that, like *Bill Brand*, featured a Labour MP, albeit right-of-centre. The resemblance between the two series went no further: as the MP Christopher Price wrote in the *Listener*, 'Hopcraft took a snapshot: Griffiths has tried to portray a political odyssey.'[23] Not surprisingly, perhaps, the network controllers were apprehensive at the prospect of a second series about a Labour politician, particularly given the poor impact of *The Nearly Man*. It took organized opposition by Griffiths and the production team to avert the series being relegated to a late-night slot. In the event, *Bill Brand* went out at 9 p.m. between *World in Action* and *News at Ten*, consistently attracting audiences of 7 to 8 million. Subsequently, the series was repeated in the early afternoon, thus reaching a largely different audience. Twelve years later, *Bill Brand* remains unequalled as an example of television drama used as a means of extended political dialogue, surpassing even the controversial *Days of Hope*, which had been transmitted on BBC1 a year earlier.[24]

Over the next four years Griffiths completed a new, idiomatic version of Chekhov's *The Cherry Orchard* for the Nottingham Playhouse and worked on a film script based on the biography of John Reed and commissioned by Warren Beatty. Beatty played Reed and directed the film, which was released in 1981 under the title *Reds*. Griffiths also collaborated with Howard Brenton, Ken Campbell and David Hare to write *Deeds*, a brutal satire on commercial power in modern Britain, which was Richard Eyre's farewell production at Nottingham Playhouse in April 1978. Later that year Griffiths began work on a dramatization of D. H. Lawrence's *Sons and Lovers*, which was shown eventually in seven parts on BBC2 in January and February 1981. Griffiths described his objectives in a *Radio Times* preview:

> Why, finally, Lawrence, *Sons and Lovers*, now, and in Britain? There are many answers, big and small, but one will have to suffice. I chose to do this work because under all the incipient mysticism of the perception, under the incipient derogation of women, under the increasingly ugly politics, there is, in *this* Lawrence, and vibrantly so, a powerful and radical celebration of dignity in resistance within working-class culture in industrial class-societies; as well as a dark, tortured cry against the waste of human resources such societies require as part of their logic. It is no bad thing to be saying, in the year unemployment will reach 3 millions.[25]

However, what emerged was a product that in terms of its visual qualities had fallen victim to the well-tried system geared to the manufacture of the 'classic serial'. In consequence, much of the work of a powerful cast and Griffiths's old collaborator Stuart Burge as director was obscured by the softening wash of period nostalgia, *le style retro* as it has been called.[26]

Up to this point all Griffiths's scripts for television had been shot either on video or on a film/video mix (fifty–fifty in the case of *Sons and Lovers*). *Country*, transmitted as a BBC1 *Play for Today* on 20 October 1981, was his first work for television both conceived as a film and entirely shot on film. The confidence that Griffiths brought to the medium was born of the long and troubled association with Warren Beatty in the making of *Reds*. Thus equipped, he was able to undertake a fundamental shift of stylistic direction in order to penetrate a new area of experience. As he said later in an interview:

> A tremendous amount of learning took place in the two recent years when I was in and out of Hollywood and I think I have made a significant technical and formal advance in this text. I've managed to concentrate meaning visually and gesturally and return to movement. That has been a movement away from the lengthy, articulated ratiocination which is one way, rather a dumb way, of characterizing my earlier plays. But that sounds as if it's form learning from form and I don't think that's the case.
>
> There's something about *Country* that forces a different way of perceiving. It's because I had no emphatic remembered experience to share with the upper class that I had to find a way of seeing them that was at one and the same both realistic and set at a considerable critical distance.[27]

Country was conceived as the first of a cycle of six films under the collective title *Tory Stories*, set in the context of significant events in British post-war history with the last taking place in the mid-eighties. The idea developed in the immediate aftermath of the Conservative election landslide of May 1979 as a response to the emergence of Thatcherism and Reaganism in Western society. The original idea was that all six scripts should be shot entirely on 16 mm. film and directed by Richard Eyre. *Country* was costed at £400,000 as against £150,000 for the average BBC television play. This indicated a series budget of £2.5 million, with all the attendant hazards of overspending and consequent cutbacks to studio video. Eventually, Griffiths decided the risks were too great and settled for *Country* alone, concentrating the meaning of the entire series within the single script. Extensively reworked and made without compromise in either production or casting, the film cost £450,000. It was shot on location in May and June 1981 at Linton in Kent. Both Griffiths and Eyre were very clear as to the filmic logic of the piece. Griffiths has said:

> ... if you watch *Country*, or indeed if you read it, you do get a sense that if there is any author in that piece it is the camera. It's like a very detached inquiring eye. Part anthropological, part sociological, part political, part psychological, always a stranger, always detached. So that you are offered entry into the spaces of these people's lives. It's not a subjectively empathizing entry; you don't go in and say, 'I am this person.' Something about the lens of the writing. You're looking through a glass at people. I don't mean literally looking at people. You get the sense of people not quite in the same room. And that's what I wanted to do. Too often, in country-house drama, that class is represented just like you and me. I wanted to get that sense of their own detachment.[28]

In another interview he elaborates on this notion of detachment, likening it to the lack in the upper classes of 'any serious ideological thought that needs airing and debating':

> I feel that I also discovered that one of the other extraordinary absences within that class is inner dialogue, or interior life. For them there is precept, there is duty, there is opportunity, and there is power – these seem to occupy all the space within these people's lives . . . In a sense they see themselves instrumentally.[29]

One has only to compare the script of *Country* with his earlier work to see the extent of the stylistic shift. While all the television plays from *All Good Men* onwards incorporate powerful visual imagery, it is used far more intermittently to concentrate or to modify verbally articulated meaning. The burden of the debate is carried by the characters. Not surprisingly, the clearest precedent for the encoded communications of the Carlion family in *Country* is found in the impenetrable conclaves of the remote surgeon and his acolytes in *Through the Night*.

In *Country*, the key to the style is Virginia, the disaffected elder daughter stalking her sometime family with dispassionate camera. As the shutter clicks after the return from the christening her despised relatives are fixed in black-and-white images – for the pages of *Picture Post*, as we later learn. Equally, as the camera tracks across the terrace at sherry time and the microphone picks up disconnected fragments of conversation, it is as though both Virginia and we, the audience, are catching the Carlions unawares. Later, a shot of Virginia outside the house at night prefaces a lengthy slow tracking shot across the still figures of gentry and hop-pickers alike, reduced to temporary equality in sleep.

Similarly, the lighting exercises an ironic effect, telling us much more of the characters' preoccupations than their clipped utterances convey. Lit and shot by Nat Crosby and designed by Geoff Powell, the film runs the gamut from the bleached exteriors of high-summer indolence to the ominous chiaroscuro of the grieving Sir Frederick alone in church or absorbing the impact of the election catastrophe in his study. The far reference point in this carefully calculated scheme is Philip, raffishly attired in 'unsuitable' lightweight suit – until, that is, he assumes the subfusc appropriate to his newly assumed authority as Chairman and Managing Director. Likewise, at the family dinner Virginia wears black as an indication of her disregard for the male hegemony.

While the entire action is punctuated and determined by the radio reports of the Conservative rout of July 1945, Griffiths's eye is fixed as ever on the present day. The viewer is being warned never to underestimate the resilience of the new pragmatic Toryism, like Philip totally unconcerned with values and only with winning. Apart from the reference to the present being indicated by the occasional planted anachronism ('really not my bag,' 'bachelor *gay*'), Harcourt's summary of the socialist threat is couched in terms that allude unmistakably to the radical aspirations of Tony Benn and the resurgent Labour Left in the early eighties: 'Confiscation of land could be on the cards, housing, property taxes, transport, insurance ... it's not inconceivable that they could close the public schools and get rid of the House of Lords altogether.' (p.294) And as the cheery labourers celebrate the overthrow of Churchill in the closing scene the Carlion's beer that they tap is an enduring metaphor for their dependence on the commodity power of capitalism, be it 'real ale' or 'weasel piss'. The original intention was for the later films in the series to develop beer as a central metaphor. As Mike Poole wrote in the *New Statesman*:

> Changes in the brewing industry – first keg, then lager, then multi-national mergers – were to have served ... as a metaphor for the restructuring of British capital. But beer was chosen because of its importance within working-class culture, the area where consumerism, the multi-nationals and, eventually, monetarism were to wreak the profoundest changes of all.[30]

In a *Radio Times* preview Griffiths drew attention to another important strand of reference running through the film:

> *Country* is a critique of a dramatic genre ... The country-house play is a lie. It is a piece of propaganda. It maintains that the aristocratic rich are just the same as us, with the same problems, the same pleasures. Well, they're not.[31]

By ironic coincidence *Country* was transmitted at the same time as the second episode of Granada's dramatization of Evelyn Waugh's *Brideshead Revisited*, which in Charles Sturridge's reverential production became the very apotheosis of the country-house genre. In the words of one critic, 'There could be no more comprehensive corrective to Waugh's romantic vision of opulence than Griffiths's rigorous class analysis.'[32]

A week before *Country* BBC1 had screened Richard Eyre's production of *The Cherry Orchard* in the same version that Griffiths had based on a literal translation by Helen Rappaport for Nottingham Playhouse in 1977. It was a text conceived as a corrective to the 'plangent and sorrowing evocations of an "ordered" past no longer with "us", its passing greatly to be mourned'.[33] What Griffiths learned from Chekhov's 'tough, bright-eyed complexity' was his distanced and laconic depiction of class-determined behaviour and it is a debt that he acknowledges in various references to the writing of *Country*. To this list of genre acknowledgements can be added Dodie Smith's celebration of the family, *Dear Octopus*, a West End hit in 1938, to which *Country* owes many plot and thematic elements.[34] Finally, too, Mario Puzo's novel and Francis Ford Coppola's film *The Godfather* suggested not only the family name Corleone (Carlion being pronounced C*o*rlion) but also the notions of 'family', dynastic succession and despotic leadership common to the Sicilian Mafia and the English 'beerage'.

One criticism levelled at *Country* is that the portrayal of the East End hop-pickers is schematic and over-romanticized. But, as John Wyver observes, the film presents them as they are observed by Sir Frederick and the family, from the point of view of *their* class. One might add that at certain points they are seen through

Virginia's camera, and hence no less objectified. Griffiths himself is apprehensive that the detailed genre references lend the film an elegance that might easily beguile the viewer, yet surely this is sufficiently counter-balanced by the cool yet vengeful presence of Virginia and by the chilling certainty of Philip's closing words. With the loss of the five remaining 'Tory Stories' *Country* was required to assume a formidable weight of meaning. Yet rarely does that compression lead to over-density or obscurity in the script. It remains Griffiths's most completely orchestrated yet most clearly articulated work to date.

Within six months a further play by Griffiths was transmitted by Central Television. The contrast with *Country* could not have been more abrupt; as Stuart Cosgrove wrote in *Screen: 'Oi for England* is a three-minute punk single recorded in a garage, set against the multi-track, concept album nuances of *Country*.'[35] The metaphor is apt: offered to Central by Griffiths in the autumn of 1981, the script of *Oi for England* was delivered at Christmas and ready for transmission on 17 April 1982. Directed by Tony Smith and shot entirely on studio video, the production was fitted into gaps in the studio schedule of the thrice-weekly soap opera *Crossroads*, from which the crew was also recruited. The idea came from a 'Race in the Classroom' conference that Griffiths had attended the previous year. His original intention was to write a short play for performance in schools, but the project grew in scale and urgency as a consequence of the inner-city riots in the summer of 1981 in Toxteth, Moss Side, St Paul's and elsewhere. The growth of Oi-Rock and its frequent association with racism suggested a focus for Griffiths's drama. Little-known bands such as The Ventz, Column 44 and Tragic Minds were being exploited by neo-fascist groups, particularly the British Movement, as they extended their recruiting activities from football matches and playgrounds to rock audiences. Inevitably, young blacks responded and a racially provocative gig by the Four-Skins at the Hamborough Tavern in Southall was besieged by an Asian crowd and the building was gutted by fire. Apart from the general urgency stimulated by the events of that summer, one specific reason for the rushed scheduling of *Oi for England* was to counteract fascist agitation in the period prior to the local council elections of May 1982. But, not for the first time, Griffiths's interventionist plans encountered institutional resistance: the IBA insisted on rescheduling transmission from a prime-time 9 p.m. weekday slot to 10 o'clock on Saturday night, when most young people were certain to be anywhere but in front of a television set. Before the start, viewers were warned: 'In the course of the play the language and atmosphere will be disturbing to some people.'

Griffiths wrote *Oi for England* on the premise that there is no simple equation to be made between skinheads and fascism:

> The play is arguing that the anger of white proletarian kids about this hulk of a society is wholly justified, but what needs to be looked at is how this anger is used. The solution for skins is not confrontation with black youths and other proletarians – that is a complete diversion that will lead them back upon themselves. Working-class youth simply has to make a common cause – to fight for jobs and fullness of life. And that's nowhere near under Thatcher.
>
> Moreover, the play is saying that the media stereotype of the skin is too unsubtle to be of any use. The skin has his tap roots in the working class. He shaves his head and makes himself distinctive, but that to some extent is cosmetic because he hasn't lost his moral relationship with his class. If we separate him as some kind of demonic tendency we tend to miss the point and tell a lie.
>
> Racism is endemic to this society. It's a white problem, not a black one. And in so far as skinhead culture evinces that racism, it reflects the broader society.
>
> But skins are available to the political process and I'd like to give them a hearing.[36]

It is a weighty subject-matter to accommodate within the limits of a fifty-minute, studio-set, small-cast play, and the strains are evident. As Stuart Cosgrove says, '*Oi for England* exemplifies the determining pressures that industrial and production constraints put on formal structures. It bears the traces of a drama restricted by its own urgency.'[37]

The pre-title video mix in bleached-out half-tones of riot footage and newspaper headlines of unemployment figures and defence expenditure vividly contextualizes the band's basement 'studio' in Moss Side. Thereafter, up to the penultimate scene the presentation of the argument is wholly verbal, apart from 'Sod the Lord – Pass the Ammunition' which acts as a powerful first-half closer. This poses problems, as Griffiths himself has agreed: 'With only six characters and a single set you have to allow them to develop a credible space of their own – and in the case of Napper and the Gavin Richards figure this meant giving a dramatic logic to some pretty unsavoury types. But this position is, I think, quite clearly challenged from within the piece by the Finn character.'[38]

True enough, though some critics were left uneasy by the insidious logic of the Man's 'Chocolate England' speech (pp.320–21), particularly when the text was later adapted for stage performance in youth club and community centre venues.[39] The pressures on the play's form are most evident in the final scene. The smashing of the band's instruments is powerfully expressive and unambiguous in meaning, but the introduction of the Irish ballad seems to pose more questions about the relevance of Finn's Irish parentage and allegiance than the action can possibly accommodate. If, once again, we are presented with a 'hard–soft' antithesis then the synthesis on this occasion seems quite impossible to locate – which of course, may well be taken as an accurate enough expression of the dilemma facing Finn and others like him. Griffiths has said:

> Finn is blocked. There's a potential tenderness there that is being denied in the subculture. I had a real problem with the

language – skinhead vernacular is detached from most forms of working-class speech. It's a display of aggressiveness for its own sake, uncontexted in other things like solidarity, gentleness, tenderness. I tried to show this through Finn's indistinct awareness of his Irishness. When he turns on the tape it's his frustration at having to deny that more tender, lyrical side of himself that, as much as anything, provokes his violent outburst.[40]

Since *Oi for England* Griffiths's output has not slackened. The last six years have seen a stage-play, *Real Dreams*, performed originally at the Williamstown Theatre Festival, USA, in 1984 and presented by the Royal Shakespeare company at the Pit in London in April 1986. Based on Jeremy Pikser's story *Revolution in Cleveland*, and set in the summer of 1969, it is described by Griffiths as an attempt 'to recover the sixties from the trashing that the seventies and eighties have given them'. Griffiths has also written the script for Ken Loach's film *Fatherland*, released in November 1986. Based on the story of a *Liedermacher* expelled from the DDR and finding an eager commercial market for his songs in the West, *Fatherland* both pursues the theme of the exploitation of art found in *Comedians* and *Oi for England* and also explores the deceptions that cloud the history of Nazism.

Also shot on film and transmitted by Central Television in February–March 1985 was the seven-part serial *The Last Place on Earth*. Based on Roland Huntford's book of the same title, this major project set out to explore the myth, enshrined in Charles Frend's reverential film *Scott of the Antarctic* (1948), that it was Captain Scott and not Roald Amundsen and his comrades who *morally* won the race to the South Pole in 1911. Griffiths describes the 'real politics' of the piece as 'the politics of social organization and leadership: collective leadership on the part of Amundsen . . . as against hierarchic, assumptive leaderships such as we have today and such as we had then in the British Empire'.[41] The point was grimly reinforced shortly after Griffiths had taken on the commission when in April

1982 the British task force invaded the Falkland Islands and a return of the Thatcher Government in May was secured on the strength of Britain's recovered 'greatness'. Griffiths used the Prime Minister's exultant 'Rejoice!' as the title for the final episode, 'because it was so neat it had to be true almost, because here we were on another crazed, impossible, vainglorious venture, and we were being invited to approve, nay we were being instructed to approve. Our whole Britishness, our status as Britons depended on our approval.'[42] While the viewing figures for *The Last Place on Earth* were disappointing, it achieved its objective by stirring up a furious controversy with the custodians of Scott's memory in the press, and by projecting Roland Huntford's book into the best-sellers list.

In an interview in Channel 4's *Off the Page* last year Griffiths said: '*Bill Brand* and *Through the Night* were the last productions where I felt that there was space around the production to make mistakes, to find what you needed to do, and then do it.'

If his work since then is any indication then it is hard to believe that Griffiths will not continue to make space to ask the questions that need asking about the times we are living through. The job may be harder now, but more than ever it is a job that needs to be done. Who, if not Griffiths among dramatists, will do it?

April 1988

NOTES

1. 'A Play Postscript', *Plays and Players*, April 1972, p. 83.
2. *Reds* (1981, directed by Warren Beatty) and *Fatherland* (1986, directed by Ken Loach).
3. Interview with John Wyver in Frank Pike (ed.) *Ah! Mischief: The Writer and Television* (Faber and Faber, London, 1982), p. 32. For an account of *Adam Smith* and all Griffiths' other work up to 1983 see Mike Poole and John Wyver, *Powerplays: Trevor Griffiths in Television* (BFI, London, 1984).
4. *Powerplays*, p. 49.
5. *Guardian*, 5 January 1974.
6. *The Times Educational Supplement*, 25 June 1976, p. 19.
7. *The Times*, 31 January 1974.
8. Raymond Williams, *Politics and Letters* (NLB, London, 1979) p. 376.
9. John Bull, New British Political Dramatists (Macmillan, London 1984) pp. 138–9.
10. 'Prickly Pair', *New Statesman*, 8 February 1974, p. 198.
11. Interview with Nicole Boireau, 2–3 May 1985, in *Coup de Théâtre*, Dijon, No. 6 (December 1986), p. 17.
12. 'Transforming the Husk of Capitalism' (interview) in *Theatre Quarterly* Vol. VI, No. 22, p. 39.
13. 'TV Selections' (unsigned), *Time Out*, 19 April 1974.
14. Quoted in *Powerplays*, p. 52.
15. Interview with Edward Braun, 8 May 1979.
16. Ibid.
17. 'Transforming the Husk of Capitalism' p. 39.
18. Letter to Edward Braun, 20 January 1980.
19. *Ah! Mischief*, p. 37.
20. 'The People Speak', *The Sunday Times*, 7 December 1975, p. 39.
21. Quoted by Griffiths in his preface to the play (p.129).
22. *Leveller*, November 1976, p. 12.
23. *Listener*, 22 July 1976, p. 85.
24. For discussions of *Bill Brand* see *Powerplays* and Edward Braun, 'Trevor Griffiths' in George Brandt (ed.), *British Television Drama* (Cambridge University Press, 1981).

25. *Radio Times*, 10–16 January 1981.
26. See *Powerplays*, Chapter 7.
27. *Ah! Mischief*, p. 38.
28. Interview with Nicole Boireau, p. 19.
29. Quoted in *Powerplays*, p. 163.
30. 'Another Country?', *New Statesman*, 30 October 1981.
31. 'A View of the Country', *Radio Times*, 17–23 October 1981.
32. W. Stephen Gilbert, 'Closed Circuits', *Guardian*, 17 October 1981.
33. Griffiths' introduction to *The Cherry Orchard* (Pluto, London, 1978), p. v.
34. See *Powerplays*, pp. 161–2.
35. 'Refusing Consent' – the "Oi for England" Project', *Screen*, Vol. 24, No. 1 (January–February 1983), p. 96.
36. 'Reds, White and Blue: The Politics of Colour', *New Musical Express*, 17 April 1982, pp. 24–25.
37. 'Refusing Consent . . .', p. 94.
38. Quoted in *Powerplays*, p. 172.
39. For accounts of these tours see *Powerplays* and 'Refusing Consent . . .'.
40. *Powerplays*, p. 173.
41. Quoted in *Powerplays*, p. 181.
42. *Judgement Over the Dead: the Screenplay of* The Last Place on Earth (Verso, London, 1986), p. xxxi.

All Good Men

Characters

EDWARD WAITE: seventy; Labour politician; born Manchester working class; life spent in trade union and labour movement. Now lives in relative affluence in semi-retirement

MARIA: twenty-eight; daughter of second marriage; teaches art in London comprehensive; married; separated

WILLIAM: twenty-three; son of second marriage; research post in history and sociology at University of Manchester

RICHARD MASSINGHAM: thirty-eight; current affairs television producer; Winchester and Oxford

MARY: Maid

Sets

Conservatory, living room, dining room, hall and principal bedroom of Waite's country house in Surrey

All Good Men was first broadcast by BBC Television as a Play for Today on 31 January 1974. The cast included:

EDWARD WAITE	Bill Fraser
MARIA	Frances de la Tour
WILLIAM	Jack Shepherd
RICHARD MASSINGHAM	Ronald Pickup
Director	Michael Lindsay-Hogg
Designer	Peter Brachacki
Producer	Graeme McDonald

INT. CONSERVATORY, DAY

Conservatory of Edward Waite's country house. Late afternoon. Crisp sun. The house is large but not opulent: twelve usable rooms, good lawns front and back, and for this home-counties territory desirably remote. WAITE *sits in a comfortable wicker chair facing the sun. He holds an open file on his knee, flicks a page from time to time, mutters the occasional word or phrase out loud. He's old, seventy, grizzled, thick-necked, fleshy not fat, hair cropped close to the scalp, yet somehow miraculously parted on the left. He wears a white shirt, red tie, gaberdine trousers with turn-ups, plaid slippers, a brown woollen cardigan unbuttoned. On a table by his left arm, a large pocket watch and a distinctive briar, unfilled, on an ashtray. No pouch, no matches. High shot. We see, ten feet from him, an Arriflex on a tripod, facing him. He stares at it. On the floor, unrigged, light battens, wiring, boards, lighting trunks and other film-production paraphernalia. He looks back at his file.*

WAITE: (*Quietly, as though to a question*) 'Twenty-six was the turning point, I suppose . . . You couldn't work in the pit as I did and not be affected. (*Pause.*) Politically, I mean.

(WAITE *turns a page, sniffs. His voice is strong still, rather harsh, the jagged Manchester consonants still glinting in the oily wash of his received standard English.* MASSINGHAM *in from the house. Late thirties, thick-haired, blond, supple. He wears an Italian suit of bottle-green thin corduroy, a splendid lacy shirt with full collar open at the neck, built-up two-tone shoes in black and brown. He returns easily to his seat opposite Waite's, in front of and beneath the camera; picks up his clipboarded notes.*)

MASSINGHAM: I'm sorry it took so long . . .

WAITE: No no.

MASSINGHAM: Anyway, we're all fixed for tomorrow. Ten o'clock.

(*A hint of a question there.*)

WAITE: Ten o'clock.

MASSINGHAM: I think the garden stuff we've just done will look good. It's a lovely house.

(*Pause.* WAITE *sucks on the empty pipe.*)

I wouldn't have thought Surrey . . . right, somehow, given your life.

WAITE: No? – No, perhaps not. (*Pause.*) It's handy for London. (*Smiling, rather pompous*) I *live* here. They haven't buried me yet.

(MASSINGHAM *shares the smile, a managed deference neatly glossing his arrogance. Silence, as he checks his notes.*)

MASSINGHAM: It's very kind of you to ask me to stay. It will help. (*Pause.*) I hope we'll . . . count ourselves friends when it's over.

WAITE: (*Grinning*) As long as you don't mind a row or two. I've never managed to last very long without a flaming good row.

MASSINGHAM: Why not? It's what the history's about anyway, isn't it? Put a bit of life in the old archive.

WAITE: (*Checking watch*) Dinner's at seven. I can't last longer than seven. Never could.

MASSINGHAM: Ah. Would you mind if I didn't this evening? I usually have dinner with the crew the first evening. It's . . . er . . . a sort of ritual.

WAITE: I quite understand. Happen you'll need a key. There's usually one on the coatstand thing in the hall.

MASSINGHAM: Thank you. (*Pause. Picks up case.*) Well, would you like a short canter over the early ground? But let's make sure we don't spoil tomorrow's spontaneity.

WAITE: Whatever you say.

MASSINGHAM: Just to get the feel and the range for tomorrow. (*Pause.*) By the way, if you don't mind I'd like to call you *Lord* Waite, if that's all right. (*Smiling*) There's no chance of your not accepting is there . . . ?

WAITE: None at all. (*Pause.*) There must be no leak, of course.

MASSINGHAM: That's understood. You see my point, don't you? By the time all this is in the can and edited, the New Year's Honours

List will have come and gone and I don't want to end up with egg on my face. (*Making note on pad*) So: Lord Waite. (*Pause.*) Tell us something about your early life. You were born in Manchester, weren't you? Well, your parents were Manchester people and you were born in Manchester, one of seven children in 1903. What was it like?

WAITE: *Six,* six children.

MASSINGHAM: (*Amending*) I'm sorry.

(*A little hold up.*)

WAITE: Do you want me to answer?

MASSINGHAM: Please.

WAITE: (*Assuming stiffish interview role at once, or merely politician's role*) They were bad times, those were. My God, but they were bad. It's hard to conceive, now, from here, how . . . viciously working people were exploited in those days. Eight of us, mother, father, four lads, two lasses, in four rooms, two up, two down, lavatory in the yard at the back. Beswick in Manchester we lived, 14 Milton Street. Dad worked as a labourer at Bradford colliery. Brought home eighteen bob a week. Don't ask how we managed . . .

MASSINGHAM: I think this part of the story is terribly important and . . . I'm keen to get the flavour absolutely right. Was it all bad, for example?

WAITE: No no. We were *alive*, for one thing. That was something. (*Pause.*) And . . . we had each other. Down the street, up the street, round the corner, down the next one. We were all in the same boat. *Bound* to each other, you might say. Aunts and uncles and cousins and . . . just neighbours. (*Pause.*) There mightn't have been much hope around, but there wasn't too much despair either.

MASSINGHAM: What about schooling?

WAITE: Schooling? Nasty, brutish and short is the phrase that comes to mind. I organized the first monitors' strike: 1912, that'd be.

MASSINGHAM: Oh, on what issue?

WAITE: I thought monitors should be paid. Some days we'd do more work than the teachers.

MASSINGHAM: What happened?

WAITE: We got a belting. Sixteen of us. Headmistress took us all into the hall, leathered us till we could hardly stand, then forced us to confess the error of our ways before the whole school.

MASSINGHAM: Did you do it?

WAITE: Yes. When I saw there was nothing else for it. She'd put the fear of God up the others. There was no point in going it alone. (*Smiling*) So I recanted: lived to fight another day, you might say.

MASSINGHAM: (*Picks up Waite's book.*) Is that in the book? I can't remember it at all.

WAITE: (*Slowly*) I don't think it is. It's a long thing, is a life. A book can't hold it all.

(*Pause.*)

MASSINGHAM: Of course. (*Puts book down and makes brief notes.*) What else do you remember? About the early days.

WAITE: Everything, bloody near. Should I say that? (MASSINGHAM *smiles him on.*)

It's what fed my politics right through my life. (*Pause.*) We might've been living on another planet for all anyone cared. (*Pause.*) I remember. (*Pause.*) Hot summer nights I'd sit on the front doorstep and just . . . listen . . . to the street. You could learn more about a community then – about its hopes and fears, its desperation and its courage – in one night on the fronts than any amount of erudite 'sociological' investigation could tell you now. (*Pause.*) The pavement was made of big smooth stone slabs, that big, bigger, bedded in soil, you know. And between each slab and the next, a little ripple of moss, dark green, soft as velvet. I used to . . . I used to . . . peel it . . . upwards . . . with my finger, see how long a strip I could manage before it broke. And then I'd take it in my hands and smell it. Close my eyes and smell it. And . . . imagine . . . whole . . . landscapes filled with . . . growing things.

(*Pause.*) And . . . I can hear it now . . . eyes closed, smelling the moss and the earth clinging to it . . . there'd be the crack, crack, crack of shoe heels on bedroom walls . . . pulverizing bedbugs gone crazy in the heat. (*He grins suddenly, relishing the tale.* MASSINGHAM *makes a note on the pad.*)

The good old days.

MASSINGHAM: And the war?

(*Silence. It's darkening a little.*)

WAITE: And the war.

MASSINGHAM: (*Silky*) Just in time, some people have said.

WAITE: In time for what?

MASSINGHAM: In time, somebody said, I can't recall who, 'in time to lance the boil of social unrest'. Ireland, women, industrial ferment, syndicalism. That's the theory, anyway . . .

WAITE: Ah, the theory.

(*There is in* WAITE, *and* MASSINGHAM *senses it, a reluctance to talk about the war.* WAITE *begins searching through his file.*)

MASSINGHAM: Well, I'm sure we can look at it later on if you'd . . .

WAITE: (*Decides to talk*) I was eleven. Just. Dad was thirty-eight, thirty-nine. Volunteered the first week of the war. Joe and Philip followed him. Nineteen and seventeen. All dead by Christmas. Joe had both legs blown off by a shell. Philip and Dad died charging machine-guns. (*Pause.*) I've still got this (*Tapping file*) letter. (*Clears throat, reading*) 'You are leaving home to fight for the safety and honour of my Empire. Belgium, whose country we are pledged to defend, has been attacked and France is about to be invaded by the same powerful foe. I have implicit confidence in you, my soldiers. Duty is your watchword, and I know your duty will be nobly done. I shall follow your every movement with deepest interest and mark with eager satisfaction your daily progress. Indeed, your welfare will never be absent from my thoughts. I pray God to bless you and guard you and bring you back victorious. Signed, George V, by the Grace of God King and Emperor, this day, August 12th, 1914.' (*Pause.*) The telegrams announcing the deaths were . . . more succinct. I think my mother burnt them. At any rate, they're not there. There she is.

(WAITE *hands photo of mother to* MASSINGHAM. *He hands it back.*)

MASSINGHAM: It must have hit you pretty hard . . . your father . . . and brothers.

WAITE: That's right. Me and a few million others. Bleak. At least I can remember him whole. You know, intact. For ten years after the war ended you couldn't leave the house without bumping into someone you used to know when he had two legs or arms.

MASSINGHAM: So how important would you say the Great War was to your political development?

WAITE: (*Sombre*) You could say . . . it made a man of me . . . (*Pause.*) I left school on my thirteenth birthday. Went down the pit. That's how I came to be involved in the trade union movement. (*Pause.*) It was suddenly all very clear to me. As I put it in my book, a Pauline revelation: if my people were going to get anywhere, they'd have to get there by Shank's, there'd be nobody giving them a lift.

MASSINGHAM: (*Checking file*) And . . . you joined the Labour Party, what, in the twenties sometime . . . ?

WAITE: ILP first. That was the Labour Party where I came from. Then the Labour Party proper, after 'twenty-four and the minority government.

MASSINGHAM: Did you ever imagine then, in those early, distant days, that you might achieve what you have achieved, in the years that followed?

WAITE: Oh yes. Oh yes. (*Pause.*) You see, we were *right.* (*Pause.*) There's nothing you can't do, if you're right.

MASSINGHAM: (*Simply*) Nothing?

(*Silence.*)

WAITE: (*Levelly*) That's right. Always provided it's possible.

(*The conservatory lights go on suddenly. The* MAID *stands in the doorway.*)

What is it, Mary?

MARY: Six thirty, sir.

WAITE: Yes, thank you, Mary.

(*She takes tea things, and leaves.* MASSINGHAM *puts his clipboard down into a small black attaché case, which he fastens and locks.*)

MASSINGHAM: I fancy that could make one section on its own. I want to put a picture researcher on it. It has a nice feel. Would you happen to know whether that pre-1914 environment still stands?

WAITE: No, I wouldn't *happen* to know, young man. I made it my *business* to know. And I can tell you it doesn't. We saw it off, rooted it up and thousands like it. (*Pause.*) Part of our history.

MASSINGHAM: Of course. Forgive me.

WAITE: I s'll have to get ready for dinner.

MASSINGHAM: And I'll drive down to the village to see the crew. (*On his feet*) Thank you. It's going to be marvellous.

WAITE: (*Drily*) It's a good story. (*Pause.*) Don't forget your key.

MASSINGHAM: No, I'm extremely grateful for all your time and trouble. I'll see you tomorrow then.

(MASSINGHAM *leaves.* WAITE *sits on, tired suddenly. He stares straight ahead, empty pipe in hand.*)

INT. WAITE'S BEDROOM. NIGHT

WAITE *stands in front of wardrobe mirror, fastening his front collar-stud. The same red tie. Dark suit jacket. The room is large, airy. He crosses to the dressing-table, swallows two tablets with a glass of water laid out for him there on a tray. He takes in the framed photographs of his second wife, Ann, his daughter Maria on her wedding day, his son William at graduation, his mother around thirty-five, dressed in black blouse and skirt, short steel-coloured hair, rimless spectacles. He picks this last frame up, studies it, puts it down, crosses to the leaded windows, stares out on to the lit drive, picks up a pair of binoculars from the window seat, attempts to pierce the blackness with them, fails, finding only his own broken reflection in the window panes. Over this image, the voice of Ramsay Macdonald announces his intention to seek George V's permission to form a national government.*

INT. DINING ROOM. NIGHT

WAITE *sits in the light at the top of the long table, the rest of the room shadowed.* WAITE *stares at the vichyssoise, puts a spoon in, retrieves it, lets it rest in the bowl. Long shot: he stares straight ahead, teeming with voices. Slow track, zoom, to close-up. Chamberlain's Croydon Peace with Honour; Attlee pledging 'responsible government' in 1945; Bevin's 'naked into the conference chamber' speech; Gaitskell's 'We will fight, fight and fight again to save the party we love.' The cheers and counter-cheers cover his stiff, sweating face in close-up. Silence. His wife's voice, in half-whisper, mock-cold, ironic and contemptuous:*

ANN: (*Voice over*) Maybe you'd better kiss me then. Go on. Get down and kiss me . . .

(*A sharp, delicate spasm. His head slumps forward, catches the edge of the bowl, tilting soup into his frozen face.*)

(*Voice over, very distant*) Isn't that what you want . . .

INT. HALL. NIGHT

Hall clock shows twelve fifteen. Light from the living room, hall darkish. MASSINGHAM *lets himself in by the front door, returns the key to the hallstand drawer, is pulled by the light, moves into the living room.*

INT. LIVING ROOM. NIGHT

MARIA WAITE, *twenty-eight, stocky like her father, dark, almost gypsyish, sits on the settee flicking a* New Statesman. *She holds a half-filled glass of something in her hand. She wears trousers, boots, thigh-length cotton smock. Sees* MASSINGHAM, *who has stopped just inside the doorway.*

MARIA: Richard Massingham.

MASSINGHAM: Yes . . .

MARIA: (*Standing*) Maria . . . Waite.

MASSINGHAM: Ah.

MARIA: Won't you come in?

MASSINGHAM: (*Frowning*) Thank you. Erm . . .

MARIA: Can I get you a drink?

MASSINGHAM: Thanks.

(*She stops by the cabinet, waiting.*)

Scotch. Thank you.

MARIA: (*Pouring*) My father's . . . (*Inching up the glass with studied precision*) . . . had some sort of . . . heart attack.

MASSINGHAM: What?

MARIA: (*Bringing drink*) Or perhaps merely a serious bout of indigestion . . . Sit down, won't you . . . The doctor can't make his mind up.

MASSINGHAM: (*Sitting, rather heavily*) I see.

(MARIA *resumes her seat.*)

I'm . . . sorry.

(MARIA *ignores this.*)

Have they . . . taken him in?

MARIA: No. They've left a nurse. (*As though savouring a recent quotation.*) He has a history of hypertension, but if it was a coronary it appears to have been a relatively minor one. As far as one can tell.

MASSINGHAM: I see.

MARIA: We'll know in the morning. When the results of the tests are through.

MASSINGHAM: How . . . how is he?

MARIA: Would you believe 'comfortable'? Floating on a sea of morphine and anti-coagulants is probably more accurate but decidedly less reassuring. (*Pause.*) You didn't mean that, though, did you?

MASSINGHAM: (*A tactical incomprehension*) I'm sorry . . .

MARIA: (*Bluntly*) He'll have to rest. (*Pause.*) But he won't die. Not this time. (*Standing*) Another?

MASSINGHAM: (*Showing glass*) Thank you, no.

(MARIA *crosses to the cabinet, pours herself another Scotch.*)

(*Suddenly*) Would you mind if I used the phone?

MARIA: Help yourself.

(MASSINGHAM *looks round the room.* MARIA *points it out. He crosses, taking a small black address book out of his pocket, stops, looks in her direction. She catches the look.*) (*Unyieldingly*) Would you like me to leave?

MASSINGHAM: No no. Please.

(MASSINGHAM *dials the number.* MARIA *returns to her seat, back to him, picks up the* New Statesman *again.*) (*Into phone*) Room 8, please.

(MASSINGHAM *waits, looks in* MARIA*'s direction.*) Eddie, Richard. Hi. Look, sorry to call you at this hour. What? No, no. Look Mr . . . Waite has been taken ill. Yes. No, it's not clear how ill at the moment, but it's obviously going to be a few days at the very least. Ahunh. Ahunh. No, I want to use the time picking up background footage. Manchester. I'll give you the details when you collect your gear in the morning. (*Pause.*) I know that, Eddie, and I'll authorize it. Eddie, I know that. All right, you travel up, that's a day, you shoot, day and a half, maybe two, travel back, no problem. (*Pause.*) So take it from Jeannie's float. (*Pause.*) In writing. You'll have it. (*Pause.*) Well, general stuff. There's an area he was born in, he claims has been pulled down and rebuilt. I want you to check it out, shoot what's there, whatever it is, old or new, we can use either, same slums or new ones, towerblock variety. And there may be a couple of interviews with people who knew him in those days, I'll get the researcher on to that first thing in the morning and let you know. No, there's no angle, save maybe a news angle, who knows? Be prepared, eh? (*Pause.*) All right, we'll talk in the morning. Thanks, Eddie. (*Phone down, he's back in the room. Crosses to the cabinet, pours himself another drink.*) Would you mind (*gestures at his chair*) if I . . . ?

MARIA: Be my guest.

(MASSINGHAM *sits down. They face each other. Silence.*)

MASSINGHAM: Is it simply distress . . . or have I offended you in some way, Mrs Bryant?

MARIA: My, but you boys do your homework, don't you?

MASSINGHAM: Well?

MARIA: Don't . . . patronize me, Mr Massingham.

MASSINGHAM: I'm sorry. I didn't mean to.

(*Silence. The question lingers.*)

MARIA: I can't decide whether your sensitivity is real or tactical.

MASSINGHAM: Ah.

MARIA: There you go again. Ah. Poor suffering *inferior* creature. Ah. (*Pause.*) He's old and he's tired and he's sick. Leave him be.

MASSINGHAM: Is that what he wants?

MARIA: No. It's what I want.

MASSINGHAM: He's a public man. A great one, some would say.

MARIA: What would *you* say?

MASSINGHAM: That's not my brief. I present; others judge.

MARIA: Ah.

MASSINGHAM: Ah?

(*A brief smile between them.*)

MARIA: Tell me about your . . . brief.

MASSINGHAM: (*Cleanly*) I'm setting up a series called *Living History*. Long hard-core interviews with living figures who embody important strands in our relatively recent past. This is the pilot. The first. They buy or reject this one.

MARIA: Why my father?

MASSINGHAM: I wrote to ten professors of politics, ten professors of modern history, outlined my brief, and asked them to list the people they considered best fitted it. Your father was mentioned twelve times. A major trade union leader, a quarter of a century in the Commons, three Cabinet posts, Party Treasurer, Party Chairman . . .

MARIA: Man of the people.

MASSINGHAM: As you say.

MARIA: What about *you*?

MASSINGHAM: What about me? I'm not important.

MARIA: Too bright for Eton. Marlborough?

MASSINGHAM: Winchester.

MARIA: Yes. I should have recognized that distinctive 'I'm not important' style of arrogance.

MASSINGHAM: It's amazing. You're exactly the way I expected your father might be.

MARIA: Don't tell me. It's chip-on-the-shoulder time. You're all the bloody same. The minute your sleek charm fails to make the requisite impression, you fall to whining about chips on the shoulder. (*Pause.*) Your dispensation isn't *natural*, you know. Or God-given. It's bred. Like my resistance. I thought they'd've told you that, while they were . . . making you.

(MASSINGHAM *stands, smiles, just a touch uncertain before the ironic onslaught.*)

MASSINGHAM: I think I'll go to bed. I – er – I'd prefer not to fight, if it's all the same with you.

MARIA: Especially with someone who insists on hitting below the intellect. I know what you mean.

MASSINGHAM: Will you . . . stay?

(MARIA *gets up, wanders to cabinet.*)

MARIA: A few days. Until he's on his feet. Term's ended. I teach. Oh, I suppose you've 'had your researcher' on that too. Did she tell you I'd left my husband?

MASSINGHAM: Good night, Mrs Bryant.

(*He leaves the room, very calm, slightly steely, reassured by the late show of vulnerability in her.* MARIA *watches him out, pours another drink, stares up at the picture of the 1945 Labour Government on the wall, her father four seats to the right of Clement Attlee.*)

INT. HALL. DAY

A battered grip, raincoat across it, in the hall.

INT. WAITE'S BEDROOM. DAY

Curtained. WILLIAM WAITE, *twenty-three, stands at the foot of the bed, staring at* WAITE*'s sleeping face on the pillow.* WILLIAM *is of middle height, brown longish hair, untidy, unkempt, with about four days' growth of beard on his face. He stands now, hands deep in pockets of olive-green combat coat, dispassionately watching his father, touches of anger and contempt nudging the unconcern from time to time.* WAITE*'s eyes open. He focuses on* WILLIAM.

WAITE: William?

WILLIAM: Rest.

(WAITE*'s eyes close. Open.*)

WAITE: Is your mother here?

WILLIAM: No.

INT. DINING ROOM. DAY

Lunch ending. Fruit. WILLIAM *and* MASSINGHAM *sit opposite each other in silence.* MARIA*'s half-eaten meal remains at the top of the table. Voices in the hall. Front door closing. Car starting up.* MARIA *in.* MARIA *removes her plate and pours herself coffee.*

MARIA: Christ, he's older and iller than father. Never stopped coughing the whole time we were up there.

MASSINGHAM: (*Handing bowl*) Fruit?

MARIA: No, thanks.

WILLIAM: What's he got to say?

MARIA: Up Friday for an hour. No repeat this time, they think. Looks as if you'll get your programme after all, Mr Massingham.

(MASSINGHAM *smiles coolly.*)

Have you seen anything of mother?

WILLIAM: No.

MARIA: (*Quiet, excluding* MASSINGHAM) I had a letter about a month ago. From Estoril.

WILLIAM: Yeah. Where's that?

MARIA: Portugal.

WILLIAM: (*Characteristically terse, bitter*) Jesus. (*Long pause.*) How is she?

MARIA: All right. She's left Frederick. Do you remember Frederick, the one with the teeth?

WILLIAM: Who was the marina developer?

MARIA: Frederick. That was Frederick. She's left him.

WILLIAM: Yeah?

(*Silence.*)

MARIA: She asked for your address.

WILLIAM: (*Standing*) What about a drink? Mr Massingham?

MASSINGHAM: Thank you, no. I have some work to do.

WILLIAM: (*Pouring at drinks table*) In this . . . new . . . golden age of unemployment it's difficult to know whether you are boasting or merely stating a fact. (*Smiles bleakly at* MASSINGHAM.) Sister?

MARIA: What is there?

WILLIAM: Sweet: Benedictine, curaçao, Drambuie. Dry: brandy, calvados . . . Canadian ginger. He must have had his Christmas presents early from his friends in the City. They *say* he used to like a glass of stout, in the old days. (*To* MARIA) Yes?

MARIA: Brandy. Stop making speeches.

WILLIAM: (*Pouring*) What do you think of my father, Mr Massingham?

MASSINGHAM: (*Equable, guarded*) I think he's a remarkable man.

MARIA: William.

WILLIAM: (*Fetching drinks to table*) Remarkable. Yes. And the programme you're doing is, what, *Living History*, that's the title?

MASSINGHAM: Working title.

WILLIAM: Oh. You might . . . change it, you mean?

MASSINGHAM: It might be changed. Producers don't usually have the final say in series titles.

WILLIAM: So it could end up as . . . *Historical Curiosities* or . . . *Anomalies of History* . . . or *A Gallery of Class Traitors*, mm?

MASSINGHAM: I think it a . . . little unlikely.

WILLIAM: Do you? (*Pause.*) I personally wouldn't mind in the least, you understand. Conceivably *he* might, though.

MASSINGHAM: (*Dry*) I believe I've already had the next speech from your sister.

WILLIAM: You think so?

(*They stare at each other levelly. The absence of empathy is palpable.*)

MARIA: I saw a book in Compendium the other day called *The Knee of Listening.* I couldn't believe it. I'm sure it's been planted by somebody making a detailed study of the double take. Mine was monumental.

(*Silence.* MASSINGHAM *smiles civilly in* MARIA*'s direction.*)

MASSINGHAM: (*To* MARIA) Would it be convenient to call in for a chat with your father now, do you think?

MARIA: Ten minutes. You mustn't tire him.

MASSINGHAM: (*Draining coffee*) Good.

WILLIAM: You haven't really said anything, have you?

MASSINGHAM: What do you want? Where I was born, early life, parents, school, relationships? What purpose would it serve, except to confirm your view that, unlike you presumably, I'm a total product of my environment?

WILLIAM: (*Gently*) I meant more the programme. (*Pause.*) I mean, you're too intelligent, too clever, really to believe that you can talk as it were neutrally about the past. So, when you choose to examine the social and political history of twentieth-century Britain through the eyes and mouth of a major Labour politician, you must have some . . . framework . . . some point of view, attitude, mm? . . . to hold the thing together.

MASSINGHAM: I don't see why.

WILLIAM: (*Gently almost*) But that would mean . . . you didn't *care.* You were indifferent.

MASSINGHAM: The conventional rules of biography and historiography will be observed. I can't see that it makes better history if one has an axe to grind.

WILLIAM: Can't you? You see – and I work in the margins of history and sociology currently, and have reason to look at the matter fairly closely – you can't look at a mainstream representative of Labourism in this century – my father, say – *without declaring an interest.* Because Labourism is itself a critique: both of extra-parliamentary revolutionism on the one hand and of parliamentary Toryism on the other. In other words, it's not a *state*, describable, with planes and surfaces and textures. Or at least, it's not in essence that. It's basically a *process*, a more or less dynamic interaction between value and value, assertion and counter-assertion, stimulus and response. You can't just . . . describe the 'Welfare State', you have to . . . account for it. And that means, inevitably, making some assessment of its 'goodness' or whatever, of its preferability to what it superseded; and of its deficiencies in terms of what was *actually realizable*, *potent*, in the period during which it was being constructed.

MASSINGHAM: I don't disagree. But I'm not writing the history. Your father is. Because he has lived it. I'm simply the film camera, the tape-recorder, the lighting man . . .

WILLIAM: The programme controller. The film editor. The picture researcher. The sound mixer. The blurb writer. The audience softener. (*Pause.*) It's not even *that.* (*Pause.*) Suppose it's the North American Indians you want to talk about. Now. How do you set about writing a history of the Red Indian in the nineteenth century or in this without mentioning the word 'genocide'? Yet merely to invoke the concept is to begin to develop a critique of American society and the economic 'necessities' of contemporary capitalism. Your answer – superficially attractive – is presumably to invite an Indian chief to tell it 'how it was'. Some Edward Waite of the Nez Percé or Arapahoe, mm? The question still remains, which chief? Spotted Tail? Geronimo? Because most of them *led* their people into obliteration. *Objectively*, most of them sold out, assimilated, *settled* for ignominy, starvation, slow death on remote and barren reservations, in face of the 'higher technology'. Yet Geronimo and others proved that objectively another way was open to the Indian, based on attritional struggle, organization, discipline, courage and will. If you want to write the history, you have to say who was right, Mr Massingham. You have to *choose* your spokesman.

MASSINGHAM: The analogy is peculiarly unapt, if I may say so. The history of your father's 'people', if I might put it that way, has been the history of increasing control over their social and work environment and the steady amelioration of the quality of life, and your father's leading role in this 'progress' I would take to be pretty well self-evident.

WILLIAM: A value. At last. (*Pause.*) Let me tell you how I see my father's role. If this coronary had killed him, I'd've suggested an epitaph from a speech from Kicking Bird, Chief of the Kiowas, who said, towards the end of his highly distinguished life, all there is to be said about my father's sort of leadership: 'I long ago took the white man by the hand; I have never let it go; I have held it with a strong and firm grasp. I have worked hard to bring my people on the white man's road. Sometimes I have been compelled to work with my back towards the white people so that they have not seen my face, and they may have thought I was working against them; but I have worked with one heart and one object. I have looked ahead to the future and have worked for the children of my people, to bring them into a position that, when they become men and women, they will take up the white road.' (*Pause.*) 'But now I am as a stone, broken and thrown away. And I fear most that my people will go back to the old road.'

(*Silence.* MARIA *stands deliberately, leaves.* MASSINGHAM *stares at* WILLIAM.)

MASSINGHAM: (*Coolly*) So you hate your father.

WILLIAM: (*Laughing tightly*) You listen but you don't hear, Mr Massingham.

(WILLIAM *stands, leaves.*)

INT. CONSERVATORY. DAY

Conservatory. Dullish afternoon. WAITE *and* MARIA *play cribbage on a small card table.* WAITE *sits in a bathchair, wears pyjamas and thick plaid dressing-gown. A car rug covers legs and feet.* MARIA *deals six cards; they carefully discard two apiece into the box; he cuts the pack; she turns up a jack, smiles.*

WAITE: Lucky at cards . . .

(WAITE *plays a seven;* MARIA *scores with an eight; they play out. He calls three. She shows seven, has six in the box.*)

MARIA: (*Moving matchstick*) Dead hole.

WAITE: All right. I'll give it you.

(MARIA *smiles ironically at the board. He's only just turned the corner.*)

MARIA: Sure?

WAITE: Don't be cheeky.

MARIA: (*Collecting cards*) Not like you to give up.

WAITE: Rubbish. When I know I'm licked, there's nobody gives up faster. There's no joy to be had fighting losing battles. How much is that?

MARIA: 30 p.

WAITE: You'll have to wait.

(MARIA *places the pack on the board.*)

MARIA: Are you warm enough?

WAITE: I'm fine. Don't fuss.

MARIA: Do you want anything?

WAITE: No. I'll go back up in a minute. I feel tired.

MARIA: You look fine.

WAITE: I feel all right. I feel better than I did before I had it. Just a bit tired, that's all.

(*Pause.* MARIA *stands, walks over to the windows, looks out down the long lawns.* WAITE *puts his hand out, touches a long, brown cardboard box on a table to the right. Looks at* MARIA. *Removes the hand.*)

MARIA: (*Back still to window*) Have you had a chat with William yet?

WAITE: I've never had a *chat* with William in my life. You can have a fight with him, or a flaming great row, or you can make the occasional interruption to his speeches. Chat, no.

(MARIA *scratches a stain from the window pane. Longish pause.*)

We exchanged . . . unpleasantries this morning. Very briefly. Why?

MARIA: He's upset about something. I don't know . . .

WAITE: Isn't he always? Vietnam, Cambodia, Industrial Relations, Wounded . . . Knee, was it? How else should he be, a lad of mine?

MARIA: Maybe. (*Pause.*) He used to cry for you, when you had all-night sittings and didn't come home. A long time ago.

WAITE: Day before yesterday. (*Pause.*) How's school?

MARIA: School . . . is school. I don't want to talk about it.

WAITE: I thought you liked teaching. Fine big comprehensive, airy classrooms, lots of equipment . . .

MARIA: Yeah.

(*Silence. She smokes a cigarette, tense.*)

WAITE: My day, it was something different.

MARIA: (*Terse*) Yes, I know about that, Dad . . .

(*Silence.*)

WAITE: (*Tentative*) Do you see anything of your husband?

MARIA: I had a letter from him, while ago. He wants to remarry. An actress.

WAITE: And you?

MARIA: Once is enough for me.

WAITE: Are you sure? It's a long time.

MARIA: (*Bluntly, turning*) My needs are relatively few and . . . not difficult to satisfy.

(WAITE *looks away, embarrassed, an old Puritan.*)

I have an address for mother, if you'd like me to write.

WAITE: (*Studying a* Guardian *he's picked up*) What about?

(MARIA *doesn't answer. After a moment,* WAITE *looks over the top of the paper at her.* MASSINGHAM *in, in good, short topcoat, carrying grip.*)

MASSINGHAM: (*Approaching*) Forgive me, I'm just off.

WAITE: Have a safe trip.

MASSINGHAM: Thank you. I've . . . I've made arrangements for the crew to arrive Monday morning, as agreed. Are you sure you'll feel up to it?

WAITE: Yes yes. They'll have to cut me up in pieces and feed me to the dogs before they'll be shot of me, don't you fret.

MASSINGHAM: Fine. Fine. Well . . . (*Moving*) Oh, would you mind if I came back Sunday evening, just to get things set up?

WAITE: Come back whenever you like. It's no bother.

MARIA: Sunday's your birthday.

WAITE: So it is. (*To* MASSINGHAM) If you get back soon enough, you'll be in time for the jelly and a piece of cake.

MASSINGHAM: Are you sure . . . ? I wouldn't want to intrude on a family . . .

WAITE: Go on with you. We've never been what you'd call struck on birthdays in our family. We'll see you Sunday dinner.

MASSINGHAM: Thank you. Goodbye.

(MASSINGHAM *leaves.* MARIA*'s distaste is fairly patent.*)

WAITE: Nice feller. (*Musing*) Do you know, I can't remember if he's BBC or the other lot.

MARIA: Does it matter?

WAITE: No. I shouldn't think so.

(MARIA *stubs her cigarette out on an ashtray by the brown cardboard box.*)

MARIA: I think I might push off home, if you're going to be all right.

WAITE: (*Taking her hand*) Do I have to be dying to get a bit of attention then?

MARIA: (*Carefully disengaging*) Don't be silly.

WAITE: What is it?

MARIA: Nothing. I don't like that man, that's all. I don't trust him. I don't think *you* should.

WAITE: Oh. I see. *That's* how you suck eggs. Well, I'd never have thought it.

(MARIA *stares hard at* WAITE, *frowning.*)

And what makes you think I trust him?

MARIA: How do you mean?

WAITE: Listen, baby. I've been in this game a long while. You don't get where I got by trusting people. And especially not the likes of him.

MARIA: He's clever.

WAITE: (*Unconvinced*) Is he?

MARIA: And he doesn't care. About you, I mean.

WAITE: He doesn't have to. It's a free country. (*Pause.*) All right? (*Pause.*) I don't understand you young people. I don't. The minute you feel something you think your only responsibility is to express it. Now, in my line of business that's tantamount to suicide. Shout when you have to, smile when you don't, Keir Hardie used to say. Mmm?

(*Silence.*)

MARIA: Hadn't you better rest?

WAITE: Sit down a minute, will you. There's something I want to ask of you.

(MARIA *sits carefully.* WAITE *draws the brown box laboriously on to his knee, breathing a little at the exertion. Looks at her. Removes the lid. Tilts it in her direction. She inspects the contents, puzzled.*)

Robes. They've just come from the tailors. I've accepted a peerage. It'll be announced in the New Year's Honours List. You're to tell no one. I wanted you to know.

(*Long silence.* MARIA *stares at the robes.*)

Say something.

MARIA: Say what? (*Pause.*) Why?

WAITE: Why not? I wasn't made for retirement and obscurity. I'm no . . . thinker, I need to be doing. (*Pause.*) It's an arena. What's wrong with that?

MARIA: How? The *Tories* put you up for it?

WAITE: It's a technicality. A deal. I was offered in 1970 but I thought I might get a safe seat in a by-election. (*Pause.*) I'll take the Labour whip. It's perfectly normal.

(MARIA *looks at the robes again, back at* WAITE.)

MARIA: (*Finally*) So do it.

WAITE: I need your help.

MARIA: (*Slightly numb*) Yes?

WAITE: There's an investiture ceremony in February sometime at the Palace. (*Pause.*) Now that your mother's finally . . . (*Long pause.*) I'd like you to . . . accompany me. Be my . . . woman. If you would.

(*They look at each other for a long time.* MARIA *is finally distracted by the sound of whistling from the garden. She looks out, stands, takes the brown box, deftly lids it, places it on the table.* WILLIAM *in from the garden.* WILLIAM *stops, surveys the scene, his lips pursed, the whistling gone silent.*)

WILLIAM: (*Finally*) The squirrels are killing that yew. You should have someone take a gun to them.

(WILLIAM *moves on into the house.* WAITE *looks at* MARIA *who's fiddling abstractedly with the box's securing tapes.*)

WAITE: I can't understand a word he says, you know. How can a squirrel kill a tree? Mmm?

MARIA: They eat the bark. When the stripped parts meet in a circle, the tree dies.

(*Long silence.* WAITE *ponders it, very pale, tired, old.*)

Let's get you inside.

(WAITE *lets himself be hauled up, shuffles slowly towards the doorway using* MARIA *as a crutch. They reach the conservatory doorway. He stops, points to the box, hangs on to the french window as* MARIA *gathers it. She returns to help him.*)

WAITE: You didn't answer.

MARIA: We'll talk. Come.

(MARIA *helps* WAITE *into the house.*)

INT. LIVING ROOM. NIGHT

Living room. Night, around seven forty-five. Some subdued talk, clink of glasses, crockery, from adjoining dining room. MARY *in, carrying a birthday cake, which she places on the coffee table before lighting the single candle. We see the pink iced message:* EDUCATE AGITATE ORGANIZE. HAPPY BIRTHDAY DAD, *in the style of a William Morris SDF banner.* MARY *takes a knife from her apron, places it on the plate, crosses to the half-open dining-room door, stands until she catches* MARIA*'s eye, nods, leaves.*

INT. DINING ROOM. NIGHT

MARIA, WAITE, MASSINGHAM. WAITE *wears a suit, looks stronger though not fully recovered.*

MARIA: One drink, the doctor said. What will it be?

WAITE: (*Pointing to wine*) Some of that'll do.

(MARIA *pours him half a glass, hands the bottle round.*)

MARIA: Now bring your glasses through. There's a surprise.

(MARIA *takes her father's arm, leads them off into the living room.*)

INT. LIVING ROOM. NIGHT

WAITE: (*Walking carefully*) All the world's a classroom to this one. Born organizer. Do this, do that . . .

MARIA: (*Squeezing his arm*) Go on . . .

(*They reach the coffee table,* MASSINGHAM *some steps behind.* WAITE *sees the cake. Stares, moved. Smiles. Approaches. Reads the inscription. Turns to* MARIA. *Looks at her.*)

Happy birthday!

(WAITE *doesn't speak. Looks back at the cake.*)

WAITE: S'elp me, God.

MARIA: Do you need any help?

(WAITE *bends carefully, blows out the candle.*)

WAITE: Isn't that something!

MARIA: Shall I cut it or will you?

(WAITE *sits down, faces it, staring still.*)

WAITE: No no. I want a picture of that before it's destroyed. Do you mind?

MARIA: (*Laughing*) Not in the least. It'll probably taste terrible.

MASSINGHAM: May I look?

WAITE *gestures* MASSINGHAM *in. He studies it.* WILLIAM *in from hall, in outdoor clothes. He carries a small package. Studies the group.*)

It's marvellous. Where's it from?

MARIA: I took it from a William Morris banner. You should see the original.

MASSINGHAM: Marvellous. Is that what you teach, domestic science?

MARIA: I teach art.

(MARIA *sees* WILLIAM *in the doorway.*)

You made it then.

WILLIAM: Yeah, I got stuck at Guildford coming back. (*To* WAITE) Sorry I missed your . . . thing.

WAITE: (*Slight brusqueness*) Come in. Get yourself a drink.

WILLIAM: (*To cabinet*) Anybody else?

(*They indicate full glasses, settle down.* WILLIAM *joins them with his glass. Approaches his father.*)

I bought you this.

(*He hands* WAITE *parcel. Stares at cake.*)

WAITE: Very kind of you.

(*A moment's hesitation. Begins to open it.* WILLIAM*'s eyes move from the cake to* MARIA, *who's watching him closely, slightly apprehensive. He smiles tightly.* WAITE *holds up a book.*)

Indian . . . Oratory. (*Pause. Looks at* WILLIAM.) Will I find this . . . instructive?

WILLIAM: You might. Tell me when you've read it.

WAITE: I will. I will. Thank you. (*Pause.*) Maria bought me the tie.

(WAITE *pulls the tails of it from his breast to show* WILLIAM.)

And . . . I had a . . . (*Searches for it on the settee where he sits, finds it*) . . . a very expensive tin of tobacco from Mr Massingham. See.

(WILLIAM *looks at* MARIA, *back at tobacco.*)

WILLIAM: Tobacco.

WAITE: That's right.

WILLIAM: Mmm. (*Takes a sip from his glass.*) Very nice.

MASSINGHAM: (*Standing*) I . . . got you something else, I don't know if it'll be of any use.

(MASSINGHAM *crosses to a chair by the door, takes up a canvas picture folder, unties the laces, takes out a sort of large black album, brings it over to the settee, sits down by* WAITE.)

It's work as well, but I thought you might just like to have it for your own use afterwards. (*He begins flicking the pages.*) I've had a picture researcher working on the period. This is some of the stuff we're likely to want for the programme. See. (*He points to a glossy pic of Waite in 1938, at the rostrum*, at the TUC Annual Congress.) I asked her to look out the best pictures of you and make them up into . . . well, this. (*He hands the album on to* WAITE*'s knee.*) If it's of any interest.

WAITE: (*Turning pages*) Interest! I should say so. Yes! Thank you. Ha, look at old Manny there . . . He never could resist a camera . . .

MARIA: You can talk.

(WAITE *stares at a picture. We close on it. It's a miners' picket in Manchester during the General Strike. He's at its head, carrying the largest placard, scrawny, fresh-faced, scarf knotted at neck, cap on head, thin trousers failing to reach his big boots.*)

WAITE: (*Very softly*) My God.

(WILLIAM *looks over* WAITE*'s shoulder at the picture.*)

WILLIAM: (*As softly*) A man could die of memories like that.

(*He walks down the room towards the french windows.* MASSINGHAM *stands.*)

MASSINGHAM: Well, I think I'll go up. You'll have plenty to talk about, I imagine.

WAITE: (*Snapping the trance*) I thought you wanted to discuss tomorrow . . .

MASSINGHAM: (*Looking around*) Not er . . . not if it's going to get in the way of . . .

WAITE: Nonsense. (*Looking to* MARIA *for support*) Be a party piece.

And it'll be something for William to get his teeth into. (*Down room*) What do you say, William?

WILLIAM: (*Turning*) What's that?

WAITE: We're going to talk about my interview. I said you'd enjoy a bit of . . . mental exercise.

(WILLIAM *looks down at his glass, up the room again.*)

WILLIAM: (*Finally*) Why not?

MARIA: (*To* WAITE) The doctor said an early night.

WAITE: I know what the doctor said and I'll still see him out. Physician heal thyself, I said to *him.* That shut him up. (*Generally*) Sit you down then. Let's get cracking.

(MASSINGHAM *takes an armchair to the side of the large fireplace. He's unhappy but senses no other option.* MARIA *retains the chair opposite.* WAITE *closes the album, rests it on his knee.* WILLIAM *refills his glass, fills one for* MARIA, *carries it to her, perches, remotely, on a small upright chair so that he can see his father's face but so as to remain physically peripheral to the action. He is taut, rather white, growing grimmer.*)

(*In good humour*) What they call a talk-in, eh? (*To* MASSINGHAM) Right. Off you go, young man.

MASSINGHAM: (*Smoothly*) I'd rather hoped you'd do the talking, Mr Waite. (*Pause. Smile.*) It *is* your story.

WAITE: (*Teasing slightly*) Aren't you going to ask me questions?

(MASSINGHAM *remains blandly silent.*)

Nay, if you don't ask me questions, I can't give you answers.

MASSINGHAM: Couldn't we perhaps . . . simply . . . talk . . . generally. I'd prefer to keep your . . . 'answers' as . . . fresh and spontaneous as possible . . . for tomorrow.

WAITE: I'm getting on, Mr Massingham. Maybe you haven't noticed it, but I'm seventy-one. And old men do tend to ramble a bit . . . Still.

WILLIAM: (*Suddenly*) I'll ask you a question.

(*Silence.* WAITE *looks at* WILLIAM.)

WAITE: Is it . . . germane?

WILLIAM: *I* think so.

(WAITE *looks at* MASSINGHAM, *who smiles assent.*)

WAITE: (*Putting empty pipe to mouth*) Ask your question.

WILLIAM: (*Very tense*) Given the power that you and your party have from time to time exercised in the last fifty years, and given the fact that your rhetoric is invariably radical in temper, how do you explain the extremely modest nature of the changes you have managed to effect?

WAITE: (*Blowing histrionically*) Is that the question, is that all of it?

(WILLIAM *makes no answer.*)

Well, let me begin by attacking the premiss. Our achievements have been *far* from modest, and only a person blinded by dogma or utterly without acumen would fail to see it. There isn't a part of this society, top to bottom, that hasn't been profoundly affected by what we have done, in office and out. The record speaks for itself, but I'll speak to it if you'd like. (*Looks in* MASSINGHAM*'s direction.*) Do you want to hear it?

MASSINGHAM: (*Alert again*) Yes indeed.

WAITE: Where to begin? Nineteen twenty-four. When we found ourselves a minority government at the mercy of a potential Tory–Liberal alliance and a hostile press, and still managed, in *months*, mind, not years, to honour our election promises over unemployment benefits, over the creation of new jobs in road and railway construction, over slum clearance and new housing subsidies, over education. Nineteen twenty-nine? Against a backcloth of shrinking world trade and a collapse in the world's financial structures – and still at the mercy of Tory–Liberal alliances – we were still able to raise and extend the pensions of widows and the aged; we were still able to make unemployment insurance more easily available; we were still able to work for international co-operation and disarmament. (*Pause.*) I make no apologies for the renegade MacDonald and the 1931 National Government. But you will remember that he was rightly and promptly ejected by the Party and shunned by it thereafter.

(*Pause.*) The great Attlee administrations of 'forty-five to 'fifty-one? There, surely, if nowhere else. I say nothing of my own part. But look at the record sometime, *objectively* – if I might borrow an overworked word from you for a moment. We said we must have full employment, and we had it. For the first time in history, outside of wars. We said we must control the commanding heights of industry, and we took coal and the railways, road transport, electricity, gas, iron and steel into public ownership. We said we must have a say in the way the country was financed, and we nationalized the Bank of England. (*Pause.*) And underpinning all of this, we created a *caring* society, a community in which people were entitled to a good education, to health services, national assistance and pensions *as of right*, not as charities doled out by this board or that. (WAITE *stops, wipes his forehead and neck with a handkerchief, half exhausted by his effort, suddenly passionate, alive, no longer patronizingly remote.*) In six short years we created a social revolution. And we did it with the consent of the people. And nobody was shot or imprisoned or tortured or . . . blown up to effect it. (*Long pause.*) And we did it against a backcloth of financial crisis, world shortages of food, fuel and raw materials, a hostile Civil Service, a rabidly Tory press, and an international community determined to make the abandonment of our socialist policies the condition of making loan capital available. (*Pause. He's angry.*) Do I bring us up to date? Or do we just let the question quietly drop?

MARIA: (*To* WILLIAM) Leave it be.

WILLIAM: (*To* WAITE) Is that what *you* want?

WAITE: (*Angry*) Go ahead.

(WILLIAM *gets up, carries his glass to the cabinet, speaking as he does so.*)

WILLIAM: Let it drop.

WAITE: The hell we'll let it drop. Finish what you started.

WILLIAM: (*Turning sharply*) Look. You're old. And you're ill. And you're my father. There's no way I can win. I asked my question, you answered it.

WAITE: (*Deliberately*) Don't patronize me, sonny.

(WILLIAM *turns back to the drinks, pours. Deliberates. Turns.* MARIA *and* MASSINGHAM *watch everything.*)

WILLIAM: (*Finally, metallic*) All right. (*Pause.*) Ramsay MacDonald boasted in 1923, 'We are going to make the land blossom like a rose and fill it with glorious aspirations.' When he came to power – the *first* Labour prime minister – a national daily argued that, 'The party of revolution approach their hands to the helm of state with the design of destroying the very basis of civilized life.' (*To* MASSINGHAM) I hope we get a chance to have a look at those . . . dangerous men in your programme . . . as they queued nervously in their bowlers and toppers and cutaway collars outside Buckingham Palace, to meet the Royal Person and prove the papers wrong. (*Back to* WAITE) You make no case at all for them, beyond the tiniest ameliorations in lives impoverished and ghastly beyond belief, so there's little point in dwelling on them, save to point out that in the likes of MacDonald and Snowden the capitalist system found two of its ablest and most orthodox defenders in this century. *Labour* leaders. Leaders of the working class. (*Pause.*) Like you. (WILLIAM *looks around the room, taking in the whole house, the whole life-style.*) Out of touch. Out of reach. Out of sympathy. Leaders.

WAITE: Nobody spent more time in his constituency than me and well you know it.

WILLIAM: Except you didn't *live* in it, did you?

WAITE: Of course I didn't. Because I worked in London.

WILLIAM: But you had a house in Manchester. Where we grew up. Only it wasn't in your constituency, was it? It was in Didsbury, four bedrooms, attics, cellars, gardens, playschools, parks . . . Not the sort of house you'd find in Beswick now, was it? Because Beswick was single-class housing. *Working* class.

WAITE: Would you have thanked me for a childhood spent in a dingy two-up two-down? Eh?

WILLIAM: (*Fiercely*) Yes! Yes! I would. Because then the rhetoric would have made sense. Because then the leaders and the led would have been part of the same *experience*, instead of just part of the same sentence.

WAITE: I never lost touch. Never. They'd've soon let me know if I had. Where it hurts most. In the ballot box.

(WILLIAM *walks about, regaining his balance, reaching for impersonality again.*)

WILLIAM: No. It was the rhetoric you never lost. So that you can describe the Attlee legislation as a *social revolution* as though what happened during that time was what socialism is all about. A *real* social revolution would have committed you to the destruction of capitalism and the social order formed and maintained by it. A real social revolution would have effected major redistribution of *wealth*, in favour of the labouring masses. A real social revolution would have smashed the bourgeois state apparatus and begun the construction of a people's state. Courts, Civil Service Departments, police, church, army, schools – nothing would have stayed the same. It wasn't a social revolution you achieved, it was a – as it turned out – minimal social adjustment. You drew a section of the working classes into the grammar schools, and allowed the public schools to continue training upper and middle-class élites. You set up national-insurance schemes and allowed private insurance to feed and grow fat on the great pond of fear remaining. You created a *national* health service and allowed the doctors to practise privately. You created municipal housing and left the building industry in the hands of the capitalists. You nationalized the ailing industries and services and allowed the strong to be run privately, for private profit. (*Pause.*) You didn't create a new social order, you merely humanized the old one.

WAITE: Have you finished?

WILLIAM: I've barely started.

WAITE: It's all so easy, isn't it? You sit there behind your little desk in your little room in your little ivory tower and you read your

Marx and your Trotsky and you get your slide-rule out and do a couple of simple calculations and you have your blueprint. Revolution. Total change. Overnight. Bang. Especially bang. You have to have your bit of theatre as well, don't you? (*Pause.*) Reality isn't like that. Reality is . . . taking people with you. Arguing with people who disagree, passionately. It's fighting hostile influences, foreign investors, currency speculators. It's sweating on a good balance of trade surplus at the end of the month. Reality is priorities. You haven't the first idea.

WILLIAM: Maybe not. But I can recognize a shabby definition of reality when I hear it. Did it ever occur to you that Edward Heath might give exactly the same definition as the one you've just propounded? Is a socialist reality the same as a Tory one then?

WAITE: We live in the same world. It doesn't change because we shut our eyes and dream.

WILLIAM: It doesn't change *unless* we shut our eyes and dream. 'I take my desires for reality, because I believe in the reality of my desires.'

WAITE: Try doing a bit of leading some day. See where it gets you.

WILLIAM: (*Tough*) You didn't fail to deliver a social revolution because reality got in the road. You didn't deliver one because you didn't *want* one. You didn't *desire* one. In fact, you desired anything but.

WAITE: You'll learn.

WILLIAM: If there's one thing marks you all out – (*with great, deliberate emphasis*) – Labour . . . leaders – it's this desperate need to be accepted. You . . . efface yourselves until there's nothing there. You all want to prove you can 'do the job as well as they can'. As though that were the summit of socialist aspiration. The need to be thought of as 'responsible' men. Examine that . . . seedy collection currently 'leading' the party. Define their reality if you can. They stand like adolescents at a dance, waiting to become men. Churchill knew it, instinctively. 'Sheep in sheep's clothing,' he called you. 'An empty cab arrived and Mr Attlee stepped out.' (*Pause.*) It's a sort of masochism you all have. It's not there in the Tories, no fear. When a Tory minister calls at his favourite whorehouse, he doesn't go to be beaten, he goes to *beat.* He's *used* to it. You never will be.

WAITE: (*Turning away towards* MASSINGHAM, *who sits, tight-lipped and intent*) I hope this is of some use to *you.* I'm damned if it's of any to me. When a man gets down to quoting Churchill at me, I know he's run out of an argument. He talks about revolution but he forgets to talk about politics.

WILLIAM: (*Fast*) Tell us about 'twenty-six then.

(*Silence. Something dangerous is registered.*)

MARIA: That's enough, William. It's been a long day.

WAITE: (*Ignoring her*) What would you like to hear?

WILLIAM: Wouldn't you have said 'twenty-six was a sort of revolutionary moment?

WAITE: On the contrary, I'd've said it was the final and crushing evidence that 'revolution', in your sense, is not the English way of doing things.

WILLIAM: Is that what you believed at the time?

WAITE: I believed in the miners' cause at the time. You'll recall I was a miner.

WILLIAM: You believed in all-out confrontation with the owners and the state then?

WAITE: Yes, I did, but I don't think I want . . .

WILLIAM: You're a liar.

(*Silence.*)

WAITE: Say that again.

WILLIAM: (*Deliberately*) You're a liar.

MARIA: (*Getting up*) All right, I've heard enough. (*To* WILLIAM) I think you'd better leave before you do any more damage.

WILLIAM: (*Lifting*) I'll leave when *he tells me to.*

MARIA: (*Going to push him out*) You'll leave *now.*

WILLIAM: (*Pulling violently away*) Leave me *alone.* I'm not a bloody infant and neither is he.

MARIA: He's ill. Christ, do you want to kill him?

WAITE: Let him be, Maria.

MARIA: I won't. And you should grow up a little, a man of your age and . . . You're like children . . . 'It's *me*, it's me.' Jesus Christ. (*She pulls away.*) All right, damn you both.

(MARIA *walks out of the room, angry, close to tears.* MASSINGHAM *has stood up, wavers uncertainly.* WAITE *and* WILLIAM *glare at each other.*)

MASSINGHAM: Would you . . . rather I er . . . ?

WAITE: (*Not looking at him*) No no. You should stay to the end, Mr Massingham. After all, it's been created in your honour.

(MASSINGHAM *sits.* WAITE *sits in Maria's chair.* WILLIAM *remains standing.*)

Let's have it then.

WILLIAM: (*Metallic again*) When I'm not devising blueprints for revolution in that ivory tower of mine the world otherwise knows as the University of Manchester, I busy myself with a doctoral thesis on the relationship between leaderships and grassroots in working-class political organizations. Now that may neither interest nor disturb you. What may come as something of a surprise is the knowledge that over the past six months I have had access to NUM files – your union – for the year 1926. The year of the General Strike. The year you made District Association executive. (*Pause.*) I've had a chance to study your record during that crucial year. How you spoke, how you voted. And I know now, absolutely, what you've always been made of. (*Pause.*) You opposed the strike before it took place and you voted on no less than six occasions after it for a return to work. You didn't want it to take place, you didn't want it to succeed. And when it was over, you acted as vice-chairman on the committee that was set up with the owners to agree on pay reductions and who would go down the road. That's the *leadership* you offered. And if that's what you call being *for* the miners, by Christ I hope you never side with me.

WAITE: It's astonishing you had to go to the files.

WILLIAM: The votes were secret.

WAITE: But I could have told you. Of course the votes were secret. But the majority always won. We each registered what we believed in our hearts to be right. And then we all pitched in, as democrats, to implement the decisions of the majority. I did nothing I'm ashamed of. Our position was hopeless, in my view, both before, and after, the strike. The strike proved nothing, achieved nothing, save more redundancies.

WILLIAM: (*Hard*) The strike proved that men can find extraordinary solidarity under the most appalling and oppressive conditions. Given a leadership basing itself on the reality of desire instead of the irreality of rhetoric, who knows what it might not have accomplished? (*Pause.*) In any case, this part of your life has hardly been an open book, has it? (To MASSINGHAM) Did you know about it?

MASSINGHAM: (*Slowly*) No, I can't say I did . . .

WILLIAM: And he's read your autobiography.

WAITE: A life's a long thing. A book can't hold it all.

WILLIAM: It will generally be found to hold what we want it to.

WAITE: (*Standing slowly*) I stand on what I've done. I've made mistakes, God knows. And usually I've paid for them. But I believe I've given more than I've taken, and helped more people than I've hurt. I agree with Beatrice Webb about the General Strike and the miners' strike that precipitated it. 'A proletarian distemper', she called it, 'that had to run its course.' Well, distemper's a kind of sickness, and you can't build a new order on a sickness. (*Pause.*) As to desires and reality, the people have always suffered from a poverty of desire, as my old friend Ernie Bevin used to put it. We could have gone faster, perhaps, but they wanted us to walk so that they could see where we were going. (*Pause.*) One day you may find yourself doing something really serious, like running a ministry, and then you'll see where dreams get you. And now I'm going to bed. (*Looking straight at* WILLIAM) You make me tired. I'll see you in the morning, Mr Massingham.

Thank you for the presents. Thank you both. (*He walks to the door. Turns.*) Oh, one more betrayal you should know about, but please keep it to yourself for the moment. I am to be elevated to the peerage in the New Year. If you wish to change your name by deed poll, I shall perfectly understand. Goodnight.

(WAITE *leaves.* WILLIAM *stares after him, numb.* MASSINGHAM *crosses to the drinks cabinet, pours himself a large Scotch, puts it back in two connected gulps, pours himself another.*)

MASSINGHAM: Excuse me.

(MASSINGHAM *walks to the french windows.*)

INT. CONSERVATORY. NIGHT

MASSINGHAM *passes through to the conservatory, puts on a single light, revealing floods and spots, in half-rigged state, for the morning. He plugs in at two different plug-boards, brings up the lights in turn, checking spot focus on the two interview chairs, general spread elsewhere. After a moment,* WILLIAM *appears in the doorway, glass in hand. He carries a small attaché case.*

WILLIAM: Lord Waite remembers. Your researchers should have found out about the pipe. It's a prop. He doesn't smoke it. (MASSINGHAM *stops working for a moment to look at* WILLIAM, *then goes on.* WILLIAM *places the attaché case on a cupboard, opens it, takes out a blue file.*) I had some copies made of the miners' strike voting . . .

MASSINGHAM: (*Looking at file*) What makes you think I'll use it?

WILLIAM: Won't you?

(MASSINGHAM *takes the file, opens it, studies it a moment.*)

MASSINGHAM: I don't know.

WILLIAM: (*Softly*) Yes, you do. (*Pause.*) You can't resist it.

MASSINGHAM: I thought . . . you were against me.

WILLIAM: Oh, I am.

MASSINGHAM: (*File in air*) Then why this?

(WILLIAM *closes the case, his back to* MASSINGHAM.)

WILLIAM: I went to see a mate of mine in London this afternoon. Alwyn Bell. Works for your lot. Know him?

MASSINGHAM: (*Guarded*) Not really. I see him at meetings from time to time.

WILLIAM: He knows you. (*Pause.*) He says you're a crook.

MASSINGHAM: Really.

WILLIAM: He says you're well known in the features field for setting up fake projects in order to get other things done.

MASSINGHAM: Does he!

WILLIAM: He says if you're supposed to be doing a whitewash on a Labour politician you're almost certainly planning a hatchet job. (*Pause.*) I trust Alwyn. (*Pause.*) He's pretty certain there's no such series as *Living History* on the stocks or projected.

MASSINGHAM: I told you, it's a working title.

(*Silence.*)

So. If I'm firing, why not use some of your ammunition, is that it?

WILLIAM: Something like that. (*Pause.*) Maybe I shouldn't even bother interfering. Leave you to each other. Maybe that way, *your* class loyalty and his . . . objective treachery . . . will stand out more clearly. (*Turning*) Attack him how you like.

MASSINGHAM: (*Quickly*) I can take it . . . you won't be speaking with him, can I?

WILLIAM: Yes. Do you think he'd listen? To me? In any case, *he* needs you as much as you need him. After all, you're both involved in . . . mystifications, aren't you?

MASSINGHAM: (*Angry now*) I've told you what I'm involved in. I'm involved in making good programmes.

WILLIAM: (*Lifting*) Sure. And if that involves ridiculing and sneering at a man who's spent the best part of his life working and slaving, however benightedly, to make things just a little bit better for people, well, so be it, that's how the cookie crumbles when the shit hits the fan, etc. Eh? Yes? Because *nobody* can take seriously, let alone imagine fit for office, a man who likes HP Sauce, or Wincarnis, or ducks in flight on the wall, can they? You can't esteem a man who looks and talks like a *grocer*, can you? How can you possibly listen to someone who's been branded on the tongue! Oh God, if only the eighteenth century hadn't gone wrong the way it did, what a fine and ordered world we'd all be living in.

MASSINGHAM: Very satirical. Perhaps you should go in for politics. You seem to have all the answers

(MASSINGHAM *begins switching the lights off, picks up the file, passes* WILLIAM *to go into the house.*) I'd still sooner be me than you. Goodnight.

(MASSINGHAM *leaves, cool, unconcerned, already working on tomorrow.* WILLIAM *stands in the barely lit conservatory. Stares at his father's chair. Approaches it. Runs his fingers gently round the top rim. Steps backwards, until he can sit facing it.*)

INT. WAITE'S BEDROOM. NIGHT

WAITE *lies awake, pillowless, staring at the ceiling, in the dark room. His wife's voice cuts the silence, metallic, like William's.*

ANN: (*Voice over: an elaborate sexual game*) Guttersnipe. Prole. Rough diamond. *Arriviste.* (*Quickly*) Stay down! (*Capping*) Collier!

(*Knock at door. Another.* MARIA *in, in dressing-gown. She stands in the doorway, listening.*)

MARIA: You awake?

WAITE: Aye. Come in.

(MARIA *closes door to, crosses to the bed, flicks on a rather harsh wall light, directed away from the bed but giving flareback from the smooth white wall. Sits carefully halfway down the bed.* WAITE *remains prostrate, fatigued but not sleepy.*)

MARIA: Are you going to be all right?

WAITE: Oh yes. I'm indestructible.

MARIA: I'll come at Christmas if you like.

WAITE: Be nice.

(*Pause.*)

MARIA: You mustn't let yourself get upset like that, you know.
WAITE: He's like his mother. Stubborn. Even looks like her.
MARIA: Get away. Spitting image of you.
(WAITE *puts his hand out for* MARIA*'s. Covers it.*)
WAITE: *You're* mine.
(*Silence.*)
MARIA: Dad.
WAITE: Mmm?
MARIA: Is there . . . any chance of your not accepting the life peerage?
WAITE: I've said yes. I can't go back on my word. (*Pause.*) Do you think I should?
MARIA: You must do what you think's right. (*Pause.*) You do . . . despise it though, don't you? You don't believe it somehow . . . honours you . . . ?
WAITE: Miner's lad to peer of the realm, or How I Slipped from Grace. (*Pause.*) No no. Say, it suits my purpose and the Party's. (*Pause.*) You will . . . accompany me, won't you?
(*Pause.*)
MARIA: (*Finally*) I don't think I can, Dad.
(*Silence.*)
WAITE: I see.
MARIA: It wouldn't be right, Dad. (*Pause.*) I can't believe in a classless society and then suddenly one day – take part in their obscene pantomime. I couldn't keep faith with the poor kids I teach, if I did that. I spend most of my working life battling against privilege and . . . hierarchy and inequalities of opportunity . . .
WAITE: You make too much of it, lass. It's nobbut a little thing.
MARIA: Maybe. But sooner or later we've got to stop being . . . picked off. Sucked in one by one, patted, flattered. We've got to stay with thc class, Dad. We've got to say no. We go when the class goes. You can't lead an army in the uniform of the enemy. (*Pause.*) I'm sorry.

WAITE: (*Smiling, patting her hand*) It's not been what you'd call my day, all in all, has it? Some days it's hardly worth getting out of bed. (*Pause.*) Maybe it'll buck up tomorrow; let me sleep now.

(MARIA *gets up, switches out the light. Bends to kiss* WAITE *on the forehead. Stands again.*)

MARIA: Take care.

(WAITE *nods, smiles.* MARIA *reaches the door.*)

WAITE: Mar. (*She turns, back-lit.*) Leave your mother's address, will you? I'll drop her a line.

(MARIA *smiles to herself at his blunt, uncomplicated pragmatism. Leaves.*)

INT. CONSERVATORY. DAY

Conservatory. Cameraman, assistant, lights, PA, etc. WAITE *sits in his chair being dabbed by make-up. The lights burst across his eyes. Voices blur around him.* MASSINGHAM *talks quietly with the cameraman, gesturing a lot; smiles reassuringly in* WAITE*'s direction.* MARIA *appears in the french windows, ready for off, withdraws.* MASSINGHAM *sees her, detaches, follows her. He carries his own file and William's.*

INT. LIVING ROOM. DAY

MARIA *waits just inside the room.*

MARIA: Goodbye, Mr Massingham.

MASSINGHAM: Goodbye, Mrs Bryant. I . . . very much enjoyed meeting you.

MARIA: (*Slowly*) Be careful with him, won't you?

MASSINGHAM: Yes, of course.

MARIA: He's a good man.

(*An uncomfortable silence between them.* MARIA *turns away finally, leaves.* MASSINGHAM *watches her, the files pulled in to his chest. Returns to the conservatory.*)

INT. CONSERVATORY. DAY

High shot of the conservatory. MASSINGHAM *takes his seat opposite* WAITE, *leans forward to whisper some encouragement. Noises subsiding, people taking up positions. They roll. Clapperboard. Close-up* WAITE. MASSINGHAM*'s voice over, muffled, distant.*

MASSINGHAM: Lord Waite, I'd like to ask you about your attitude to some of the really crucial moments in the history of our society in this century. Take 1926, for example, and the General Strike. How would you summarize your view of it now, half a century later, and how would that view differ from your feelings at the time? You were, of course, deeply involved in the miners' strike of that year that directly precipitated the General Strike.

Close-up WAITE. *All sound out. Light very white, bright, washing out the shapes and textures of his face. His lips begin the answer. Pull back very gradually, back and up until eventually beyond the conservatory, mute, to reveal him in his chair, alone, the room empty of equipment and people, his baronet's robes draping his still form. Fade out.*)

Absolute Beginners

Characters

LENIN
NADEZHDA KONSTANTINOVA KRUPSKAYA
JULIUS OSIPOVITCH MARTOV
VERA IVANOVNA ZASULICH
GEORGES VALENTINOV PLEKHANOV
LEON TROTSKY
N. E. BAUMAN
TUPURIDZE
ALEXANDROVA
LIEBER
MARTINOV
NICHOLAS II
VON PLEHVE
LANDLADY
KRASIKOV

Non-speaking

ALEXANDER POTRESOV, PAVEL BORISOVITCH AXELROD, GUARD, SHOTMAN, LENGNIK, KRZIZHANOVSKI, AKIMOV, 'Centre' delegates to Congress, other 'Hard' delegates, 'Right' delegates, PLEKHANOV's teenage daughters (twelve, fourteen)

Sets

State room, Tsarskoe Selo; Holford Square; study/bedroom, kitchen/living room; commune, Sidmouth Street (one room); Plekhanov's study; warehouse office, Brussels; Lecture Theatre, London; caucus room

Telecine

Von Plehve's armoured carriage, Tsarskoe Selo; estates, Tsarskoe Selo; British Museum, forecourt, etc., train to Geneva; Highgate Cemetery

Absolute Beginners was first broadcast by BBC Television on 19 April 1974 in the series *Fall of Eagles*. The cast included:

LENIN	Patrick Stewart
KRUPSKAYA	Lynn Farleigh
MARTOV	Edward Wilson
ZASULICH	Mary Wimbush
PLEKHANOV	Paul Eddington
TROTSKY	Michael Kitchen
BAUMAN	Peter Weston
TUPURIDZE	Julian Fox
ALEXANDROVA	Svandis Jons
LIEBER	David Freeman
MARTINOV	Raymond Witch
NICHOLAS	Charles Kay
VON PLEHVE	Bruce Purchase
KRASIKOV	Robert O'Mahoney
Director	Gareth Davies
Designer	Allan Anson
Producer	Stuart Burge

INT. TSARSKOE SELO: STATE ROOM. DAY

VON PLEVE, *large, massy, bearded, at the huge window, looking down at the formal lawns and curved drive at the front of the house. His coach stands there, four armed police at ease around it.*

EXT. DRIVEWAY. DAY

The policemen share a cigarette. We examine the coach through the movement. It is heavily armoured, with thick zinc plating at the windows and double locks at the door.

INT. TSARSKOE SELO: STATE ROOM. DAY

VON PLEHVE *turns as the door is opened at the far end of the long room and* NICHOLAS *enters.* VON PLEHVE *bows low.* NICHOLAS *advances briskly into the room, untrapping his shirt collar as he goes.*

NICHOLAS: Von Plehve.

PLEHVE: Your Majesty.

(NICHOLAS *sits at the head of the long table, where* PLEHVE *had laid his 'report': files, dossiers, photographs.*)

NICHOLAS: (*Reading, studying*) I've been . . . shooting . . .

(*Shy smile at* PLEHVE; *polite smile back.*)

Mmm. Is this everything?

PLEHVE: If your Majesty would care to compare it with last year's report, I think he will find an agreeable improvement in the country's security.

(NICHOLAS *already beginning to use files as cover.*)

NICHOLAS: I think you should know, Plehve, that only yesterday I received a security report from Colonel Zubatov. Admittedly his provenance is limited to labour unrest . . . but there is little doubt in his mind that there has been a disagreeable deterioration in security. (*Pause.*) Mmm?

PLEHVE: With respect, Majesty, I do what I can. (*Pause.*) It is precisely Zubatov's police-union policies that undermine my own efforts to promote discipline and the rule of law.

NICHOLAS: (*Studying pictures again.*) *He*, of course, lays exactly the same charge against *you*. (*Looking at* PLEHVE *seriously, like a young boy, but with irony too*) I would like some guidance.

PLEHVE: Majesty, the state has no business organizing workers to present economic demands to employers. There are plenty of . . . revolutionists around to do that, God knows. The state's job is containment. We put out fires. And we eliminate fire-raisers. The market and tradition . . . will take care of the rest.

NICHOLAS: (*Enjoying his game: somehow incapable of proper seriousness, yet not joking*) But it *was* Zubatov who organized 50,000 workers or more in a demonstration of loyalty to the throne in Moscow last month, wasn't it?

PLEHVE: (*Hard*) Majesty, in Zlatoust, last week, one of those same . . . unions stormed the offices of the Urals Mining Federation . . .

NICHOLAS: (*Quickly*) Why do I not know about this?

PLEHVE: It's in the report. (*Pause.*) It is hardly a singular event, Majesty. (*Pause.*) I have the situation under control.

NICHOLAS: I'm relieved to hear it. (*Pause.*) Jews, was it?

PLEHVE: Jews, anarchists, revolutionists . . . fortunately they're all the same size in a gun-sight. (*Pause.*) Sixty-nine rioters killed, a hundred and forty-three wounded; over two hundred arrests. Two dozen already hanged. (*Pause.*) It's all there.

(PLEHVE *points to large file.* NICHOLAS *opens the file rather woodenly, psychologically too weak by far for a close scrutiny.*)

(*With an advantage*) I ordered a Grenadier regiment up from Orenburg to burn a few houses and restore order. (NICHOLAS *nods several times.*)

And . . . I . . . took the liberty of drafting a message of

congratulations to the officers commanding. (PLEHVE *plucks it from a file, hands it to* NICHOLAS.) It would be a considerable boost to morale if you would consent to sign it, Majesty.

NICHOLAS: (*Putting it down.*) Yes, of course.

PLEHVE: (*Relentless*) We will win the war if we have the will to, Majesty. But . . . they must be made to understand that we are serious. And if we are to be serious we must be coherent, we must be ruthless, and above all we must be intelligent. That is the message you will find in every page of my report, Majesty.

(NICHOLAS *bites his lip, breathes deeply, gets up, turns to the window. Silence.*)

NICHOLAS: I shot seven crows this morning. (*Pause.*) Are they all . . . my enemies?

PLEHVE: Potentially. As they are all your loyal and devoted friends and subjects. The people . . . are simply the stakes, Your Majesty.

NICHOLAS: And whom do we . . . play for them?

PLEHVE: They're all there. (PLEHVE *waves an experienced hand across the files of pictures.*) Socialist Revolutionaries. Anarchists. Liberals. Social Democrats . . .

NICHOLAS: (*At table again, studying pictures.*) Jew. Jew. Jew. Aren't there *any* Russians?

PLEHVE: Onc or two, Your Majesty.

(PLEHVE *begins spreading mug shots on the table.* NICHOLAS *crosses reluctantly to look at them.*

NICHOLAS: Look at them.

(*We see their distasteful faces: Plekhanov, Axelrod, Zasulich, Potresov, Strove, Bauman, Martov, Trotsky . . . Krupskaya . . . Lenin.*)

(*Voice over*) Who are these?

PLEHVE: (*Voice over*) Social democrats. Dreamers mostly. Marxists, they call themselves. (*Plekhanov*) Plekhanov, Geneva. The leading figure.

NICHOLAS: (*Martov*) This one. Jew, yes?

PLEHVE: Martov. Born . . . Tsederbaum.

NICHOLAS: (*Lenin*) And this?

(PLEHVE *turns picture over for legend.*)

PLEHVE: Ulyanov. Agitator. Fourteen months in the Marinka awaiting trial. Sentenced to three years exile, ninety-seven. Menusinsk. Last report has him in . . . Munich. Married to this one here. (*Krupskaya. Voice over, drily*) Maybe she'll give him some babies . . . make him settle down, in Germany.

(*Back to Lenin picture. Mix to close-up Lenin;* PLEHVE*'s voice continues.*) (*Voice over*) Of course my political police abroad are monitoring their every movement.

INT. HOLFORD SQUARE. DAY

The Lenins' two-room flat. The study/bedroom. LENIN, *trousers, boots, doing his fifty press-ups. He's at forty; says it under his breath. Half-opened cases litter the room. Track into next room, the kitchen/living room: forty-four, forty-five.* KRUPSKAYA *prepares a frugal breakfast, turns to watch him through the open adjoining door. Knocking at door.* LENIN *stops, at full stretch. They look at each other.* LENIN *hits fifty, stands, dons vest, shirt, waistcoat, jacket, all neatly hung for him.* KRUPSKAYA *opens door.*

LANDLADY: Mrs . . . (*Looks at her book*) Richter? (KRUPSKAYA *makes no answer, beyond a vague, staying frown.*)

I'm . . . your landlady. Pleat, Mrs Pleat. (*She's advancing into the room.*) I believe my husband let you in last evening . . . (*She's clocking everything, talking to cover it.*) I was at my sister's, she's had another of her turns, it's this weather I'm afraid, you'll find it the very devil to get used to, I shouldn't wonder. From . . . Germany, isn't it?

(LENIN *in from the bedroom, dressed, a perfect bourgeois.*)

And you'll be Dr Richter, I presume.

(LENIN *looks at* KRUPSKAYA.)

I'm your landlady, Mrs Pleat. Well . . . welcome to London. I hope your stay will prove a happy one.

KRUPSKAYA: Thank you. I'm sure it shall.

LANDLADY: (*Near door again*) Ah. While I remember. There is the matter of . . . erm . . . marriage lines.

KRUPSKAYA: I'm sorry . . . ?

LANDLADY: Please don't imagine I am in any way attempting to pry . . . It is simply that the authorities do demand that I satisfy myself, as your legal landlady, as it were, that you are . . . well . . . married. A . . . marriage certificate would . . . (*Fade into silence.*)

KRUPSKAYA: (*To* LENIN) Isn't that in the large trunk?

(LENIN *nods.* MRS PLEAT *smiles expectantly.*)

Yes, I thought so. I'm afraid the large trunk is travelling separately and won't be here for some little while. (*Pause, studying effect*) There is a *ring* . . . if you'd care to see it . . .

(KRUPSKAYA *crosses to a box on the mantelpiece. Produces their crude copper ring.* MRS PLEAT *takes it, relieved.*)

MRS PLEAT: Ah. How . . . er . . . unusual. Yes, that's er . . . Not that *I* doubted for one . . . Well, thank you.

(MRS PLEAT *turns to* LENIN, *who remains silent, aloof.*)

Nice to make your acquaintance, doctor . . .

(MRS PLEAT*'s gone.* KRUPSKAYA *pulls a cool, amused face at* LENIN. *He's very serious. Approaches her.*)

LENIN: I didn't know . . . you still had it.

KRUPSKAYA: (*Simply*) I thought it might be useful some time.

(KRUPSKAYA *smiles very seriously.* LENIN *touches the hair on her forehead with the backs of his fingers.*) (*Still held*) Come. You'll be late for the printer. And you have Martov and Zasulich to contact.

(LENIN *nods. Releases* KRUPSKAYA *from his gaze.*)

(*Looking down, almost shy*) I made breakfast.

EXT. BRITISH MUSEUM. DAY

LENIN *stands on pavement outside British Museum, the building clearly visible behind him through the railings. He carries a roll of galleys under his left arm; stares sombrely at the entrance of the pub across the way.*

MARTOV *emerges, studying a piece of paper in his hand, looks around until he sees* LENIN, *breaks into a smile, hurries, despite the limp, across the road. He's thin, smallish, bearded, untidy; papers and pamphlets bulge from his person.*

MARTOV: Volodya! (*Closing in, hugging him passionately*) Volodya, Volodya.
(*They kiss. A love kiss of sorts.*)
It's good to have you with us, comrade. (*Steps back.*) Let me look . . . We expected you Wednesday.

LENIN: (*Smiling gently*) That's what Zasulich said.

MARTOV: Ah.

LENIN: She told me I'd find you . . .
(*He waves towards the pub.*)

MARTOV:(*Serious*) You know me. I need an argument. I need . . . dialectic.

LENIN: (*Softly*) Today *is* Wednesday, Julius.
(MARTOV: *frowns, looks about him eccentrically, as though for confirmation, gropes at his pockets, smiles owlishly.*)

MARTOV: You know, I believe you're right, comrade. Shall we drink to that? Your note (*Paper in his hand*) forced me to defer my destruction of the anarchists' position. It's a great place for anarchists is London, Volodya . . .

LENIN: (*Indicating British Museum*) Let's talk, eh?

MARTOV: (*Serious*) Of course.
(*We watch them walk, arm in arm, into the British Museum forecourt.*)

EXT. BRITISH MUSEUM: PORTICO. DAY

LENIN *and* MARTOV *stand beneath the portico.* MARTOV *has his glasses on the end of nose, totally engrossed in their exchange. He's studying a page of Lenin's* Iskra *galleys. Looks up at* LENIN, *perhaps for an answer.*

LENIN: A year. (*Pause.*) Not less.
(MARTOV *thinks.*)

MARTOV: Can we do it in a year?

LENIN: Yes. With work.

MARTOV: What does Plekhanov think?

LENIN: Does it matter? Plekhanov couldn't organize a coach to the theatre, and God knows he's had enough practice. In any case, he's a *theoretician*. Organization isn't . . . abstract enough for Georges.

MARTOV: But has he approved the broad strategy?

LENIN: Plekhanov and Axelrod have agreed to leave it to my judgement. That's to say, they support my view that we should not undertake a full Party Congress until our own tendency has been strengthened at the expense of all other tendencies. When the *Iskra* men have a strong position within the Party on the ground, then we can convene a Congress that will recognize us as the leading element. And that won't happen until *Iskra* (*Indicates the galleys*) has won the minds of the Party workers.

MARTOV: (*Grinning suddenly*) Oh, how we've *missed* you, comrade.

INT. COMMUNE: MAIN ROOM. DAY

Table in centre. LENIN, MARTOV, KRUPSKAYA, ZASULICH. *On the table, the* Iskra *galleys and Krupskaya's pinned map of Russia.*

ZASULICH: *Fifty, tall, handsome still but seeding fast, in dressing-gown, cigarette in mouth, cuts up bacon into tiny pieces with a pair of nail scissors throughout* LENIN*'s speech. On a board before her, chopped carrots, potatoes, onions, etc.*

LENIN: (*Bringing speech to a close*) What we have now is a fragile chain of agents and contacts spread thin across Russia; in a year, we must have built the embryo of a party, each cell working implicitly from the nucleus, the centre, the source of power. At the moment, *they* are strong. It's we who are weak. We're . . . émigrés. Dilettante, intellectual. Unreliable. We must change that. We must begin with ourselves, if we are to create an organization of professional revolutionaries whose duty is to devote not only their free evenings but their whole life to working

for the Revolution. And when we have such an organization we will begin to shape the Party in its image.
(*A small silence develops*.)

ZASULICH: What does Georges say?

LENIN: (*Looking at* MARTOV) He agrees. (*Pause.*) I don't argue there isn't important work to be done *with* the liberals, as with other elements. I simply say that we must distinguish ourselves *organizationally* from them, based on our profound theoretical differences.

MARTOV: Ilyich is right. We have to establish an entirely new relationship between centre and periphery. Just how to achieve the delicate balance to strengthen central direction without endangering local responsibility and initiative is another matter.

LENIN: Do you have . . . suggestions?

MARTOV: One or two. I think I'd probably want a wider membership than you appear to envisage. And I'd want more power in the hands of the local committees. But they're very minor. As I say, on the whole I agree with your perspective.

LENIN: Vera Ivanovna?

ZASULICH: Well, if Georges says so, I don't suppose I'll object. It seems a pity about the peasants.

LENIN: What does?

ZASULICH: They have revolutionary potential too. They need . . . organizing too.

LENIN: They won't make the Revolution. The question of the peasant arises after the Revolution, when they are forced to bow to the dictatorship of the proletariat. We'll see then how revolutionary they are.

ZASULICH: It seems a bit late leaving it till then, comrade. What do you propose to do about it *then*, may I ask? Shoot them all? There are millions of them.

LENIN: I'll discuss that at length with you some other time, comrade Zasulich. At the moment, I'd prefer we stayed with the agenda.
(ZASULICH *lights a cigarette, angry at the snub.* MARTOV *catches*

LENIN*'s eye, tells him to go easy.*) That becomes the policy then. (LENIN *stands up, preparing to go.*)

We're building an army, comrades. And an army must have its general staff. (*He spreads a hand.*) Us, comrades. We have a newspaper. We have an organization. Now we must find the will. Then we will be fit to lead.

LENIN *leaves,* KRUPSKAYA *follows, kissing* ZASULICH *and muttering good night.* ZASULICH *sweeps up food in a bowl, walks towards kitchen.*)

ZASULICH: (*To* MARTOV, *over shoulder.*) Comrade Robespierre: you're too *soft* with him, Julius.

(MARTOV *looks as though he might follow* LENIN, *stops himself, rubs his nose, thinking.*)

INT. HOLFORD SQUARE: STUDY/BEDROOM. NIGHT

Beds as before. Light from the street. Lenin's watch ticks on the bed cupboard. After 2 a.m. KRUPSKAYA *and* LENIN *lie on their backs, awake.* LENIN *withdrawn, brooding.*

KRUPSKAYA: Do you want me?

LENIN: No.

KRUPSKAYA: Do you want to talk?

LENIN: (*Finally*) Perhaps we're the wrong people.

KRUPSKAYA: No.

(LENIN *turns to look at* KRUPSKAYA, *plays with the hair on her forehead a moment.*)

LENIN: They're turning into fossils, Nadya. (*Long, tough pause.*) Émigrés.

INT. HOLFORD SQUARE: KITCHEN/LIVING ROOM. NIGHT

KRUPSKAYA, *expressionless, beginning delicate job of heating a coded letter. On the wall behind her, the map, red pins slightly more numerous. We see the cyrillic begin to take shape between the lines of the visible letter.*

A stew bubbles on the stove which, from time to time, she stirs, but functionally, undomestically. ZASULICH *sits at the table drinking a glass of tea and smoking.*

ZASULICH: Will we ever go back, Nadya, do you think . . . ?

KRUPSKAYA: (*Not turning, absorbed in the letter*) Oh yes.

ZASULICH: I want to believe that. Here we become . . . nothing. Living or dying . . .

INT. HOLFORD SQUARE: STUDY/BEDROOM. NIGHT

LENIN *writes at his desk, whispers what he writes, but only half intelligibly.*

LENIN: (*Whisper, finding the words*) . . . not time to think about . . . toy forms of democracy . . . an organization of real revolutionaries will stop at nothing . . . rid itself of an undesirable member . . .

INT. HOLFORD SQUARE: KITCHEN/LIVING ROOM. NIGHT

ZASULICH: Nobody'll miss me, depend on it. When I go you'll say, dear me, we're drinking one glass of tea less . . . and that'll be me. Aiii.

KRUPSKAYA: (*Turning, serious*) The Revolution will not forget Zasulich, Vera Ivanovna. (*Pause.*) The revolution will honour her.

INT. HOLFORD SQUARE: STUDY/BEDROOM. DAWN

KRUPSKAYA *sleeps in the bed.* LENIN *sits forward, head on one hand, pale, awake, the same taut, hunched position, reading what he has written. He flexes his writing hand, turns a final page or two. Three huge, spaced bangs on the front door knocker below.* LENIN *sits up, looks at the bed.* KRUPSKAYA *sits, wide awake.*

KRUPSKAYA: Was it three?

(LENIN *nods.*)

Then it's us.

LENIN: (*Checking watch*) At ten to five?

(KRUPSKAYA *sweeps into dressing-gown and slippers, leaves quickly*.)

INT. HOLFORD SQUARE: FRONT DOOR/HALL. DAY

KRUPSKAYA *at door. She sees outline figure through glass. Opens door as hand goes up to knocker.*

KRUPSKAYA: Yes?

(*A young man*, TROTSKY, *twenty-three, tall, good-looking, a bit of a dandy, in the doorway, a running taxi beyond.*)

TROTSKY: Mrs . . . Richter?

KRUPSKAYA: Who wants to know?

TROTSKY: (*Importantly*) Trotsky.

(*He waits. No response.*)

Bronstein.

(*Still no response.*)

Erm . . . The Pen.

(KRUPSKAYA *smiles slowly, opens the door to admit him.*)

KRUPSKAYA: Welcome, comrade. I'm . . . M. Never forget the forms, comrade. We heard you were on your way. (*She looks at her watch.*) But I won't pretend we were . . . expecting you exactly. Come.

(KRUPSKAYA *moves for the stairs.*)

TROTSKY: Comrade.

(KRUPSKAYA *turns.* TROTSKY *takes out a bank note.*) Would you be so good as to pay the cabbie for me. He seems to be having difficulty making himself understood. (KRUPSKAYA *smiles, takes the money.*)

KRUPSKAYA: First on the right, on the next floor.

(TROTSKY *smiles, heads for the stairs.*)

INT. HOLFORD SQUARE: KITCHEN/LIVING ROOM. DAY

The door is open. TROTSKY *knocks, waits, enters.* LENIN *appears in the adjoining doorway.*

TROTSKY: Comrade Lenin?

(*Pause.* LENIN *looks* TROTSKY *over, gives nothing.*)

Trotsky. The Pen. Your wife let me in . . . She's paying the taxi.

LENIN: Trotsky? I thought you were Bronstein.

TROTSKY: Bronstein I got tired of.

(*Pause. Still little give there.*)

Trotsky I borrowed from a gaoler . . . just before I escaped. (*Pause*) Do you think it suits?

(LENIN *still scrutinizing, ignores the question and its irony.*)

LENIN: Do you have a letter? Something?

TROTSKY: (*Finally, to inside pocket*) Of course.

(TROTSKY *hands the letter over.* LENIN *breaks open, reads. He looks over at* TROTSKY *once. Folds it neatly, returns letter to envelope.*)

LENIN: Welcome to London, comrade.

(*They break at last, take each other in arms, hug.*)

TROTSKY: It's an honour to be here, comrade Lenin. I'm in your hands. Tell me what I can do.

LENIN: (*Watch*) Are you tired?

TROTSKY: No. Why do you ask?

LENIN: (*Closing watch. Small smile*) It doesn't matter. (*Pause.*) Come. (*Beckoning into study.*) Sit down then. First of all you can tell me what you know. People, organization, trends – everything . . . A centre cannot hold without intelligence . . .

(KRUPSKAYA *appears in the adjoining doorway.*
LENIN *breaks off.*)

KRUPSKAYA: Tea?

LENIN: Coffee. You've met our new comrade.

KRUPSKAYA: 'The young eagle', wasn't it, Zaphorhets called him?

TROTSKY: It's something to do with the way I hold my nose, I think.

(KRUPSKAYA *laughs.*)

KRUPSKAYA: (*Leaving*) We need all the eagles we can get.

(TROTSKY *returns his attention to* LENIN.)

LENIN: Tell me.

TROTSKY: Do you mind if I remove my shoes?

LENIN: (*Puzzled*) Not at all. Please.

TROTSKY: (*Beginning to slip them off*) Ahh. *They* belonged to Trotsky too. You'd think the least they could do is provide warders with sensible feet.

(TROTSKY *grins, wiggling his toes.* LENIN *smiles, sits back, studies him, liking the confidence, the style.*)

INT. HOLFORD SQUARE: KITCHEN/LIVING ROOM. MID-EVENING

Dark again outside. Trotsky's shoes where they were. LENIN *sits in his desk chair, facing* TROTSKY. TROTSKY *reads from his recent pamphlet* Optimism and Pessimism. KRUPSKAYA *at the kitchen table, coding a stack of Lenin letters, mounds of* Iskra *around her, awaiting despatch. Lenin's room has grown cluttered through the day with cups, plates, books, papers. The two men have talked non-stop.*

TROTSKY: (*Reading*) 'If I were one of the celestial bodies, I would look with complete detachment upon this miserable ball of dirt and dust . . . I would shine upon the good and the evil alike . . . But I am a *man*. World history . . .'

(*Cut to* KRUPSKAYA, *coding in kitchen.* TROTSKY*'s voice in background.*)

'. . . which to you, dispassionate gobbler of science, to you, book-keeper of eternity, seems only a negligible moment in the balance of time, is to me everything! As long as I breathe, I shall fight for the future, that radiant future in which man, strong and beautiful, will become the master of the drifting stream of his history, and will direct it towards the boundless horizon of beauty, joy and happiness. It seems as if the new century, this gigantic newcomer, were bent at the very moment of its appearance, on driving the optimist into total pessimism and civil nirvana . . .'

LENIN: (*Very slow, broken up. Low, voice over*) Are you doing anything at all about *organization* . . . Once again I earnestly beseech and demand that you write us more often and in greater detail. In particular – do it *at once*, without fail, the very same day you receive this letter. Let us know you have received it, even if only a couple of lines . . .

(*Cut to* TROTSKY.)

TROTSKY: 'Surrender, you pathetic dreamer. Here I am, your long-awaited twentieth century, your future.'

'No,' replies the unbowed optimist. 'You are only the present.'

(*Silence.* TROTSKY *closes the pamphlet, looks almost shyly at* LENIN. LENIN *stares back.*)

LENIN: Have you shown it to Plekhanov?

TROTSKY: No. He's seen other things of mine.

LENIN: And?

TROTSKY: He thinks my style is . . . florid and rhetorical. (*Pause.*) What do you think?

LENIN: He's right.

(TROTSKY *frowns suddenly.*)

But Georges has always put style first. He's a great . . . European. (*Smiling chillily*) He once said, not long ago even, that I had . . . no style at all . . . in the French sense, of course.

(TROTSKY *grins suddenly.*)

It's not the style that bothers me. I think it's too . . . soft.

TROTSKY: I don't understand . . .

LENIN: All right. How do we achieve that 'future' you talk of?

TROTSKY: By struggle. How else?

LENIN: But against whom?

TROTSKY: The state. And the classes whose interest it protects. (*Pause.*)

LENIN: The duty of a revolutionary is to fight those forces and personalities . . . that obstruct and impede the Socialist Revolution . . .

TROTSKY: That's what I said . . .

LENIN: No. It isn't what you said and you must see the difference. The 'future' is less than six months away. We make the future with every new theory we evolve, every organizational change we set in progress. (*Pause.*) There will *be* no *Revolution – Millions* will not be mobilized to overthrow the Tsarist state – unless *we* make it possible. We are Marxists: we understand, as liberals and anarchists cannot, the nature of power, of the state and so on. But it is not enough to *know* the world; we must learn how to change it. And that means, first and foremost, building an organization – a party – to develop the theory and lead the revolutionary struggle. (*Pause.*) Do you see what I'm saying . . .? (*Deliberately*) Objectively, the enemy can be your best friend, your lover, your party colleague, the chairman of your local committee, the editor of your party journal . . . The enemy is he who impedes the course of the Revolution. (*Pause.*) The real battle for now is not with the Tsar, Comrade Trotsky, it's with ourselves.

(LENIN *breaks off.* KRUPSKAYA *appears in the doorway.*)

KRUPSKAYA: If comrade Trotsky doesn't leave soon he'll miss Vera Ivanovna's mutton stew.

LENIN: All right.

(KRUPSKAYA *returns to the kitchen.*)

Think about it. I want you to stay for a while. Work with *Iskra*. Find yourself. (*Pause.*) A word of warning. Don't become . . . an émigré. These capital cities . . . fat, bourgeois . . . they suck you in, if you let them. Live only for the Revolution in Russia. Do you understand me?

TROTSKY: Yes. I saw a fair bit of it in Paris on my way here.

LENIN: You'll see it here too. (*Another discussion already in mind . . .*) Tell me about Paris . . .

TROTSKY: (*Squeezing shoes on painfully*) Paris . . . is like Odessa. Only Odessa is better. (*Standing up*) I'm sorry, comrade. I mustn't miss my mutton stew. (*They shake hands.* TROTSKY *passes into kitchen area, where* KRUPSKAYA *gives him an address and a hand sketch of the block. He kisses her forehead gently, leaves.* KRUPSKAYA *closes the door after him. Comes back into the study/bedroom.* LENIN *has already begun work at his desk. She stands behind him. Gently massages his neck and shoulder muscles.* LENIN *releases his pen, sinks a little into the massage.*)

KRUPSKAYA: Was there anything for me?

(LENIN *weary; the news is old; he's known it for years now.*)

LENIN: The Jewish Workers' Alliance are determined to fight for control over their own affairs within the party. (*Pause.*) The 'Southern Worker' group argue that we 'underestimate the role of the peasant', deplore our sharp attacks on the liberals, and . . . seek to control their own affairs within the Party. The 'Economists' group continue to argue in favour of strictly industrial action and agitation, with the problem of revolution to be left until the bourgeoisie have captured power in Russia . . . and seek to control their own affairs within the Party. (*Pause.*) It's not a party they want, it's a gentleman's club.

KRUPSKAYA: Come to bed now.

LENIN: I have less than a fortnight to finish my draft programme for the board meeting . . .

KRUPSKAYA: You'll work better tomorrow when you've slept. Come. I'll sing.

INT. HOLFORD SQUARE: STUDY/BEDROOM. NIGHT

They're in bed, LENIN*'s head in* KRUPSKAYA*'s arms. She sings a Russian song, low, husky. She finishes; strokes his head gently.*

KRUPSKAYA: Do you think we'll ever go home?

LENIN: Yes.

KRUPSKAYA: When?

LENIN: When the Revolution needs us.

KRUPSKAYA: Shall I sing 'Katya'?

LENIN: No. No more music. It's too . . . moving. (*Pause.*) It softens.

INT. HOLFORD SQUARE: STUDY/BEDROOM. NIGHT

KRUPSKAYA *sleeps. A clock booms 3 a.m.* LENIN *sits at his desk, writing, muttering, scratching out.*

INT. COMMUNE: MAIN ROOM. DAY

MARTOV *pours wine round the table.* LENIN *in the chair;* ZASULICH; KRUPSKAYA (*taking notes*); TROTSKY (*though not an* Iskra *board member*) *at end opposite chair.* LENIN *has no glass. The others receive refills. Room rather cool.* ZASULICH *fuming silently at* LENIN. LENIN *steely.*

MARTOV: (*Talking gently*) Now let's keep calm. We're *comrades.* These are honest differences and it's right we should talk them out. But I see no need for personalities and name-calling. Surely we're beyond that sort of thing. I beg you, comrades . . . (MARTOV *finishes his conciliatory libation, returns to his chair, makes a worried face at* LENIN.)

LENIN: (*Deliberately*) Do you have more criticism of my programme, Vera Ivanovna?

(ZASULICH *goes to answer but is headed off by* MARTOV.)

MARTOV: (*Quiet, firm*) I think Vera Ivanovna has made her point, Ilyich. It's quite simple. She prefers Plekhanov's draft to yours. As do Axelrod and Georges himself. You, Potresov and I prefer yours. If you press for a vote, you give comrade Plekhanov, as chairman of the *Iskra* Board, the opportunity of casting the deciding vote in his own favour. (MARTOV *waits a moment, drinks some wine.*) May I make a suggestion?

LENIN: Please do.

MARTOV: Give me the two drafts. I'll see if I can't get something out of them to please everybody.

(LENIN *considers this.*)

LENIN: What do you think, comrade Trotsky?

(*Some frowns.* TROTSKY *surprised.*)

As a comrade, I mean.

TROTSKY: I think it's probably possible to safeguard your salient points within Plekhanov's text. Personally, I think Plekhanov's draft is better suited for a textbook of economics than a party programme.

ZASULICH: Look, young man, Georges Plekhanov was running a revolutionary movement when your father and mother were still holding hands in the front parlour!

TROTSKY: (*Softly*) Yes, I know. He told me.

LENIN: All right. I accept what you say, Julius. But it's important to preserve the notion of an all-out attack on both absolutism *and* capitalism; and it must be clearly understood, through the programme we eventually agree, that the 'dictatorship of the proletariat' means *just that* . . . It does *not* mean the dictatorship of the proletariat in conjunction with the peasants. With those conditions, I concede the need to prepare a new programme based on both drafts.

(*Long pause.* MARTOV *winks at* ZASULICH.)

It looks like July, comrades. We are strong and as ready as we'll ever be. If Julius's Organizing Committee does its work properly, there should be no difficulty in winning a majority for our programme and party rules. What's the latest on Congress venue, Julius?

MARTOV: Plekhanov and Axelrod favour Brussels. (*Pause.*) The Organizing Committee is still undecided.

LENIN: (*Nodding*) Questions? Good.

(LENIN *starts to get up.*)

MARTOV: Would you mind staying a little longer, Ilyich?

(LENIN *looks surprised.* MARTOV *looks at* ZASULICH *and* TROTSKY *before going on.* LENIN *sits down, frowning.* MARTOV *takes an opened envelope from his pocket, removes the letter, opens it up.*)

A . . . comrade has asked if he might address the board? He's waiting upstairs now.

LENIN: Upstairs? (*Pause. To* KRUPSKAYA) Why is it not in the agenda?

(KRUPSKAYA *is bewildered.*)

MARTOV: Comrade Miliutin arrived only this afternoon. From Orlov. I raise the matter only now because I didn't want the main body of the meeting to be disrupted.

LENIN: (*Already sensing something*) I see. What does comrade . . . Miliutin want?

MARTOV: I think he should be allowed to tell us that himself.

LENIN: (*Finally unbudging*) Nevertheless . . .

(*Silence.* MARTOV *undecided.* LENIN *waits.*)

MARTOV: Comrade Miliutin has laid grave charges against one of our agents.

LENIN: (*Fast*) Who?

MARTOV: N. E. Bauman.

LENIN: What charges?

MARTOV: Bauman got Miliutin's wife with child during his exile in Orlov. After his excape, he began to . . . slander her, labelled her 'the whore of Orlov', even used our own underground networks to . . . revile her. It wasn't long, naturally, before Party workers in Orlov picked up the stories. (*Pause.*) To . . . (*Long pause.*) . . . 'defend her honour', as she put it, she . . . hanged herself. (*Holds up letter.*) This is her suicide note. It's addressed to the Party. Vera Ivanovna has already seen it.

(MARTOV *pushes the note towards* LENIN, *who picks it up, reads it impassively, pushes it back down the table.*)

LENIN: (*Mildly*) So. (*Not a question: a sort of new paragraph.*)

MARTOV: Will you see him?

LENIN: No.

(*Silence. A slow stunned reaction.* ZASULICH *bangs her huge fist into the table, spilling wine all over it in her anger.*)

ZASULICH: By Christ you will though! You what? You won't see a comrade who's travelled 4000 miles to ask for justice from the party . . . what does it say? (*Scans the letter.*) . . . 'the party of the struggle for the freedom, the dignity and the happiness of man'? I'll fetch him in myself. You're a disgrace to the party. A scourge and a monster.

(ZASULICH *storms towards the door.* MARTOV *calls her name, hurries after her. Silence around the table. Aruging on the stair outside.* KRUPSKAYA *picks up the note, reads it.* LENIN *looks at* TROTSKY.)

LENIN: (*Very calm*) I have written to Plekhanov urging you be co-opted on to the *Iskra* board. (*Pause.*) That is, if you still want it?
(LENIN *gestures at the door.*)

TROTSKY: (*Calm too*) More than ever.
(KRUPSKAYA *puts the letter down. She is simply moved.* MARTOV *in, without* ZASULICH. *He wipes his hands with a raspberry-coloured handkerchief.*)

MARTOV: She . . . won't come back. But she won't bring in Miliutin unless we send for him.
(MARTOV *sits down where* ZASULICH *sat.*)

LENIN: Anything else?

MARTOV: (*Very tense*) Yes. I haven't finished. (*Pause.*) I want to know what you intend to do about Bauman.

LENIN: Nothing.

MARTOV: (*Deliberately*) I think there should be an inquiry.

LENIN: Nadya, tell comrade Martov comrade Bauman's role in the *Iskra* network . . .

MARTOV: (*Flashing*) I know his role . . . don't play the grandfather with *me*, comrade. It doesn't wear . . .

LENIN: (*Hard*) Then don't be so *childish*. Bauman is an *outstanding* agent; not average; not good; outstanding. In Party matters I would trust him above anyone I know. Now you're asking that he should be disciplined . . . how? Expelled . . . ?

MARTOV: Yes, certainly, if it's true . . .

LENIN: Expelled because of personal misdemeanours? Let me tell you, comrade, I rule an inquiry out of order, as being outside the competence of *Iskra* and detrimental to the interests of the party. If you want my *private* views on the matter you can have them . . . privately.

MARTOV: (*Losing control*) You can't separate private from public like that, can't you see it, man! We are what we *do* . . . you, me, Bauman, all of us. Party morality is more than just loyalty to the party . . . it's the highest level of ethical consciousness yet afforded the human species . . .

LENIN: Metaphysics, Julius. Another time, perhaps, we may speculate. Just now we're trying to make the revolution *possible*. (*Silence.* MARTOV *disturbed, thrown, shivering a little, unused to being in conflict with* LENIN.)

MARTOV: So you'll do nothing.

LENIN: (*Standing*) I will do my duty. That's to say, I will protect comrade Bauman from any move on your or anybody else's part to expel or discipline him. Be warned. (*To* KRUPSKAYA) I think we should go.

KRUPSKAYA: You go. I want to speak with Vera Ivanovna.

(LENIN *stares at* KRUPSKAYA, *searching for betrayal. She touches his hand.*)

I'll follow.

(LENIN *nods. Leaves.* MARTOV *turns away from the table, his head in his hands. The front door bangs below.* MARTOV *is crying, shaking and trembling.* KRUPSKAYA *goes to him, presses his face into her belly, nurses him with shushing sounds.* TROTSKY *remains at the table, reaches for the suicide note with his pen, opens and reads it without taking it in his hands.*)

INT. HOLFORD SQUARE: STUDY/BEDROOM. NIGHT

LENIN *in bed, sick, at night. He's suffering from inflammation of the nerve terminals of back and chest (shingles?) naked, a thin sheet covering his loins and legs untidily, he bucks and rears, screams, his flesh red and blotched, his eyes fevered, remote.*

LENIN: (*Explaining crazily*) It's simple. See. I am the Party. Right. Party organ . . . unh? (*He indicates his head.*) . . . Unh? Central Committee . . . (*He indicates a clenched fist.*) . . . Right? Central Organ, Central Committee . . . (*He begins again.*) See . . . I am the Party, eh? I am the Party . . . No, I . . . mmm? mmm? . . . Julius, you're not listening. (*Big shout*) *Martov!!!*

(LENIN *opens his eyes, blinks.* KRUPSKAYA *just in from kitchen, bowl of iodine and cloth in hands. She soothes him gently, begins to bathe his chest and back with the solution.* LENIN, *awake now, takes the pain with stiff face.*)

KRUPSKAYA: You can't go on like this, Volodya. Let me get a doctor . . . please.

LENIN: (*Quietly*) I want you to pack the trunks and prepare to leave.

KRUPSKAYA: We can't *leave*. You're ill, man . . .

LENIN: (*Fierce*) Do it! (*Pause. Almost absent-mindedly*) Do it!

KRUPSKAYA: (*Dish of milk and bread*) Try to take some of this.

LENIN: (*Still in great pain*) Listen! Tell Martov I want to see him.

KRUPSKAYA: Julius is in Paris, *en route* for Geneva. There's a meeting of the Organizing Committee.

LENIN: Did he call?

KRUPSKAYA: It blew up very suddenly. He left the day he heard of the meeting. (*Pause.*) He's . . . still hurt and bitter . . .

LENIN: Who called the meeting of the Organizing Committee?

KRUPSKAYA: I don't know. Rest, love.

LENIN: Rest? I'll rest when they rest! (*Pause.*) It looks as though Julius is making his bid for power.

(LENIN *says this with some sadness, resignation, as well as foreboding.*)

KRUPSKAYA: No . . . No, no.

LENIN: I say the Party must be built like a fist, like a brain balled. He wants a party like a saucerful of calves' hearts put down for the cat. I must show him he is wrong.

(KRUPSKAYA *covers* LENIN *gently with the thin sheet. He closes his eyes. She stands, picks up the bowl.*)

(*Eyes open*) Thank you comrade.

(KRUPSKAYA *smiles, almost shy now, leaves.*)

INT. TRAIN COACH AND CORRIDOR. DAY

LENIN *and* KRUPSKAYA *in empty coach. Cutaways of Swiss scenery. Every lurch of the train gives* LENIN *pain. He is pale, drawn; sweat on forehead.* KRUPSKAYA *watches him carefully. The train is slowing. A* GUARD *in the corridor calls 'Secheron. Secheron, Geneva next stop.*

Secheron, Secheron . . .' BAUMAN, *hard, heavy, pushes down the corridor towards them.* LENIN *sees him, stands.*

LENIN: Bauman.

BAUMAN: There'll be police in Geneva. Are these yours?

(LENIN *nods.* BAUMAN *takes the cases easily, leads the* LENINS *from the train.*)

INT. PLEKHANOV'S STUDY. GENEVA

Large, expensive, tastefully and expensively got out. Double doors join it to the next room. A view of mountains from the window. The room is full of books and 'objects'. LENIN *sits on a wooden chair. He is totally withdrawn: almost rapt in his self-absorption. The double doors open and* PLEKHANOV *appears. He is forty-five, the father of Russian Marxism; aristocratic, élitist, intellectual, vain; beautifully dressed, and with his own dignity. He holds his hand out to greet* LENIN. LENIN *stands, takes the hand.*

PLEKHANOV: Ilyich! We meet again. Sit down, sit down. How are you? We were worried about you.

LENIN: (*Sitting*) Recovered . . . thank you.

(*They study each other for several moments. They hide their distrust and dislike well.*)

PLEKHANOV: Well, we're almost there. (*Pause.*) You've worked hard.

LENIN: The operative word is 'almost', Georges.

PLEKHANOV: (*Ignoring him*) I've dreamed of this Congress for a quarter of a century. Do you know that? The Congress that will unify the Party.

LENIN: With *Iskra* as its organizational and theoretical centre.

PLEKHANOV: Precisely, comrade.

LENIN: (*Softly*) But will it?

PLEKHANOV: What do you mean?

LENIN: We have forty-one votes out of a total of fifty-one, our principal opponents being the Jewish Bund, with five votes, and the Workers' Cause and the Southern Workers' factions with a further two votes each. Theoretically, we cannot fail to dominate the Congress, push through our own resolutions and elect our own people to the central committees of the Party. (*Pause.*) The question remaining is: Who will control *Iskra*?

PLEKHANOV: (*Getting the measure of it now*) Doesn't *Iskra* speak with one voice?

LENIN: What do *you* think?

PLEKHANOV: You surprise me. I know of course there have been personal frictions . . . the Bauman affair, things like that . . . but surely there's no evidence of ideological division, is there?

(LENIN *pushes slightly, disliking the constraints.*)

LENIN: Georges, Martov has tabled his own draft rules for party membership . . .

PLEKHANOV: (*Testily*) Yes, I have seen the agenda. (*Pause.*) I must say, I've read them both side by side, yours and his, and I'm damned if I can see much difference between them, if you allow for necessary differences arising from stylistic capabilities.

LENIN: (*Resolute*) I'll tell you the difference in a sentence, Georges. His rules allow anyone, any opportunist, any windbag, any 'professor', any 'high-school student' to proclaim himself a party member, while my rules – *our* rules, Georges – confine membership to a narrow vanguard of professional revolutionaries owing strict allegiance to the Party centre. That's the difference.

PLEKHANOV: (*Defensive now*) I'm not sure I'd accept the interpretation of Martov's formulation that you offer, Ilyich . . .

LENIN: (*Deadly*) Well, I think you should, Georges, because comrade Martov certainly does.'

(*Silence.*)

PLEKHANOV: Are you sure?

LENIN: Perfectly.

PLEKHANOV: Then I'd better have a word with him.

LENIN: It might make matters worse. (*Pause.*) I think we should simply see to it that his rules are defeated.

PLEKHANOV: How?

LENIN: Canvass. Argue. Persuade. Make sure of our votes. Secure them. Keep them hard if they look like softening. (*Pause.*) I think we are the right people to lead the revolutionary party, comrade Plekhanov. Theory and organization drawn together like that . . . (*He clasps his hands in front of him.*) What do you think?

(PLEKHANOV *leans forward, places his hand on* LENIN*'s.*)

PLEKHANOV: Let's build the Party, comrade.

(*They look at each other for several moments, sealing the compact.*)

I've always been fascinated by your hardness. It always seems so . . . unrelative.

LENIN: (*Simply*) I was a gentle enough child.

PLEKHANOV: (*Trying the reassertion*) One thing I insist on. There will be no place for the man Trotsky on the new board of *Iskra*. He's too young and he's too arrogant.

LENIN: (*Finally, making the point*) All right, I withdraw the suggestion. (*He stands.*) Is it still London if the police stop us in Brussels?

PLEKHANOV: (*Standing*) That's right.

(*He shows* LENIN *the door.*)

I can't think why there should be trouble though.

(*Plekhanov's two teenage daughters, in riding habits, burst in.*)

Ah, you won't remember these two, will you? (*Takes them by shoulders. To girls*) Say hello to comrade Lenin and go and get dressed, you scamps.

(*They laugh, say 'Bonjour, cher comrade' in turn, and leave the room.*)

Well . . . till Brussels . . . Give my love to Nadya, won't you? *Au revoir.*

(LENIN *leaves.* PLEKHANOV *crosses to the upright piano, picks out a few bars from a Beethoven sonata with skill and precision.*)

INT. BRUSSELS: LARGE OFFICE IN FLOUR WAREHOUSE. DAY

The Congress is convening. A growing noise from the warehouse proper: shouting, laughter, occasional snatches of song. The office is crowded. The Organizing Committee and the Congress praesidium are trying to resolve matters of procedure before the first session. A good deal of all talking at once, as delegation leaders try to have their business recognized by chairman PLEKHANOV. MARTOV, ZASULICH, POTRESOV, TROTSKY, ALEXANDROVA *and several others sit round a large desk.* LENIN, *flanked by* KRASIKOV, *stands behind the seated* PLEKHANOV. *Before and all around them, the 'Economists'* MARTINOV *and* AKIMOV, BROUCKERE *of the Southern Worker,* LIEBER *and* GOLDBLATT *of the Jewish Bund,* EGOROV, POPOV *and others of the 'centre'.*

LIEBER: (*Above the noise; angry*) So let me get this straight, comrade. If the Jewish Bund refuses to surrender to party control over its *own* organization, this Congress is prepared to expel us from the Party? Is that the meaning of Resolution 2 on the Agenda? Now I'm asking you a straight question, comrade . . .

PLEKHANOV: (*Lofty, in all the moil*) The answer is yes, comrade. How many times must I *tell* you . . . *yes!!*

LIEBER: Then I demand that this Procedures Committee rule that the resolution be deferred. There should be a commission. Some of my people have travelled the length of Europe to be here . . . We're Party too, you know.

MARTOV: (*Suddenly*) Shall we put that to a vote then?

LENIN: You know what our collective view is on the Bund, comrade . . .

MARTOV: (*Coolly*) We are now the Procedures Committee of the Second Congress of the Russian Social Democratic Party, comrade. Not the editorial board of the Party organ *Iskra*. (*To desk*) Shall we vote it?

(LENIN *ready.* PLEKHANOV *uncertain.* POTRESOV, *next to* MARTOV, *nods.*)

ZASULICH: Yes.

ALEXANDROVA: Yes.

PLEKHANOV: All right. Those in favour of deferring the vote on the expulsion of the Bund?

(MARTOV, POTRESOV, AXELROD, ZASULICH, ALEXANDROVA.)

Against?

(LENIN, KRASIKOV, PLEKHANOV.)

Carried.

LIEBER: Thank God. Thank you, comrades.

PLEKHANOV: Next.

(MARTINOV *begins arguing for a similar concession for his group.* LENIN *and* MARTOV *glance at each other, impassive but surly stares.* LENIN *catches* ZASULICH*'s eye.* POTRESOV*'s. His chill anger is patent.* BAUMAN *in fast from the warehouse. He pushes through the throng until he reaches* LENIN, *whispers.* LENIN *nods, bends over* PLEKHANOV*'s shoulder, whispers.* PLEKHANOV *nods, stands, bangs the desk with his feet.*) Comrades, comrades, listen to me.

(*The din subsides. Sounds of movement, the odd shout from next door.*)

Six delegates have been arrested in their hotels. I'm informed that the Belgian police are on their way to break up the meeting.

(*Consternation, chatter.*)

Comrades. The contingency plan is now effective. Congress will convene in London in four days' time. Go now.

(*People move at speed.* PLEKHANOV *begins gathering up conference papers.*)

LENIN: (*To* BAUMAN) Take care of Krupskaya.

(BAUMAN *stands, frowning, emphatic.*)

Take care of Krupskaya.

(BAUMAN *leaves, impassive, with* KRUPSKAYA. *The room is almost empty.* LENIN *fills his briefcase with papers from the table.* TROTSKY *remains.* LENIN *looks up, sees him.*)

Comrade. How fortunate, we'll travel together.

(*Pause.* TROTSKY *says nothing.*)

(*Weighing words*) I'm sorry I couldn't get Plekhanov to co-opt you on to the board. There was nothing I could do.

TROTSKY: No, of course.

LENIN: Nothing, comrade.

TROTSKY: No.

LENIN: (*Ready*) Well. Are you coming with me?

TROTSKY: No. (*Pause.*) I'll make my own way.

LENIN: (*Crossing to door, turning*) Avoid . . . personalities, comrade. They could prove your downfall.

(*He leaves.* TROTSKY *watches him.*)

INT. LECTURE HALL, TOTTENHAM COURT ROAD, LONDON. EVENING

The 22nd and crucial motion in progress. The room is half tiered on two sides, with a demonstration area and desk at the focus. PLEKHANOV *sits behind the demonstration desk, in the chair.* LENIN *at a small table in front of the desk, as one of the vice-chairmen. As* MARTOV *speaks, we track around the room, clocking faces, groupings, group titles crayoned on pieces of cardboard . . . All votes.* LENIN *flicks from* MARTOV *to his 'support . . .' The sequence should suggest a hard-fought decision, when the vote is taken . . . Some votes* LENIN *is unable to assign:* TROTSKY, *for example;* ALEXANDROVA *and others of the original Organizing Committee.*

MARTOV: If we adopt comrade Lenin's formula we shall be throwing overboard a section of those who, even if they cannot be directly admitted to an organization, are nevertheless Party members. We are a party of a *class*, comrades. We must take care not to leave outside the Party ranks people who consciously, though perhaps not very actively, associate themselves with our party. Indeed the more widespread the title of Party member, the better.

(*Applause from* BUND, AKIMOV, MARTINOV, EGOVOV, POPOV, ALEXANDROVA . . . LENIN *makes a note on a piece of paper, missing nothing.*)

For me, a conspiratorial organization only has meaning when it is enveloped by a broad social-democratic working-class party.

LENIN: (*Shouting suddenly*) You're confusing a *party* with a *movement*, comrade. They're not the same thing.

MARTOV: (*Flaring as quickly*) No, comrade, it is you who are confused. You confuse the Party with a bunch of professional . . . thugs who will do your or somebody else's bidding without question . . .

(*Uproar. Applause for* MARTOV; *boos and shouts from hard* Iskra *men* (BAUMAN, KRASIKOV, LENGNIK, SHOTMAN, NOSKOV *and others*). LENIN *white but perfectly controlled.*)

PLEKHANOV: (*Drily, as it dies*) Confine yourselves to argument, comrades. Reserve your abuse for the enemy.

MARTOV: I look forward to the day, comrades, when every striker, every demonstrator against the Tsar and his regime, accounts for his actions by stating: I am a member of the Social Democratic Party of Russia. If you share that hope, you will support my motion.

(MARTOV *sits down, flushed, a little elated, dazed. Applause again, especially among the Bund.*)

PLEKHANOV: Comrade Lenin.

LENIN: (*Standing*) Thank you, comrade chairman. Comrades, you have heard the arguments . . . Martov's and mine. What we're arguing about is both an image and a reality. If you accept my motion, you vote for coherence, organization, discipline, above all, power at the *centre*. You will say, in effect, that it is essential to distinguish between those who belong to the Party and those who associate themselves with it. You make the necessary distinction between an *entire class*, shaped by *capitalism*, and its *vanguard*, the Party. The title 'Party member' is a *fiction*, if it cannot be made to correspond to facts. Capitalism is bound to weigh down wide sections of the working class with disunity, oppression and stultification. Social Democracy seeks to lift the worker from his present level of consciousness to a genuinely *revolutionary* one.

But if we fail to recognize the distinction, there is no way we can achieve that end. Vote for Martov's proposal, and you create a tea party, not a party of revolutionaries ready to lead a class into battle.
(LENIN *sits down. Applause, counter-applause.*)

PLEKHANOV: (*Reluctantly*) Well . . . I suppose I should order that . . . the vote be taken.
(*He tries to catch* LENIN*'s eye; fails.*)
In favour of comrade Lenin's proposal on Party membership?
(*Twenty-three votes. We need clock only key ones:* LENIN*'s two, for example.*)
Twenty . . . three. And comrade Martov's . . . ?
(*The Bund vote five; Economists and other rightists swell the number.* MARTOV*'s two hands go up. A small knot of* Iskra *people –* ALEXANDROVA, *for example – join in.* ZASULICH, AXELROD, POTRESOV *go up in turn. And* TROTSKY. KRUPSKAYA, *who sits next to* TROTSKY, *can't look at him.*)
(*Grimly, writing it down*) Twenty-eight. Comrade Martov's resolution carried.
(*Hubbub. Shouting. Banging of fists on desks.*)
The chair suggests a fifteen-minute adjournment.
(*Carried by acclamation.* LENIN *sits silent, white, but held in.* MARTOV *passes by his desk. Gives* LENIN *an odd smile.*)

MARTOV: (*Tense, nervy*) Good fun!

LENIN: (*Bitterly*) Oh yes. There's nothing funnier than watching a man commit political suicide.

MARTOV: (*Trying to laugh it off*) You think so?

LENIN: Today you have entered into an opportunistic alliance with centre and right-wing elements. You have surrendered your political credibility.

MARTOV: I doubt it. In any case, you left me little option in the matter. You forced me to beat you.

LENIN: (*Bleakly*) You have won a battle, comrade. The war has only just begun.
(MARTOV *limps out. Hall empty.* LENIN *surrounded by* Iskra *hards:*

principally BAUMAN, KRASIKOV, LENGNIK, SHOTMAN, NOSKOV.) Full caucus meeting tonight, to decide on our list for the central committee and the Party council. Seven thirty sharp. Questions? (*None.*)

Bauman, when does the commission on the Bund propose reporting back?

BAUMAN: Next week some time, according to Tupuridze.

LENIN: I want the report and the vote tomorrow morning. You see Tupuridze, I'll see Plekhanov. Do it now.

INT. CAUCUS ROOM. EVENING

A small, cramped room. LENIN *in chair; a dozen 'hards', including* BAUMAN, KRASIKOV, SHOTMAN, LENGNIK, NOSKOV, KRZHIZHANOVSKY, TUPURIDZE. KRUPSKAYA *as secretary. A broom handle has been wedged in the double-swing-door handles, to lock it. One of the 'hards' stands guard by it. The door shifts slightly as* MARTOV, *locked out, bangs and calls on the other side. He has been there protesting since the meeting started. His tone is now a little desperate, unreal.*

MARTOV: (*Off*) Let me *in*! I demand to be admitted. It is directly forbidden by Party rules to exclude members of the executive from caucus meetings.

(MARTOV *goes on with this throughout the scene that follows.*)

LENIN: (*Dictating to Krupskaya*) . . . Comrade Lengnik . . . Comrade Noskov. (*Turning to meeting*) That concludes the lists for the central committees. I don't need to remind you that the voting will be *solid*. We have outlived the wavering days. The Bund . . . (*Pausing, looking for Tupuridze*) I've seen Plekhanov. The Bund problem will be taken first thing tomorrow. Is your commission able to report, Tupuridze?

TUPURIDZE: It will be by morning.

LENIN: Good . . . No problems?

TUPURIDZE: No problems.

LENIN: Good. (*Standing*) That's all. (*To man at door*) Let comrade

Martov in when the comrades have left, will you?

(*They disperse swiftly, brushing past* MARTOV *in the doorway, the doorman's big hand on his chest.* KRUPSKAYA *tidies her files.*)

KRUPSKAYA: Do you want *me*?

(LENIN *shakes his head. She leaves. She meets* MARTOV *a few paces into the room. He barely sees her. Stands staring at* LENIN. LENIN *is writing something on a piece of paper. Looks up at length.*)

MARTOV: (*Pleading*) What is happening, Volodya?

LENIN: I don't know what you mean. I was in caucus . . .

MARTOV: (*Almost screaming*) You had me locked out. (*He tries to get himself together.*) Why?

LENIN: Simply . . . you no longer belonged to the caucus.

MARTOV: Why? Because my motion won the majority in Congress?

LENIN: No. Because your 'majority' was based upon an openly opportunistic alliance with the 'swamp', with the right and centre elements of the Party, the elements we as a tendency have been fighting for the last year.

MARTOV: There was no . . . *alliance*. I haven't spoken to the Bund since Brussels. Believe it!

(*Silence.* LENIN *impassive.* MARTOV *gets closer, gathering.*)

Volodya . . . comrade, there are no fundamental differences between us. (*Pause.*) Can't we simply sit down and talk it out? We share the *same* vision, comrade . . . We spent the whole night talking, the night before Siberia . . . do you remember? On and on. Building the vision . . . (*Pause.*) Tell me what I should do.

LENIN: (*Softly*) I can't do that, comrade. You must find that for yourself. The *choices* are clear. If you are not to be tainted with the Bund for the rest of your days, you must make it clear tomorrow that your position is as it always was, that total authority over the activities of members shall be exercised *by the Party centre*. (*Catching* MARTOV*'s surprise*) The Procedures Committee have decided that the question of the Bund should be tackled at once.

MARTOV: But the Bund Commission hasn't reported . . .

LENIN: That's being taken care of. (*Pause.*) If, on the other hand, you decide that you need the votes of the Bund and other centre elements to gain control of the Party, you will be exposed as an opportunist and a counterfeit revolutionary. (*Pause.*) The choice is yours.

MARTOV: (*With growing hauteur*) There can be no question of my cynically changing my position on national autonomy within the party. My positon is identical with yours, as you very well know, comrade.

LENIN: The point is not that *I* know it. The point is that everyone in the Party, *including* the Bund, knows it.

(*Pause again.* MARTOV *is wondering whether the rupture has begun mending.*)

MARTOV: I wanted to . . . talk to you . . . about the composition of the central committees . . . There is good argument for building on the existing Organizing Committee . . .

LENIN: There is nothing to talk about. We have decided our lists.

(MARTOV *stunned a little, breathless. He turns away, walks a few paces to the door. A delayed reaction.*)

MARTOV: I see. I see. (*Pause. Vicious now*) Have you made recommendations on who should be elected Dictator of the Party too? Eh? Or will you be able to manage without that?

(LENIN *folds his papers away, walks past* MARTOV *without a glance, leaves the room.*)

(*As* LENIN *passes*) I asked you a question, comrade. Vera Zasulich was right; Potresov was right, Axelrod was right. You think you're Robespierre . . . that's what they think . . . By God, they're right.

(*The door swings shut.* MARTOV *kicks a chair over, in a swift freak of anger.*)

INT. LECTURE HALL. MORNING

The following morning. Congress in progress. The groupings – MARTOV*'s,* LENIN*'s – now very clearly delineated in the way they sit.*

TUPURIDZE: (*Winding up*) . . . I repeat, the Commission this

Congress set up to inquire into the question whether the Jewish Workers' Alliance could lawfully remain within the Party without subjecting itself to Party disciplines is of the opinion: (a) that no grounds can be found why the Bund should not accept Party constraints and (b) that therefore Congress should proceed to vote at once on whether the Bund should be allowed to exercise rights in the Party and, in particular, in this Congress.
(*He sits down.*)

PLEKHANOV: Thank you, comrade. Questions?
(LIEBER, *leader of the Bund, on his feet.*)

LIEBER: I must protest, comrade chairman. We were given unequivocal assurances by the Procedures Committee in Brussels . . .

BAUMAN: Out of order, comrade chairman!

KRASIKOV: 'This man has no right to speak, Comrade Chairman', eh?
(*Hubbub, as hard* Iskra *men keep up a flow of interruptions.* LENIN *stands up; his men subside.*)

LENIN: Comrade Bauman is right, comrade chairman. The Commission's recommendation is that we proceed directly to the vote.

MARTOV: (*Nervous, uncertain*) The Commission cannot determine what Congress may or may not do, comrade chairman.

PLEKHANOV: Very well. Would Congress like to hear argument on this matter or move at once to the vote? Show, please. Those in favour of moving to the vote? (*The* Iskra *vote, about twenty, solid.*) (*Repeating himself, very deliberately*) Those in favour of moving forward to a vote . . .
(AXELROD *puts hand up;* ZASULICH, TROTSKY, POTRESOV . . . MARTOV *joins them . . . the 'centre' follows suit. About forty hands lifted now.*)
Carried.

LIEBER: I protest, chairman! This is monstrous.
(*Counter-boos and hisses.*)

PLEKHANOV: (*Over din*) And now the vote itself. Those against the Bund's being allowed to remain within the Party, please show . . . (*The same procedure.* MARTOV *trapped, unable to run risk of being labelled a political opportunist, but conscious that he is voting his own majority away.*)
Forty . . . one. An overwhelming majority for expulsion.
(*The Bund consults.* LIEBER *stands up. Some jeering from the 'hards'.* LENIN *impassive.*)

LIEBER: There is no question of staying, comrades. The insult and humiliation you have dealt us will live with us many a day. Like you, we dream of and work for the Socialist Revolution. All we have asked is that we be allowed to do it in our own language with our own people. You deny us that basic right, because of some . . . Napoleon who craves after personal power.
(*A storm of booing and hissing.*)
It's true! See it now before it's too late.
(PLEKHANOV *calls for order; gets it finally.*)
Well . . . we will continue to fight for the Revolution . . . with or without the aid of the Party we helped to form.
(LIEBER *leaves. The others file out with him, in silence.*)

MARTINOV: The Workers' Cause group wish to demonstrate solidarity with the Bund against the . . . dictatorial tendencies that are emerging inside the Party apparatus. We hereby withdraw from the Congress. (MARTINOV *and* AKIMOV *withdraw. Cheering from the 'hards'.* MARTOV *approaches* LENIN*'s table.*)

MARTOV: You see. If history seeks an opportunist, it will not be in my direction that it will look, comrade.

LENIN: (*Smiling icily*) If it does not label you an opportunist, it may well conclude that you're a fool. (*Pause.*) I believe it may very well call you both. (*Sequence of minimally notated mixes, in which Congress votes in* LENIN*'s lists for central committee and Party council. Each time,* MARTOV*'s group abstains.* PLEKHANOV *duly announces the election of the* Iskra *'hards' . . .* LENGNIK, KRZHIZHANOVSKY, NOSLOV – *Central Committee, etc.*)

PLEKHANOV: Elections for the board of *Iskra*, the party journal. Comrade Lenin?

(LENIN *stands at his desk. He waits for the Congress, seething and boiling, to subside.*)

LENIN: You have already, in an earlier vote, affirmed the place of *Iskra* as the ideological centre of our Party. It is now our task to elect its editorial board, whose role it will be to create political guidelines for Party action in the struggle against the Russian state. (*Pause.*) I have, as you know, been associated with *Iskra* since its birth three years ago. And I think I can say, with all modesty, that the work we have done on the *Iskra* front has been of decisive influence in the shaping and development of our party. But it is the future, not the past, that calls us on. Times change: capacities change; objective circumstances change. What our Party journal requires now is a small nucleus of trained ideologues and organizers capable of launching the work far and wide across the Russian empire. (*Pause. Very resolute*) It is for this reason that I propose that we should decrease the number of seats from six to three; and further, I nominate, as *Iskra* editors, myself, Comrade Plekhanov . . . and . . . Comrade Martov .

(*He sits down. Stunned silence, at least in* MARTOV *ranks.* MARTOV *gets up, rather dazed, unable to take it in.*)

MARTOV: (*Weakly*) This is not possible, comrade chairman. Have we not already voted for the continuance of the *Iskra* . . .

(VERA ZASULICH *begins to scream; like a Cossack charging.*)

ZASULICH: You . . . bastard! You dirty stinking bastard! Jesus God, if I had a pistol I'd blow your rotten brains out! You're not a comrade, you're a dictator . . . You're a bloody *Tsar*. I see your game, Lenin. By hook or by crook, isn't it? Any way so long as it's your way, with your 'hard' men all around you. What do you care about loyalty . . . and service . . . and dedication . . . ? I've spent a lifetime . . . so has Axelrod, Potresov . . . of devotion to this Party. And now you . . . cut us off. Just like that. To fall into the swamp. (*Broken already*) You are no man to lead this great movement . . .

(*To* PLEKHANOV) And you . . . you whom I have worshipped as a great mind and comrade . . . one day this man will eat you for breakfast . . . (ZASULICH *walks out, avoiding* KRUPSKAYA*'s outstretched hand of sympathy. The 'hards' hurl epithets and derisory shouts after her.*)

MARTOV: (*With dignity*) May I remind those comrades who now revile comrade Zasulich . . . that you are reviling the comrade who shot the infamous Colonel Trepov of the Moscow secret police, when he ordered the flogging of workers who had demonstrated against the Tsar.

(*Derision tails off. The Conference waits for* MARTOV*'s move.*)

(*Quietly*) I refuse to accept nomination under these arrangements.

PLEKHANOV: You are not allowed to refuse, comrade, under the rules you yourself voted in only days ago.

MARTOV: (*Very quiet*) I will not serve with *that man*! That man is . . . not a good man!

(MARTOV *walks out.* POTRESOV *and* AXELROD *follow.* TROTSKY *stands.*)

TROTSKY: (*Measured, eloquent*) If this is comrade Lenin's 'image of the Party', then I want no part of it. What he has done today shames and degrades all of us. Zasulich and Axelrod in particular have fought all their lives to build the Party. And now here, on the brink of success, they are ruthlessly cut off and sent out into the wilderness, to satisfy the insatiable lust for power of one individual.

(*Waves of protest, etc.* TROTSKY *listens to it.*)

Comrades, we are privileged to be listening to the sound of Party debate – new style.

(TROTSKY *leaves with a flourish, to jeers. The remainder of* MARTOV*'s group follows him.*)

LENIN: (*Calmly*) I so move, comrade chairman.

EXT. MARX'S GRAVE, HIGHGATE. DAY

Around the grave (as it was on November 1903), split into factions, LENIN*'s to the left,* MARTOV*'s to the right;* PLEKHANOV *in the centre. They stand in silence. We scan the strain and tension in hands and faces. Finally . . .*

PLEKHANOV: (*Almost under breath*) We dedicate this great . . . unifying Congress . . . to the memory of the great man whose body is laid herein.

(*They stand on a little longer.* LENIN *flanked by 'hards',* BAUMAN *and* KRASIKOV *prominent.* KRUPSKAYA *stands at the back, staring at* ZASULICH *who is distraught and totally destroyed.*)

(*Furling his umbrella*) Well, comrades. Good luck, wherever your work may take you . . .

(PLEKHANOV *steps back on to the path.* ZASULICH, AXELROD, POTRESOV *join him in a group; some small departing chat. The 'hards' drift away. Some handshakes from* LENIN, *etc.*)

KRUPSKAYA: I must speak with Vera Ivanovna.

LENIN: Leave it . . .

KRUPSKAYA: (*Levelly*) I must.

(LENIN *nods finally.* KRUPSKAYA *hurries off after* ZASULICH. TROTSKY *approaches* LENIN.)

TROTSKY: I did what I had to.

LENIN: But what you had to do was not what had to be done.

TROTSKY: At least, I did not destroy the Party.

LENIN: (*Slowly*) Yesterday the Party was *made*, not destroyed. What is more, history will prove it to be the only party – the only sort of party – capable of capturing state power. You seem to think a party is an organization for the deliberation of complex moral choices, a sort of political sewing circle. (*Pause.*) You will not find the Tsar and von Plehve, and Trepov and Witte, and the state apparatus, sitting around 'deliberating moral choices' . . . They are *organizing* their defence . . . There is only one slogan that will defeat them. *Salus populi lex suprema est*. In revolutionary language, the success of the Revolution is the supreme law. Until you can say that, comrade, and mean it, history will have no use for you.

(TROTSKY *looks over his shoulder. Only* MARTOV *remains at the graveside.*)

TROTSKY: I suppose it will depend who writes the history.

(TROTSKY *walks off.* LENIN *and* MARTOV *left. They are about twenty feet apart. They look at each other for several moments, openly, without venom.* MARTOV *wants to speak but controls it. He turns eventually, limps off.* LENIN *watches him.* LENIN *stands by the tomb, alone, in longshot. Close-up, he stares at the head of Marx. Crows flap past, unexpected.*)

EXT. TSARSKOE SELO. DAY

NICHOLAS, *on his estates at Tsarskoe Selo, fires. The huge flock of crows flaps on across the sky. Close-up, frowning. We hear him reload.*

EXT. MARX'S GRAVE, HIGHGATE. DAY

KRUPSKAYA *rejoins* LENIN.

KRUPSKAYA: Zasulich wept. She can't understand why you've done what you have done.

(LENIN *looks at her, pushes stray floats of hair out of her eyes.*)

LENIN: Remember Minusinsk. Remember the peasant crouched over in the field? It was impossible to say what he was doing. And when we'd walked across the field and reached him, we saw at once that he was sharpening his scythe on a stone. From the path it was impossible to say . . .

KRUPSKAYA: She has nothing left, she said.

LENIN: (*Quietly*) There is nothing to be done about that.

(*They look at each other. Turn, walk off towards the gate, two simple bourgeois on a Sunday morning stroll. Fade out.*)

Through the Night

Preface

Of all the outlets available to a playwright for his work, television seems to me at once the most potent and the most difficult; the most potent and *therefore* the most difficult, one's inclined to add. Film boasts a 'global audience' (as one celebrated English director put it, perhaps as a way of justifying his new Californian existence) but has never afforded the writer a status in the power structure much above that of, say, a second-unit director. With relatively few exceptions, film uses (and has usually always attracted) writers for whom wealth* and ease and a certain sort of localized (i.e. American) celebrity are or have become inseparable from the writing impulse itself; so that the consequential loss of regard (and self-regard) will be measured against more tangible and presumably more consumable gains. The global audience will then be surrendered by the writer to the expert ministrations of other 'ideas men': studio chiefs ('We could have bought into North Sea oil with what we paid for this shit'), distributors ('It's too long/short/frank'), directors ('Do I get the cut?'), stars ('I *know* what they want. They want me.') and so on.

Theatre is in important ways the converse; that's to say, while at its most secure it offers the writer a greater degree of control than any other medium over the production of his work, it is incapable, as a social institution, of reaching, let alone *mobilizing*, large popular audiences, at least in what is more and more desperately referred to as the Free World. Success in the theatre can confer fame, prestige, wealth, critical acclaim and a place in literature, but all of them will be

*The current top-price for a screenplay that's made into a film is around $400,000 and perhaps 5 per cent of the gross profit. Most screenplays are never made, of course; another aspect of writer's impotence.

pickled in a sort of class aspic. To write only for the theatre is to watch only from the covered stand; you stay dry but there's a pitch dividing you from another possible, and possibly decisive, action on the terraces.

There are fewer cinemagoers in Britain now than there are anglers; fewer regular theatregoers than car-rallyers. For most people, plays are television plays, 'drama' is television drama (though it's a word used almost exclusively by those responsible for *production*, rarely if ever by audiences). A play on television, transmitted in mid-evening on a weekday, will make some sort of contact with anything from 3 to 12 million people (20 if it's a series), usually all at the same time. And the *potential* audience, because of television's irreversibly network nature, is every sighted person in the society with a set and the time and desire to watch. Not surprisingly, a medium as potentially dangerous as this one will need to be *controlled* with some rigour and attention to detail. 'To inform' and 'to educate' may well be in the charter alongside 'to entertain', but information that inflames and education that subverts will find its producers facing unrenewed contracts and its contributors mysteriously dropped. (Who took the decision, and on what grounds, not to repeat the brilliant *Days of Hope*? Or not to renew the contract of Kenith Trodd, producer of *Leeds United* and the suppressed *Brimstone and Treacle*?) It would be odd, of course, if it were otherwise. In a society predicated on the exploitation of the many by the few, in a world a large part of which operates according to precisely the same capitalist principle, yet where the necessary tactical avowal of democratic process had led to its actualization, however shallowly, and not always so, in the minds and actions of the exploited, the shaping of consciousness, the erection of the superstructure of consent, will become the major cultural concern of the state and the dominant class or classes it represents. What Enzensberger calls 'the consciousness industry' (cf. H. M. Enzensberger: 'The Industrialization of the Mind' in *Raids and Reconstructions*, Pluto Press, 1976) has become, more than steel, coal or oil or motor cars, the critical industry in the efficient management of modern societies, capitalist and Stalinist alike; as television has increasingly come to be located as that industry's key sector.

The constraints and difficulties of writing for television can then be easily described. Certain sorts of 'language', certain sorts of subject, certain sorts of form – an urban terrorist saying 'Fuck off' straight to camera pithily embodies all three – will inevitably trigger discreetly placed control-mechanisms on the floor above the floor you're working on. And a writer's arguments *ad rem* or *hominem* will never be enough to overcome the blandly prepared positions of a television controller. (Theatres have directors; films have chiefs; only television has the need and the confidence to let nomenclature reveal function in this way.) Yet in important ways, the experience cannot be reduced to the simple equation of company diktat = writer's accommodation, as many talented writers and intellectuals of the Left have for too long tried to assert, in a puny apology for a theory of the media. For one thing, as Enzensberger points out, a communications system beyond a critical size cannot continue to be centrally controlled and must then be dealt with statistically. 'This basic "leakiness" of stochastic* systems admittedly allows the calculation of probabilities based on sampling and extrapolations; but blanket supervision would demand a monitor that was bigger than the system itself . . . A censor's office, which carried out its work extensively, would of necessity become the largest branch of industry in its society.' Moreover, direct leakage is not the only sort: for example, the 'meanings' or 'messages' of plays are often encoded in such a way that the controllers of television output are incapable of decoding them with any precision. (In particular I'm thinking of plays where working-class idioms, speech patterns, behaviours suggest one thing but imply, by defensively developed irony, something quite other, which only a person of that class or with a deep knowledge of it could be expected to recognize readily.

* i.e. systems based on *conjecture* rather than certainty.

I suspect much of *Bill Brand* worked in very much that way, with a working-class audience.)

To argue, then, as many still do, that television is part of a *monolithic* consciousness industry where work of truly radical or revolutionary value will never be produced is at once to surrender to undialectical thought and to fail to see the empirical evidence there is to refute such an argument. If the medium weren't of the highest critical importance in the building and maintenance of the structures of popular consent, there'd be no need for controllers; conversely, the presence and activity of controllers rigorously monitoring and modifying the nature of the output is one index among many of the medium's importance. To work in television as a playwright will be to seek to exploit the system's basic 'leakiness', so as to speak intimately and openly, with whatever seriousness and relevance one can generate, to (though it must in time be *with*) the many millions of cohabitants of one's society who share part of a language, part of a culture, part of a history, with oneself; as not so to work, the opportunity *there*, will be to settle for less, a sheltering myopia or praise from the cell.

And let there be no cant, finally, about television's 'moving wallpaper', about 'advertising fodder' and the 'manipulable masses' and all the rest of the sad copy of minds tired of the problem and eager for revenge on those who would not listen. 'The "telly-glued" masses do not exist; they are the bad fiction of our second-rate social analysts. What the masses, old or new, might do is anybody's guess. But the actual men and women, under permanent kinds of difficulty, will observe and learn, and I do not think that in the long run they will be anybody's windfall.' The words are Raymond Williams's and, as with so much he has written in the last twenty-five years, I wish they were mine.

Through the Night was transmitted on BBC1 on 2 December 1975, to an estimated audience of more than 11 million people. Close to a hundred phone calls were 'logged' by the BBC's duty officer on the night of its broadcast; the producer's office and *Radio*

Times received a heavy postbag during the following weeks; and I received personal mail amounting to some 180 letters. The *Sunday People* opened its columns to readers inviting them to send in their own experiences of mastectomy treatment. More than 1,800 letters were received over the next ten days. Few critics saw (or at least wrote about) the piece; and the critic of the *Observer* spoke for many, perhaps, when he said: 'I found this week's episode of *The Nearly Man* by Arthur Hopcraft sufficient excuse for not watching *Through the Night* (BBC1), a Trevor Griffiths play about breast cancer which I lacked the nerve to face.' It is, without question, my best-known piece.

T.G.
14 February 1977

Characters

CHRISTINE POTTS
DR PEARCE
MR STAUNTON
DR SEAL
MRS SCULLY
ANNA JAY
JOE POTTS
SISTER WARREN
NURSE O'MALLEY
STAFF NURSE BRENTON
NURSE CHATTERJEE
REGISTRAR
NIGHT SISTER
THEATRE SISTER
NIGHT NURSES
ANAESTHETIST
DR MOUNT
LUCY
PORTER
MRS GOODWIN
MARTHA PAISLEY
OUTPATIENTS SISTER
AUXILIARY
TEA LADY
RELIGIOUS VISITOR
MOTHER
WOMAN PATIENT
JOAN
AGNES

Through the Night was first shown on BBC Television in December 1975. The cast was as follows:

CHRISTINE POTTS	Alison Steadman
DR PEARCE	Jack Shepherd
MR STAUNTON	Tony Steedman
DR SEAL	Thelma Whiteley
MRS SCULLY	Anne Dyson
ANNA JAY	Julia Schofield
JOE POTTS	Dave Hill
SISTER WARREN	Andonia Katsaros
NURSE O'MALLEY	Phylomena McDonagh
STAFF NURSE BRENTON	Sheila Kelly
NURSE CHATTERJEE	Rebecca Mascarenhas
REGISTRAR	Richard Wilson
NIGHT SISTER	Patricia Leach
THEATRE SISTER	Wendy Wax
NIGHT NURSES	Sue Elgin, Angela Bruce, Anna Mottram
ANAESTHETIST	John Rowe
DR MOUNT	Richard Ireson
LUCY	Jeillo Edwards
PORTER	Louis Cabot
MRS GOODWIN	Anna Wing
MARTHA PAISLEY	Jane Freeman
OUTPATIENTS SISTER	Rachel Davies
AUXILIARY	Barbara Ashcroft
TEA LADY	Shirley Allen
RELIGIOUS VISITOR	Peter Lawrence
MOTHER	Kathleen Worth

WOMAN PATIENT	Myrtle Devenish
JOAN	Jeanne Doree
AGNES	Lucy Griffiths
Director	Michael Lindsay-Hogg
Designer	Sue Spence
Producer	Ann Scott

INT. EXAMINATION ROOM. DAY

Long shot, CHRISTINE POTTS, *around thirty, in examination room of large general hospital. She wears a white cotton gown over skirt, etc; is naked from waist up beneath it.* CHRISTINE *sits on a canvas chair, alone, in the bottle-bright room. She listens. From the next room, through the thin wood wall, the oddly distinct sounds of an examination being conducted. The connecting door opens suddenly and a* SISTER, *spruce, young, bright, appears. She carries a small bunch of brown open files in her arms.*

SISTER: (*Studying top file cover*) Are you ready, Mrs . . . Potts? The doctor will be with you presently.

(*The* SISTER *smiles, withdraws immediately.*

CHRISTINE *feels her breast, catches sight of herself in a glass cupboard filled with instruments. The connecting door opens and the* SISTER *returns, leading in the examination team.*) This is Mrs Potts, Mr Staunton.

(*She hands* STAUNTON *the file.*)

(*To* CHRISTINE) Would you just lie on here for me, Mrs Potts? And we'll have this off for a moment, shall we?

(*The* SISTER *removes the gown, helps* CHRISTINE *on to the black leather couch.*)

There we are . . .

(STAUNTON, *the consultant, has been studying the file. He's tall, gaunt, around sixty; wears a three-piece pin-stripe suit, discreet tie, half-glasses over which he appears to do most of his seeing. As he steps to the examination couch he hands the file to the blonde house surgeon on his right, who (when she's read it) hands it to the other member of the team, a young* HOUSEMAN *with three days' growth of stubble on his face and longish hair, tatty white coat and basketball shoes. The young* HOUSEMAN *wears a T-shirt (i.e. no tie) under his coat.*)

STAUNTON: Well, Mrs Potts. Let's see what we have here, shall we? (*He feels the left breast with both hands, palpating the lump. Measuring it, tracing gland paths up into the armpit.*) Yes. Yes. Yes. Yes. Now. You discovered it when?

CHRISTINE: Erm. About three weeks ago, doctor. Just after Christmas I think it were . . .

STAUNTON: Yes. And when did you get round to seeing your doctor?

CHRISTINE: Well, I went that week.

STAUNTON: (*Pausing fractionally*) I see. Yes.

CHRISTINE: (*Helpfully*) I've been waiting to be seen . . .

STAUNTON: Yes. (*To* HOUSE SURGEON, *low, confidential, patient-excluding voice*) Tell me what you think, Doctor Seal.

(SEAL *moves into his space, feeling breast thoroughly, examining it visually. She speaks over her shoulder to the consultant.*)

SEAL: No pain, so we can probably rule out a cyst. Clearly not a haematoma. Absence of discharge suggests it's not an intraduct papilloma . . . I think we can rule out fat necrosis . . . More likely fibroadenoma . . . At this age particularly, sir . . .

(SEAL *smiles, steps back.* STAUNTON *looks at the* HOUSEMAN.)

STAUNTON: Is that a *beard* you're growing, Dr Pearce?

PEARCE: I suppose it is really, Mr Staunton.

STAUNTON: Would you care to give an opinion?

(PEARCE *comes forward slowly, some unexplained resistance in him to the procedure.*)

PEARCE: (*Smiling*) Hello, Mrs Potts.

(CHRISTINE *smiles, a little uncertainly.*)

Would you mind if I examined your breast?

(PEARCE *speaks in an unsmoothed Leeds voice: undoctorlike.*)

CHRISTINE: No, doctor . . .

(PEARCE *begins his examination. Finishes it.*)

PEARCE: Thank you.

(*He hands* CHRISTINE *the gown, to cover her chest with.*)

Has it grown at all, since you first noticed it, Mrs Potts?

CHRISTINE: Yes, it has, doctor. It were quite a bit smaller . . . (*Pause.*)

STAUNTON: Ideas?

PEARCE: (*Looking at* CHRISTINE) It's all a bit speculative, isn't it? I don't think I'd want to rule out neoplasm.

(STAUNTON *looks quickly at* CHRISTINE, *to reassure himself the word has no meaning for her. Frowns at* PEARCE. *The* SISTER *opens the connecting door, speaks to the woman in the next room.*)

SISTER: Are you ready, Mrs . . . Banton? The doctor will be with you presently.

(*Returns, closing door silently.*)

STAUNTON: Yes. (*Pause. Practised smile at patient.*) Right you are, Mrs Potts. We'll arrange for you to come in so that we can do a tiny operation and find out what it is.

CHRISTINE: Will it be for long, doctor? I've two little girls, you see . . .

STAUNTON: A couple of days. I don't think there's anything to worry about . . . (*To* SISTER) Biopsy, sister.

(*The* SISTER *asks with her pen which of two columns this should be entered under.*)

Non-urgent.

(*The* SISTER *copies it into file.*)

I'll see you again, Mrs Potts . . .

(*They file out behind the* SISTER. PEARCE *winks at* CHRISTINE *as he leaves.*)

PEARCE: All right?

(CHRISTINE *smiles, grateful.*)

CHRISTINE: Dr Paignton said he were sure it were nothing . . .

PEARCE: I'm sure Dr Paignton knows what he's talking about.

(PEARCE *leaves, closing the door behind him.* CHRISTINE *sits up, stands. Long shot. She looks down at her breast. Quite audible, the next examination starting up in the next room.*)

INT. WARD. DAY

Ward 20 (Women's Surgical). Mid-morning. Several discrete but overlapping actions convey the mood and sense of the place. Mid-morning tea is being served by a young West Indian woman with ornamental spectacles: a SENIOR REGISTRAR *(George) and* DOCTOR SEAL *are studying a patient's (*MRS GOODWIN*'s) notes at the bottom of the ward.* PEARCE *and a* NURSE *are taking a history from a newly admitted woman with acute appendicitis; a woman in a wheelchair, happy, well-looking, is slowly pushed along the ward by an ambulance man on her way home;* PUPIL NURSE CHATTERJEE, *slim, small, girlish, Indian, does temperatures as though the system's reputation depended on it.* CHRISTINE *arrives at the top of the ward, in nightdress and nylon quilted dressing-gown.*

TEA LADY: (*Local accent*) No sugar, Joan. How you like it.

JOAN: (*Old, gaunt*) Bless you, Maria, bless you. I'm fair clemming.

TEA LADY: (*Delicately placing it, quiet, matter-of-fact*) How was the stout?

JOAN: Grand. Gave me the runs.

TEA LADY: Said it would.

(*The* REGISTRAR *and* SEAL *with* MRS GOODWIN, *opposite sides of the bed. They talk across the old lady, who follows them with her eyes as they knock up.*)

REGISTRAR: (*Studying file*) Looks like another one . . .

SEAL: Yes, I think so.

REGISTRAR: Who did the last one? (*Thumbing a file*) Oh, I did. (*He smiles at* SEAL.) All these years. Let it be a lesson, doctor. Can't win 'em all.

SEAL: Seven years. I don't call that bad.

(*A burst of laughter from across the ward. They turn to look.*)

Mrs Paisley. Going home.

REGISTRAR: His nibs'll be pleased.

SEAL: He *is*.

(MRS PAISLEY *is talking to a cluster of ambulants in the sink and table area.*)

MRS PAISLEY: (*About fifty, ruddy complexion*) . . . You're not kidding. If the old feller ever finds out where they've had their hands, he'll never speak to me again. (*Laughing unforcedly*) Still, what he doesn't know won't hurt him. I'll see you at the Three Tuns a week Satday, Agnes . . .

AGNES: (*Pale, thin*) Nay, I'm not so sure, Martha . . .

MRS PAISLEY: Don't be daft, course I will, I'll get you a port in – and I don't drink port – so you'd better be there. Bye, bye, bye, bye, Carmel, Mildred, Kath . . .

(*A chorus of 'Bye, Martha . . .' as* MRS PAISLEY *trundles up the ward.*)

JOAN: (*Calling, remembering*) Don't forget your boyfriend now, Martha . . .

(MRS PAISLEY *turns, grins.*)

MRS PAISLEY: Don't be naughty!

(MRS PAISLEY *arrives at the bed area where* PEARCE *and a* NURSE *take the history.*)

PEARCE: (*To* PATIENT) What would you say, all the time, every so often, once in a while, what?

WOMAN: Phww. I don't rightly know. Sometimes it's all the time, sometimes it's now and again. Then again every so often it's just once in a while . . .

(PEARCE *frowns, clears his throat, looks across at the* NURSE.)

PEARCE: (*Slowly*) Did you get all that, nurse?

MRS PAISLEY: (*Out of vision*) I'm just off now, doctor. Come to say goodbye.

PEARCE: Excuse me.

(*He walks towards* MRS PAISLEY.)

Oh, you're off then, sexpot? What am I supposed to do at nights now, eh? (*To* AMBULANCEMAN.) Watch this one, Peter. She'll have your pants off as you push her . . .

MRS PAISLEY: Here, that'll do. I've a husband and four kids . . .

PEARCE: It's not all you've got, Martha. (*He kisses* MRS PAISLEY*'s cheek. Very serious*) Take . . . care.

(*He's close to her face. She looks at him in silence.*)

Terra.

MRS PAISLEY: Terra.

(PEARCE *watches* MRS PAISLEY *up the ward before turning back to his patient. We see* CHRISTINE *still in doorway, stepping aside to let* MRS PAISLEY *pass.*)

Cheer up, lass. Naught to be feared of.

(*A clean, plain, pleasant smile.* CHRISTINE *smiles back, rather timid. The doors slap behind her, she pushes into the ward, past* CHATTERJEE, *the tea trolley,* PEARCE, *until she reaches her bed, the number of which she checks before surveying it and the area and furniture about it.* NURSE O'MALLEY *arrives, carrying a cheap plastic suitcase.*)

O'MALLEY: Here it is, Mrs Potts. Your clothes is here, ready for your man this evening. He can bring 'em in when you're ready for home.

SISTER: (*Out of vision*) Nurse O'Malley!

O'MALLEY: Coming, sister! (*To* CHRISTINE) Better slip into bed for a while, Mrs Potts. Best place, out of the way.

(NURSE O'MALLEY *slips the case behind the locker, joins* SENIOR SISTER WARREN *and* STAFF NURSE BRENTON, *who are directing the* THEATRE PORTER *where to place a trolley. On it, on blood drip,* MRS SCULLY, *late sixties, very thin, white, still under anaesthetic. Who could be dead. The* PORTER *is very young, in tight-fitting jeans, a 'Save the Watergate 5000' T-shirt, and plimsolls. Grubby white coat, open and torn. Straight light brown hair a good six inches beyond his shoulders.* WARREN, *blonde hair, black roots, amazingly spruce in white with black belt, court shoes and American-style hat, supervises proceedings.* MRS SCULLY *is being returned to her bed next to Christine's. Through all of this,* LUCY, *fat morose West Indian cleaner, wetmops the ward floor.*)

WARREN: Watch those bottles.

(*The* PORTER *stares at* WARREN *as though she's just revealed a long-suspected insanity.*)

PORTER: (*Guiding trolley in*) Them bottles'll see you out, sister.

WARREN: I'd sooner they saw Mrs Scully out actually.

BRENTON: (*Short, chunky*) Right. Thank you. Screens, nurse.

(O'MALLEY *draws the curtains on the rails that surround the bed area.* CHRISTINE*'s view has been replaced by green curtain.*)

WOMAN'S VOICE: (*Out of vision*) Is this seven?

(CHRISTINE *turns. A young girl (*ANNA JAY*), nineteen or twenty, in dressing-gown and slippers, stands at the bottom of next bed.*)

CHRISTINE: Yes, it will be. (*She turns to look at the plastic number plate on the bed head.*) I'm eight.

ANNA: Oh yes. Thanks. (*She flops on to the bed. Surveying room*) God, what a dump.

(CHRISTINE follows ANNA*'s eyes round the twenty or so beds they can see. Their eyes meet eventually.*)

I'm in for a biopsy. I've got a lump on my breast.

CHRISTINE: Me too. I've just arrived.

ANNA: Snap. Anna Jay.

CHRISTINE: Christine Potts.

ANNA: I'm at the university.

CHRISTINE: Oh. (*Pause.*) I'm a housewife.

ANNA: (*Surveying ward*) You wouldn't want to lance a *boil* in a place like this, would you?

CHRISTINE: (*Not understanding*) It's my first time in a hospital. I suppose they're pretty much alike.

(O'MALLEY *jerks the curtains on Mrs Scully's bed back with a sharp scraping sound. The* PORTER *begins skating his trolley back up the ward, one foot propelling, the other resting on the rear transverse strut. The* NURSES *disperse.*)

WARREN: (*Passing Anna's bed, not stopping*) I think you'd be better in your bed, Miss Jay. (*To* BRENTON) X-rays for those two, staff nurse.

(BRENTON *follows* WARREN *to the windowed nurses' room at the top of the ward.* O'MALLEY *stays at* MRS SCULLY*'s bedside for a moment scraping wisps of scraggy grey hair back from the forehead.* ANNA *stands, stares at* MRS SCULLY*'s ashen face, the drips.*)

ANNA: Oh God.

INT. WARD. DAY

O'MALLEY *dry-shaves* CHRISTINE*'s armpit.* CHATTERJEE *shaves* ANNA*'s. The food ritual has begun at the top of the ward,* BRENTON *serving,* NURSES *handing out.*

O'MALLEY: (*To* CHATTERJEE) Ryan's up the spout.
(CHATTERJEE *blank.*)
Pregnant. Do you know Ryan? Third year, she's on 15. (*Pause.*) Sorry, did I hurt you? (*Pause.*) Leaving at the end of the month to get married. Lucky pig. (*Pause.*) Just got a job on agency too. Sixty quid a week doing the same job she's doing now for peanuts. (*Pause.*) We muster been born mugs, Chatty.

CHATTERJEE: (*Serious innocent*) Don't you like it here?

INT. WARD. DAY

CHRISTINE *dozes, mid-afternoon. Out of vision,* SEAL*'s voice, repeating 'Mrs Potts' several times. She opens her eyes. The curtains have been drawn round her bed.* SEAL *sits on a chair by the bedside, the file on her knee.*

SEAL: Having a nap, were we, Mrs Potts?

CHRISTINE: I must have dropped off, doctor.

SEAL: I'd like to take another look before tomorrow, Mrs Potts.
(CHRISTINE *slips her nightdress over her head.* SEAL *begins the examination.*)
How long ago was it we saw you?

CHRISTINE: Just coming up to three weeks, doctor.

SEAL: Yes. (*Still feeling*) Still no pain?

CHRISTINE: No.

SEAL: Good. Yes. Good. (*She feels again under the armpit.*) Is it about the same size, would you say?

CHRISTINE: No. I think it's a bit bigger.

SEAL: Yes. Good. You can put your thing on now.

(CHRISTINE *puts the nightdress on.* SEAL *opens her file, finds a form, takes out her pen.*)

I'd like you to sign the consent form, Mrs Potts.

(*She hands the form in the file to* CHRISTINE, *and the pen.*) We're not permitted to do anything without the patient's consent.

(CHRISTINE *does her best to read it.*)

It's just to say that you give your consent to the biopsy . . .

CHRISTINE: (*Finding the word*) Biopsy . . .

SEAL: Yes. We'll cut a piece of the lump and er do some tests on it . . . and the tests will tell us what to do next, if anything. Sign there, if you will.

(CHRISTINE *signs on the line indicated.* SEAL *takes the file and pen, stands.*)

Good. We'll see you tomorrow in theatre, Mrs Potts.

CHRISTINE: Thank you, doctor.

(SEAL *pulls the curtains back, revealing the ward, inert and littered. Leaves.*)

ANNA: (*Watching her go*) She's the one with cold hands, isn't she? Still, you know what they say, cold hands . . .

(*She smiles, leaves it unspoken. An old woman hobbles past on a Zimmer frame, says something neither of them catches.* MRS SCULLY *begins to moan and mutter in the next bed. She lies half propped, eyes open, staring at the far ceiling.*)

SCULLY: Oh the bastards. The bloody bastards. Oh the bastards. They are. Bloody bastards. Wait till I see him. He's nothing else.

INT. WARD. NIGHT

Close-up, JOE POTTS. *Early thirties, broad, powerful, squat face, balding, weather-beaten with big roughened hands. He's a brickie, straight from work. Beyond him, the sounds of a busy evening visiting time.*

JOE: The kids are all right. They're at your mother's.

(CHRISTINE *purposive, alert, a different person.*)

CHRISTINE: Linda'll need her dinner money on Monday, tell her, if I'm not home. Sixty p.

JOE: I thought you said you'd be out Friday.

CHRISTINE: Well, you know what these places are. Who took their clothes?

JOE: Your Renee met 'em from school. I left a key under the brick.

CHRISTINE: Have you spoken to anyone?

JOE: How do you mean?

CHRISTINE: *Here.*

JOE: Oh. No.

CHRISTINE: Have a word with the sister 'fore you go.

JOE: What for?

CHRISTINE: Well . . . Ask her if I'm going to be out Friday.

JOE: I thought they'd told you.

CHRISTINE: She won't bite you.

JOE: What's the point. I mean, if she's told you . . . They know what they're doing.

(*Silence.* JOE *shifts uneasily on his chair. Looks at the clock at the bottom of the ward.* CHRISTINE *looks over his shoulder at* ANNA, *who nuzzles her boyfriend's ear. At* MRS SCULLY *who sleeps.*)

What's wrong with *her*?

CHRISTINE: I don't know.

(*Silence.*)

JOE: When do you have it then?

CHRISTINE: Tomorrow morning. Sister says I'm first on the list.

JOE: Oh. Good. (*Pause.*) Have you got everything you want?

CHRISTINE: Yes. Don't forget the case.

JOE: It hardly seems worth it, does it? I thought of calling in at t'Working Men's . . .

CHRISTINE: (*Firm*) Take it. They said you've to take it.

(*Pause again.*)

JOE: (*Finally*) Do you want your crisps?

(CHRISTINE *shakes her head.*)

I gave your mother two pounds. Is that all right?

(CHRISTINE *nods.*)

She said she didn't want it, but . . .

CHRISTINE: Make sure you get something to eat, won't you?

JOE: Stop fussing. Bloody'ell.

O'MALLEY: (*Arriving*) Temperature, Mrs Potts.

(O'MALLEY *slots the thermometer under* CHRISTINE*'s tongue, takes her pulse, studying watch.*)

INT. CORRIDOR. NIGHT

PUPIL NURSE CHATTERJEE *ushers the last of the visitors from the ward. In the open corridor by the nurses' room,* JOE *lingers, watching* WARREN *entering something in her report book. A surge of leavers blocks his view for a moment. When it clears, she's picked up the phone. He leaves, the case in his hand.*

INT. WARD. NIGHT

In the ward, two ambulant PATIENTS *help to vase assorted flowers left behind by the visitors.* BRENTON *is already giving out drugs from the trolley, mainly sleeping pills. She's one up from Anna's bed, pouring water for a feeble* OLD WOMAN, *helping her to take her two capsules. She watches* ANNA, *who has taken foil from her handbag, swallows a yellow pill with some water.* BRENTON *moves to the foot of Anna's bed, consults her chart briefly.*

BRENTON: Do you have anything, Miss Jay? There's nothing written up for you.

ANNA: How're you fixed for a couple of grams of cannabis resin? That usually does the trick.

BRENTON: Could I ask what that pill was you just took? You're not supposed to take pills in here, you know, not unless they're given you, you were told when you came in.

ANNA: Nobody told me a thing. Believe me.

BRENTON: Well, you took a pill . . .

ANNA: It wasn't a pill. It was *the* Pill.

(BRENTON *looks at the chart again.*)

BRENTON: Just a minute.

(CHRISTINE *eats her crisps, sitting up.*)

MRS SCULLY: Give us one, will you, love?

(CHRISTINE *turns, startled.*)

CHRISTINE: Are you . . . supposed to?

MRS SCULLY: Sod it, give us one. I'm starving.

(CHRISTINE *holds the bag out.* MRS SCULLY*'s white arm extends waveringly, the hand emerges with seven or eight. She pushes them into her mouth as* WARREN *and* BRENTON *return to Anna's bed.*)

WARREN: Staff Nurse Brenton tells me you're on the Pill.

ANNA: That's right.

WARREN: Oh, Christ. That's another five-day bed wasted. Didn't anybody tell you?

ANNA: Tell me what?

WARREN: (*To* BRENTON) I'd better ring Rogers. (*Consults watch.*) He'll have gone. And don't leave the drugs trolley unattended in the middle of the ward again, staff nurse. How many more times . . . ? (*Across the ward to* O'MALLEY, *cutting daffodil stalks*) Nurse, leave those, get a pan for Mrs Scully, she's throwing up . . .

(WARREN*'s gone.* O'MALLEY *rushes on to the scene. Green bile drips from* MRS SCULLY*'s mouth on to the pillow and beyond.*)

O'MALLEY: God, you devil, you've been eating, haven't you? What have you been eating? You know what I told you . . .

BRENTON: Sleeping tablets for you, Mrs Potts. A good night's sleep for tomorrow.

CHRISTINE: I'm . . . fine, thank you.

BRENTON: (*Placing them on locker*) There we are. Take them with some water . . . (*She smiles, leaves. Studies Mrs Scully's chart. Preparing Stemetil injection*)

You don't deserve any, Mrs Scully.

MRS SCULLY: Sod off.

(O'MALLEY, *trying to sponge* MRS SCULLY*'s sick-streaked hair, smiles with pleasure to herself.*)

INT. WARD. NIGHT

Night lighting. Clock says 10.15. Coughing, low muttering, moaning, creaking. A NURSING AUXILIARY, *small, old, dumpy, talks to* ANNA, *who lies listening.* CHRISTINE *is looking at a picture of her two children, six and three.* AUXILIARY *watching out for the* NIGHT SISTER *in nurses' room.*

AUXILIARY: . . . I prefer men's wards. They're just like babies, once you get 'em in. And there's always a chance of a flash here and there. Dirty buggers. The older the dirtier. Eeh, they're always so grateful . . . I like nights though. It's a rest from the old feller's coughing . . .

(PEARCE *arrives, in old tracksuit, basketball shoes. He remains about three days unshaven.*)

Evening Dr Pearce.

PEARCE: Hello, Nancy. Still at it?

AUXILIARY: (*Leaving*) Cheeky.

PEARCE: (*To* ANNA) Hello.

ANNA: Hello.

PEARCE: There's been a bit of a balls-up.

ANNA: Really?

PEARCE: Yeah. Somebody should have told you to stop taking the Pill.

ANNA: Who, for instance?

PEARCE: (*Smiling*) Ah, well, there's some . . . dispute about that. (*Pause.*) Listen, we can't do a biopsy with that lot inside you. There's a risk of thrombosis . . .

ANNA: Listen, I've been waiting nine weeks for this . . .

PEARCE: I know. I'm sorry. Really.

ANNA: So how long will I have to wait?

PEARCE: It's not my case . . . (*He stops himself, hating the words.*)

You'll have to get back on cycle. We'll work it out and let you know . . .

ANNA: Bloody hell.

PEARCE: (*Standing*) I'm sorry.

(PEARCE *stands, moves fractionally towards Christine's bed.*

CHRISTINE *smiles at him shyly.* PEARCE *crosses his fingers, smiles back at her, leaves.*

ANNA *lies there for a while, then swings her feet on to the floor and pulls a long white paper carrier from under her bed, takes her clothes out, begins to get dressed.*)

CHRISTINE: Anna . . . ?

(ANNA *puts jeans on under nightdress.*)

What're you doing?

ANNA: I'm off. No point staying here.

CHRISTINE: Did he say you could go? Shouldn't you . . . see somebody?

ANNA: (*Clipping bra*) Yes. My feller.

(CHRISTINE *watches her anxiously as she completes her dressing.*)

(*Finally*) Hey. Hope it goes OK. See you.

(ANNA *strides off down the darkened ward.*

CHRISTINE *watches her to the open doors leading past the half-lit nurses' room, sees her path blocked by the* NIGHT SISTER *and* STAFF NURSE. *Waves of verbal exchange meet her. Finally* ANNA *strides off into the dark.* CHRISTINE *turns to her locker, begins taking her pills.*)

MRS SCULLY: What've they taken this time? Feels like half me insides. This is me third. Eeeh there'll be nowt left. The Queen Mother's had one, you know. And Petula Clark. Sister thing told me. Poor buggers. I hope they don't feel like me (*Pause.*) They made me sick, them crisps.

INT. WARD. NIGHT

CHRISTINE *sleeps. Wakens suddenly. The middle of the night. Low gasps and hisses from Mrs Scully's bed area. She focuses on two young* NURSES *who've been changing her blood bag. They talk in harsh whispers.*

FIRST NURSE: Jesus Christ, look at it, it's all over . . .

SECOND NURSE: Shh. Don't wake her, for God's sake. She'll pull the place down. Take the bag, take the bag . . .

FIRST NURSE: All right, I've got it.

(*They stare at each other, momentarily lost.*)

What are we going to *do?*

(CHRISTINE *edges forward, until she can see* MRS SCULLY. *Her face, hair, neck and pillows are splashed with blood from the bag the* FIRST NURSE *holds in her bloody hands.*)

SECOND NURSE: You're a clumsy sod, I showed you how to do it.

FIRST NURSE: My hand slipped.

SECOND NURSE: 'My hand slipped.' Sister'll love that.

(*The* FIRST NURSE *sees* CHRISTINE *peering at them.*)

FIRST NURSE: We'd better pull the curtains.

(*The curtains are drawn.* CHRISTINE *lies back, half hearing the muffled exchanges that persist.*)

SECOND NURSE: Well, you'd better tell her. (*Pause.*) Look at it!

(*Suddenly they're giggling, shushing each other.* CHRISTINE *turns over, returns to sleep.*)

INT. WARD. DAY

ANAESTHETIST *is preparing syringe and tray for injection.*

ANAESTHETIST: (*Out of vision*) All right, Mrs Potts? This'll just make you feel nice and drowsy.

(CHRISTINE *sits propped in her bed, eyes quite heavy, but watching.* CHATTERJEE *has just finished taking* MRS SCULLY'*s blood pressure, mutters 'Good morning, doctor' shyly, as* SEAL *arrives with a file.*)

SEAL: Mrs Potts. All ready.

(CHRISTINE *smiles.*)

Now then, (*sitting*) there's just another form here we'd like you to sign. Do you feel up to that?

CHRISTINE: What is it, doctor?

SEAL: It's nothing to worry about. Mr Staunton thought it might be as well if you signed an open consent form too. Just in case. (*Here show the modified consent form being held by* DR SEAL. *Casually pick out key words . . . 'Frozen section (biopsy)? Proceed? mastectomy.'*)
(*Soothing voice over*) Then if there *were* anything, well, nasty, he could deal with it on the spot, instead of having to send you home and call you back again.

CHRISTINE: I see.

SEAL: Just there at the bottom. (*She guides* CHRISTINE*'s signature.*) That's it. Good. (*She stands.*) See you in theatre, Mrs Potts.
(SEAL *leaves.* CHRISTINE *frowns a little, uneasy now.*)

ANAESTHETIST: (*Who has been waiting.*) Here we go then.
(*He begins preparing the arm.* CHRISTINE *watches, fearful.* ANAESTHETIST *sees her.*) (*Smiling*) No need to look, Mrs Potts.
(*The* ANAESTHETIST *directs* CHRISTINE*'s gaze away from the syringe. She looks at* MRS SCULLY, *scrubbed white again.*)

MRS SCULLY: (*To no one*) I'm being buggered about.
O'MALLEY *and* CHATTERJEE *help* CHRISTINE *on to the theatre trolley. The* PORTER *stands by, blowing gum bubbles, in, out.* O'MALLEY *ties an ident-disc round* CHRISTINE*'s left arm.* CHATTERJEE *places her file between her feet.*)

O'MALLEY: All ready, Mrs Potts. Have a good time.
(*The* PORTER *trundles* CHRISTINE *up the ward.*)

INT. CORRIDORS. DAY

We take CHRISTINE*'s trolley-view of the journey, through the ward, past* WARREN*'s open door, out into the old tiled corridor. Past laundry, kitchens, clanging lift cages, X-ray (follow the white line), the inner semaphore of a Victorian general hospital.*

INT. ANAESTHETIC ROOM. DAY

CHRISTINE *lies, almost out, in pre-op. The* ANAESTHETIST *and his trainee talk out of vision, as they give her a second injection. The trainee prepares the arm, but the assistant gives the actual injection.*

ANAESTHETIST: Put it in the right, Charlie. Left breast, right arm, OK?

INT. OPERATING THEATRE. DAY

CHRISTINE *is lifted on to operating table. The* REGISTRAR *(George),* SEAL, PEARCE, *masked, stand around waiting.*

REGISTRAR: Any sign of Mr Staunton yet, sister?

THEATRE SISTER: On his way, Dr Williams.

(*The* REGISTRAR *checks the time.*)

We're going to be pushed again . . .

PEARCE: Why not go ahead?

(*The* REGISTRAR *stares at* PEARCE *for a long time, his eyes searching* PEARCE*'s for some sign, a gleam of irony perhaps, that might save him from irredeemable certification. He finds nothing approaching it.*)

REGISTRAR: (*Deliberately*) Doctor Pearce. I hope by the time you finish your training in this hospital you will have learnt the answer to that question.

(*Close-up clock above theatre door: 9.55.* STAUNTON *arrives, gowned, capped, but not gloved, glasses halfway down his nose. A chorus of 'good morning' greets him. The* THEATRE SISTER *hands him the file, with bred deference.*)

STAUNTON: Good morning. George. Dr Seal. (*To* SISTER) Thank you. Dr Pearce. (*Quick look in file.*) Yes. Yes. Yes. Good, let's get started. (*To* REGISTRAR) Off you go, doctor. We're waiting for you . . .

INT. OPERATING THEATRE. DAY

Close-up the REGISTRAR *working on the cut. Close-up* STAUNTON, SEAL, PEARCE. *The* REGISTRAR *looks up at* STAUNTON. *They exchange a longish look.*

STAUNTON: Take it on a bit, George, mm?

Close-up REGISTRAR, *returning to the cut. Close-up* PEARCE, *staring intently. The* REGISTRAR *looks across the table again at* STAUNTON.)

Do the section.

(*The* REGISTRAR *teases out a sliver of flesh, scraping it into a small round plastic container.*)

REGISTRAR: (*Out of vision*) Path lab, nurse. Oh, and phone Dr Mount, tell him we might have something for his mice in an hour or so . . .

(*Close-up* CHRISTINE, *in repose.*)

STAUNTON: (*Out of vision*) How old is she?

(*Pan round table. Return to close-up* CHRISTINE. *Close-up* PEARCE.)

PEARCE: (*Out of vision*) Twenty-nine.

STAUNTON: (*Out of vision*) Twenty-nine.

REGISTRAR: (*Out of vision*) Any point waiting, do you think?

(*Close-up* PEARCE.)

PEARCE: (*Half muttering, barely audible*) We've waited three weeks, another twenty minutes won't make any difference . . .

STAUNTON: Say something, Dr Pearce?

PEARCE: (*Finally, looking away*) No.

INT. OPERATING THEATRE. DAY

Close-up file, containing histologist's report on the section, in the SISTER*'s hand while the* REGISTRAR *reads from it. She then holds it for* STAUNTON, *who is now scrubbed-up and gloved. He scans it briefly.*

STAUNTON: Well, I suppose we knew as much. Let Dr Seal and Dr Pearce see it, will you, sister? Well, George, shall we have a look at the nodes . . .

(*They close around the table. Close-up clock: 10.35.*)

INT. OPERATING THEATRE. DAY

CHRISTINE*'s head in close-up as she's wheeled out of the theatre into the post-op area. Draw back to reveal the process: the clock is at 12.40. Drip bottles – saline only – attached. The doctors have retired to wash up. Two* NURSES *are cleaning the couch area, etc, another lays out new instruments, etc.*

INT. POST-OP. DAY

Post-op area. O'MALLEY *stands a few paces away from Christine's trolley, waiting for a porter.*

O'MALLEY: (*To* NURSE *passing through*) Did you see that porter feller anywhere?

(NURSE *shakes head, leaves.*)

He's an idle man.

(CHRISTINE *moans, stirs a little.* O'MALLEY *frowns, makes an impatient noise in her throat.*)

INT. ANAESTHETIC ROOM. DAY

DR MOUNT *in a white coat, passes through the anaesthetic room and raps on the theatre doors. The* THEATRE SISTER *pokes her head out.*

MOUNT: Dr Mount. You've got some tissue for me.

SISTER: Yes, it's in the theatre, doctor. I'll just get it for you.

(*The* SISTER *disappears back into the theatre.* MOUNT *waits. She returns, and hands him a small round plastic lidded bowl containing tissue.*)

It's about fifty grams. Will that be enough?

MOUNT: That's fine. Is that it?

SISTER: (*Out of vision*) That's it.

MOUNT: Frozen section say anything about the type?

(PEARCE *enters from the theatre.*)

SISTER: Medullary, I think. I'll send a copy down, if you like.

MOUNT: Thanks.

(MOUNT *talks on, though both grow aware of the silent, brooding figure at their side.*)

Medullary'll do nicely. (*Staring at tissue bowl*) I'm trying implants on immune-deprived mice.

Subcutaneous. Intramuscular. Intravenous.

Intrahepatic. If that goes well, I'll try a second passage of tumour solution by injection into the pleural and peritoneal cavities.

PEARCE: How long before you crack it then?

MOUNT: Hard to say. Believe it or not, a major problem is the shortage of tumour tissue.

PEARCE: (*Short, snapping laugh*) Yeah? Well, we'll have to see what we can do, won't we . . .

(PEARCE *leaves abruptly.* SISTER *coughs.* MOUNT *pockets his tissue.*)

MOUNT: I'd better get this to the fridge . . .

SISTER: Odd to think of it . . . living on like that.

MOUNT: Yes.

(MOUNT *turns to go. As he does so another* PATIENT, *out, is wheeled into the anaesthetic room, ready for the next operation.*)

INT. POST-OP. DAY

O'MALLEY *and* CHRISTINE *still in post-op. Close-up* CHRISTINE, eyes open. A long moment.

CHRISTINE: (*Starting very low, a drunken mumble.*) What have they done? What . . . ? What've they . . . ? (*Louder*) What have they done? What have they done?

O'MALLEY: Shh, you're all right, Mrs Potts . . .

CHRISTINE: (*Louder*) What have they done? Eh? What have they . . . ?

O'MALLEY: You're all right, Mrs Potts . . . You've had your operation and we're just waiting . . .

CHRISTINE: (*Scream, harsh*) . . . *What have they done to me?*

INT. WARD. NIGHT

Ward 20. Evening, minutes before visitors. Tea things are still being cleared, NURSES *finish off bed-rubs (soap and powder) for the elderly frail. Everything that moves creaks, rumbles, clanks; a Second World War combat area.* CHRISTINE *lies in her bed, propped, awake but sedated, under her saline drip. Her face is very red, blotched with crying. She stares up the ward at the ward doors, which remain closed. The large puff bandage over her left breast is slightly stained with blood.* WARREN *emerges from the dayroom pushing a creaking dirty-linen skip before her. Surveys ward. Looks up at clock: 7.40.*

WARREN: Let them in, nurse. We're ten minutes behind again.

(SEAL *emerges from a curtained bed area, a* NURSE *pulls the curtains back.*)

SEAL: Give me a second or two, will you, sister? I don't want to get caught by the hordes . . .

WARREN: Quick as you can then, doctor.

(SEAL *leaves up the ward.* WARREN *approaches Mrs Scully's curtained bed area, peeps in.*)

Nearly finished, nurse?

O'MALLEY: Not really, sister.

(O'MALLEY *and* CHATTERJEE *are about to change Mrs Scully's dressing.*)

WARREN: Quick as you can then. I'll get your temperatures started for you . . .

(WARREN *recloses the curtain, moves on to Christine's bed. Visitors surge in down the ward.* CHRISTINE *watches them in a sort of dull anxiety.*)

How are we feeling now, Mrs Potts?

CHRISTINE: (*Seeing her*) Sore.

WARREN: We'll give you something to help you sleep. You'll feel better tomorrow.

(CHRISTINE *returns to the visitors.*)

I shouldn't be letting you have visitors, according to regulations, Mrs Potts . . .

(CHRISTINE *looks at her again, some slight aggression mounting in her.*)

Tell your husband to pop in on his way, I'll have a word with him, just to reassure him . . .

(WARREN *pushes the trolley off up the ward, passes* JOE *on his way in, carrying a bunch of daffodils.* CHRISTINE *sees him, begins to fill up and spill over. He takes her hand nervously, anxious at once, ignoring her tears, wishing them not there.*)

JOE: I'm sorry I'm late, love. I went down the market and got you these, we're working on Chaucer Street, you know, the flats. (*Pause.*) What you crying for?

CHRISTINE: They've taken it off, Joe.

(CHRISTINE *tries to stem the flood of tears with a Kleenex but it gets worse.* JOE *can't find anything to say, in the shock and fear of the moment.*)

JOE: (*Finally*) I thought they were just doing tests, love. (*Pause.*) You weren't even ill. (*Looking round at the ward, embarrassed*) Listen, don't cry.

CHRISTINE: (*Working on her face with Kleenex*) I can't help it. I'm sorry. (*She makes the effort.*) I'm . . . (*She won't say it: 'frightened'.*) I don't know why they did it. Nobody's said.

JOE: I suppose they know best, Chris.

SCULLY: (*Screeching from her curtained bed area*) Oh dear gentle Jesus they're killing me! God Almighty don't, don't do that, oh, oh, oh, don't do that, please, no, no, oh, oh . . .

O'MALLEY: Nearly finished, Mrs Scully. We'll have you right as rainwater in a tick, you see.

(*The exchanges continue.* CHRISTINE *stares ahead of her, deep in her fear.* JOE *stares at her in some desperation, anxious for some word from her that will restore their normality to them.*)

JOE: (*Finally*) What shall I do with the flowers?

CHRISTINE: Oh . . . Take them up to the nurses' room, they'll look after them . . .

(JOE *stands gratefully.*)

Speak to the sister will you . . . (*She's desperate.*) Please.

JOE: (*Pinned again*) Do you think I should?

CHRISTINE: Please. (*Pause.*) She said it'd be all right.

(JOE *nods, leaves.* CHATTERJEE *unzips Scully's bed area,* O'MALLEY *pushes the squeaky trolley with the soiled dressing into the main aisle.*)

O'MALLEY: You're a brave lady, so you are, Mrs Scully.

(MRS SCULLY *lies back, drained of all reply. The* NURSES *move off up the ward through the glass partition of the nurses' room.* CHRISTINE *can just make out* JOE *talking to* SISTER WARREN.)

SCULLY: I've had it this time. I'll not see this through.

(CHRISTINE *looks at her, hasn't even the energy to console her.* MRS SCULLY*'s hands are on her midriff.*)

There's nowt left. How'ma gonna get to the post office like this?

(CHRISTINE *turns away, looks back up to the nurses' room.* JOE *leaves it, walks back into the ward and down to her bed.*)

JOE: (*Sitting down again*) I've seen her, love. She's quite nice really.

CHRISTINE: What did she say?

JOE: Well, she said when they opened you up it were pretty nasty and that there were some sort of infection, so the specialist decided you'd be better off without . . .

(*Pause.*)

CHRISTINE: How long will I be in for, Joe?

JOE: Oh, she said about a fortnight. They have to do some more tests and that.

(CHRISTINE *has studied his face and manner for hints, clues to her condition, yet she's eager to take the hope offered.*)

CHRISTINE: Am I . . . going to be all right?

JOE: Course you're gonna be all right. That's why they did what they did. They're not fools, you know, these people.

CHRISTINE: (*Bleak*) It's to be hoped to God they're not.

JOE: Hey, there's no point talking like that, our Chris. You've got to start getting well again. You've got two kiddies and a husband to look after.

(CHRISTINE *begins to weep again, gently hopeless.*)

CHRISTINE: What am I going to do? Nothing'll fit me . . .

JOE: Sister said they fix you up with something. (*Gentle, embarrassed, frightened by her unfamiliar despair*) Hey. It'll be all right, chuck.

INT. WARD. NIGHT

Two a.m. by the ward clock. Old women cough, wheeze, croak, ramble in their sleep. Noise everywhere. Track in on CHRISTINE, *lying awake, staring at shadows. After a moment, her right hand moves along the bedspread until it contacts the vacated breast area.*

INT. WARD. DAY

Morning, 10.15. Ward 20. STAFF NURSE BRENTON *hurries her nurses along, in expectation of the consultant's weekly round.*

BRENTON: Come along, Nurse Chatterjee. Let's get that finished, shall we.

(CHATTERJEE *shakes down a thermometer at Mrs Scully's bed, enters temperature on chart, smooths the coverlet several times.*)

CHATTERJEE: Just finished, staff.

(O'MALLEY *comes into the ward.* BRENTON *turns to look at her.* O'MALLEY *nods, goes out again, enters nurses' room, where* WARREN *is adjusting her cap in a mirror. Some laughter at bottom of ward.*)

BRENTON: All right, ladies. Settle down now. Mr Staunton is about to start his round and Mr Staunton likes a little quiet on the ward. (*She's turning, sees a crushed grape on the floor, begins to tease it up with her finger, puts the skin into her pocket, borrows a Kleenex from a locker to wipe up the juice. To herself*) God Almighty, what do those cleaners *do*! (*She's satisfied, strides off into the nurses' room.* CHRISTINE *sits up in bed, still red, but rested.*)

SCULLY: He's your man, inne, Staunton?

CHRISTINE: Yes.

SCULLY: I have Price. Had him for years. (*Pause.*) Wait till I see him.

(*The doors open and round begins, in all its rich and subtle ritual.* STAUNTON *has eleven patients in the ward, the first two up from* CHRISTINE. *We take her point of view as she sits and watches.* STAUNTON, *George the* REGISTRAR, SEAL *and* WARREN *stand at the foot of the bed.* WARREN *hands* STAUNTON *file and bed-chart, says the patient's name clearly. The* PATIENT *is not addressed.* STAUNTON *shows the* REGISTRAR *something in the file. Some brief, low discussion.* SEAL *asks a question, almost unaudible.* WARREN *answers, after hesitation.* STAUNTON *says something to* SEAL *which she writes up. They move to the foot of the next bed. Apart from a marginal (but still ineffective) increase in audibility, the procedure unfolds as before. Close-up* CHRISTINE, *her face tensing as her turn approaches. They arrive at the bottom of her bed.*)

WARREN: (*Handing file*) Mrs Potts, sir.

(STAUNTON *half turns with the file, so that he's in less than half-profile from the bed, as though shy or embarrassed.* SEAL *acknowledges* CHRISTINE *with a slight smile. The* REGISTRAR *asks a question of* WARREN. *All the exchanges are indistinct, barely audible, the odd word floating down the bed to* CHRISTINE. *Square brackets indicate dimension of unclarity, for the patient.*)

REGISTRAR: [No problem with the] wound, sister?

WARREN: [None] at all, doctor.

SEAL: [Is she de]pressed, would you [say]?

WARREN: [Just a bit] down, doctor. [It's only] natural, I [sup]pose.

REGISTRAR: [What about the] radivac?

SEAL: [About a] hundred ccs.

(STAUNTON *says something wholly inaudible, his back almost wholly turned to* CHRISTINE. *The* REGISTRAR *looks up the bed at her, studies her for a moment.*)

REGISTRAR: (*Audibly*) Possibly. What do you suggest, sir?

(STAUNTON *replies after a moment, again wholly inaudibly. The* REGISTRAR *speaks to* WARREN, *who nods. They move on, in order, beyond Mrs Scully's bed, towards the bottom of the ward.*)

WARREN: (*Cheerfully*) Thank you, Mrs Potts.

(*She joins the doctors.*)

SCULLY: (*Racking whisper*) Doesn't he look like Prince Philip! He's going bald, you know. Spent thousands on hair restorer. I read it in the *People*.

WARREN: (*Up the ward*) Thank you, Mrs Scully!

(MRS SCULLY *deliberates a reply for a moment, then reaches for her plastic water jug and glass. Her frail hand sets up a rattling in the sepulchral quiet of the ward. She winks at* CHRISTINE; *wicked. The water begins to splash over the locker.* WARREN *gestures to a standing* NURSE *at the top of the ward. The nurse,* O'MALLEY, *approaches Mrs Scully's bed area, takes the jug off her.*)

O'MALLEY: (*Sotto voce*) You're nothing but a little girl, Mrs Scully. What are you?

(MRS SCULLY *stares at her.*)

SCULLY: (*Finally*) Thirsty. It's like the bloody desert, this place, it's so full of dust.

O'MALLEY: (*Minatory, mopping floor with Kleenex*) That'll do now, Mrs Scully.

INT. WARD. DAY

Afternoon, towards 3 p.m. The ward rests desultorily, thin sunlight washing the floors. Ambulants gather in clusters about beds. The woman with the Zimmer frame wanders from bed to bed, trying to cadge some Lucozade. The PORTER *and* BRENTON *are wheeling in the last of the day's theatre patients, restoring her to her bed. The trolley shop works its way down the ward.* CHRISTINE*'s bed area is curtained. Inside,* CHATTERJEE *has just begun dressing the wound.* CHRISTINE *lies half on her back, her head averted, her left arm extended only slightly, but enough to give her pain.*

CHATTERJEE: Will it go any further, Mrs Potts?

(CHRISTINE *shakes her head.*)

Come on, I'm sure it will, just a weeny bit more . . .

(CHRISTINE *closes her eyes on the new pain.*)

That's it . . . There. I'll try not to hurt you . . . (*She begins removing puff-bandage dressing with textbook devotion. Lifts the final dressing. Examines the wound.*) That's an excellent wound, Mrs Potts.

(CHATTERJEE *looks at* CHRISTINE, *who tacitly but unequivocally refuses the oblique invitation to look. She begins to clean it, doing her throttled best.*)

You know, they say Mr Staunton's the best surgeon in the hospital. Sister told me he could have been in Harley Street . . . You were lucky to get him, really . . . Good stitches. Excellent. (*She works on, eyeing* CHRISTINE*'s still-averted face from time to time.*) Your husband can bring your children in on Sunday. They'll cheer you up . . . (*She works on finally.*) I'm applying the new dressing now, Mrs Potts.

(*She waits.* CHRISTINE *makes no response.*)

All right?

(*She begins the new application.*)

BRENTON: (*Out of vision from ward*) Nurse Chatterjee.

CHATTERJEE: Here, staff.

(BRENTON*'s head pokes in.*)

BRENTON: Lend a hand with Buckley, she's back from theatre.

CHATTERJEE: Nearly finished, staff.

BRENTON: Have you seen O'Malley?

CHATTERJEE: No, staff.

(BRENTON *withdraws.* CHATTERJEE *begins taping the bandage.* CHRISTINE *turns at last, to look at it.*) That wasn't so bad, was it?

CHRISTINE: Thank you.

(CHATTERJEE *stands, begins to reorganize her trolley. Begins to unzip the curtains.*)

Nurse, do you think I could have a word with sister?

CHATTERJEE: (*Turning*) What is it, Mrs Potts?

CHRISTINE: It's nothing. I just wanted a word with her.

CHATTERJEE: (*Finishing curtains*) I'll see if she's free. All right?

CHRISTINE: Thank you.

(WARREN *moves down the ward, eyes flicking from side to side. She straightens a couple of visitors' chairs, adjusts some tulips in a vase, picks something up from the floor and pockets it, arrives at Christine's bed.*)

WARREN: Hello, Mrs Potts. What can we do for you?

CHRISTINE: (*Low voice*) I think I've started my period, sister. It shouldn't be till next week, I'm usually very regular . . .

WARREN: Not to worry. It does happen sometimes . . . I'll get you some tampons. All right?

CHRISTINE: Do you think I might have a bath, sister?

WARREN: It's all right, Mrs Potts, we'll clean you up. I'll send a nurse down, we can't have that wound getting wet . . .

CHRISTINE: Couldn't I have a bath, sister?

WARREN: (*Thinking a moment*) Well, we'd have to be careful.

(*Pause.* CHRISTINE *pleads silently.*)

I'll see what we can do . . . All right?

CHRISTINE: Thank you, sister.

WARREN: (*Leaving*) Any time.

INT. TOILET AREA. DAY

Bath filling with hot water. O'MALLEY *tests the water, turns off the taps, moves out of the bathroom into the general toilet area, where* CHRISTINE *sits, in bathrobe, in wheelchair. A frail, elderly* WOMAN *comes in, goes into a lavatory cubicle, closes the door.*

O'MALLEY: Here we go then.

(O'MALLEY *pushes* CHRISTINE *into the bathroom, begins to help her to her feet.*)

Now for God's sake don't let us get that wound wet or you'll have me shot.

(O'MALLEY*'s massive arms support* CHRISTINE *as she sinks into the water.* CHRISTINE *sits facing the door.*)

How is it? Not too hot?

CHRISTINE: It's lovely.

O'MALLEY: Don't splash.

(*A loudish cry of 'Shit!' from the cubicle across the room.*)

Oh God, that sounds like Mrs Goodwin's Translet gone for a burton again . . .

(O'MALLEY *leaves the bathroom, the door stays open behind her, crosses to the cubicle.* CHRISTINE *watches her.*)

Mrs Goodwin, are you all right?

GOODWIN: (*Behind door*) It's my bag. I dropped it getting it off.

O'MALLEY: Let's have a look. You should have emptied that hours ago.

GOODWIN: I couldn't get it off . . .

O'MALLEY: I showed you myself how to take it off . . .

GOODWIN: It wouldn't come off, it doesn't fit properly . . .

O'MALLEY: Wait there. Don't move.

(O'MALLEY *goes out, clucking.* CHRISTINE *stares through the two open doors at the seated woman, who sits vacantly for a while before becoming aware of her.*)

GOODWIN: It's a bugger, innit? (*Pause.*) She didn't show me how to do it, you know. Two minutes she spent. (*Pause.*) What's up wi' you?

CHRISTINE: Breast.

GOODWIN: Oh. (*Sniffs.*) What a caper. I'll be well shut of this place. I will.

(CHRISTINE *withdraws into her bathing.* GOODWIN *goes on muttering to herself.* O'MALLEY *returns with* LUCY, *the cleaner.* LUCY *looks at the bag.*)

LUCY: Here, I'm supposed to be on 18 now. Are you sure sister's talked to Mrs Prince?

O'MALLEY: Lucy, it'll only take you a minute . . .

LUCY: I'd better see sister. It's more than my job's worth . . . If the Organizer says so, that's a different matter. Ward 18's where I'm supposed to be . . .

(LUCY *leaves.* O'MALLEY *follows her. Another* PATIENT *comes in, about thirty, looks at* GOODWIN. GOODWIN *pushes the door to aggressively with her hand. The* PATIENT *pulls a face, changes her mind, walks out.* CHRISTINE *tries to wash her legs with her right hand, the left one, bent at the elbow to clear the water, pretty well unusable.)*

INT. WARD. DAY

CHRISTINE *sits on her bed, an unopened copy of the* Sun *on her thighs. A* RELIGIOUS VISITOR *makes his way down the ward, placing a four-page leaflet on every bed and uttering magic formulas to their occupants. He reaches* CHRISTINE.

VISITOR: (*Short, bald, about forty-five*) Good news, sister.
(CHRISTINE *looks for it.*)
The Lord Christ is risen. And the Lord Christ loves you. (*He hands* CHRISTINE *the pamphlet.*) Read the Lord's Word. For the Lord will make you whole. (*He smiles, inconsequentially, passes on to* SCULLY.) Good news, sister.

SCULLY: What's that then?

VISITOR: The Lord Christ is risen.

SCULLY: I should hope he is, it's bloody teatime. Is he on nights then?

VISITOR: And the Lord Christ loves you.

SCULLY: That's nice.

VISITOR: (*Handing her pamphlet*) Read the Lord's Word. For the Lord will make you whole.

SCULLY: Gonna get me foot back, then, am I? And me bowels?

VISITOR: (*Unnerved*) Have faith, sister. Faith can move mountains.

SCULLY: I bet it can't move this place.

VISITOR: Read the Lord's Word . . .
(*He's leaving, the same irrelevant smile forming.*)

SCULLY: Piss off. I'm a Catholic.
(*The* VISITOR *proceeds down the ward, restoring his ritual.* CHRISTINE *flicks the pages of the pamphlet, which is laid out in question-and-answer format, with clinching quotes from the New Testament in heavy type.*)
I could fancy a drink of someat.

CHRISTINE: I've got some lemon squash.

SCULLY: You haven't a drop of gin, have you? No, I thought not. I like a drop of gin.

(CHRISTINE *looks at the* Sun. *She must have seen the front page twenty times. Opens it. On page 3, half-page, a nude dolly, both stunning breasts on display. She closes it again.* SEAL *arrives.*)

SEAL: (*Checking watch*) Thought I'd just drop in before visitors, Mrs Potts. How are you?
(*She looks at charts at bottom of bed.*)

CHRISTINE: A bit better, doctor.

SEAL: Good, good. The physiotherapist will probably call tomorrow, get that arm of yours moving. If things go well, we'll have the first lot of stitches out within the week.
(*Pauses, looking at file.*)

CHRISTINE: Yes, doctor.

SEAL: That's all right. Perfectly normal. Nothing to worry about.

CHRISTINE: (*Tentative*) Everybody looked . . . very serious, this morning, doctor . . .

SEAL: Serious? No, no. (*Pause.*) Mr Staunton does a very formal round. He's of the old school you know. But you're in good hands.

CHRISTINE: He didn't seem to want to . . . look at me, doctor.

SEAL: You mustn't imagine things, Mrs Potts. He's always pressed, that's all . . . He's done all that's needed. Now we just wait until you're well enough to go home. Mr Williams, the Registrar, will probably want a word with you early next week, when the results of the tests are through . . .

CHRISTINE: Tests?

SEAL: Nothing to concern yourself over, they're just routine tests we carry out in cases like yours. (*She looks at watch.*) Good. Your iron pills aren't giving you trouble, are they?

CHRISTINE: No, I don't think so, doctor.

SEAL: Good. Good.

CHRISTINE: What happened to that young one?
(SEAL *frowns, not understanding.*)
With the hair . . .

SEAL: Dr Pearce. I think it's his day off. Did you want something?

CHRISTINE: No. (*Pause.*) I just wondered.

SEAL: (*Watch again*) Well, I'll look in tomorrow. Keep smiling.

(SEAL *off up the ward. As she reaches the far doors,* BRENTON *begins locking them back to admit evening visitors.* SEAL *wades through the 'waves of the great unwashed', her expressionless gaze fixed on the corridor. We follow a short, sturdy, grey-haired* WOMAN *of fifty-five back down the ward. She wears a bottle-green longish coat, flat shoes, a handbag, frowns as she searches for the bed. Sees* CHRISTINE *eventually, moves towards her.*)

WOMAN: There you are. (*Bending, to kiss* CHRISTINE*'s hair*) Thought I'd got the wrong ward. How are you, lass?

CHRISTINE: Hello, Mum.

(*She reaches for a Kleenex, begins to blow her nose, her eyes leaking again.*)

WOMAN: (*Sitting*) Let's have a look at you.

INT. WARD. NIGHT

Ward 20. Beyond midnight. A WOMAN *coughs and coughs, remorselessly, at the bottom of the ward.* MRS SCULLY *snores and snorts. Beds creak. Moans. Occasional sleep calls.* CHRISTINE *lies wide-eyed, her fingers beating time to the* WOMAN *coughing. She peers up the ward at the lit nurses' room. Looks back at the ceiling. Close-up. Fear and tension growing, an unresolved dialogue somewhere inside her head. She shakes her head several times, answering herself. She sits up, watches the ward: drips, bottles, trolleys, lockers, sleeping heads, then white hair, scrawny, arthritic arms on counterpanes. Listens. A crash from the day room, unexplained, unnoticed, unaccounted for. Slowly, she pushes her feet to the floor, feels for her fluffy slippers in the locker, drops them between her legs, houses her feet in them, unhooks her dressing-gown, stands waveringly to put it on. She holds her left arm in a hard defensive curve. Looks at clock: 12.55. Begins to walk, with infinite care, up the ward. She reaches the ward doors that lead to toilets on left and nurses' room on right. Leans her right side on flap to open a wing, shuffles through.*

INT. CORRIDOR. NIGHT

CHRISTINE *stands for a moment, only feet from the* NIGHT SISTER *and* TWO NURSES *who sit in the nurses' room. Walks past the door unseen and into the toilet area, now only dimly lit.*

INT. TOILET AREA. NIGHT

CHRISTINE *closes the door behind her, clicks on a switch, which lights the bathrooms, clicks it off, clicks on the lights over the two lavatory cubicles, moves towards the first one – occupied that afternoon by* MRS GOODWIN. *She turns into the other cubicle. Locks the door. Sits heavily, exhausted, on the closed lavatory seat, stares at the dull green door.*

INT. ENTRANCE HALL. NIGHT

Vestibule, block entrance, poorly lit. PEARCE *goes very slowly round and round in the swing doors. He wears an old broad-stripe double-breasted Italian suit, an anonymous old trilby, three days' stubble, shiny pointed Italian shoes, dirty white mac over his shoulder. He's had a fair few, is gently slewed. As he creaks round, he sings contralto to himself.*

PEARCE: 'When you walk through the storm keep your head up high
And don't be afraid of the dark . . .
(*The clock over the door says 1.30.*)

INT. WARD. NIGHT

Ward 20. A STAFF NURSE *and a* STUDENT NURSE *do the hourly round. They're three beds up from Christine's; the* STAFF NURSE *shines a torch on to* MRS GOODWIN*'s face.*

STAFF NURSE: Thank God she's sleeping . . . Did you hear about her this afternoon . . . ?

NURSE: In the lavatories, you mean?

STAFF NURSE: Keep an eye on her tomorrow morning, that's all.
(*Torch out, they move on to next bed, flash light on sleeping face, study it*

a moment, listening, light out, move on, flash light on Anna's empty bed.)

(*Disgusted*) Look at that. That's that student, you know. Wasted. A whole week. With people clamouring to get in.

INT. VISITORS' TOILETS. NIGHT

Inside, PEARCE *switches on the lights in the tiny, two-stone room; is immediately assailed by the stench; looks down at the floor, half-flooded with stagnant urine and water. Paper and other rubbish fill the drain channel. The stones are urine-stained, dark brown and yellow. He wades to the nearest stone, prepares to piss.*

PEARCE: (*To wall*) No, it's not the consultants' day room, your worship, it's the male visitors' lavatory. *Regal*, sir, wonderful choice of word if I may say so. Fit for a king. Preferably a king in his wellies. What was that, sir? Seafresh, we call it. Ozone. Delightful, isn't it? Well, sir, you know our motto here at St Luke's – 'Es bildet ein Talent sich in der Stille, Sich ein Charakter in dem Strom der Welt.' 'Genius is formed in quiet, character in the *stream* of human life.' (*Pause.*) Natürlich.

INT. TOILET AREA. NIGHT

CHRISTINE *is in the lavatory, hugging herself, face white. Knocking on the door.* CHRISTINE *ignores it; sits on, impassive.*

STAFF NURSE: (*Out of vision*) Come along, Mrs Potts. I know you're there. (*Knocks again.*) This is ridiculous, come along now. (*Sounds of others entering.*)

She's in here, sister. The Lord knows how long she's been here . . .

SISTER: (*Out of vision*) Is she all right?

STAFF NURSE: (*Out of vision*) I don't know. She won't answer me.

SISTER: (*Out of vision, gently*) Mrs Potts. Mrs Potts. It's sister. Open the door.

CHRISTINE: I'm all right. Leave me alone.

SISTER: (*Out of vision*) You can't sit in there all night, Mrs Potts. What is it? Come on, you can tell me.

(CHRISTINE*'s face sets. Silence.*)

(*Out of vision*) Mrs Potts. Mrs Potts.

(*Nothing.*)

All right, we'll have to get you out.

(*The* SISTER *begins giving instructions.* CHRISTINE *looks up to the top of the cubicle. Crane up to take the reverse shot:* CHRISTINE *looking up on one side, the* SISTER *giving instructions on the other.*)

(*To* STUDENT NURSE) You'll find a ladder in the kitchens, I think. Staff, you'd better help, no, better still, keep an eye open for Senior Sister March – we could do without her for the next ten minutes . . .

(*They leave, the junior* NURSES *in a hurry. The* SISTER *turns in the doorway.*)

This is very childish, Mrs Potts. And you a mother . . . with two growing girls . . .

(*The* SISTER *waits for some response. In the cubicle,* CHRISTINE *stands, puts her hand on the bolt, withdraws it again as the door closes behind the* SISTER.)

INT. CORRIDOR. NIGHT

PEARCE *wanders along another corridor, his coat collar turned up, mac over shoulder, trilby pulled down over eyes: a regular Philip Marlowe. He feels in his pocket for a Camel, flicks one clumsily but effortlessly up into his nostril, makes the necessary adjustment, fails to get his throwaway briquet to work. The* STUDENT NURSE *comes out of the kitchens behind him carrying the steps. She looks at him warily.*

PEARCE: I should put some nail varnish on that, nurse. Stop it running. Here, let me have that.

(PEARCE *goes to take it from the* STUDENT NURSE. *She frowns.*)

It's all right, I'm a doctor. Aye, well, takes all sorts . . . (*He fumbles his plastic ident card from his top pocket.*) See . . . doctor. All right? (*He takes the ladder.*) Where do you want it?

NURSE: Ward 20, doctor. Women's Surgical.

PEARCE: Right.

(PEARCE *hunks it off. The* STUDENT NURSE *follows.*)

Admitted a giant, have we?

(*The* STUDENT NURSE *looks at* PEARCE, *he looks at the ladder.*)

NURSE: Oh. No, a patient's locked herself in the lavatory.

PEARCE: While the balance of mind was disturbed, presumably?

(*They reach the doors. The* STUDENT NURSE *holds them open for* PEARCE. *he's confronted by the* NIGHT SISTER *and the* STAFF NURSE.)

I was passing. Can I help?

SISTER: (*Doubtful*) Well, I think we can handle it, Dr Pearce . . .

PEARCE: I'd like to, if that's all right . . . Who is it?

SISTER: Mrs Potts in 8. She had a radical two days ago.

(PEARCE *nods he knows.*)

She's been in for an hour, I estimate. She won't say why, won't come out.

(PEARCE *thinks for a moment.*)

PEARCE: (*Very serious*) Let me see what I can do. OK? Is there a wheelchair about?

INT. TOILET AREA. NIGHT

Inside the cubicle. CHRISTINE *has resumed her seat. Sounds outside.* PEARCE*'s head appears above the door.*

PEARCE: (*Perfect Bogart*) Here's looking at you, kid.

(CHRISTINE *looks at him.* PEARCE *tics his lips across his teeth, Bogart to the inch.*)

Listen, sweetheart, we gotta stop meeting like this.

(CHRISTINE *laughs.*)

No foolin', honey, this ain't no ladder of fame I'm currently negotiatin' . . . believe me . . .

CHRISTINE: What do you want?

PEARCE: (*Own voice*) I've lost an 8s needle, I wondered if you'd seen it. What do you think I want, you daft haporth, open the door.

(CHRISTINE *doesn't move.*)

Come on, I can't stop up here all night. It's undignified, a man in my position. What do you think Staunton'd say if he were to walk in now?

(CHRISTINE *laughs again.*)

It's all right laughing, you could be witnessing the termination of a thoroughly promising career . . . (*He appears to slip, manages somehow to hang on, pulls himself up, turns into Norman Evans, massages his left breast with pain-clenched face.*) Ooh, that's the third time today on the same wun, I'll cut his breath off, the little bugger . . .

(CHRISTINE *laughs again.*)

I'm getting down now. All right?

(*Toilet area.* PEARCE *reaches the floor, moves the ladder. Watches the door. Eventually it opens.* CHRISTINE *stands in the doorway.*)

Hi.

CHRISTINE: Hello.

PEARCE: Fancy a cocoa?

CHRISTINE: How?

PEARCE: Come on.

(PEARCE *takes* CHRISTINE*'s arm, leads her out past the collected* NURSES, *winks at the* SISTER, *sits* CHRISTINE *in the chair, pushes her out into the corridor.*)

INT. CORRIDOR. NIGHT

PEARCE: (*Over shoulder*) Won't be long, sister. Just having a cocoa.

INT. PEARCE'S ROOM. NIGHT

Pearce's cramped, untidy room, lit by fierce but local Anglepoises on floor, desk and shelf. Work litters most surfaces. He pours hot milk into two cups of cocoa, stirs, sugars, carries them to where CHRISTINE *sits in her wheelchair. He still wears his clothes as before, though he's dropped the mac.*

CHRISTINE: I suppose you think I've . . . gorra screw loose or someat.

PEARCE: (*Cocoa up; toast*) Here's looking at you, kid.

(CHRISTINE *smiles, looks down into her cup to taste it. Is suddenly overcome by it all, fatigued, desperate, very low.* PEARCE *sits down opposite her in a mothy old armchair, half disappearing in it.*)

We could have some music, but my violin's at the menders.

(CHRISTINE *stares on at the cocoa, miserable, not looking at* PEARCE.)

I don't want to ask what it is, because I *know*, and it's a sort of impotence, knowing what causes someone grief and not being able to do anything about it.

CHRISTINE: (*Small voice*) I just want to get better.

PEARCE: Yeah.

CHRISTINE: Nobody says anything. They treat you as if you were already dead. The specialist, he never even looked at me, let alone spoke. (*Long pause.*) I know it were serious. I'm not a child. You don't cut a thing like that off for nothing. (*Long pause.*) I don't want . . . fobbing off. (*Pause.*) I don't know, maybe I'm being . . . stupid. *They* know what they're doing, that's what me husband says, that's what me mother says . . . Just . . . let 'em gerron with it . . . don't be stupid . . .

(CHRISTINE *looks at* PEARCE *suddenly. He takes the look, sunk in his chair.*)

I just want to get better. (*Pause.*) But I want to know what I'm facing.

PEARCE: I'm . . . not in charge of your case, you know that, don't you? I'm a trainee.

(CHRISTINE *draws back in her chair, sensing another evasion.*)

I'll tell you what I know. Which is most of what there is to know. The lump in your breast was a malignant tumour. A cancer.

(CHRISTINE *swallows, looks back at her mug of cocoa, faint with fear yet oddly relieved.*)

Can I go on?

(CHRISTINE *nods once.*)

We couldn't have known it, not your own doctor, not us in out-patients; a hundred thousand and more breast lumps are seen every year and very very few are malignant like yours. Particularly at your age. Equally, you did everything you should have done. As soon as you spotted it, you told your GP. Your GP informed the hospital. The hospital sent for you as soon as it could. (*Pause.*) Three weeks later. You were a low-cancer risk, marked non-urgent. We were wrong, but we weren't to blame. Yet, if there hadn't been 600,000 people competing for 500,000 hospital beds, we'd have seen you within a fortnight, and maybe taken it out before it had a chance to move. You know, even when it is cancer, we don't always have to remove the breast. (*Pause.*) Well, it did move. At any rate, we found traces of it in some lymph nodes under the arm . . . sort of glands . . . So we took those out too. (*Pause.*) As far as we know we've cleared the site. But just to make sure, when the stitches are out and the wound's healed, it's possible we'll treat the whole area with radiation – it isn't very pleasant, but it might be worth it. (*Pause.*) It's . . . hard to explain why you haven't been told all this, why we go on talking about this 'infection' and 'nasty tissue' . . . I mean, there are a thousand reasons, most of them decent and honourable. Mainly, I think, it's because we have lost all idea of you as a whole, human being, with a past, a personality, dependants, needs, hopes, wishes. Our power is strongest when you are dependent upon it. We invite you to behave as the sum of your *symptoms*. And on the whole you are pleased to oblige. (*Long pause.*) Mr Staunton's a good man. He's just . . . not used, not equipped . . . to deal with you as a person. The gap is too great. (*Pause.*) And there's something else. The reason he can't speak to you, look at you, after the operation is that for him you represent a failure, even

when the operation is a success. Because each time we use surgery we fail, medicine fails, the system fails, and he knows it, and he bears the guilt. He really can't bear to see what he's done to you, Mrs Potts. It makes him feel crude . . . and insensitive . . . and ignorant in the real sense; without knowledge. But if he can't face the inadequacies of his profession, who else is allowed to? The junior doctors, struggling to become consultants? The nurses, struggling to make sense of the mad world they've inherited . . . ? (*Very long pause.*) In spite of which . . . you're better off now than you would have been if you hadn't come forward for screening. (*He stops. Sits up, leans forward.*) Listen. The father of medicine was a man called Hippocrates. Two and half thousand years ago he said something we've forgotten. He said: 'Whoever treats of this art should treat of things which are familiar to the common people. For of nothing else will such a one have to inquire or treat, but of the diseases under which the common people have laboured, which diseases and the causes of their origin and departure, their increase and decline, unlettered persons cannot easily find out for themselves, but still it is easy for them to understand these things when discovered and expounded by others . . . For whoever does not reach the capacity of the common people and fails to make them listen to him, misses his mark.' Well, we're all missing the mark, Mrs Potts. And we need to be told. Not just doctors and nurses, but administrators and office men and boards of management and civil servants and politicians and the whole dank crew that sail this miserable craft through the night. (*Long silence. His cocoa's cold. He puts it down.*) Do you know something? My mother's proud. (*He laughs drily.*) Wow . . .
(*Another silence.*)

CHRISTINE: Thank you.

PEARCE: Don't thank. Demand.

CHRISTINE: (*Slowly*) What are the chances . . . ?

PEARCE: Your chances are good, Mrs Potts. We'll know how good when we've seen the full results of the tests. But they're good. But from now on, you live every day for keeps. The rest of us may continue to cherish the illusion that we're immortal. You know you're not. (*He stands, smiles at* CHRISTINE.) I'll probably get sacked for this. Unethical behaviour. (*Pause.*) I wouldn't mind, but I hardly laid a hand on you.

(CHRISTINE *blushes a little, laughing with pleasure.* PEARCE *leans across the wheelchair, looks into her eyes.*)

Here's looking at you, kid.

INT. WARD. DAY

Ward. 20. CHRISTINE *lies in her bed, having alternate stitches removed by* CHATTERJEE. *She observes the procedure in silence, but very carefully. The scar, still very red, runs from deep armpit to sternum in a long bent diagonal. At the bottom, a rubber drain is sunk under the skin.*

CHATTERJEE *raises the knot of each stitch, snips it on the clean side and pulls the clean side through the skin. When she's finished the stitches,* CHATTERJEE *carefully lifts the drain out. Swabs the wound with sterile water. Prepares a small dressing.* CHRISTINE *looks at the cut critically.*

CHRISTINE: It's a mess.

CHATTERJEE: It's a *beautiful* scar.

CHRISTINE: What did he do it with, a bottle?

(CHRISTINE *grins at* CHATTERJEE, *ribbing her.* CHATTERJEE *relaxes, applies the dressing. Packs her trolley. Unzips the curtains.*)

CHATTERJEE: I'll be glad to see the last of you, Mrs Potts.

(CHRISTINE *smiles, lies back.* ANNA JAY *leans across from the next bed.*)

ANNA: Hi.

CHRISTINE: Hello. You're back then?

ANNA: (*Cautious*) Couldn't keep me away. Thought you'd've gone.

CHRISTINE: So did I. (*She undoes her nightdress, shows* ANNA *the dressing.*) They took it all.

ANNA: (*Closing eyes*) Oh God. I'm sorry . . .

CHRISTINE: Yes. (*Pause.*) Can't be helped.
(*Pause.* ANNA*'s very tense.*)
Where there's life, eh?
(*Pause.* ANNA *offers* CHRISTINE *some fruit.*)
When do you go?
ANNA: Day after tomorrow, I think.
CHRISTINE: You'll be all right.
(*She eats a grape.*)

INT. WARD. NIGHT

CHRISTINE *sleeps.* ANNA *stands over her, on Mrs Scully's side, blows on her face to waken her. She awakens slowly.*

ANNA: (*Whispering*) Shh. Mrs Scully's having a drink-up. She's going home tomorrow, she says.

CHRISTINE: What? She's not going home tomorrow . . .

ANNA: Well, she wants you to say goodbye . . . Bring your glass.

CHRISTINE: (*Chuckling*) She's batty. (*Getting out of bed*) Let's have a look.
(*A door closes at top of ward. They stare up it, towards nurses' room. In it,* SISTER *writes up unending notes; two* NURSES *play liar dice. They let themselves into Mrs Scully's curtained bed area with silent stealth.* MRS SCULLY *plays hostess, pouring from a large lemonade bottle. Three other* PATIENTS *in the drink-up.* MRS SCULLY *beams wickedly at* CHRISTINE.)

SCULLY: Give us your glass. Gin. Our Ethel brought it, bless her. Come on . . . (*She pours a large helping.*) There y'are . . . How're you ladies, all right, are you? A toast.
(*She looks round. The* NURSES' *hands shield the throw; three queens.*)

CHRISTINE: You're never going home tomorrow . . .

SCULLY: I know. Sod it.
(MRS SCULLY *drinks. Looks at* ANNA *owlishly.* ANNA *raises her glass.*)

ANNA: (*Repeating toast*) Sod it.

(*She looks at* CHRISTINE.)

CHRISTINE: (*Grinning*) Sod it.

(*The other three whisper 'fuck it' in unison. They begin to laugh as they drink. Shot of the curtained cubicle from the aisle. Suppressed snorts of laughter. Fade out.*)

Such Impossibilities

Preface

Such Impossibilities was written in 1971, commissioned by the BBC as part of a series entitled *The Edwardians.* Though I had explained at some length what I wanted to write, the play was rejected and has never been seen. The ostensible grounds were cost – they often are – but it's at least as likely that the play offered too brutal and too overtly political a contrast with the remainder of the series, which included, if you remember, pieces on E. Nesbit, the Countess of Warwick, Marie Lloyd, Baden-Powell, Conan Doyle, Horatio Bottomley, Rolls-Royce and Lloyd George. Tom Mann might well have roughed the series up a bit, but it's arguable he might also have done something towards redressing its 'balance' too. Still, it must count, till now at least, as a failure. Should it ever be produced, it can then be tested against the severest of its intentions: to restore, however tinily, an important but suppressed area of our collective history; to enlarge our 'usable past' and connect it with a lived present; and to celebrate a victory.

T.G.
14 February 1977

Characters

TOM MANN
SHIP'S DOCTOR
SHIP'S OFFICER
SEAMAN
GERARD GROARK, steward, Maritime Hall
NIGHT PORTER
JAMES FRANK PEARCE, Secretary, Ship Stewards' Union
TERENCE DIXON, Secretary, Seamen and Fireman's Union
THOMAS DITCHFIELD, Secretary, Mersey Quay and Railway Carters' Union
BILLAL QUILLIAM, Solicitor, Mersey Quay and Railway Carters' Union
JAMES SEXTON, Secretary, National Union of Dock Labourers; magistrate
MARTHA CLARKE, stenographer
MILLIGAN, Secretary, No. 12 Branch, Dockers' Union
CUTHBERT LAWS, General Manager, Shipping Federation
POLICE SUPERINTENDENT
HEAD CONSTABLE
LORD MAYOR OF LIVERPOOL
MONTAGUE, General Manager, shipping lines
CARRINGTON, General Manager, shipping lines
MENTEITH
ELLEN MANN
SAWYER
DOCKERS, SEAMEN, ARMY, POLICE

EXT. LIME STREET STATION. DAY

5.30 am. A swathe of steam clears around TOM MANN, *grip on platform, a small notebook in his hand. He consults it briefly, picks up the grip, walks towards the barrier. He's short, stockily built, lithe and powerful, a very young fifty-odd. His thick hair is only slightly grey; his full walrus moustache good and black. He wears a good serge three-piece; a watch-chain across his middle. Song: 'Rise Up Jock' (Bob and Carole Pegg) begins.*

EXT. LIME STREET APPROACH. DAY

It's bright day. At this time, the city is quiet, save for an odd delivery cart here and there. MANN *strides down the approach, comes out by St George's Hall, stops to watch a cavalry detachment pass at the canter. Song – second verse: 'O the first come was a soldier'.*

EXT. PRINCE'S DOCK. DAY

Signing-on hall of the White Star Line, incorporated member of the Shipping Federation. A knot of SEAMEN *stand by the entrance to the great draughty shed.* MANN *stops to talk with them. Song – third verse: 'And the next come was a sailor'.* SEAMAN *hands* MANN *a white card – his Shipping Federation ticket – and* MANN *continues in. Song ends on third chorus of 'Rise up, Jock'.*

INT. SIGNING-ON HALL. DAY

Long straggles of SEAMEN *attend the eight or ten inspection and call-in tables scattered throughout it. The men wear only trousers, carry boots, socks, shirts, coats and hats in their hands. At each desk, a* MEDICAL

SUPERVISOR *and a* LINE OFFICIAL. MANN *stands, observes, grip in hand. A* LINE OFFICIAL *approaches.*

OFFICIAL: You for calling?

MANN: That's right.

OFFICIAL: You'd better get in line then. You won't do yourself much good standing there.

(*The* OFFICIAL *moves off.* MANN *slowly joins a queue. Ahead of him, the* SEAMAN *at the table is removing his trousers. The* MEDICAL SUPERVISOR, *who remains seated, motions him to turn round and bend over, then parts his buttocks with a ferrule and briefly inspects his anus. The man then turns round, has his legs parted by the ferrule and his penis raised. All this time, he tries to keep a hold on his clothing. Finally, he presents his ticket (held between his teeth) and signs on. All round the hall, variations on this simple, brutal procedure can be observed. Finally,* MANN *reaches the table.*)

What's wrong with you then?

MANN: Nothing. How do you mean?

OFFICIAL: Clothes, man, clothes. What do you think you're playing at? We haven't got all day, you know. (*Pause. Looking hard*) You got a ticket?

MANN: Yes.

OFFICIAL: Let's have it then.

(MANN *hands it over. The* OFFICIAL *studies it.*)

According to this you're twenty-eight.

MANN: Aye. It's a hard life.

(*The line begins to laugh, growing interested, behind him.*)

OFFICIAL: Oh. A joker. (*He blows a whistle, hanging from a lanyard round his neck.*) We'll see about that.

MANN: Don't bother. I'm just . . . looking.

(*Two* DOCK POLICE *arrive; big.*)

OFFICIAL: Troublemaker. Move him.

(*They step forward.* MANN *turns, crouches, arms curved downwards, like an orang-utan, the grip poised for swinging use.*)

MANN: Easy now. I can find the way on my own.

OFFICIAL: (*Finally*) Let him be.

(POLICE *draw off.* MANN *turns to the table.*)

MANN: Let's hope your line can show as much good sense. (*He smiles gently.*) The ticket.

(*The* OFFICIAL *hands it over, reluctantly and without grace.*)

OFFICIAL: Don't try anything here again, I'm telling you. We've got ways of dealing with troublemakers.

MANN: (*Gently*) Good. You're going to need them. (*Turning, a few paces towards the entrance*) If you bump into Mr Cuthbert Laws today, tell him you showed Tom Mann the door. He might strike you a special medal.

(MANN *walks off through the waiting* SEAMEN.)

OFFICIAL: Who'd he say he was? Who was it he said?

SEAMAN: Tom Mann, he said.

OFFICIAL: And who's Tom Mann when he's at home?

SEAMAN: Nobody. When he's at home. But he ain't at home, is he? He's in Liverpool.

EXT. BY GRAIN DOCK. DAY

MANN *strides slowly along, taking in everything.*

EXT. CITY STREET. DAY

MANN *stops by a news-vendor's stall, buys a* Manchester Guardian, *asks for something else, is offered a small pad, gestures bigger with an angler's stretch of the hands, finally receives a large street map of Liverpool, which he pays for and tucks into his grip.*

EXT. EXCHANGE STATION HOTEL. DAY

MANN *stops, walks in.*

INT. HOTEL FOYER. DAY

Red plush, deep curtaining, the odd discreet frond. The NIGHT PORTER, *a young man, dozes at the desk.* MANN *approaches, pings the bell.*

PORTER: (*Startled*) Yes, sir.

MANN: Could you tell me, do you have a Mr Cuthbert Laws, Secretary and General Manager of the Shipping Federation, staying here?

PORTER: One moment, sir, I'll have a look. (*Rummages through book.*) Er . . . yes, we do, sir. Room 7. Just along the corridor. I imagine he'll be sleeping just now, sir.

MANN: (*Consulting watch*) Yes. Would you mind telling him there's a Mr Tom Mann to see him?

PORTER: What, now?

MANN: Now.

PORTER: (*Slowly*) Is he . . . expecting you?

MANN: Mmmmm. Yes. I think you could say that.

PORTER: (*Going finally*) All right. If he's expecting you.

(*The* PORTER *leaves.* MANN *fiddles the map out of the grip, spreads it on the desk, begins to study it. The* PORTER *returns after a little while. He's not pleased.*)

PORTER: (*Stiffly*) Mr Cuthbert Laws has no wish to speak with you, sir.

(MANN *studies the map a moment longer, then folds it, packs it away.*)

MANN: Is that so? Didn't he like being wakened?

PORTER: No, he didn't, sir. Not at all.

MANN: Tell him, will you, later on, you know, tell him he may have no wish to, but in a day or two he will have no choice in the matter. Will you tell him that?

PORTER: As you wish, sir.

MANN: You know, you say 'sir' as if you enjoyed it.

(MANN *leaves briskly, grip swinging.*)

EXT. DOCK AREA. DAY

MANN *passes the dock offices of the large shipping lines, finally approaches the Maritime Hall, headquarters of the National Union of Seamen and Firemen, the Ship Stewards' Union, the National Union of Dockworkers and the Mersey Carters. He stands looking at the crazy over-busy façade for a moment, then walks in.*

INT. MARITIME HALL. DAY

A long dark corridor, doors on either side, a long straight staircase directly ahead. MANN *stands, sunlight behind him, sniffs, pokes a door open to the right, looks, pulls it to, repeats the process to the left. A youth (*GROARK*), sixteen, seventeen, small, skinny, carries mop-bucket and mop down the stairway. Stops about four up as he sees the stranger.*

GROARK: Was there something?

MANN: (*Seeing him*) Aye. I'm looking for Committee Room A, son.

GROARK: Oh. (*Pause.*) Well, it's up here.

(*Stands a moment longer, then begins to plod back up the stairs, bucket splashing freely.* MANN *follows.*)

INT. COMMITTEE ROOM A. DAY

Large, roomy, four windows on two walls, one pair giving out on to the veranda that dominates the front of the building, the other providing a fair view of the docks. Down the centre, a long shiny deal table, with a dozen or so hardback upright chairs. At the top of the table, a single captain's chair, with arms and a bit of class. A door in one corner leads to a small office. GROARK *pushes the door open, lets* MANN *in.*

GROARK: And less of the 'son'. All right?

(MANN *smiles, back to* GROARK.)

MANN: Sorry.

GROARK: (*Sniffing*) 'S all right. I do a man's work.

(MANN *is by the window, surveying the docks.*)

Strike Committee, are you?

MANN: Ahunh.

GROARK: Thought so. North End, is it?

(MANN *puts his grip down on the captain's chair, takes out the map, opens it, fiddles thumbtacks from his top pocket, carefully pins the map to the table in front of his chair.*)

(*Uneasy*) Hey, that's er, that's er, the, that's the chairman's place, that is.

MANN: (*Evenly*) Aye.

GROARK: Jesus Christ! (*Closing eyes, opening them*) Eh, you coulda said. Bloody'ell. You're him, aren't you?

MANN: (*Busy*) Him. Yes.

GROARK: (*Stepping forward, wiping hand on apron*) I'm . . . I'm very pleased to make your acquaintance, brother. I am that.

MANN: (*Taking his hand*) Greetings. Comrade.

GROARK: (*Stunned by the word, hand back too sharply*) Aye. Aye. (*Lost now*) Gerard Groark. That's me, that's my name.

MANN: Good. Do you work here?

GROARK: Yes. I'm the er, I'm a steward. Waiting to go on the boats.

MANN: (*Surveying room*) Fine. I'd like some breakfast, Gerard. That all right?

GROARK: It is that, Mr . . . brother. Egg and bacon do you?

MANN: Eggs.

GROARK: Eh?

MANN: Eggs and bacon.

GROARK: Oh. Eggs and bacon. I have it. No more than a jiff. (*He moves towards the door; turns, very formal.*) I think I should like to say, on behalf of the Maritime Hall management committee, how . . . honoured and . . . privileged we are . . . to have you with us here . . . in Liverpool. (*Pause.*) I don't think I step out of line by extending that . . . greeting to you on behalf of . . . my colleagues.

MANN: Thank you, brother Groark. It's an honour and a privilege to be here. (*He takes out his big watch, clicks it open.*) Could you get a word through to brother Frank Pearce? Tell him I've come.

GROARK *stands staring, still realizing it all, then nods and leaves.*)

INT. MARITIME HALL: CORRIDOR AND STAIRWAY. DAY

*We see it from halfway up the stairs. It's crowded with men spilling out from the bar parlour on the right, jugs of porter in their fists. A door on the left opens. Two men (*GROARK *and* FRANK PEARCE*) appear, carrying a large wooden filing cabinet. They shunt and buffet drinking men in their way, as they approach the stairs.*

PEARCE: (*Thirty-five, dark, swarthy, short*) Shift your bloody carcases, will you. I'm not taking this thing over youse.

(*Some groans and oaths.*)

(*Last,* GROARK *already on the stairs*) Now take your time, lad, now take your time. We're not bloody mountain goats, you know. Leastways, I'm bloody not. Just nice and steady and we'll get the blinding thing up in one piece.

(*They begin the arduous ascent.*)

Now steady. Steady does it. STEADY FOR CHRIST'S SAKE.

(*They stop, disaster thinly avoided.*)

Christ almighty, what *are* you doing? (*Props cupboard with knee, mops face with scarf.*) I swear, it's a bloody madman we've gorrup there. We're supposed to be going on strike and I've never worked so bloody hard in me life. Right, come on. Let's get his blinding cabinet up while I've strength left.

(*They lumber on,* PEARCE *spattering the stairs with oaths and admonitions.*)

INT. COMMITTEE ROOM A. DAY

The whole of the Strike Committee as at present constituted – six men, counting PEARCE *– is assembled. It's noon or just after. The room is already dense with smoke and heavy with noise.* MANN *is pouring himself a glass of water at a table by a wall. He brings it back to his chair, sits down. He sits, sipping his drink, until the heated chat cools: the chair is deferred to.*

MANN: (*Looking around*) Well.

(*Slow slide around the table: as we frame each member of the Strike Committee, he makes his response.*)

JAMES SEXTON: All right. If we're ready. We'll certainly take it back to the dockers.

THOMAS DITCHFIELD: We'll leave it to the seamen.

BILLAL QUILLIAM: The carters are ready for a signal. Have been for a week or more.

(*The door opens and* PEARCE *and* GROARK *appear with the cabinet.*)

PEARCE: Easy, lad, easy. Right, now back towards that wall, *that* wall . . . right, right, down gently, gently, there she is. (*He stands, mops forehead with neckerchief, sniffs.*) One filing cabinet. Liverpool Strike Committee 1911 for the use of. (*To* GROARK, *handing him a halfpenny*) All right, go and get yourself a mineral water.

(GROARK *grins and leaves.*)

MANN: Thank you, Frank.

(PEARCE *takes his seat at the bottom of the table, picks up pen, inspects the open ledger book in front of him.*)

PEARCE: Where are we then?

MANN: Still on timing, Frank. Dockers and carters generally in favour.

PEARCE: (*Writing something*) All right. (*Finishing*) If I can speak for the ship stewards for a moment, we're already on record. We can go any time. From now. (*Pause.*) Same goes for cooks.

(MANN *nods, begins the ascent of the table up the other side.*)

MANN: What about the seamen and firemen, Terence?

TERENCE DIXON: Our call's been out for a week. We'll go tomorrow, if that's the time to go.

MANN: (*Finally*) Good. Thank you, brothers. (*He gets up, walks over to the filing cabinet, pulls a couple of drawers open, looks inside, pushes them to again, turns.*) I shall want some files to go in there, Frank. Tomorrow'll do. First thing. (*To whole Committee*) I'm not a great one for the past. It's what we do now that counts. But there's one or two lessons to be learnt. (*Pause.*) I was involved in the big one, 'eighty-nine, some of you will remember. I remember this. In negotiation with the employers, time and time again there'd be a point at issue – a particular rating, the status of a special process – and the employer would go straight to it, he'd have his documents neatly pigeon-holed for reference. And us? Ours'd be all over the floor, half a ton of it perhaps. It finished up we had half a dozen men permanently on their knees trying to sort it all out. (*Pause.*) I want to *win*, brothers. And I think we can. But it'll only happen if we *organize.* And that means – (*He points to the cabinet.*) a system. I want that filling. With information. I want copies of all agreements for the past five years between employers and the unions involved. I want detailed day-by-day accounts of all negotiations undertaken by and on behalf of this Joint Strike Committee. I want duty rosters on file, so that *responsibility* can be accurately assessed when things fall down. And I want background on all the major shipping lines involved in the Port of Liverpool. (*Grinning*) All yours, Frank.

PEARCE: Eh, now wait a minute, I'm a full-time officer of a union, brother, I can't be . . .

MANN: We'll get you some help. It must be done. (*On quickly, moving back to the table, remaining standing*) Look, we are about to declare war. It's not summer manoeuvres we're about, brothers. It's war. Now then, this Strike Committee had better begin to get a few things straight. First, this Committee is the workers' general staff. Second, the job of a general staff is to deliver a victory by whatever means it has at its disposal. Third, I see myself as CGS, and it would help if you saw it that way too. (*He sits down.*) Questions.

DIXON: You'll have to find someat different to say to my seamen when you put it to 'em. They didn't elect *you* and you're not responsible to them.

(*Some nods, grumbles of assent.*)

MANN: All right, Terence. I'll find . . . different words. I'm trying to make an important point about unity. Unity of purpose; unity of planning; unity of action. That's why I'm Secretary of the Transport Workers' Federation. That's why, isn't it, your union affiliated. All my life I've watched the single union fight its solitary battle against the full weight of employers and state. All my life, I've watched 'em getting hammered for want of support and solidarity from brother unions. (*Pause.*) There are, need I remind you, brothers, eleven hundred and sixty-eight trade unions in this country. I reckon we need no more than fourteen. (*Pause.*) I'm not up here to run a tea-party. Either we're fighting an all-out war or I'm off to Lime Street for the next train back. (*Silence. A few coughs.*)

PEARCE: (*Finally*) I could put: 'Brother Mann's opening address on strategy was greeted with approving silence.'

QUILLIAM: (*Grinning*) Aye, you could do that, Frank. Ever think of lawyering for a trade?

PEARCE: One lawyer's enough on this Committee, Billal. Couldn't afford the fee, else.

(*Some relieved laughter. The room relaxes.*)

DIXON: How do you see it, then?

MANN: First, nobody goes home tonight. Send messages or whatever, but I reckon we won't be shut of here till noon tomorrow. Second, by nightfall, we should have entered the first phase.

DITCHFIELD: I've two branch meetings to attend tonight.

MANN: Important ones?

DITCHFIELD: Well . . .

MANN: Send someone else. You're needed here.

(*Silence.* DITCHFIELD *purses lips, makes to rejoin, stays silent.*)

SEXTON: Go on.

MANN: Basically, this is a seamen's dispute. And it has both national and international ramifications. Perhaps a dozen ports in Europe and America are likely to be affected, as well as just about every port in Britain. But each port will have to look to its own resources on the ground, to bring things to a successful conclusion, which is why we have represented here officers of all the other major dock unions, and promises of support from some of the smaller ones, like the Coal Heavers, the Coopers and the Bakers. (*Pause.*) So. We begin with the Seamen, the Stewards, the Firemen. See how it goes. It's . . . unlikely (*Grinning slightly*) they'll accede to *all* our demands right away. At the correct moment we shall extend the strike. Perhaps to the dockers, if they'll come. Perhaps to the dockers and carters both. Now it's not only passengers, it's cargo and mail as well. This is the second largest port in Britain. About a fifth of all the food we buy abroad comes in through our front door. And not only food; raw materials; cotton for Lancashire; wool for Yorkshire; iron and copper and tin for the Midlands. (*Pause.*) We turn the screw.

SEXTON: Be careful. I reckon you suck an egg as good as anyone, but you should be warned about Liverpool dockers. If they come out, they'll want someat for coming.

DITCHFIELD: Aye. Carters too.

MANN: Well, we'll bear that in mind. That's not the end, though. We've to be ready for the day when, to all intents and purposes, this Strike Committee controls not only the whole of the waterfront, but the whole of this city. When not a vehicle – tram, train, cart, bus – moves, nor a person nor piece upon it – without we give our say so.

PEARCE: Sounds a mite fanciful, does that.

MANN: Maybe. Now. Be ready, none the less. When the day comes, it's statesmen we'll be. So be warned. (*Pause.*) All right, let's have the facts, there's plenty to be done. Brother Dixon, the floor's yours.

DIXON: (*Standing; producing papers*) I've drawn up a list of demands, based on grievances tabled times without number at conferences with employers over the last God knows how many years. Shall I read 'em out?

MANN: Surely.

DIXON: One, the constitution of a conciliation board. Two, a minimum rate of wages. Three, a manning scale for stokehold, deck and galley. Four, the abolition of the medical examination by a doctor appointed by the Shipping Federation. Five, the abolition of the engagement of seamen in the Shipping Federation offices. Six, the right of seamen to a portion of their wages in port during a voyage. Seven, the right of seamen to have a union representative present when signing on. Eight, hours of labour and rates and overtime to be fixed. Nine, improved forecastle accommodation.

MANN: The minimum rate, Brother Dixon. What are you asking?

DIXON: Six pounds and five pounds ten a month on mail steamers; five pounds ten and five pounds on ordinary cargo.

MANN: That's an increase of what?

DIXON: Ten bob a month on the best rates paid at present; about a pound on the worst.

MANN: Good. Thanks, Brother Dixon.

(DIXON *sits.*)

Frank?

PEARCE: (*Standing*) The stewards are demanding a minimum wage of four pounds a month, that's an increase of around thirty bob for most grades. We're asking for perquisites to be excluded from the reckoning. Galley staff are asking the same four pounds, plus four and six a day for work done in port. We're demanding the abolition of deductions to cover silver loss on voyage and we're asking for improved accommodation, like the seamen. We've had enough of the bloody 'glory hole'.

MANN: Thank you, Frank. (*Blowing cheeks*) Right, answer me this then. How many men can we *count* on? I mean *really* count on? Brother Dixon?

DIXON: All of 'em. Twelve thousand.

PEARCE: And I've another ten and they're keen as pigeons to be off.

MANN: So where do we start?

DIXON: The Federation. If we crack them, we crack the lot. If they hold out, we sink.

MANN: Go on.

DIXON: The Shipping Federation controls 60 per cent of all shipping in this port. What they say goes. And they're the buggers who won't even *meet* the unions, let alone let us speak for the men. It's got to be them.

MANN: Frank?

PEARCE: 'S right. Federation's the master.

MANN: But they control mainly cargo, isn't that right?

DIXON: That's right. About 80 per cent.

MANN: And the passenger boats are controlled by the big independent lines?

DIXON: That's right.

MANN: How many passenger boats are waiting crewing in port just now?

DIXON: Three.

MANN: What are they?

DIXON: Well, there's the *Baltic*, that's White Star. Then there's the *Teutonic*, she's White Star too. And erm . . . *Empress of Ireland.* Canadian Pacific.

MANN: Sort of average is it, three a week, say?

PEARCE: Summer, yes. There's another four due the end of the week. Two for America, bringing back the swells for the Coronation.

MANN: Tut tut. What a pity. I suppose we could be arraigned for treason or something if *they* didn't get away.

DIXON: I'm not sure what you're driving at, brother.

MANN: (*Quietly*) I'm trying to see whether there isn't a better way of cracking the Federation than by hitting it square on. You're closer to the ground than I am, but it occurs to me that we might be better off initially striking at the independents. Cargo's a funny thing. You don't fetch it this month, you fetch it next. You can't take it now, you take it when you can. Passengers're another story. They won't wait. If they can't go, they don't go. And that's a loss to the company that's irrecoverable.

PEARCE: So we put pressure on the independents through passengers. That makes some sense, I suppose. What then?

MANN: Well, we'll have to see. If things go well, we'll have the advantage of a sort of tide of successes to approach the Federation on. And there's nothing like success to bind a workforce together.

SEXTON: So where do *we* come in?

MANN: Dockers and carters carry on, at least for the time being. (*Grinning*) But it wouldn't do any harm to do a bit of . . . what do they call it? – contingency planning for a week or two ahead.

DITCHFIELD: That's all right by us. Just so long as we know what's happening.

MANN: (*Tough*) You'll know what's happening, brother Ditchfield, because this Committee will be meeting every day of the strike until we've brought it safely home. And you'll be here, helping to decide its policy. (*Looking at watch*) I think we might break for a bite of someat now, brother Secretary –

(PEARCE *nods assent.*)

– before we launch into detailed strategies (*Chairs screak back.*) *Before* you go, could I just outline what I think it's going to be useful to talk about for the rest of this particular meeting?

(*Silence resumes.*)

Perhaps you'd take some of this down, Frank. It might serve as a sort of rough agenda, bearing in mind that other members might wish to table quite other matters. (*Pause.*) We've to discuss pickets. Nature, number, *style* of same. We've to discuss co-ordination of all our activities through and by this Joint Committee. We've to discuss communications, both with the press and, more important, the workers. To tell truth, I couldn't give a cuss what the great, brutal British public thinks, as long as the people I lead *know* what's going on, understand it, agree with it, and are prepared to abide by it. Strikes aren't won by public sympathy; they're won by ruthless organization, concerted action, and understanding between leaders and led. So: we shall need to discuss news-sheets, demonstrations, speeches and the like. (*Pause.*) We shall need to discuss our relations with the police and, if and when the time comes, with the army too. It's idle to think that the Federation and the independents won't try to mobilize blackleg labour from somewhere or other. So we've got to be on our guard from the outset, if we want to avoid bloody clashes between the picket lines and the law. Let's get one thing clear: I'm not against violence. I *am* against unarmed workers fighting street battles against superior forces, be they police or the army. (*Pause.*) Well, that's some of the things I think we should be talking about. Oh, two things before you go off. I think we should have a leaflet run off right away – perhaps you could put this in hand, brothers Dixon and Connor – letting the seamen know it's tomorrow. And, I think it would be nice if we could let everybody know we were in business. Be nice if we let off a few rockets, the minute the strike's declared. Sort of . . . symbolic. (*He smiles sweetly. The men return the smile, begin to leave.*)

PEARCE: (*Consulting watch*) Back at three, brothers, if you will. (*They file out.* PEARCE *remains.*)
You're riding them hard, brother.

MANN: (*Slowly*) It's . . . a hard life, Frank.
(PEARCE *smiles, closes book, leaves.* MANN *gets up, stretches, walks to the window overlooking the docks, looks out. After a moment, a knock at the door, and* GROARK *enters.*)

GROARK: What about some grub, brother?

MANN: (*Turning*) Mmmm. Good. Anything'll do. (*Pause.*) Oh. Do something for me, will you? Find a mattress and a blanket from somewhere and put 'em in there. (*Gestures towards small office door.*) Here's as good a place as any, I reckon. (*Grinning*) I like to live . . . close to my work.

GROARK: (*Smiling*) Right you are, brother Mann. I'll do that. Right after grub.
(GROARK *leaves.* MANN *returns to the table, begins to trace routes through the docks on the map.*)

EXT. THE DOCKS. NIGHT

Gaunt ships against the sky. Suddenly, a sheaf of rockets rakes the skyline, and another, and still more.

INT. OFFICE. NIGHT (5 a.m.)

MANN *under a blanket, stretched out on his mattress, a lamp by his head, reading. The book is by Carlyle. He studies it closely. His voice over, as he reads.*

MANN's VOICE: 'There is not a horse in England willing and able to work but has due food and lodgings . . . And you say it is impossible. Brothers, I answer, if for you it be impossible, what is to become of you? It is impossible for us to believe it to be impossible. The human brain, looking at these sleek English horses, refuses to believe in such impossibilities for Englishmen.' (*He stops reading, touches his nose with his finger, returns to it again, says out loud:*) 'The human brain . . . refuses to believe in such impossibilities for Englishmen.' (*Pause.*) I like that. (*Pause.*) I do. (*Pan to floor by side of mattress. On it, the* Red Handbill: '*It May Be Tomorrow*'.)

EXT. SLOW, EARLY MORNING SHOTS OF WATERFRONT. DAY

The three passenger steamships, Baltic, Teutonic *and* Empress of Ireland *lie in dock. A picket of four men, equipped with armbands, guards a gangway, well wrapped against early-morning chills. A* SMALL BOY *approaches, two brewcans in his hands. They tousle his hair, pour tea and drink it, handing the lids round.*

Mix to:

EXT. MARITIME HALL. DAY

Very quiet.

INT. COMMITTEE ROOM. DAY

*A woman (*MARTHA CLARKE*), thirty maybe, sits typing on a table by a wall and window. There's a heap of files by her chair, papers on both sides of her table. She is neat, attractive, mature-looking. She wears her hair pinned close to the head; long-sleeved, high-necked brocade blouse and full ankle-length, very straight skirt. She is absorbed in her work.* MANN *comes in from the 'office' room, fiddling his jacket on over broad shoulders. He stops when he sees the woman.*

MANN: Good morning.

MARTHA: (*Finishing line, answering through it, then turning*) Morning.

MANN: (*Studying watch*) Will you be . . . working here?

MARTHA: Mr Pearce set me on.

MANN: (*Yawning*) Ah. (*Still at watch*) Still, it's early.

MARTHA: Seven thirty. Mr Pearce said there was plenty to do. (*She gestures at the files on the floor.*)

MANN: I take it you're . . . union.

(MARTHA *opens her handbag, takes out a small card, hands it to* MANN. *He looks at it, smiles, hands it back.*)

Good lass. (*Pause.*) Sorry.

MARTHA: That's all right. You're right to ask.

(MARTHA *turns back to her work.* MANN *strides to the door, calls into the passageway.*)

MANN: Gerry!

GROARK: (*Out of vision*) Yeah!

MANN: Eggs.

GROARK: On the way.

(MANN *closes the door, crosses to the table, sits down, begins to study some papers.* MARTHA *strips a page from the machine, clips it to some others on the desk, types a file heading on a strip of paper, licks and sticks it on to a file, puts the papers inside and carries it to the cabinet. She bends to place it into the bottom drawer.* MANN *watches her.*)

MANN: I'm sorry, I haven't introduced myself. My name's Mann. Tom.

MARTHA: (*Standing*) Yes, I know. (*Pause.*) I've seen your picture in the papers.

MANN: (*Grinning*) Don't flatter me, do they? Mek me look like an old walrus, 'stead of what I am . . . deeply handsome.

(MARTHA *laughs.*)

Oh!

MARTHA: I didn't mean that. It just sounded so funny.

MANN: What's your name then?

MARTHA: Martha Clarke.

MANN: (*Standing, hand out*) I'm pleased to meet you, Martha.

(MANN *and* MARTHA *shake hands, rather solemnly, then break and stand looking at each other.* GROARK *enters the room with a tray.*)

GROARK: Morning. Eggs and papers.

MANN: Morning, Gerry. Put 'em on the table, will you.

(MARTHA *returns to her seat rather quickly, resumes work.* GROARK *makes a great play of laying the breakfast out.*)

MANN: (*Standing behind him*) Come on, Gerry, bloody hell, you're not on the boats yet, you know.

GROARK: (*Refusing to be hurried*) Got to get my hand in though. (*Standing back, surveying*) Mmm. That looks all right. (*Moving to the door*) Oh, there's a picture of you in the *Manchester Guardian.* (*Grin.*) Can't say it does much for you. (*Pause.*) Still, there isn't really that much to work on, is there?

(MANN *makes a mock-menacing move towards the door;* GROARK *exits fast.* MANN *sits at table, begins to eat, spreads* The Times, Manchester Guardian *and the* Mail *out around him, begins to read. We catch a* Guardian *headline: 'Seamen's Strike: a beginning made at several ports: Liverpool firms' offer'. There's a knock at the door and* PEARCE *and* DIXON *enter.*)

PEARCE: Morning, Tom. (*To* MARTHA) Ah, you've arrived. Hello, Martha.

(*He crosses to* MARTHA, *begins to discuss the work with her.*)

DIXON: (*Coldly*) Good morning.

MANN: (*Finishing breakfast*) Morning, brother.

(DIXON *stands for a moment, then takes a seat at the table.*)
(*Finally*) What's going on then?

DIXON: (*Taking note from pocket*) I'm not having this.
(*He throws the note on to the table.*)

MANN: (*Taking note*) Oh. Why not?

DIXON: I take orders from Wilson in London. Nobody else.

MANN: (*Looking at note again*) I can't see any orders.

DIXON: I'm not having it. I'm not being told how to run my strike.

PEARCE: (*Returning*) Easy, Terence, easy now. There's no need to go . . .

DIXON: Bugger easy. Either I run my bloody union or I don't. It's as simple as that. That note says I don't.

MANN: (*Reading*) 'Advise you reach no accommodation with leading independents until line has been agreed by Joint Committee. Signed Tom Mann, President, Joint Strike Committee.' I don't see how that stops you running your union, brother Dixon.

DIXON: Look, I'm telling . . .

MANN: (*Hard*) No, *you* look. You took a unilateral decision to meet with representatives of three major lines last night. The first we knew about it was when a *Manchester Guardian* reporter let it slip after the public meeting at the docks. Now, this is a *Joint* Committee. If we're going to get anywhere, we're going to have to work *together.* I sent that note with the full approval of the Committee – your *brothers*, brother Dixon – because I didn't want you to reach any agreements that might weaken our *overall* position. (*Pause.*) I'm sorry if the tone offended you. I am. Really.
(DIXON *looks slightly mollified.*)
But I had to put the Committee's position to you and fast. Hence the note.

DIXON: I had the full backing of my executive for the meeting with the companies.

MANN: I'm sure you did. But somebody's going to have to tell your executive you're not in this on your own. You won't take the knocks on your own; and you won't take the perks either. (*Pause.*)

Perhaps I ought to have a word with 'em.

PEARCE: (*Quickly*) I reckon that's brother Dixon's job, Tom.

MANN: Aye. Happen.

(*The situation appears defused.* MANN *gets up, strides to door, opens it, steps into passage.*)

Gerry!

GROARK: (*Out of vision*) Yeah!

MANN: Coffee!

GROARK: (*Out of vision*) Right.

MANN: Four cups! (*He closes the door, returns to the table.*) So what happened?

DIXON: We met Cunards, Holts and White Star.

MANN: What level?

DIXON: General Managers.

(MANN *pulls a wondering face.*)

MANN: And?

DIXON: (*Smugly*) They've conceded pretty well everything.

MANN: Oh?

DIXON: It's true. Full agreement on eight of the nine demands. If we can carry on like this, we'll be home and dry within a week.

MANN: Ahunh. And the stewards?

DIXON: (*Looking at* PEARCE) Stewards weren't present. I imagined they'd be meeting . . . later on.

PEARCE: No. We . . . didn't meet. We brought it back to the Joint Committee.

(*Long silence. Some discomfort, for* DIXON.)

DIXON: We'll not settle without the stewards. There's no question of that.

(*Another silence.*)

MANN: When you say 'full agreement', are you talking about . . . particular ships, or about all ships of the three lines you mentioned?

DIXON: Well, we were talking initially about particular ships . . .

MANN: The *Baltic*, the *Teutonic*, so on.

DIXON: But I see no reason why . . .

MANN: But as yet you have agreement only on the basis of half a dozen *ships.* (*Pause.*) Is that right?

DIXON: That's right.

(*Pause.*)

MANN: *Did* you sign anything?

DIXON: (*Defiantly*) No.

MANN: And when do you meet again?

DIXON: Today.

MANN: Where?

DIXON: Exchange Station Hotel.

MANN: Make it . . . here.

DIXON: Why?

MANN: You've met there once already. They should meet on your ground now. And I want to be present. In a leading role.

DIXON: (*Finally*) They won't come.

(GROARK *in with coffee.*)

MANN: Ah, thanks, Gerry. (*Pause; watching*) And one for Martha over there.

(MARTHA *smiles to have it.*)

Grand. Many thanks.

(GROARK *out.*)

They'll come.

EXT. MARITIME HALL APPROACH AND EXTERIORS. DAY

Three automobiles neatly parked in line. The DRIVERS *lean on wings, in a knot, chatting.*

INT. COMMITTEE ROOM. DAY

MANN *in chair.* DIXON *on his right hand.* PEARCE *on left.* MARTHA *with notepad, facing* MANN. *The three company men down table sides. They are:* MONTAGUE *(Cunard);* CARRINGTON *(Holt);* MENTEITH *(White Star).*

MANN: Well, there are actually several reasons why your boats might not get away on the evening tide, Mr Menteith. In the first place, you have made no agreement with the stewards' union. In the second, we are simply not interested in agreements that cover individual ships. Let me quote from this morning's *Manchester Guardian*, gentlemen, though I'm sure I've no need to. Mr Cuthbert Laws, General Manager of the Shipping Federation, is reported as saying, I quote: 'Even if the men win better wages now, it will not do them much good. We shall be here day after day, every time a crew signs on, whittling away the increase until it disappears. We are always here. The men's union is here only once and again.' (*He looks benignly up, smiles.*) Mmm. We want that changing. The agreement we put our names to will cover every ship in your line. In return, every ship in your line will be immediately placed on the white list of every port in the country. (*Pause.*) Those are our conditions, gentlemen. (*Standing abruptly*) I think we can leave the detailed negotiations in the hands of brother Dixon and your good selves.

(*The three* COMPANY MEN *stands, not at all sure of their ground.*)

MENTEITH: You realize we'll need full board approval for agreement covering the whole company.

CARRINGTON: That's right.

MANN: Yes I do. (*Pause.*) May I suggest the telegraph service? It has many advantages. Especially as time and tide wait for no man.

MENTEITH: We'll see what can be done.

MANN: Thank you for coming, gentlemen. Your good sense is an example to the whole shipowning fraternity. I've little doubt it will be seen as such.

(*The three* COMPANY MEN *leave, stiff bows but no handshakes.*)

(*Grinning*) We're on the way, brother.

(DIXON *grins back.*)

EXT. MARITIME HALL: UPSTAIRS VERANDA. DAY

Immediately outside the committee room windows, on the wall, INTERNATIONAL SEAFARERS' CLUB AND INSTITUTE: SEAMEN'S UNION: FEDERATED WITH ALL THE SEAMEN'S UNIONS OF THE WORLD. *And below:* MARITIME HALL. *Sounds of large crowd gathered. Some banners obtrude; one in particular: 'War is now declared. Strike home and strike hard for liberty' (there is a very good picture of this, that can be worked while* MANN*'s speech is in progress).* MANN, *in close-up, addresses the crowd.*

MANN: Brothers.

(*Noises down.*)

Brothers, we have come a long way. In twelve days we've won massive concessions from more then 65 per cent of owners: the full ten shillings a month for seamen and firemen, full union recognition, an agreed minimum wage, vastly improved conditions and accommodation, and much, much more. For the stewards, well, we fell five shillings short of the four pounds a month we laid claim to, but we've improved on everything else: short duty pay, conditions and accommodation, overtime pay. (*Pause.*) We're doing well, brothers.

(*Loud and prolonged cheering.*)

But we've some way to go before we reach port. Having so far won the strike and gained all these benefits from the biggest shipping firms of the country, we must now extend our operations to the remaining lines, most of which are controlled by the bitterest enemies of the workers – the Shipping Federation. These firms have absolutely refused – and refuse still – to consider our demands or recognize the unions. (*Pause.*) the District Joint Strike Committee have therefore decided to withdraw all union sailors and firemen and cooks and stewards from the boats of the Federation firms, beginning Monday morning, June 26th.

(*Great cheering.*)

Any men continuing to work on these vessels will be considered and dealt with as blacklegs. They will be no different – and will receive no different treatment – from those . . . things that crawl off the Federation's depot ships anchored off Prince's Dock, collected, one imagines, in jamjars, like maggots, from every upturned stone in Britain, and brought to Liverpool in a feeble, festering attempt to break the strike. (*Pause.*) I must say, while I'm on the subject, how responsibly the pickets continue to handle this . . . difficult situation. Let it remain so. (*Sombre*) Few of you will need reminding that a picket was shot through the head in Hull two days ago, and died later in hospital. (*Pause. With grim emphasis*) It must not happen here. If the flow of blackleg labour continues, now, the shipowner will be forced to rely upon our fellow unionists, the carter, the docker, the coalie, the craneman, the scaler, the railwayman and the engineer to wage war against his brothers now on strike, in loading, discharging, and working at his blackleg vessels. (*Pause.*) Our fellow transport workers in Glasgow, Goole, Hull and Southampton have refused to be the catspaws of the shipowner, and all eyes are now turned upon Liverpool men, anxiously watching whether they will exhibit solidarity, or whether the evils of sectionalism shall curse our movement once more and seal the fate of the seafaring man for years to come. The Strike Committee are confident that no such calamity shall happen, and that our brothers, now that they are appealed to, will immediately put their already expressed sympathy into direct action, and refuse to be guilty of handling any goods or in any way assisting the vessels of Federation lines. (*Pause.*) The strike begins first thing on Monday morning. Strike at once, strike hard, and as men be men!

(*Sustained cheering.* MANN *waves, steps off balcony into committee room, followed by rest of Strike Committee. The cheering continues.*)

Right. I think we might be hearing from Mr Cuthbert Laws before long.

DITCHFIELD: We'll have to get busy. I've to get this through eighteen carters' branches before I can call 'em out.

SEXTON: I've twenty-two. At four meetings a day, that's nearly a week.

MANN: I've a feeling we shan't need you. Neither dockers nor carters. I've a feeling we've won already, brothers. There's a strong wind blowing up around Mr Laws's house of cards.

INT. EXCHANGE STATION HOTEL: VESTIBULE. DAY

MANN *sits in a plush armchair, under a huge rubber tree. He's asleep, head forward. A* PORTER *approaches.*

PORTER: Mr Mann.

(*Nothing.*)

Mr Mann.

(*Nothing. He leans forward and pokes* MANN*'s shoulder with his finger.*) Mr Ma . . .

(MANN *has his finger inside his fist. They look at each other for a moment.*)

Mr . . . Laws will see you now, sir.

(MANN *sniffs, slowly releases the finger, gets up. The* PORTER *turns and leads him off down a heavily carpeted corridor.*)

INT. LAWS'S ROOM. DAY

LAWS, *in dressing-gown, drinks a brandy, smokes a corona. The remains of a room dinner rest on a tray on the table. It's a big, comfortable, tasteful room, a little heavy, perhaps, in its furnishings.* LAWS *is youngish; late thirties say. Haut-bourgeois, bland, cool, able. He has some wit but no humour. Knock at door.*

LAWS: Come.

(*The* PORTER *enters.*)

PORTER: Mr Mann, sir.

(*The* PORTER *stands aside as* MANN *enters.*)

LAWS: Ah, Mr Mann, how nice to see you. (*To* PORTER) Thank

you, that will be all. (*Looking around*) Well, then, won't you have a seat. Can I get you a drink?

MANN: (*Sitting down*) No, thanks.

LAWS: (*Catching something in the tone*) Oh. Don't you approve?

MANN: I don't mind if you drink. I don't . . . approve of it for myself.

(LAWS *smiles, raises his glass in an ironic salute, drains it, pours another.*)

LAWS: Good of you to come so soon.

(MANN *impassive.*) We've . . . we've studied your demands. And . . . we don't think a great deal of them. (*Pause.*) I thought I should let you know, there's a strong move afoot to start laying up.

(*Silence.*)

I take it you know what that could mean for the men. Let alone the country.

MANN: Let alone the employers.

(*Silence.*)

LAWS: Yes. (*Pause.*) Fortunately, I think we've managed to stave off that particular . . . extreme line of action.

MANN: Glad to hear it.

LAWS: (*Very straight*) The Federation is not in a position at this moment in time to grant recognition to the unions. We cannot accept the total defeat that that would imply. If you . . . persist in demanding it, I think several of the lines would almost certainly lay up their ships and wait until the clouds cleared. However long that took. (*Pause.*) Do you take my meaning?

MANN: You have, I take it, a compromise to offer.

LAWS: Yes. (*Pause. Gathering*) I've suggested that each company within the Federation enters into individual negotiation with the appropriate unions. That way, the issue can be speedily resolved without compromising the Federation's stance. (*Pause.*) How does that strike you?

MANN: (*Slowly*) I think we'd probably view that very favourably. Pragmatically, we achieve our ends. I don't think we're bothered about the protocols. (*Pause.*) I'll take it back.

LAWS: It's not just seamen, firemen and stewards. You'd have to call off the threatened strike of all port workers – dockers, carters, coalheavers, railmen, all of them. While the negotiations are in progress, I mean.

MANN: The Strike Committee controls the port, Mr Laws. If we say work, there is work.

LAWS: (*Smiling bleakly*) That must give you . . . immense satisfaction, Mr Mann.

MANN: Objectively, yes. Personally, none at all. I'd sooner be working a farm. Growing things. (*He stands up abruptly.*) I should be able to let you know by tomorrow.

LAWS: I look forward to a favourable reply.
(*Their hands waver, as though a handshake is called for, but nothing happens.* MANN *makes for the door.*) My father used to tell me about you. He fought you in 'eighty-nine. Perhaps you remember.

MANN: Yes. I remember.

LAWS: Why do you do it? Go on doing it, I mean.

MANN: (*Simply*) To rid the world of people like you, Mr Laws.
(*He leaves.*)

INT. HOTEL VESTIBULE. DAY

PEARCE *paces anxiously up and down.* MANN *appears, sees him first.*

MANN: Hello, Frank. Keeping in trim, are you?

PEARCE: Christ! Tom. Look, I don't know what you've been saying to Laws but we've got problems.

MANN: I don't doubt it. Talk.

PEARCE: (*Terse*) The dockers are out.

MANN: How do you mean? Called?

PEARCE: No. Just out.

MANN: How many?

PEARCE: Five thousand. Mebbe more. Half the blinding work force.

MANN: Sexton?

PEARCE: Down there. Working like a goblin.

MANN: And?

PEARCE: They don't like goblins.

MANN: Let's go.

(MANN *and* PEARCE *leave quickly.*)

ACTUALITY FILM

Food, fuel, etc., stands on trucks and carts. Knots of dockers stand idle. Nothing moves.

EXT. DOCKSIDE. DAY

MANN *and* PEARCE *on dockside. Speak to group of men, who point them in direction of large hut. They continue towards it.*

INT. HUT. DAY

Meeting place of Dockers' Union No. 12 Branch. Inside, SEXTON, *a gash in his head, being attended to by another union official. The room is empty save for them.* MANN *and* PEARCE *in.*

MANN: What's it about, brother?

SEXTON: (*Savage*) It's a bloody insurrection, that's what it's about. They're out, Tom.

MANN: I know they're out. What I want to know is why.

SEXTON: I told you. Don't say I didn't tell you. Liverpool dockers . . .

MANN: Shag Liverpool dockers! I'm not interested in sodding *Liverpool* dockers, I'm interested in *workers*. What's this *about*, brother. We've got the Federation in the palm of our hand, all we need is two days more, of discipline and unity and solidarity, and what do we get!

SEXTON: (*Standing, groggy but angered*) Look, don't start blaming me. If I'd spent more time with the men instead of up there with your blasted Strike Committee, perhaps this'd never've happened. Any of it.

MANN: (*Cooling*) All right. All right, Jim, I'm sorry. How's the head?

SEXTON: All right. Bloody awful, actually. If I get hold of the bastard who threw it, he'll learn a thing or two.

MANN: You spoke.

SEXTON: Yeah. Mass meeting, north frontage. They wouldn't listen. 'Strike, strike,' they yelled. 'Strike, strike.' I put the Joint Committee line, they just didn't want to know. There's a dozen branches gone already, more to follow, I should think.

MANN: And what're they after? Do you know?

SEXTON: Aye. Union recognition. Twopence an hour. New overtime rates. And a fifty-four-hour week.

MANN: Christ almighty! They don't want a boat each for Christmas as well, do they? (*Pause.*) Who's in charge, Jim?

SEXTON: (*Offended*) *I'm* in charge!

MANN: Come *on*, James. You're sitting with a hole in your head.

SEXTON: (*Reluctant*) Word has it, Milligan, No. 12 Branch.

MANN: Who's he then?

SEXTON: Nobody. Just a bloody straightforward foursquare up and down honest as the day is long firebrand.

INT. MARITIME HALL: STAIRWAY. DAY

A young man, MILLIGAN, *steps in from the bright sunshine. He's lean, hard, lithe, a little over average height; wears a short, full-face beard and longish hair. He stands in the hallway, adjusting to the shadows.*

GROARK *opens a door, enters the corridor.*

MILLIGAN: (*Irish*) Committee Room A.

GROARK: Upstairs, first right.

(MILLIGAN *hits the stairs hard, takes them two at a time, reaches the door, knocks once, opens on the knock.*)

INT. COMMITTEE ROOM A. DAY

MANN*'s at the filing cabinet.* MARTHA CLARKE *works at her little table.* MANN *continues his search, though he's aware of* MILLIGAN *'s presence.*

MILLIGAN: Milligan.

MANN: (*Turning finally*) Mann. Come in.

(MILLIGAN *shuts the door, looks round the room.*)

MILLIGAN: You wanted words.

MANN: That's right. Sit down, won't you.

(MILLIGAN *sits reluctantly.* MANN *goes on with his search.* MARTHA *half turns, smiles at* MILLIGAN*; who half returns the smile, but not quite.* MANN *makes the table finally, dumps three files untidily down in front of him, sits down to face* MILLIGAN. *Stares at him for a long time.*)

(*Slowly*) More than five thousand dockers out. In flat contravention of the union's declared policy of *selective* support for the seamen's claims. Sexton says it's you.

MILLIGAN: Sexton should know better.

MANN: How do you mean?

MILLIGAN: Can't be one man. However . . . gifted.

(*Pause.*)

MANN: How do *you* see it?

MILLIGAN: I think we've gorra case.

MANN: I'm *sure* you've gorra case. *Now's* just not the time to be presenting it.

MILLIGAN: Who says so?

MANN: I say so. Your union says so. The Joint Committee says so.

MILLIGAN: The dockers say you're wrong.

MANN: (*Bleakly now*) Do they?

MILLIGAN: Ask 'em. They'll tell you.

(*Silence.*)

MANN: Martha, could you nip out for some sandwiches? Couple of big uns. (*To* MILLIGAN) All right? Cheese and onion, love.

MARTHA: Do you want sauce?

MANN: (*Looking at* MILLIGAN) No. No sauce. (*He hands* MARTHA *a sixpence.*) And get something for yourself. (MARTHA *leaves. He closes the door after her, stands, leans with back against it.*)
(*Finally*) You wouldn't be working for them, would you?
MILLIGAN: You want a belt in the mouth, brother, you just carry on like that.
MANN: (*Unperturbed*) I can't think of any other explanation.
MILLIGAN: Look, I'm warning you, I don't care who you are or how old you are, you go on . . .
MANN: Can you? Eh? How else can you explain it? Eh?
MILLIGAN: . . . with that rubbish and I'll put you down, I'm war . . .
MANN: You must be. A Laws man. You must be.
MILLIGAN: Right. I've told you.
(MILLIGAN *lunges,* MANN *catches him with a perfect short uppercut to the stomach, takes him, with immensely powerful arms, by the shoulders and bangs him head first into the door; then throws him at the table, where he lies spreadeagled across it, moaning and clutching his stomach. His nose bleeds quite a lot.* MANN *wipes his hands fastidiously on his handkerchief, crosses to the table, takes* MILLIGAN *by the lapels and helps him to a seat.*)
MANN: I'm sorry. I provoked that. I couldn't help myself. I just needed . . . that release. Are you all right?
MILLIGAN: (*Struggling to breathe*) I've . . . I've . . . I've known . . . days I've . . . felt better. Jesus Christ.
MANN: (*Dabbing* MILLIGAN*'s nose*) Here. Let's clean you up.
(MILLIGAN *takes the handkerchief, dabs his nose and mouth with it, lurches to his feet, does a few deep squats, begins to breathe more steadily.*)
MILLIGAN: Christ. Someone shoulda told me about you.
MANN: I'm sorry. I really am.
MILLIGAN: Yeah. Yeah. It's all right.
MANN: (*Hand out*) All right?
MILLIGAN: (*Taking it, blowing*) All right.
MANN: I had to be sure.

MILLIGAN: Yeah.

(MANN *and* MILLIGAN *sit down again.*)

MANN: You've . . . put us in a spot, brother. Now I want you to help us out of it. If the dockers stay out, the carters'll probably follow, and there'll be no settlement for the seamen with the cargo companies. That's to say, with the Federation.

MILLIGAN: I thought the Federation wouldn't play anyway. If the dockers don't strike, they'll go on using black labour till the seamen have all died in their boots.

MANN: No. We've got a deal. Supplies of blacklegs are running low. And the good weather's making most of the cargo particularly vulnerable to delay. They've offered to negotiate on an individual company basis. (*Pause.*) We've as good as won.

(*Long pause.*)

MILLIGAN: I see.

MANN: Now. What do we do?

MILLIGAN: I don't know. (*Pause.*) These aren't wild men making wild demands, you know. These are people driven daft by overwork and underpay.

MANN: You don't have to tell me, son.

MILLIGAN: I can't see 'em going back without someat.

MANN: Go on.

MILLIGAN: Well, at the very least, total recognition of the union by the whole Port Authority. And clear and unequivocal union preference in hiring practice.

MANN: Mmm.

MILLIGAN: Even so, it's hard to say what they'll do.

MANN: Well. We'd better get started. (*Pause.*) I'd . . . er . . . like you to join us.

MILLIGAN: Mmm?

MANN: Joint Strike Committee.

MILLIGAN: No, no. That's not me at all. Jesus Christ!

MANN: Mebbe not then. But it is now. I'll see that appointment's ratified by this evening.

MILLIGAN: What about Sexton?
MANN: I think you should get started.
MILLIGAN: All right. Whatever you say.
(*They shake hands, rather formally.*)
MANN: Seven o'clock sharp. Here.
(MILLIGAN *nods, leaves.* MANN *paces the room, looks out of the window, fretting.* MARTHA *comes in with the sandwiches wrapped in thin muslin.*)
MARTHA: Two cheese and onion.
MANN: (*At table*) Thanks. (*Opening one*) No sauce?
(MARTHA *goes to answer.* MANN *grins. She grins back.*)
MARTHA: I saw Milligan on the stair. He looks as if he'd had a fall. His nose was a mess.
(MANN *chews his sandwich impassively.*)
Oh. Gerry gave me this. (*She hands* MANN *a note.*) A Federation messenger brought it by hand. I said I'd bring it up.
(MANN *rips it open. Reads it carefully; face tight.*)
Bad news?
MANN: (*Stony*) Not good.

INT. COMMITTEE ROOM A. NIGHT

Full Strike Committee meeting. Full of smoke. It's late into the night. MARTHA *takes notes.* MILLIGAN, MANN, DIXON *and* DITCHFIELD *are in shirtsleeves.* QUILLIAM *remains fully suited, as do* SEXTON *and* PEARCE. *It's a hot, sultry night. From below, the noise of carousing seamen.*
SEXTON: Well, I don't think there's any doubt they'll stay out. How long is anyone's guess. But I've had reports from every branch during the day, and there's no sign of 'em budging, for the present.
MANN: Brother Milligan?
MILLIGAN: 'Fraid so. They're listening to nobody. And I think the picket clash with the police up the North End's just the first of many.
MANN: Ahunh. I think we can take it that the owners aren't bluffing

either. (*Reading a note on the table before him*) 'Failing a return to work by 6 a.m. Friday, the shipping dock employers will declare a lock-out of all dockers in the port.' I like the economy of style. Whatever else they waste, it's rarely words.

PEARCE: So. What do we do?

DIXON: We've got to get them back.

QUILLIAM: And how do you suggest we do it?

DIXON: I don't know. It's not *my* union.

SEXTON: I've called dockgate meetings for tomorrow. I suggest every Strike Committee member attend at least one. And I think we should start running off handbills and posters spelling out the Committee's case for discipline and unity.

MANN: I suppose that's a start. Anything else?

DITCHFIELD: I reckon we ought to do something about staunching my lot. They'll be next, I can feel it in me water.

QUILLIAM: Somebody ought to be talking to the employers. At least we ought to have a go at persuading them to postpone the lock-out, if only on the grounds that it'll lead inevitably towards worsening the overall situation. (*He receives doleful looks all round.*) All right. It was only a suggestion.

(*Silence.*)

MILLIGAN: (*Putting it together carefully*) Quite frankly, I don't think we've got a chance in five thousand of getting the dockers back before the lock-out. Whatever we do, things've gone too far now. So, in a way, aren't we starting at the wrong end?

SEXTON: (*Hostile*) Meaning?

MILLIGAN: Meaning, wouldn't we be better backing the dockers' claim than making fools of ourselves trying to get them to do something they quite clearly aren't going to do?

(*Momentary silence. Then a whole spate of rejections from the members, especially* SEXTON, DITCHFIELD *and* PEARCE (*all top union officials*).)

SEXTON: You can't ratify unofficial action just because it has the upper hand, man. Surely you . . .

DITCHFIELD: Bad practice. No union could hold its head up after that, believe you me.

PEARCE: No. Let them come to us. That way there's discipline. The other way there's only anarchy and chaos.

MANN: (*Matter of fact*) Much as I hate disagreeing with old and trusted colleagues, I think he's right.

PEARCE: You what? You think he's what?

MANN: I think he's *right*. Sooner or later, we have got to face the cruel but incontrovertible fact that we have *lost control*. We can no longer, if you'll pardon the expression, deliver the goods. Now, the longer we go on trying to whip the dockers in, the more evident that fact becomes. And all the time, of course, we lose sight of the enemy who remains, need I remind you, the capitalist employer.

(*Pause. Some mutters.*)

Let's anyway, just for . . . argument's sake, examine the case for an offensive. No, listen.

(*They subside.*)

Suppose we endorsed the dockers' claims – not all of 'em, but enough to carry them with us. Suppose, then, brother Ditchfield, we invite the carters to join them. With one or two claims of their own, of course. Take it a step further. There are signs that the railwaymen in these parts are looking for an opportunity to kick over the 1907 Conciliation Boards and do some face-to-face bargaining. Now, imagine us taking the railwaymen with us. Mmm? And suppose, too, that the tramwaymen came out; and the sanitary men; and the scavengers; and the electricity plant workers; and the gas workers; and the bakers. Mmm? Where do you think we are *then*, brothers? Cap in hand? Or boot on the collar?

(*He sits back, aglow with the prospect.*)

PEARCE: That's a mite fanciful, init Tom?

MANN: You say that line . . . beautifully, Frank. Every time.

DIXON: Still, it's a far cry.

DITCHFIELD: Aye.

QUILLIAM: Is it feasible?

MANN: I shouldn't think so. (*Grinning hugely*) Why don't we just *do* it. We could start by issuing a statement of unequivocal support for the dockers. How's this Martha? Erm . . . 'The Strike Committee are of the opinion that the dockers, who have rendered such effective service to the seamen and firemen, stewards and cooks, are acting quite within reason in asking that, in return, those unions should now assist them to obtain the recognition of their union, to which they attach so much importance and which, we agree, is a matter of vital concern. Erm . . . in only a few instances will that involve any immediate increase of pay, and even then it will only mean a return to the conditions which formerly obtained.' How does that sound?

PEARCE: (*Ironically*) Sounds grand, Tom. *Sounds* grand. If I were to try to put my finger on a weakness in your case – and God forbid it should fall to me to have to do it – I think it would be round about where you slip in . . . the railwaymen. Now you see, without them, I don't think your case is worth a bag of cold peas. And I can't for the life of me see how you're going to get them involved. Unless you've someat up your sleeve. (*Grinning*) Always likely, of course.

MANN: Arms, Frank. Only arms. (*Pause.*) Though, strangely enough, I did take a quiet stroll yesterday around St George's Square with the North-West Secretary of the Amalgamated Society of Railway Servants, who is of the opinion that, if their grievances are not met by the end of the week, he can see no alternative but to put the matter . . . in the hands of this Committee.

(*A long silence.*)

(*Very grave now*) I'm sorry to have been so light in manner over this. It is, indeed, our most important moment. Almost by accident we find ourselves on the brink of a major offensive, in which the whole of this city will be our battlefield, and where victories and defeats will be of moment to others far and wide throughout this land. It seems to me that we have no choice but to go on. But if we do go on, we must do so with iron purpose and resolute intent. There is no such manoeuvre as an apologetic attack. We must aim to deliver a crushing defeat to the shipowning fraternity, one that they will remember for years and years to come. (*Pause.*) In the meantime, we must prepare ourselves for counter-offensives of much greater power and magnitude than any we have had to deal with before.

(We mix to actuality sequences (still or film) of the army arriving; foot soldiers and cavalry; rotting food on trucks; soldiers and police escorting food convoys through the streets of Liverpool; police on horseback pursuing demonstrating strikers; pickets clashing with police and army; gunboats in the Mersey; soldiers on the railways; armoured cars patrolling the streets; newspaper headlines detailing the state of civil strife that has developed; women and children proclaiming rent strikes; mass meetings of striking workers. A gradual build-up of sound is required too.)

As we aim to control the day-to-day life of the city, so the state and the civic authorities will aim to wrest that control from us. We will be confronted not merely by staves and truncheons but by rifles and cold steel. Gunboats may well guard the depot ships and the docks. Every effort will be made to discredit our cause and undermine our morale. We will need the highest possible sort of self-discipline, if we are not to offer ourselves up to the slaughter. (*Back to* MANN, *now, close-up*) And even then, we may not escape it.

EXT. ST GEORGE'S SQUARE. EARLY MORNING

A bright summer day. MANN *and* QUILLIAM *walk around St George's Square and Plateau, deserted save for the pigeons and a few labourers erecting the speakers' platforms for the afternoon's rally and demonstration.* MANN *is reading something aloud,* QUILLIAM *listening intently.*

MANN: 'Don't disgrace your parents, your class, by being the willing tool any longer of the master class. You, like us, are of the slave class. When we rise, you rise; when we fall, even by your bullets, ye fall also. You no doubt joined the army out of poverty. We work long hours for small wages at hard work, because of our poverty. And both your poverty and ours arises from the fact that Britain belongs to only a few people. Think things out and refuse any longer to murder your kindred. Help us to win back Britain for the British, and the World for the Workers.'

QUILLIAM: It's good.

MANN: I know it's good. Is it actionable?

QUILLIAM: (*Thinking*) I'm not rightly sure.

MANN: Well, you're the lawyer, Billie.

QUILLIAM: Yes. It probably is.

MANN: Right. So do I say yes to printing it?

QUILLIAM: Well, if you mean are they likely to bring charges against the *publishers*, the answer's almost certainly no.

MANN: (*Sniffing*) Wouldn't matter anyway. It needs saying. Now more than ever. We'll publish.

(MANN *and* QUILLIAM *reach a platform.*)

How many do you reckon, 's afternoon?

QUILLIAM: A lot. Perhaps a hundred thousand counting the wives and kids. (*Pause.*) It . . . hardly seemed possible, only weeks ago.

MANN: What?

QUILLIAM: All this. Seamen, dockers, carters, coalies, cranemen, engineers, tramwaymen. And now five thousand railmen, and growing ever day. Nothing moves, but we say it should.

MANN: (*Smiles.*) It's . . . as it should be, Billie. No more than proper. (*Pause.*) It'll be good today. It's what we need. And it'll serve to demonstrate –

(*A squad of horses clatters past.*)

– to that lot, that we have both spirit and discipline greatly in excess of their own.

QUILLIAM: Let's hope so.

MANN: It will. It will.

(*A short wiry man walks towards them, a sort of rough-hewn stave in his hands.*)

STRANGER: Are you brother Mann?

MANN: Aye. I hope that thing doesn't mean mischief.

STRANGER: So do I. I work for Terrell's, the sawyers by Harvey Brew. We've had this order in for three hundred staves. Like this one. I tried to find out who for, but no one were saying. This morning, police came round to fetch 'em. I thought you should know.

(MANN *takes the stave, weighs it in his hands, hands it back to* STRANGER.)

MANN: Thank you, brother.

(MANN *holds his hand out. The* STRANGER *takes it.*)

STRANGER: You're welcome, brother. (*Pause.*) See you on the march.

(*The* STRANGER *leaves.* MANN *looks at* QUILLIAM.)

MANN: What do you think?

QUILLIAM: I think you'd better go and find out.

INT. POLICE HEADQUARTERS: THE OFFICE OF THE CHIEF SUPERINTENDENT. DAY

The SUPERINTENDENT *sits trimming his moustaches before a mirror placed on his desk. He's a tall, florid, handsome man, about forty-five; rather vain and showy. A knock at door; a constable opens it, says 'A Mister', and* MANN *is in.*

MANN: Mann. Good morning, Superintendent.

SUPERINTENDENT: (*Only momentarily surprised*) Morning, Mr Mann. Nice to see you again. (*To door*) All right.

(*The* CONSTABLE *leaves.*)

Just let me finish this perishing thing, will you. Seems to grow faster in the heat. (*He tweaks away at it, rather lovingly.*) Can't think why.

(*He finishes, regards himself affectionately in the mirror, sweeps his equipment into the drawer, the clippings into his hand and thence a basket, and turns to devote his whole attention to* MANN, *who is seated in a bucket chair opposite.*)

Well, Mr Mann. To what do I owe the erm pleasure, as they say?

MANN: (*Quiet, contained*) Just a last-minute precaution. I wanted to be quite sure we understood each other regarding this afternoon's proceedings.

SUPERINTENDENT: Why, of course we do, Mr Mann. We spoke only, what, two or three days ago. Is there something wrong?

MANN: I hope not, Superintendent. As I understand it, we have agreed to marshal the four marches and the assembly in the Plateau. You, in turn, have indicated a willingness to remain out of sight and unobtrusive as possible.

SUPERINTENDENT: That's right.

MANN: And you have seen and approved Mr Shelmerdine's permitting letter for the use of the Square and Plateau.

SUPERINTENDENT: What is all this about, Mr Mann?

MANN: (*Tersely*) Just this. A hundred thousand people – mostly men, but some women and children – will come to the centre of Liverpool this afternoon. You haven't agreed to let us 'police' them because you like surrendering your power and authority; you've done it because you know perfectly well that if you even tried to do it you'd probably be trampled underfoot. (*Pause.*) There's a very thin line, Superintendent, between order and chaos. You tread it this afternoon. A foot wrong and the Mersey'll rise a foot more by nightfall. With largely innocent blood. (*Pause.*) Do you take my meaning?

SUPERINTENDENT: Perfectly, Mr Mann. It's no more than you said the other day. A bit more . . . poetical, perhaps, but basically the same message. One, as you know, I've already taken delivery of.

MANN: I believe you took delivery of several hundred specially prepared staves this morning.

SUPERINTENDENT: Did we? Is it . . . to the point?

MANN: You know . . . nothing about them?

SUPERINTENDENT: Nothing. They could be drill sticks, I suppose. Now that we're working closely with the army, we're having to improve our training procedure. Yes, I think you'll find they're probably drill sticks.

MANN: But nothing to do with this afternoon?

SUPERINTENDENT: Good lord, no. Whatever gave you . . . Look, man, our job's to minimize tension and conflict. We'll stick to our side of the bargain, as long as you stick to yours. That's a promise.

MANN: (*Standing*) That'll do me. (*Stopping*) Oh. You might be interested to know, we've arranged for two cinemaphotographers to take a film of the proceedings. It'll make a useful . . . record, later on. (*Pause.*) I hope it keeps fine.

(*He leaves.*)

SUPERINTENDENT: So do I, Mr Mann. So do I.

(*The* SUPERINTENDENT *sits down, strokes his moustaches reflectively, humming a rather tuneless melody. After a moment, a slight knock and the* HEAD CONSTABLE *walks in. The* SUPERINTENDENT *stands up sharply.*)

HEAD CONSTABLE: All right, George.

(*The* SUPERINTENDENT *sits down again. The* HEAD CONSTABLE *stands in the doorway.*)

Everything . . . ready for this afternoon?

SUPERINTENDENT: (*Slowly*) Everything, sir.

HEAD CONSTABLE: (*Nodding, lips pursed*) Good. (*Pause.*) Good.

ACTUALITY

Still work and studio combined, perhaps.

MANN *addressing this vast gathering from No. 1 platform. Enormous build-up of sound, songs, bands, etc., subsiding during the speech. We cut, from time to time, to squads of police moving at the double through deserted streets, staves at the port.*

MANN: (*Throwing off coat and waistcoat*) Comrades. Citizens. It is good to see you. You lift an old man's heart. Your spirit, your will, your courage and the rightness of your cause will see us through.
(*Great cheering.*)
We're gathered here today, peacefully, to demonstrate our great determination to win this long and terrible battle against the employing classes and the state, their lackey. You should know that the railwaymen have joined us, have asked us to fight their fight for them. Now, all the transport workers of Liverpool are arm-in-arm against the class enemy. We have sent a letter to the employers, asking for an early settlement of our grievances, and a speedy return to work. If that brings forth no satisfactory reply, if they ignore us, the Strike Committee advise a General Strike all round.
(*Great cheering.*)
We cannot, in face of the military and police drafted into the city – to say nothing of the two gunboats sent down by the government to clutter up the mouth of the Mersey – we cannot, I say, have effectual picketing; and we cannot but accept this display of force as a challenge.

EXT. GREAT NELSON STREET. DAY

Edges of vast crowd, near Great Nelson Street. Three or four LADS *stand on shop windowsills to try and get a sight of the platform. Two* POLICEMEN *appear, order them down. The* LADS *are loath to move. The* POLICEMEN *drag them roughly down. One* LAD *crashes badly on to a shoulder. A section of the crowd advances on the two* POLICEMEN, *edges them out of the street. Suddenly, round the corner, a tight phalanx of forty policemen, with staves at the port. They double silently towards the strikers, who simply stand and watch them, incredulous. The police make contact, crack skulls like mangoes, ruthless, disciplined, mechanical. They show no anger; behave as soldiers doing drill. Charge after charge occurs, a new wave building as the first one breaks. It is terrifying. The square is filled with shrieks and groans; the ground seethes with wounded men, women and children. Here and there some strikers try to organize an effective counter, but they are outclassed and outmanoeuvred.*

INT. MARITIME HALL. NIGHT

Corridors and stairway bulging with wounded. MANN *picks his way through them, giving tightlipped comfort where he can. From lead-off rooms, the sounds of others receiving attention.* QUILLIAM *steps in from the street.*

MANN: (*Sharp*) Did you see them?

QUILLIAM: Yes.

MANN: So?

QUILLIAM: Police got there first. Confiscated all the film.

(MANN *stands up, stretches, looks at nothing in particular, very tense.*)

MANN: (*Finally*) They will pay. They must be made to. (*Pause.*) Have you got a count?

QUILLIAM: (*From notebook*) A rough one. Thirty-five in the Northern, one hundred and forty-two at the Royal, twenty at the Southern, eleven at the Stanley, around three hundred at the East Dispensary. With what we've got on our own premises, it's about a thousand.

MANN: Police?

QUILLIAM: About a dozen. It's hard to say.

MANN: (*Bitter, tough*) We must take it . . . as a lesson from history, Billie. (*Pause.*) No deals . . . with the state.

(*He turns, picks his way upstairs, bending to comfort the injured who litter his path.*)

INT. TOWN HALL. DAY

Vast committee room, gleaming, oaken, emblazoned and escutcheoned. Towards the bottom of the huge table in the centre of the room sit MANN, QUILLIAM *and* PEARCE. *Silence. They sit very still, indifferent to the room, incurious, unmoved. The top door opens and a liveried* ATTENDANT, *staff in hand, enters.*

ATTENDANT: (*Boomy*) His Worship the Mayor.

(*The* MAYOR *appears, in morning suit and chain. He is small, dapper, a baronet. The* ATTENDANT *walks him to his ornate chair at the head of the table, bangs the floor three times with the staff, pulls the chair out and backs it for the* MAYOR, *then retires to the door.* MANN, QUILLIAM *and* PEARCE *remains seated and inattentive throughout.*)

MAYOR: Gentlemen. I'm . . . very gratified you consented to this meeting. Would you be good enough to inform me who it is I have the pleasure of addressing?

MANN: My name is Mann. This is Mr Quilliam. This is Mr Pearce.

MAYOR: How do you do. (*Pause.*) Gentlemen, let me come to the issue with all the expedition I can muster. When the . . . national railway strike ended in agreement and, in consequence, the dock owners agreed to end their lock-out of dockers, it was assumed by all men of goodwill here in Liverpool that the transport strike would, in fact, be at an end, and . . . that . . . work would be resumed forthwith. It . . . er . . . seems, at any rate to me, that employers have been . . . more than generous in acceding to your demands, not only in respect of seafaring men, but also dockers, carters, and all other classes of transport workers in the port. (*Pause.*) Now, I know there are one or two grievances outstanding, but in the interests of the community – and that includes workers' wives and children, you won't need reminding – is it not now possible to sanction a full return to work, pending a satisfactory settlement of the outstanding issues? (*Pause.*) Gentlemen?

MANN: (*Slowly*) I speak for the Strike Committee. (*Pause.*) The answer's no.

MAYOR: Mr Mann, please see reason. There really is no point in . . .

MANN: I think you must allow us to decide whether there is point. (*Pause.*) A settlement is, as you well know, entirely in your hands. Reinstate the three thousand tramwaymen who struck in support of our just claims, and we will effect a full resumption within forty-eight hours. Unless and until that happens, not a ship, not a cart, not a bottle of milk or bucket of coal will move, without we say so.

MAYOR: I quite appreciate your . . . loyalty to the tramwaymen, but you must see how it stands with us. Eight hundred men refused to strike. It would be a gratuitous insult to their loyalty if we agreed to reinstate unconditionally.

QUILLIAM: Equally, you should appreciate how far we have ourselves come in this matter. We have had to resist repeated demands from the men themselves that no settlement should be accepted until the eight hundred 'blacklegs' were dismissed.

MAYOR: That is, of course, unthinkable.

MANN: Of course. We are agreed. (*Pause.*) Is it Petrie?

MAYOR: Sir Charles *is* taking it all . . . very personally.

MANN: He must learn to be more . . . pragmatic. There is no room for pride in politics. Perhaps you need a new chairman for your Highways Committee.

MAYOR: Sir Charles is a very powerful man.

MANN: I'd be surprised if he remained one. (*Pause.*) I hear the Board of Trade have called him down to London. Is that so?

MAYOR: Well . . . Sir Charles *is* in London at the moment. Whether it is to talk over matters at the . . .

MANN: (*Standing*) Good. That will do *us*, I think, Mr Mayor. Mr Askwith will tweak his nose for him. The tramwaymen will be back by the weekend. If you're a wagering man, place your sovereigns on it.

MAYOR: (*Standing*) I shouldn't be too sure of that, Mr Mann.

MANN: (*Smiling faintly*) Sometimes I wonder how you get where you do, you people. You read the world like a page of Swahili in the dark. Sir Charles is not a very powerful man. He is a jackal among puppies. Now he has fallen among tigers, you will hear nothing but the tearing of flesh. The strike is all but over. Take my word for it. Good day, Mr Mayor.

(MANN *walks out, fast and straight,* PEARCE *and* QUILLIAM *flanking him. The* ATTENDANT *opens the door sharply. The* MAYOR *looks dismally round at their backs.*)

EXT. LIME STREET STATION. EARLY MORNING

MANN *and* QUILLIAM *on the platform, a train in.*

QUILLIAM: Straight back, is it?

MANN: Aye. I'm due in Paris Monday. Conference.

QUILLIAM: It's been good.

MANN: Yes. Not a bad seventy-two days. We'll do better, though.

QUILLIAM: Keep in touch.

MANN: Mmm. (*Hand out*) Goodbye, brother.

QUILLIAM: (*Taking it*) Goodbye. Tom.

MANN *walks down platform, grip in hand. The* SUPERINTENDENT *and a* CONSTABLE *step out from the shadow.*)

SUPERINTENDENT: (*Easily*) Morning, Mr Mann.

MANN: (*Halting; hard*) You got business with me?

SUPERINTENDENT: Yes we have, Mr Mann.

MANN: Well?

SUPERINTENDENT: It's going to take a bit of time. You'll have to forget this one (*At train*), I'm afraid.

MANN: Oh? Have you got a charge?

SUPERINTENDENT: Oh yes indeed. Had it drawn up myself. Incitement to mutiny.

MANN: What?

SUPERINTENDENT: The article you published in your paper. You know: Don't shoot on your fellow workers. We're having you. (*Nice smile.*) I'm pleased to say. (*Pause.*) Shall we go?

(*They walk off,* MANN *between* TWO POLICEMEN. *Fade. Fade up*:)

INT. CELL BELOW COURT. DAY

MANN *sits in it alone. After a while,* QUILLIAM, *in court dress, arrives outside the door, is let in.*

QUILLIAM: Well. There we are.

MANN: (*Quiet, impassive*) Aye.

QUILLIAM: I'm sorry. I handled it badly. I didn't expect . . .

MANN: No, Billie. You did fine. Really. I could do with nine months' rest. (*A small grin.*)

QUILLIAM: Erm . . . Ellen's here.

MANN: Aye. Does she . . . ? (*Nodding*) Show her in, then, will you, Billie?

(QUILLIAM *knocks on cell door, is released, the door closes.* MANN *stands and faces the door. It stays shut a long time. It opens finally and* ELLEN MANN *enters. She's late forties, small, grey, tired, dowsed. She speaks with a Suffolk accent still, after all these years. She is hesitant, tiredly in control, but a little bewildered.*)

Hello, Ellen.

ELLEN: Hello, Tom.

MANN: How've you been love?

ELLEN: All right. Are you . . . ?

MANN: Yes, I'm fine.

(*Long silence.*)

ELLEN: Mr Quilliam said you might appeal or something.

MANN: Aye. We might. Don't fret.

ELLEN: No.

MANN: Billie'll sort the money out. He knows what to do. And I've written to William.

(*Silence again.*)

ELLEN: I'll never understand, Tom.

MANN: No. I know.

ELLEN: Why you do what you do. It's beyond me.

MANN: I . . . have to, love. You know *that.*

ELLEN: I know that.

(MANN *closes with* ELLEN, *draws her in to him.*)

MANN: You know, when they buried the Duke of Wellington, 1840 something, one hundred and twenty thousand people turned out for the funeral. They said then, no funeral could ever touch it, for size and scale and dignity. Forty years later I went to a worker's funeral. Alfred Linnell he was called – a general labourer, killed by police in a demonstration in Hyde Park. The mourners at that funeral were estimated at one hundred and fifty thousand. For an unknown worker. In forty years. And we're only just starting.

(ELLEN*'s crying at his shoulder. He notices.*)

Hey hey hey hey hey. You can't be crying. I'll not have you crying. The working class don't cry, lass. We've nothing to cry for. We're winning.

(*He kisses her on the forehead very gently. Pull out.* MANN *and* ELLEN *stand there. She leaves finally. He stands and watches her go. Roll: 'Actions that aim only at securing peace between employers and men are not only of no value in the fight for freedom, but are actually a serious hindrance and a menace to the interests of the workers. Political and industrial action direct must at all times be inspired by revolutionary principles. That is, the aim must ever be to change from capitalism to socialism as speedily as possible. Anything less than this means continued domination by the capitalist class.' Tom Mann 1856–1941.*)

Country: 'A Tory Story'

Characters

SIR FREDERIC CARLION
DAISY CARLION
PHILIP CARLION
VIRGINIA CARLION
DOLLIE VAN DER BIEK
ALICE CARLION
ROBERT CARLION
LINDSEY CARLION
EDWARD CARLION
SIR PIERS BLAIR
JAMES BLAIR
ANDREW OLIPHANT (SEN.)
ANDREW OLIPHANT (JUN.)
MATTHEW HARCOURT
MARGARET HARCOURT
TEDDIE HARCOURT (their son)
ELIZABETH HARCOURT (their daughter)
GUY WHELDON
NIGEL WHELDON (his son)
FAITH
ASHFORD (the butler)
NANNY POTTS
MINISTER
MR JOSEPH
PHOTOGRAPHER
DETECTIVE INSPECTOR
SQUATTER

Country: 'A Tory Story' was first shown on BBC Television in the autumn of 1981.

The cast included:

SIR FREDERIC CARLION	Leo McKern
DAISY CARLION	Wendy Hiller
PHILIP CARLION	James Fox
VIRGINIA CARLION	Penelope Wilton
DOLLIE VAN DER BIEK	Joan Greenwood
ALICE CARLION	Jill Bennett
ROBERT CARLION	Julian Wadham
LINDSEY CARLION	Suzanne Burden
EDWARD CARLION	Bryan Coleman
SIR PIERS BLAIR	Alan Webb
JAMES BLAIR	David Neville
ANDREW OLIPHANT (SEN.)	Tim Seely
ANDREW OLIPHANT (JUN.)	Piers Flint Shipman
MATTHEW HARCOURT	Frederick Treves
MARGARET HARCOURT	Eliza Buckingham
TEDDIE HARCOURT	Edward Hicks
ELIZABETH HARCOURT	Tamsin Neville
GUY WHELDON	Richard Durden
NIGEL WHELDON	Aubone Tennant
FAITH	Deborah Norton
ASHFORD	Frank Mills
NANNY POTTS	Madoline Thomas
MINISTER	Donald Eccles
MR JOSEPH	Ralph Nossek
Director	Richard Eyre
Photography	Nat Crosby
Producer	Ann Scott

EXT. ETON COLLEGE. DAY

Long, calm, rural shot of Eton College. Sound of raised voices, very distant. Pulsing fragments, coming and going, of Churchill announcing the fall of Germany. Camera begins long, measured, insistent track towards the main building. An organ sets up a single keynote. Boys' voices sing, unaccompanied, chapel acoustic, the words of 'Roll Out the Barrel' (chorus) to the tune of the 'Eton Boating Song'. The main building looms. From behind it, slow trails of white smoke drift and clot above the roof.

INT. COLLEGE. DAY

Boys leaping through smoke into air, a steady stream, on a sharp command from somewhere behind them. The boys are toppered, collared, frock-coated, carry pickhelves on their hips. Over this, begin voice over.

CHURCHILL'S VOICE: (*First election broadcast*) '. . . How is an ordinary citizen to stand up against this formidable machine which, once in power, will prescribe for every one of them where they are to work; where they may go and what they may say: what views they are to hold and within what limits they may express them; where their wives are to queue up for the state ration; and what education their children are to receive to mould their views of human liberty and conduct in the future . . . ? Here, in Great Britain, the cradle of free democracy throughout the world, we do not like to be regimented and ordered about and have every action of our lives prescribed for us . . .'

(*Second-storey window, from within room of old outbuilding. Smoke canisters billow thickly on the window ledge. Boys stand poised between them briefly, disappear, the voiced 'out' closer, in the room. Pan slowly, along the line of toppered boys who queue to leap. Smaller boys chew stiffly on their fear. Churchill pushes on. The queue stretches into the corridor beyond. Pan back, the voice closing in, till we find* ANDREW OLIPHANT (JUN.). *He leans against the wall, facing in towards the line of boys. He's tall, lithe, fair-haired, remote, seventeen. He calls 'out' in a dead, accurate way, scarcely looking, as he scans his* Financial Times. *He gives a cursory glance out of the window at some boys' babble from below. Cut to that point of view, piercing the smoke: six identically accoutred boys on the flags below stretch taut a piece of canvas. A boy has just bloodied his face landing on it. The catchers are laughing.*

Cut to in int. the room. ANDREW OLIPHANT *turns back to his paper, restarts the line's forward propulsion.*)

BOY'S VOICE: (*out of shot*) Best I could do, Oliphant.

(*He looks up. That point of view of* NIGEL WHELDON (*thirteen*), *sallow, small. He holds out a gleaming Sam Browne and swagger stick.*)

Shall I put them in your cupboard, Oliphant?

(ANDREW OLIPHANT *takes them, examines them in turn, Sam Browne first, which he returns. Then the stick, which he hangs on to.*)

ANDREW: Put them in my bag.

(*A boy leaps, another takes his place on the ledge.* NIGEL WHELDON *dwells.*)

What is it, Wheldon?

NIGEL: Erm . . . My father has arrived, Oliphant. I wondered if I might cut off.

(*Several boys in the line add their requests to* WHELDON*'s.* ANDREW OLIPHANT *standing upright, scanning the dwindling line.*)

ANDREW: Out.

(*The call quells a queueing boy's attempt to ask to be excused.*) I can't think why not, Wheldon. (*Looks at him*) Can you?

(NIGEL WHELDON *looks away uncomfortably:* OLIPHANT*'s tone is always difficult to judge.* OLIPHANT *still holds the swagger stick.* NIGEL *decides to assume he's hearing 'Yes'.*)

NIGEL: Well . . . thanks awfully, Oliphant. Erm. Father wondered whether we'd be seeing your people at the Carlion fest . . .

(OLIPHANT *looks at him for a second, then returns to the line of boys.*)

ANDREW: *Natürlich*. Out.

(*He holds out the stick.* NIGEL WHELDON *takes it, grateful, wary; leaves. The last boy climbs on to the ledge.* ANDREW OLIPHANT *approaches the window, looks down through the boy's legs at the canvas below.*)

(*Dead, quiet*) Out.

(*The boy leaps, lands, bounces to a cheer, rolls off.*)

FIRE OFFICER: (*Looking up*) Is that it?

ANDREW: Wait. (*We retreat with him briefly back inside the room, as he plunges the smoke canisters into fire buckets. He returns to the ledge, mounts it lithely, stands perfectly still, arms at full stretch in front of him.*)

EXT. COLLEGE. DAY

Steep, vertical shot of sky, from ground below the window ledge. ANDREW OLIPHANT *swallow dives perfectly through the frame in slow motion. We hear the cheers, etc. below,* OLIPHANT*'s curt 'Go to your homes.* Raus,*' but remain framing the blue white sky. Superimpose Title caption. Clear frame. A single-barrel ·410 enters, pointing up, is aimed, fired, retracted. The frame clears. Superimpose subtitle caption.*

EXT. SEAL PARK. DAY

A hand reaches for a blood-splashed woodpigeon spread like a hankie in thick shrub. Long backview of SIR FREDERIC CARLION, *through shrubbery. He stands stock still, gun in one hand, bird in the other. He stares up the lawn, past the old beech, to the house one or two hundred yards away. Eventually he turns to face camera. He's seventy, tough, tall, weathered. His face is empty, his mind on ahead somewhere. Crows flap past noisily. He looks up, on a reflex, but does nothing. A woman's voice calls something from the terrace. The voice floats down the long lawn. Long shot of house,* CARLION *in frame. A woman* (FAITH) *stands on the terrace.* CARLION *turns, waves vaguely; the woman calls something else;*

he waves again. Cut to short sequence of static shots of the scene, each one further receded, until we're on the ridge that marks the eastern boundary of the Carlion estate. The house sits snug in the rich Kentish distance, two miles of Weald away. Over the sequence, start voice over.

CHURCHILL'S VOICE: (*4 June broadcast*) 'It is not alone that property, in all its forms, is struck at, but that liberty in all its forms is challenged by the fundamental conception of socialism.'

(*The camera holds on the ridge,. It's windy here. Slow pocks of a ·410 can be heard from below somewhere. Sound of car idling close by. Something flaps, wisps, across the lens. It takes a moment to establish itself as a woman's dark brown hair. Cut to shot of woman from rear, scanning the estate.*)

WOMAN: (*Out of shot*) It's all right. I know the way.

EXT. TERRACE. DAY

FAITH*'s point of view of* CARLION *approaching her on terrace. He carries gun and bird.*

FAITH: (*Out of shot*) They're gathered at the front. You have three minutes . . .

(*Reverse on* FAITH, CARLION*'s approaching point of view. She's mid-thirties, slim, in tweed skirt, light wool sweater, good shoes. She holds his morning coat up ready for him. On a table by the french windows, his hat and a tray with a box of pills and some water.* CARLION *props his gun, lays the bird on the table, fingers for his cuffs, accepting the coat.*)

CARLION: Thank you, Faith.

FAITH: (*Straightening his collar*) Lady Carlion would like a word some time today about numbers for the dinner . . .

(*He barely hears.*)

. . . Here.

FAITH *hands* CARLION *his box of pills. He places two on his hand, takes the proffered water, palms them to his mouth, swallows, hands her the glass, takes the proffered hat, picks up the gun and enters the ballroom/ drawing room. She follows him.*)

INT. BALLROOM. DAY

CARLION *ambles purposefully for the far door,* FAITH *behind him.*

FAITH: Mr Benson telephoned again.

CARLION: Mmm.

FAITH: (*Calm*) He needs to know the date of the next board meeting by Friday at the latest.

CARLION: (*Not a question*) Does he.

(*They reach the passage by the stairs, cross it and pass into the study.*)

INT. STUDY. DAY

CARLION *places his gun against the fireplace, straightens his tie in the glass-framed portrait of Frederic on the wall. We see him dimly, behind the correct portrait of his eldest son in major's uniform. A moment.* CARLION *has retruded: sees only Frederic.*

FAITH: (*Out of shot, quite quiet*) Sir Frederic, they're waiting, we must go . . .

(CARLION *turns, looks at his fobwatch, head down and slightly averted, as he resurfaces.*)

CARLION: (*Returning watch*) One more for the tub.

(*He ambles out of the door and into the hall.*)

EXT. HOUSE. DAY

FAITH *follows* CARLION, *shrugging a coat over her shoulders. He moves quickly, emerges on to the porch, where she joins him. He stands for a moment, settling his hat, studies the families as they stand, in looseish groups of affinity and interest, around the waiting cars at some distance from the front porch. They're a relaxed group, dullish, rather inert. Tiny flurries of energy come off* DAISY*'s clot of people, and off the mother-and-child area; but mainly they just stand.*

CARLION: Philip?

FAITH: Called from the station.

(CARLION *turns to look at her. He's alert; dangerous suddenly.*)
(*Calm, threatened*) You were down the garden. It was a public telephone . . .
(*He nods her on, tersely.*)
He'll go straight there.
(*They look at each other.*)

DAISY: (*Out of shot, from some distance, the irony unmistakable*) Ah, I believe we can proceed.
(*The look holds. Sounds of cars being started up.*)

CARLION: (*Almost minatory*) I want him first, Faith.
(DAISY *calls* FAITH *to hurry.* FAITH *breaks eye contact with* CARLION, *calls 'Just coming', doesn't move. A woman,* NANNY, *about eighty-five, walks between them from the house. Shouts of 'Nanny do get a move on' from the car area.*)

NANNY: (*Explaining to* SIR FREDERIC) I *couldn't* find my umbrella. (*She shows it to him.*) In the nursery! Young Virginia up to her tricks again, I'll wager . . .

CARLION: Do bugger off, will you, Nanny, there's a good girl.
(NANNY *ignores him, smiles nicely at* FAITH, *walks off towards the waiting cars.* FAITH *looks once more at* CARLION, *quite levelly, then walks on towards the embarking clusters.* CARLION *remains with his back to them for a moment. Looks down at his left hand, which is balled into a taut fist. Opens it to reveal the two pills. He shakes them off the palm , which is dappled with pigeon blood. Organ music up.*)

EXT. CHURCH. DAY

The cars are parked on verges, skewed untidily on the lane outside. The organ plays mindless chords, held for ever within the convention of filling an awkward hiatus.

INT. CHURCH. DAY

Front pews occupied by the families, seated in unconcerned silence before a

High Church MINISTER *in vestments, who carefully checks the time on his watch and smiles frequently. Scan the families.* DAISY *and* CARLION *sit in the middle.* DAISY *is bored, stoical;* CARLION *is recessed. They could be in different hemispheres. On* DAISY*'s right are* ALICE, *her daughter-in-law, and* ROBERT *and* LINDSEY *and* INFANT *by the aisle. On* CARLION*'s left sit* MARGARET, *his eldest daughter, her husband* MATTHEW, *and their children,* ELIZABETH (*fourteen*), *and* TEDDIE. *Behind them, clone-like, sit the* OLIPHANTS PÈRE *et* FILS, NIGEL WHELDON, *his father* GUY, EDWARD CARLION, SIR FREDERIC*'s brother, and* FAITH. *They wait, to waiting music. The music stops. The* MINISTER *nods discreetly in the direction of the organ. The music starts up again. The* MINISTER *walks forward, speaks deferentially, bending from the waist, to make it discreet, with* LADY CARLION, *who turns to speak with* FAITH. FAITH *leaves the pew and walks towards the door at the rear of the church. Reverse on* FAITH, *walking up aisle. Behind her the* MINISTER *is guiding the party towards the font.* FAITH *reaches the doorway. The music has cut mid-chord. The* MINISTER*'s bland brown voice eases in to the short baptism service.* BABY CARLION *senses danger, begins some fairly unrefined resistance.*

FAITH*'s point of view from church doorway. A man stands in quarter-profile before a gravestone, smoking a black cigarette, a spray of wild rose in his hands. There's a battered valise by his feet. The man wears a finely cut lightweight suit, elegant and perhaps a fraction raffish.* FAITH *watches him calmly, analytically, for some moments. He turns suddenly, sensing presence; sees her. Smiles. Picks up the valise and approaches, dropping the cigarette butt* en route.

PHILIP: (*Smiling*) Had to do some walking. Cab ran out of petrol by Fagg's Corner. I'm whacked. How are you, Faith?

FAITH: (*They're in the porch*) I'm well.

(*They shake hands, rather formally.*)

PHILIP: You look radiant, Tats. (*Looking past her down church*) Oh God. The gathering.

FAITH: (*Dry*) Would you care to join them? I'll take your bag.

PHILIP: (*Starting in, then remembering*) Wait.

(*He turns to the small stone water-holder on the porch wall, places the spray in it, smiles at* FAITH *and walks down the aisle. Cut to shot, over* MINISTER*'s shoulder, of the families round the font,* PHILIP *advancing, almost casually.* MARGARET HARCOURT *and* GUY WHELDON *have moved forward as godparents.*)

MINISTER: (*To* MARGARET HARCOURT *and* GUY WHELDON) . . . dearly beloved, dost thou, in the name of this child, renounce the devil and all his works, the vain pomp and glory of this world, with all covetous desires of the same, and the carnal desires of the flesh, so that thou wilt not follow . . . (PHILIP *arrives almost invisibly by* GUY WHELDON*'s side*) . . . nor be led by them.

MARGARET: I renounce them all.

WHELDON: I renounce them all.

PHILIP: (*Perfectly arrived*) I renounce them all

(*The* MINISTER *looks up from his book.*)

MINISTER: Good morning.

PHILIP: Good morning to you.

(DAISY *frowns.* CARLION *chuckles suddenly, gives no indication why, becomes as suddenly grave. Cut to* FAITH*'s long point of view of the proceedings, from the porch.*

The MINISTER*'s voice reaches us clearly at this calm distance.*)

MINISTER'S VOICE: Frederic Charles Carlion, I baptize thee in the name of the Father and of the Son and of the Holy Ghost . . .

(*Close up*) FAITH, *watching. She turns, to look at the rose spray in the water-holder. Touches it.*)

EXT. CHURCH YARD. DAY

The MINISTER *bows and handshakes people out of the porch and in to the yard. They come at a leisurely pace in dribs and drabs, clustering and clotting as they emerge to regroup. For a few moments a click arrests them into* Tatler *stills of the class at church, without disrupting the scene's development. A few locals gaze at them from the road: not envy, not deference – a sort of guarded interest. The* Tatler *photographer, formally dressed, coaxes pics from the disinterested families: all is ease, distance.* DAISY *is handed her grandson: she holds it with calm disdain, her eyes on the church porch.* ROBERT (*twenty-two*) *and* LINDSEY (*twenty*) *stand with her.*

DAISY: Robert, I think you should consider the offer of Nanny Potts very seriously . . . She's aching to get her hands on one of these things again and I cannot be expected to carry her for ever . . .

ROBERT: (*Irish Guards, with discreet black armband; pleasant, empty*) I'll have a word with Mother, Grandmother . . .

(*He sees his mother, talking with* OLIPHANT PÈRE, WHELDON *and* HARCOURT.)

LINDSEY: (*Middle-class, strong, pretty*) He has two teeth, Lady Daisy. (*Showing her how*) You can feel them.

DAISY: (*Looking at child stonily*) I'm sure one can. (*Sees* PHILIP *emerge.*) There you are! (*To* LINDSEY) Here, take it. (*She moves forward to take* PHILIP*'s kiss on the cheek.*) Famously on time. Faith said you would be.

PHILIP: Good old Faith. How are you, Mother? For you. May the bloom last for ever.

(*He gives her the wild rose. She smiles drily.*)

DAISY: Ha. 'Tongue of Silver'.

PHILIP: 'Heart of stone'.

DAISY: (*An intercepting call*) Faith, we seem to have lost Sir Frederic again . . .

FAITH: (*Carrying* PHILIP*'s valise towards car*) Still inside, Lady Carlion. I'll bring him home . . .

PHILIP: Let me take that . . .

FAITH: (*Unfalteringly in motion*) It'll go in the car . . .

DAISY: (*To groups*) Shall we go? Margaret, you're getting fat again, girl.

(*She leads* PHILIP *towards the main group of* HARCOURTS, WHELDONS, OLIPHANTS, ALICE, *who've now been joined by* ROBERT, LINDSEY *and babe.*)

Say hello to your godson. Got your father's eyes, don't you think?

ALICE: I was just thinking how like a Wheldon the mite is . . .
PHILIP: Really. (*He studies the infant.*) Poor sod.
(*He's greeted by the families, rather formally, neither liked nor liking, but all amiably masked. A moment with* ALICE: *eyes.*)
LINDSEY: Mummy thinks he's a Parker . . .
(*No interest.*)
At least from the photographs . . .
PHILIP: (*Reaching* ROBERT*: a handshake*) How's my nephew then?
ROBERT: Good shape, really, Uncle Pip. Windsor next week, to hand this lot in (*Uniform*) . . . and then it's back to whatever again . . . (*Smiles pleasantly.*) Thank you for your note about Father . . .
DAISY: Come everyone come . . . The promenade is over.
(*They drift towards the waiting cars.*)
ROBERT: (*Quietly*) I hadn't realized quite how much he meant to you, actually . . .
PHILIP: Oh yes. Under the envy, great love . . .
DAISY: Faith, get Sir Frederic, will you . . .
(FAITH *moves towards porch. The* PHOTOGRAPHER *has detained* MATTHEW HARCOURT, *is taking down details of his constituency and government post. Drifts of* HARCOURT*'s confident predictions of a Tory victory.*)
Don't be all day, Matthew, you'll miss lunch . . . Philip, walk me back, I want a word . . .
(PHILIP *takes some steps towards* FAITH *and the porch.*)
PHILIP: I thought I'd drive Father back . . .
(*She waits.*)
A pleasure. With you in a tick . . .
(*People drift off. Summer haze settles over the emptying yard. Car doors bang. Engines hum.*)

INT. CHURCH. DAY

PHILIP *joins* FAITH *at the church inner door. Outside, they can see* DAISY, *standing, rose in hand, staring at the grave* PHILIP *stood by earlier. Down the church,* CARLION *stands looking at a wall-plaque.*

PHILIP: They're taking it hard, Tats.

(*She looks at him.*)

Freddie's death.

FAITH: It was a hard death.

(*Beat. They regard each other; almost friends.*)

PHILIP: How's Mother?

FAITH: Strong.

PHILIP: (*Slight smile*) Aren't all women?

FAITH: Don't keep her waiting. And don't tell your father you've spoken . . . He wants you first.

(PHILIP *chuckles.* FAITH *smiles.*)

Welcome home.

PHILIP: Oh yes.

(FAITH *walks down the aisle towards the motionless* CARLION. PHILIP *watches a moment. Leaves for his mother. We see* FAITH *join* CARLION *in long shot, stand quietly by his side, as* DAISY*'s voice trails over from next scene. Eventually we cut to* CARLION*'s point of view: a newly erected plaque commemorating the death of Major Frederic Carlion, killed in action in France, 23rd March 1945.*)

EXT. SEAL PARK. DAY

The redwood fir walk to the house. DAISY *and* PHILIP *walk arm in arm.* NIGEL WHELDON *and* TEDDIE HARCOURT *lead phantom platoons on a surprise raid against the Hun. Odd shouts bobble on the air. Towards the end of the scene the boys stalk the adults on both sides of the grove.*

DAISY: (*Voice over for beginning*) He's crumbling . . . God knows he's always been a singular man but this is not that . . .

PHILIP: (*Laughing, easy*) Mother, you always say that. Every time.

DAISY: Philip, whether I say it or not, your father is . . . ppp. Do you have a cigarette?

(*He hands her a black russian from a gold case.*)

That's new.

PHILIP: A present.

DAISY: Kind friends. (*At cigarettes*) Oh God.

(*He lights it for her. They walk on.*)

Well, you'll see for yourself soon enough . . .

(*They walk in silence, detached now.*)

You brother's to be given some posthumous award.

(*Silence.*)

I'm sorry you had to miss his funeral.

PHILIP: Couldn't be helped. I was in Ireland.

DAISY: Yes. (*Pause.*) His widow made some noises.

PHILIP: About me?

DAISY: Mmm.

(*He smiles. The house is looming. He senses the boys in the background, stalking them.*)

PHILIP: (*Aware it isn't*) Is that it?

DAISY: (*Handing him her butt for disposal*) Philip, it was not *my* idea to resume the annual dottiness of Carlion Week. And if I'm fortunate enough to survive the dance for the Loyal Subjects, I am almost certain to expire at the Grand Family Dinner. Do you see what I'm saying?

PHILIP: It's your birthday tomorrow. He wants to celebrate. I find that touching.

DAISY: Ha.

PHILIP: You think the old feller's after something, eh?

(*She says nothing. He smiles, loving her timing.*)

Well, what do you imagine that might be?

DAISY: I dreamt about Virginia last night.

(*She stops, looks at him carefully. He carefully looks away.*)

What is he after? Well, among other things, he's after you.

(*Silence.* PHILIP *turns eventually to take her look. He wants to smile; can't. Takes out another cigarette: she takes one.*)

(*As he lights hers*) Your father has lost his eldest son. The fifth baronet has lost his heir. The Chairman of the Board has lost his managing director. He's seventy years of age. The families are

pressing for Robert to take Freddie's place.
(*Their eyes meet briefly.*)
I think your father wants to go to his grave knowing things will go on much as they have done.

PHILIP: (*Quietly*) It's out of the question.

DAISY: (*Walking on towards steps*) It would seem so.

PHILIP: Mother, it is.
(DAISY *turns at the top of the step, stands over him to listen.*)
Mother, I'm thirty-five, I have two rooms at the Hyde Park, I earn my own living writing salacious copy for the *Evening Standard* and I live, absolutely, my own life. He mustn't be serious.
(DAISY *says nothing.*)
Has he spoken with you about this?

DAISY: Ha.

PHILIP: Mother, it's not on. Really it isn't.
(*Pause.*)

DAISY: (*Simply*) Then tell him.
(*She walks off towards the house.* PHILIP *stubs his cigarette. In close up, his fine face grows unexpectedly relaxed, a small smile threatening the edges of his mouth. A faint rustling of dead wood behind, which* PHILIP *barely registers, until he whips round with terrifying speed and plugs the two boys with his phantom Sten gun. They fall laughing and groaning into the bracken.*)

EXT. SEAL PARK. DAY

Binocular shot of DAISY *crossing to the front porch, past parked cars. Sound of approaching car as she enters the house. The binoculars scan down the drive to the stables area, where a blacksmith is at work cold-shoeing. A car edges round towards the house. Is panned back to the porch.* FAITH (*driver*), CARLION, ANDREW OLIPHANT *and his* FATHER *decant.* FAITH *gets out Philip's valise from the boot. The scan picks out* CARLION, *as he moves abstractedly indoors, then returns for the*

OLIPHANTS, *who stand a moment conferring, then disappear through the front doors.* FAITH *bangs down boot lid and carries the case in. Voices over, boomy, from the hall, as those people disperse. Cut to long shot of woman, in trees, scanning the house. She removes the glasses momentarily. We see a camera slung round her neck. She wears belted mac, black beret: her hair is dark, long. Sounds of boys running, feet on gravel, a shriek. The glasses go up. Cut to* NIGEL *and* TEDDIE *rushing into the house. The binocular pan moves right, to pick up* PHILIP *walking in, some paces behind them. The scan follows him in, waits as he stoops to pick something up from the ground. Hall acoustic over:* NIGEL *and* TEDDIE *disappearing into the bowels of the house.*

INT. HALL. DAY

PHILIP *stands there, on the threshold, his valise just in front of him. He takes the place in: portraits, ceilings, furniture, fireplace, geography. He smells it. Hears the sounds of the house. His face in close up is still, unyielding, feeling held at some ironic distance.*

FAITH: (*Out of shot, arriving from study.*) You're in Upper Grey. Next to Alice. Who would like a word.

PHILIP: Grisly. I feel it. There are times I wish *I* were a penurious third cousin, Tats.

FAITH: Your father's in his study.

(PHILIP *looks at the study door, picks up his valise.*)

PHILIP: I think I'll clean up first. (*Looks at case in his hand.*) I suppose it's the war. The absence of coolies . . . (*He moves off then turns.*) Oh. Your flowers.

(PHILIP *hands* FAITH *the spray. She takes it. Her eyes dip for a second, then steady.*)

FAITH: Waste not, want not?

(*He grins, charming, leaves.* FAITH *watches him, flowers at her breast.* CARLION *comes out of his study, stands stock-still, seeing little. Sees* FAITH. *Says 'Philip.' Pats his pockets. Retreats into the room.* FAITH, *in close up, smells the single spray of roses, drops it into a cane basket.*)

DAISY: (*Out of shot, arrived*) He wears scent. Have you noticed?
FAITH: Does he? I haven't.
DAISY: I think he did see Virginia.
FAITH: Did he say so?
DAISY: No. That's what makes me think it. He's like his father. In better days.
FAITH: Mrs Van der Biek arrived.
DAISY: Good for Doll. Good old horse. All the way from Johannesburg and only a day late. How did she look?
FAITH: Extraordinary.
DAISY: (*Pondering, less pleased*) Mmm. Mmm. She damned well would. I need a drink.
(*She leaves for the sitting room.* FAITH *stoops, to retrieve the spray, sets it in a vase on a cabinet.*)

INT. UPSTAIRS CORRIDORS. DAY

Long, upstairs corridor, dark save for the far window light. PHILIP *is in long shot, framed by the window. He has just reached Upper Grey, opens door, places case down, pauses, looks at the room door a little above his own, crosses to face it. He knocks.*

INT. ALICE'S ROOM. DAY

Shot of door, over PHILIP*'s shoulder. He knocks again. It's opened by* ALICE CARLION, *in dressing-gown. She's resting.* ALICE *is forty-three, tallish, handsome in dark glasses.*
ALICE: Philip, come in.
(*He kisses her on the cheek, passes into the room, notes the rumpled bed, the drawn curtains.*)
PHILIP: Look, this is probably a bad time, Faith mentioned you'd like a word . . .
ALICE: Please, it's all right. I was resting. I'm glad you came.
(*She shows him a chair by the bed. She sits on the far side from him, her*

back on the bedhead, virtually in profile to him. The table lamps, on each side of the bed, light them. ALICE *lights a cigarette. Rubs her eyes under the shades.* PHILIP *watches her with quiet, wary ease.*)

PHILIP: (*Finally*) I'm sorry I wasn't able to be there to bury Frederic.
(ALICE *says nothing.*)
I had to go to Ireland.

ALICE: Of course.

PHILIP: Can you cope?
(*She looks at him, smiles drily.*)

ALICE: Can you?
(*He laughs a little. She smiles on, not joining him.*)

PHILIP: Well. Here I am.

ALICE: Yes. The question is: why?
(*It hangs, in the silence.*)

PHILIP: Oh. (*Pause.*) You know me, Alice.
(*Silence. She stubs her cigarette. Takes off her shades. She has fine eyes, dark with long-term fatigue.*)

ALICE: (*Factually*) There's a feeling, a strong feeling, in the families, that Robert should take his father's place at Carlion's.
(*Silence.* PHILIP *sits, interested but neutral. She looks at him.*)
Your father can't go back to doing both. And not even your father believes he can. (*Pause.*) My son, God knows, is not ideal. But (*Carefully*) as there is no other possible alternative . . . he is a Carlion and could probably be induced to act like one, given coaching. (*Pause.*) Therefore.
(*Silence.* PHILIP *studies her. She looks away.*)

PHILIP: That's a pretty gown.

ALICE: Is it? (*Pause.*) How's Nikki?

PHILIP: (*Easily*) Nikki's fine. Nikki's fine.

ALICE: (*Quite serious now, calm*) I asked why you were here, Philip.
(*He stands, stuffs his hands in his trouser pockets, strolls a little.*)

PHILIP: When I'm not flogging upper-class droppings in the *Evening Standard*, I spend a smidgeon of my spare time working unpaid on a tiny satirical magazine turning over *real* dirt. To my discredit, I have managed to spike – for what are purely personal reasons – two extremely unattractive stories, recently. Both concerned you, Alice. I would find it quite distasteful to have to elaborate. The cast of the first was fairly extensive, from the evidence I've seen. As was the ducal yacht which served as setting. (*Pause.*) In Cork they say: 'Never quarrel when the guns are loaded.' (*Pause.*) In Gaelic it sounds subtler.

(*He begins to head for the door. She puts her glasses on. He stops in doorway, is quite angry, suddenly quite pale, but under control.*)

I'm here because this is where I was born and grew up and I have some odd, whimsical, probably quite selfish love for my crazed parents. It is my whim to be here. (*Very quietly*) That's all, Alice. (*He smiles, brow quizzical. A credible version of Noël Coward.*) Be it ever so humbug, there's no place like home.

ALICE: (*Yielding slowly to amusement*) You're still like a pigeon with three wings. And an awful rat, you know.

PHILIP: (*Coward again*) My reputation's terrible, which comforts me a lot.

(ALICE *chuckles. Lies back on the bed. They look at each other for a long time.*)

ALICE: (*At length*) Two, you said.

PHILIP: (*Simply*) Yes.

(*He leaves, closes door behind him. She removes her glasses, lights a cigarette. She's full length on the bed. She stares at the ceiling, smokes: her face is impassive, unreadable.*)

INT. UPSTAIRS CORRIDOR. DAY

PHILIP *approaches second-floor stairway, passes room with door ajar on his right. He turns to look into the room.* DOLL VAN DER BIEK *sits crumpled by fatigue on the bed, her back to the door, a fine feather hat raked absurdly across her head. Bags everywhere.* DOLL *has never travelled light. Part of her collapsed face can be seen in the mirror.*

PHILIP: (*Gentle*) How's Doll?

DOLLIE: (*Not moving*) Doll's done for. Who's that? That Philip?
PHILIP: Welcome.
DOLLIE: How's your mother?
PHILIP: Radiant.
DOLLIE: (*Unexpectedly*) How's your father?
PHILIP: (*Beat*) Haven't seen him, Doll.
(*He watches* DOLLIE *some moments longer, as* CARLION*'s toast voice over comes up, before drawing the door gently to on her.*)

INT. STUDY. DAY

*Slow point of view (*PHILIP*'s) scan of glass-covered display of Carlion Breweries International Gold awards.* CARLION*'s voice, trailing from last scene, over.*

CARLION: (*Out of shot*) . . . The sign of the soothsayer, Greek, you know, hung outside the office . . . was two eyes. One looking forward, one looking back. Soothsayers were the first Tories. I give you the future. The old whore.
(PHILIP, *glass at lip, watches* CARLION *drink his Madeira, then wander back to an upright chair and sit vacantly in it.* PHILIP *crosses to sit opposite in another.*)
Old whore.
PHILIP: I'm sorry I couldn't get up in the spring . . . I've been pretty busy. (*Pause. It's difficult.*) . . . I wish I could have been of more help . . .
CARLION: Help? Oh yes. No, no.
(*There's silence in the room. A horse whinnies somewhere.*)
What is it you're doing now, exactly?
PHILIP: (*Fractionally surprised*) Do some journalism. Pays rather well. And I've been handling a few things here and there.
(*Pause*) I see Randolph and co., now and again, in the Commons bar, but they're not much fun these days.
(*Pause*).
CARLION: I killed a man with my bare hands once. In France.

(PHILIP*'s face tightens very slightly.*)

Why didn't you serve?

PHILIP: Father, you know why I didn't serve . . .

CARLION: You look all right to me.

PHILIP: I am all right. Except for military duties.

CARLION: I could've put in a word. Didn't you want to fight?

PHILIP: (*Distinctly*) I was declared unfit to fight. Whether I wanted to fight never was and is not now material.

(*They look at each other for a moment.* CARLION *grins.*)

CARLION: We always play games, you and me. Frederic was serious and the girls were silly darlings or invisible . . . With you I could play games . . .

PHILIP: I come from a long line of sober villains. (*Waves glass along ancestral portraits.*) Gamblers to a man. Good God, Black Bart won the brewery and the whole caboodle on the throw of a single dice, didn't he?

CARLION: (*Seriously*) Not at all. It was cards and he played all night for it.

(PHILIP *laughs, liking him.* CARLION *chuckles.*)

Is that what you call him, Black Bart?

PHILIP: (*Laughing again*) Yes it is. Actually it was Ginnie called him it first . . .

CARLION: Very funny.

(*The laughter fades.* CARLION *stands to pour more wine. They drink, eye each other.*)

Have you spoken with your mother?

PHILIP: (*Fluent*) I said hello for a moment.

CARLION: Good. Your mother understands none of this. (*Pause.*) Let me speak a little. Let me say one or two things. I am not the man I was. As a matter of fact, I am sometimes not even the man I am. (*Pause.*) In a year, two at the most, I want to be done and on my way. (*Pause.*) Frederic . . . Frederic's son Robert is a great disappointment. Very stupid. Quite sloppy. (*Grave suddenly*) I have to *care*, Pip.

(PHILIP *nods, blinks, the feelings difficult.*)
He can't be given Carlion's. Might as well sluice it down the loo. (*Pause.*) Edward's too old, not the man for the times. That leaves the families – Oliphant, probably, Wheldon perhaps. Or there's you.
(*A long moment. It's as if* PHILIP, *knowing it was coming, had failed to prepare himself for how it would feel to hear it. He gets up, crosses to a bookshelf, touches things softly.*)

PHILIP: Pop, I broke with all this . . . ten years ago.

CARLION: You weren't my eldest son then.

PHILIP: (*Gently*) With respect, Pop, I don't consider that to be the most important thing about me. (*Pause. Turns. Tries a grin.*) Don't even drink the beer . . .

CARLION: We don't make beer to drink it, we make beer to . . .

PHILIP: *You* do.

CARLION: (*With force*) *We* do. (*Pause*) You are what you are, have what you have, *because* we do. Eton, Oxford . . .

PHILIP: I loathed Eton . . .

CARLION: Nevertheless. (*Pause.*) Beer made you a gentleman. As it did us all. And you're still that, whatever your other deficiencies.

PHILIP: (*Smiling*) What, my fallen arches you mean?

CARLION: (*Matter of fact*) I mean your lack of wife, clubs and decent clothes.
(PHILIP *inspects his suit carefully. Takes cigarette from gold case, lights it.*)

PHILIP: It's a perfectly good suit . . . (*Eventually*) Do the families know it's what you want?

CARLION: Haven't told 'em, but they know.
(*The gong sounds sharply for lunch. There's a knock at the passage door and* ASHFORD, *temporary part-time butler, limps in. The gong sounds again. He waits until it subsides, fingering his loose-fitting jacket.*)

ASHFORD: Lady Carlion wished me to let you know that luncheon is served, Sir Frederic.

CARLION: Thank you, Ashford.

(*The gong sounds again. He waits.*)

Thank her ladyship and tell her I am not yet so decrepit that I cannot hear the bloody gong being struck outside my door by what would seem to be an aboriginal brandishing a crowbar.

ASHFORD: I will, sir.

(*He limps out.* PHILIP *has watched* ASHFORD, *puzzled.* CARLION *has stood for the tirade; looks now at his watch, suddenly distracted.* PHILIP *watches* CARLION; *sees the sudden frightening frailness.*)

CARLION: Would like an answer, Pip. Tomorrow evening latest. Like to put a stop to the chatter.

PHILIP: (*Carefully*) In the meantime . . . what about a spot of lunch?

CARLION: If we must.

(*He opens the hall door, precedes* PHILIP *out.*)

INT. HALL. DAY

Movement as people converge on dining room. CARLION *stops, a few paces in.*

CARLION: Where's the nearest lavatory?

PHILIP: (*Pointing through study*) On the right.

CARLION: Oh yes.

(*He returns to study.* PHILIP *goes on, overtaken by* NIGEL *and* TEDDIE. *Laughter from the stairway area, as people descend.* NANNY *in from outside. She carries a large shovelful of horse manure.* ALICE *and* DOLL *approaching from stair area.*)

PHILIP: Hello, Nanny.

NANNY: (*At once*) Hello, Master Philip. I'm taking this to my room. I've had my eye on it for a couple of days.

PHILIP: Looks just about ready, Nanny . . .

(*She's gone, smiling sweetly.* FAITH *has appeared.* PHILIP *offers* DOLL, *resplendent in couture and maquillage, his arm.* ALICE *walks through him, calm, amused.* PHILIP *and* DOLL *walk elegantly in. Behind them,* HARCOURT *explains the problem of India to*

MARGARET. *Cobs of it bounce around the room, as it empties.*)

HARCOURT: . . . India's a geographical not a *national* entity. You might just as well call the equator a nation as call India one. Poor bloody wogs'd be at each other's throats before we'd packed our puttees. That's the current thinking, anyhow . . .

MARGARET: (*Fading*) It's odd, I'd always somehow imagined they were all just . . . Indians . . .

(*It's empty. Stillness.*)

EXT. TERRACE. DUSK

Bring up clink of glasses, hubble, church clock striking six. Slow mix to Seal Park. On the edge of evening. Terrace. Long developing shot, one large relaxed group fringed by children. The sound is wild-track, fractured from the action. The scene is half real, half spectral. DAISY *and* DOLL *are close, enjoying each other, friends and competitors since schooldays.* NANNY *walks the baby in a tall pram. The boys rag* TEDDIE'S SISTER *about something. She works at being above it.* LINDSEY *sits on a fringe, neglected, husbandless.* PHILIP *sits between* ALICE *and* MARGARET, *quite close to his mother, doing tricks with coins, glances occasionally at* FAITH, *who sits quietly by* LINDSEY *on the observational side of participation.* ASHFORD *limps out through ballroom french windows, to speak with* DAISY. ROBERT *appears, approaches* PHILIP, *stoops to say something.* PHILIP *shakes his head, easily. Says something. Laughter from* DAISY, DOLL, MARGARET. ALICE *smiles.* ROBERT *straightens, walks back towards the house, stops to pass a word with* OLIPHANT FILS *and* JAMES BLAIR, *in uniform, who stand by the parapet, and who seem to be discussing the world quite importantly. Whiffs of tapeshot.*

DAISY: And how have you found South Africa? Odd to think of you out there, Doll . . .

DOLL: It's not *jungle,* Daisy. There *is* the odd settlement, that sort of thing . . . (*Grinning*) God, but it's a dreary place . . . And it's not as if it's *near* anywhere . . .

DAISY: What's the name they're giving Kensington, Margaret?

MARGARET: (*Interrupted*) Fremantle.

DAISY: Fremantle. Yes, I thought so. (*To* DOLL) Telephone exchange.

DOLL: (*Reflecting*) What's wrong with Kensington?

DAISY: Couldn't say. Some . . . clerk didn't like it, shouldn't wonder. You heard about the Trees?

DOLL: Heard what about the Trees?

DAISY: I'll tell you later.

DOLL: What, *scandale*?

DAISY: Later. Philip, do you have a *white* cigarette? You should've stayed on the stage . . .

DOLL: I couldn't act.

DAISY: Ladies *don't* act. Ladies are.

PHILIP: Saw a young man doing this one to a cinema queue in Leicester Square. (*Matched, though not synchronously, with a shot of two pennies svelting across the knuckles of his two hands. The pennies disappear. The fists roll and open, revealing them.*)

ALICE: (*Amused*) Is it true you saw *Peter Pan* six times in a week when you were a boy, Philip?

PHILIP: Six times in four days. It remains to this day my favourite work of dramatic literature. I was also rather smitten by the young woman playing Peter.

(*Laughter.*)

ALICE: I bet you were . . .

ASHFORD: (*Kentish*) Cook says she needs numbers for the big dinner this evening, milady.

DAISY: Thank you, Ashton.

ASHFORD: Ashford, ma'am.

DAISY: Yes. I suggest you have a word with Sir Frederic about the big dinner, Ashford . . .

MARGARET: Where *do* you get them, Mother?

DAISY: Enough, Margaret. Servants is not a subject I wish to discuss. This war has treated no one well . . .

LINDSEY: I still haven't worked them out. *Who* they are, I mean. I've been married to Robert almost two years and I still have no idea who these people are to each other . . .

FAITH: It takes time. It'll come.

LINDSEY: How long did it take you? I mean, to be accepted?

FAITH: Accepted? Ah, I see. That's something else entirely.

LINDSEY: I bet it was years, wasn't it . . .?

PHILIP: Blackie. Blackie Ashford.

MARGARET: Blackie what?

PHILIP: Ha . . .

INT. BALLROOM. DAY

Track ROBERT *through ballroom, being stripped and rolled back for the dance. Terrace sounds recede, click of billiard balls, slow, measured, begins to grow, as he crosses the sitting room.*

OLIPHANT (SEN.): (*From billiard room*) Does this thing *have* to wait for Philip before we can hear it?

CARLION: (*From billiard room*) We'll wait, if it's all the same, Andrew. Harcourt thinks he might get something big in the next government.

(ROBERT *reaches the doorway, stands discreetly inside it, awaiting a moment.*)

Housing, was it, Harcourt?

INT. BILLIARD ROOM. DAY

CARLION *stands by the table, cue in hand.* EDWARD CARLION, OLIPHANT PÈRE, MATTHEW HARCOURT, GUY WHELDON *sit in shirt sleeves, randomly dispersed around the room on leather wall-benches. They drink whisky from fat glasses. There are half-forgotten cues between legs.*

HARCOURT: Housing or something like it. Wouldn't mind something at the Foreign Office, as a matter of fact . . .

(CARLION *sees* ROBERT *in doorway. Looks his question.*)

ROBERT: Can't budge him, Grandfather, sorry. Says he's enjoying himself too much on the terrace.

(CARLION *nods tersely. He sits down by* EDWARD, *cradling the cue.*)

HARCOURT: (*Exchanging look with* OLIPHANT) Bachelor gay.

(ROBERT *resumes his seat on the edge of the group.*)

EDWARD: (*Looking at* CARLION) Makes no matter, Freddie.

HARCOURT: (*Taking* OLIPHANT*'s look easily*) Seems my father-in-law's in one of his gnomic moods. If it's Carlion's you want to talk about, the Board's all but assembled . . . (*Waves round room.*) . . . I'm sure Robert here can speak for Alice . . .

(*A horse neighs, quite close to the house.* CARLION *has begun chalking his cue.*)

WHELDON: I certainly think we *should* talk, this week. (*Pause.*) We have to begin filling the vacuum.

CARLION: (*As if just asked about his own*) How old's *your* boy now, Guy?

(WHELDON *blinks, frowns, thinks, but reluctantly, can't work it out.*)

WHELDON: (*Finally*) Twelve.

CARLION: Twelve, eh. Mmm. (*Pours a glass of whisky.*) I'm seventy. (*Looks at* EDWARD, *his only ally in the room. Grins.*) In another ten or fifteen years I'll be on the shelf. (CARLION *cackles, pleased with himself, stands.*) Is it me?

(CARLION *prepares to continue the game.*)

OLIPHANT: (*Slightly stiff*) I think I've had enough of games, as a matter of fact . . .

(*The door opens and an old man pushes a bicycle into the room. He's dressed in baggy shorts, leather shoes, white short-sleeved shirt and elasticated green sun-shield. His skin has been flushed red and brown by the sun. He's* SIR PIERS BLAIR, *seventy-two, flea-like, a tallish, upper-class Frank Randle.*)

CARLION: (*Mildly, not fazed*) Peephole, what the hell are you doing here?

BLAIR: (*Faint Scots trace*) I'm looking for somewhere to put my bike, Freddie. Last time I was here I had a set of Indian clubs lifted . . .

Ha.I'll have a whisky.
(*He props his bicycle against the wall, takes the glass from* CARLION. *No discernible surprise at his appearance or behaviour.*)

CARLION: We were just talking about young Jimmy.

BLAIR: (*Sitting next to* EDWARD) Back from India. Is he here?

CARLION: Arrived this afternoon. And your sister Doll.

BLAIR: You don't say.

EDWARD: Didn't expect you, Piers.

BLAIR: Wasn't going to come, Eddie. Changed my mind, got on my bicycle. (*Looks up the room.*) Who's that?
(HARCOURT *smiles.*)

CARLION: Matthew. Margaret's husband. Member for Heathfield.

BLAIR: Course it is. That's Guy Wheldon. Oh, and Oliphant, is it?
(OLIPHANT *smiles stiffly,* EDWARD *trying to head him off.*)

EDWARD: You rode from *Scotland*?

BLAIR: Left Election Day. How did it go, by the way?

EDWARD: Still counting. Soldiers' vote.

BLAIR: Something to tell you, Freddie, can't remember what it is.
(*Noise of several horses, close to the house.*)
(*With a lot of power*) Well, we beat you Oliphant. Fair and bloody square. And your bloody nahzee friends'll be dancing on the end of a rope by Christmas. Hee hee.

OLIPHANT: (*Bored*) Sir Piers, will you please not persist in this ludicrous calumny. You are senile, sir.

BLAIR: (*Contained*) Wrong, sir. You kissed von Ribbentrop's arse, do you deny it? Before the war.

CARLION: (*Standing*) Come on, Peephole, we'll get you a room.

OLIPHANT: (*Almost at the same time as* CARLION, *patient*) Yes, I knew von Ribbentrop, as did Lord Halifax, the Astors . . .

BLAIR: More *dogshit*. (*He stands. To* CARLION) Remembered. What's a horse doing in the hall?
(FAITH *enters quite quickly. No panic, more puzzled concern.*)

FAITH: Someone appears to have turned the horses out of the barn, they're all over the place. The stable lads are rounding them up.

CARLION: (*Bored by it already*) Tell whatsisname, Faith. We're playing.

FAITH: It's under control. Only there appear to be people in the barn.

CARLION: People? What people?

(FAITH *shakes her head.*)

Well, call the police.

FAITH: (*Levelly*) I did. They're coming.

CARLION: Good. Maybe they could stay to dinner.

(FAITH *leaves coolly, untouched by his casual cruelty.* CARLION *goes to the table, plays a slow, deliberate in-off red in top pocket. Looks down the room, at* BLAIR, *then at* OLIPHANT.) Gentlemen. This war is over. We will *all* need each other, when the peace comes.

(*Pause. Nobody speaks. The darkening room has grown grave.*)

EDWARD: I think we might drink to that.

(*He wanders round, topping up. Distant shouts from the lawn, as horses are cornered and caught.* CARLION *holds his glass up. The others are raised, finally. He drinks. We hold him in close-up for some time, master at any rate of this moment. Very slow mix, through his face, to:*)

INT. HALL. DUSK

A white horse stands stockstill inside the open doorway, feet slightly spread, as it noses the room. Bring up fiddle and concertina music, singing, jollity, very vivid, boisterous sound.

EXT./INT. STABLES. NIGHT

Stables, box doors open, a fiddler playing, squatters dancing, singing, drinking cider. Dogs bark, kids watch from high vantage points. A small fire crackles under hanging pots. There's a Grapes of Wrath *lorry parked untidily in the courtyard.*

EXT. SEAL PARK. NIGHT

CARLION *and* EDWARD, *in evening dress, and* JAMES BLAIR, *in Captain's Blues, stand watching the stables some way away. Behind them, the lit house. Their point of view. Two policemen, one in uniform, have reached the stables door. One knocks. The three men again, staring dispassionately. The stables music stops. We become aware of the music from the house, a five-piece strict tempo hokey-cokey.*

INT. BALLROOM. NIGHT

About fifty people gathered, gentry and acceptable professionals from the area, most of them bloodlessly following the royal example of the Queen Mother in the new democracy of the dance floor. Flashes of DAISY, *getting in the nods, circling the room's perimeter. The dancing is vulgar, but without gut. The 'whole side in' is particularly anaemic.*

EXT. SEAL PARK. NIGHT

CARLION *watching the stables intently. The music has started up down the slope. On the reverse, we see the two policemen approaching the waiting group. The constable removes his helmet as they arrive. Brief talk:* CARLION *terse, peremptory; his brother soothing; the plainclothes man placatory, deferential.* CARLION *turns on heel towards the house.*

INT. BALLROOM. NIGHT

Dispersal of hokey-cokeyers. DAISY *fixes* FAITH *across the room, nods tersely in the direction of sitting room.* FAITH *returns the nod, crosses to the glass doors, as the bandleader discreetly trails the imminence of the last waltz.* MARGARET, *on duty, joins her mother.* DAISY *ignores her.*

INT. SMALL DRAWING ROOM. NIGHT

FAITH *enters through glass door.* SIR PIERS *and* NANNY *play backgammon.* OLIPHANT (SEN), ROBERT *and* LINDSEY, HARCOURT, WHELDON *and* ALICE *sit down the room talking seriously.* FAITH *approaches.*

OLIPHANT: He wouldn't dare. No, no. The man's an outsider. Utterly unfitted . . .

HARCOURT: He's a Carlion. And therefore no fool.

ALICE: (*Seeing* FAITH*'s approach*) Ah, the plain and simple Faith, in whom there are reportedly no tricks . . .

FAITH: Lady Carlion would like you to join the company in the ballroom for the Last Waltz . . .

ALICE: Oh God. I knew it. Death by trampling . . .
(LINDSEY *laughs, innocently.* ALICE *blinks once at her.*)

HARCOURT: (*Relieved*) Yes, yes of course, Faith, glad to. 'D like a word, actually . . .

FAITH: (En route) Could it wait, Matthew, I have to tell the others . . .

INT. HALL. NIGHT

JAMES BLAIR *is addressing fellow officers and girlfriends.* OLIPHANT (JUN) *is listening to* ELIZABETH.

ELIZABETH: The games mistress has warts and veins all over, she looks like cheese . . .

OLIPHANT: (*Desperate*) Cheese doesn't *have* warts.

ELIZABETH: Veins. Cheese has veins.

JIMMY BLAIR: I don't think there's much to worry your pretty head about, my dear . . . We can handle the Russians, provided the Americans don't welch on the thing . . .
Personally, I don't believe anyone who matters has fallen for this Uncle Joe nonsense. They're our enemies . . . and will be treated as such . . . when the time comes . . .

(FAITH *arrives, begins her gather of the families.*)

FAITH: Lady Carlion wonders if you would care to join the company in the ballroom for the Last Waltz . . .

(*They disperse.* FAITH *moves off to the ballroom.*)

INT. BALLROOM. NIGHT

FAITH *walks back through ballroom, building for the Last Waltz.* DAISY *watches her as she listens to a woman describing the East End evacuees they'd taken in.* FAITH *passes* DAISY, *waiting for the troops, crosses to the door leading to hall.*

DAISY: (*As they advance*) At last. Margaret, Doctor Rankin, the bald man in the corner . . . (*Suppressing* MARGARET*'s ritual protest*) . . . off you go. Matthew, Canon Partridge's daughter, see her, with the eye-glasses . . .

(HARCOURT *accedes.*)

I don't see Doll . . . Alice, by the window, Mr Joseph . . .

ALICE: (*Glass in hand*) The Jew?

DAISY: (*Pleasantly*) The Jew. He's perfectly civil.

(*The waltz is about to begin.*)

ALICE: (*Looking for* DAISY) I was hoping for Philip.

DAISY: I believe Philip is spoken for.

(*Music: action.*)

ALICE: I believe I'll sit this one out, Daisy, if it's all the same . . .

(*The two look at each other calmly, almost sub-textually.* ALICE *moves back towards the sitting room.* ROBERT *and* LINDSEY *pass* ALICE en route.)

ROBERT: (*On move*) Not dancing, Mother?

ALICE: Not dancing, darling. (*Glass*) Drowning.

(ROBERT *smiles, frowning, and has gone, closing doors behind them.*)

INT. SMALL DRAWING ROOM. NIGHT

ALICE *walks the length of the room.* ASHFORD *appears, with a tray of drinks.* ALICE *takes one.* ASHFORD *limps on to the backgammon players.*

SIR PIERS: Where'd you get the leg, young man? Catch a jerry bullet?

ASHFORD: Caught in a trap, sir.

(ALICE *drinks, on slow fuse.* ASHFORD *limps back into frame. She holds the glass out for him to take.*)

NANNY: We called them wellingtons, after the Duke . . . my father saw him ride by once. Such a fine man. Very musical. (*Rolls dice. Little gasp of delight. It's another double.* SIR PIERS *clutches his head.*) I always had a soft spot for Mr Chamberlain, you know . . .

SIR PIERS: (*Muttering*) In the bloody head, I presume, Nanny . . .

INT. BALLROOM. NIGHT

We watch the families progressing round the room. DAISY *invigilates.* JIMMY BLAIR *comes in through hall passage door, shepherded by* FAITH: *he spends some time selecting a partner.* FAITH *stands for a moment, fraying very slightly, masking well: mainly though, she's avoiding* DAISY*'s insistent stare for information.* PHILIP *looms suddenly, face by her shoulder.*

PHILIP: Damn. I've just remembered I promised this dance to Alice, but you look . . . (*Coward*) . . . so perfect in this light, this . . . setting. May I?

FAITH: Dare I make an enemy of Alice?

PHILIP: Dare you make her a friend?

FAITH: You may.

(*It's fast, unforced, perfect patter. He takes her to the floor and into his formal arms. Smiles up the room at his mother.*)

PHILIP: What are *your* people like, Tattie?

FAITH: Father was a bank manager. Mother was a bank manager's wife.

PHILIP: Oh yes, I did know that.

FAITH: Why do you ask?

PHILIP: (*Laughing*) I may need to get married. Rather quickly.

FAITH: You? How bizarre.

PHILIP: (*Chuckling*) Yes, isn't it?

FAITH: I see. So this is a sort of vetting.

PHILIP: You have it. Good girl. We'll have to see if we can't get you on to *The Brains Trust*.

(*They laugh*.)

Why haven't you married?

FAITH: (*Thinking*) I don't like men particularly . . .

PHILIP: Really? There was a time I thought you were sleeping with the Old Man . . .

(FAITH *looks at him coolly: laughs. He laughs*.)

Never wanted children then.

FAITH: Yes. I've wanted children.

(ASHFORD *appears in the hall passage doorway, waves awkwardly at* PHILIP, *who draws* FAITH *to the door*.)

ASHFORD: Sir Frederic wondered if he might have a word, Sir Philip. He's in the big 'all.

PHILIP: Can it wait?

ASHFORD: He told me to tell you it was important, Sir Philip.

PHILIP: Thank you, Blackie.

(ASHFORD *blinks, turns, limps off towards the hall.* PHILIP *smiles briefly, gestures* FAITH *to join him. She puts her arm in his*.)

INT. CORRIDOR. NIGHT

FAITH *and* PHILIP *walk slowly arm in arm, down to the corridor to the hall.*

FAITH: Why do you call Ashford Blackie?

PHILIP: Why does he call me Sir Philip?

FAITH: Playing safe, I should think. I suspect it's his first post, actually . . .

PHILIP: What happened to Blinkers?

FAITH: He died.

PHILIP: Oh.

(*They arrive at the doors to the hall. Strains of waltz from the ballroom. Applause. Hum of chatter.*)
I hadn't actually finished.
(*Her brows lift.*)
The vetting.

FAITH: (*Amused*) Shouldn't you see what your father wants?

PHILIP: Another time?
(FAITH *is dry, within the game.*)

FAITH: By all means.
(*He looks at her quickly, judging the tone. She's pleasant, inscrutable.*)

PHILIP: (*Slim smile*) Your room or mine?
(*She smiles.*)

INT. STAIRWELL. NIGHT

By the drawing-room door, a youngish balding man stands in his mac, hat in hands, unattended and uncomfortable. EDWARD *hobbles from him to* PHILIP *and* FAITH, *who approach from the hall.*

EDWARD: Good, you're here . .

PHILIP: Anything the matter, Uncle?

EDWARD: (*Indicating*) Have a word with the inspector chappie there, will you, Pip . . . Your father stomped off, refused to speak with him . .

PHILIP: Yes, of course.
(EDWARD *smiles at* FAITH, *excusing himself.*)
Philip Carlion, Sir Frederic's son, how do you do.

INSPECTOR: (*Kentish*) Inspector Cotton, sir. Tonbridge CID. The Chief Constable asked me to look into this barn thing . . .
(PHILIP *gestures, they move into the drawing room.*)

INT. DRAWING ROOM. NIGHT

PHILIP: Very decent of him. Will you have a drink?

INSPECTOR: I won't, thank you, sir.

(*He's distracted for a moment by* ASHFORD *as he limps by. Stares, frowns, trying to fit the face.* PHILIP *smiles thinly, looks at* ALICE, *who raises ironic salute with glass, which he returns, and on to the* INSPECTOR.)

PHILIP: What news do you bring, Inspector?

INSPECTOR: Well, sir, as I tried to explain to your father, sir, we'll get them out just as soon as we can, but it'll take a little time . . . I know it's a very unpleasant thing to happen, valuable horses sleeping out and that, but we'd all be wise to go a bit steady, sir, if you take my meaning . . .

(PHILIP *is neutral: takes cigarette from gold case.*)

PHILIP: Steady.

INSPECTOR: (*Eyeing case*) There's been quite a rash of it, sir . . . Houses, mostly. First barn we've encountered. Still, the principle holds; it's trespass and they're for it. But I think we should . . . keep our heads about it, sir . . . Things are quite delicate just now . . . There's a widespread feeling that people have earned the right to a decent roof over their heads . . . You know the sort of thing, sir . . .

PHILIP: Yes.

(*Music reaching final slowed-down chords.*)

INSPECTOR: . . . and I've had word there's a couple of reporters down from London snooping around in the area, so all in all we'd counsel patience and understanding for a day or two . . . at least until the election's declared and so on . . . if you take my meaning, sir.

PHILIP: Yes. I think I take your meaning, Inspector.

(JIMMY BLAIR *wanders in.* HARCOURT *and* MARGARET, GUY WHELDON *follow.*)

It was good of you to call.

INSPECTOR: Not at all, sir.

(*He's distracted by shout from up the room:* SIR PIERS *has spotted* JIMMY BLAIR.)

SIR PIERS: (*Shouting*) Jimmy boy, come here and tell your

grandfather how we licked the nahzees . . . (*He crows, a little pissed, at* OLIPHANT *on his right.*) I don't think Oliphant here actually believes it . . .

(PHILIP *takes the* INSPECTOR *to the stairwell and thence to the hall.*)

INT. STAIRWELL. NIGHT

INSPECTOR: We'll be in touch. Nice party, sir.

(*He leaves. In the hall* DAISY *is saying goodbye to guests, helped by* FAITH. ALICE *has approached, glass in hand, stands quite close in the doorway to the drawing room.*)

ALICE: Imagine doing this for the rest of your life. Strike a chill?

(PHILIP *smiles, shivers ironically.*)

There was a telephone call for you . . . you were dancing . . .

PHILIP: No message?

ALICE: (*Shakes head.*) None needed.

(*He nods, meaning taken.*)

Very bold, aren't we . . . It must be the war gives us our . . . courage . . .

(PHILIP *looks at Alice's glass.*)

PHILIP: Very likely. (*To* FAITH, *who's fetching something from the stair recess.*) Where's the nearest telephone, Tats?

(FAITH *points to the one in the stair recess. He shakes his head.*)

FAITH: Sir Frederic's study, then . . .

(FAITH *moves back to* DAISY *in the hall.*)

ALICE: (*Casual*) What a capable girl.

(*They exchange a look.*)

What did you say to your father?

(PHILIP *studies* ALICE *for a moment. The grandfather clock begins striking: eleven.*)

PHILIP: I said I'd think on it. (*Pause*) Playing for time, sister-in-law.

ALICE: Did he mention I was thinking of seeking a Royal Warrant for the title Frederic would have had?

PHILIP: Really? How quaint. No, he didn't. Excuse me.

(*He leaves for the study.* DAISY *and* FAITH *approach from the hall.* DAISY *watches* PHILIP *leave.*)

DAISY: *Now* where's he going?

FAITH: He said he had a business call to make . . .

DAISY: Business? What business? Slippy man.

(*She goes into the drawing room.*)

INT. DRAWING ROOM. NIGHT

DAISY: (*Pours whisky.*) I'll take this to bed.

(LINDSEY *and* NANNY *say their goodnights.* DAISY *smiles tiredly.*) (*To gathering*) Breakfast in the Dining Room tomorrow, I've asked Frederic to have the wireless put in there . . .

(*Men stand to say goodnight to* DAISY. *She moves towards staircase passage,* EDWARD *with her.*)

INT. STAIRWELL. NIGHT

DAISY: Have you seen Frederic?

EDWARD: Daisy, am I my brother's keeper? Probably gone for a walk.

DAISY: And Doll? I don't see Doll.

FAITH: (*Casual*) Bed, I think. Said she had a head.

(DAISY *sniffs, nods, sips, sees* NIGEL *and* TEDDIE *in dressing-gowns squatting on the stairs. Glares at them, suddenly fierce. They scarper. She follows them slowly.*)

DAISY: (*To* EDWARD, *over shoulder.*) Don't let him tire himself, will you.

INT. DRAWING ROOM. NIGHT

People begin sorting themselves out in the large room. A man appears suddenly from the ballroom. One of the guests, but a stranger to everyone in the room. They look at him for a moment. It's MR JOSEPH.

JOSEPH: (*Embarrassed, hopeless*) Oh, excuse me, I'm terribly sorry, I've been trying to find my way out . . .

FAITH: (*Smiling*) Well, you made it. Straight ahead.

JOSEPH: Much obliged.

(*He crosses the hall, smiling tightly, deference and panic sharing his soul. A brief silence.* ALICE *laughs once, a bright bark.*)

INT. BILLIARD ROOM. NIGHT

Close up CARLION, *in darkness, pressed to wall, a single desk light from the adjacent study passage faintly establishing his face through the half-open door. We hear several lines of the telephone call through the study's open door, before cutting to* CARLION*'s point of view. During the call, cut in* PHILIP*'s face, as he studies the picture of* VIRGINIA *in silver frame on* CARLION*'s desk; and to* PHILIP*'s cigarette case, which he plays idly with as he talks.* PHILIP*'s voice, perspectived but quite distinct.*

PHILIP: (*Out of shot, persuasive, intimate*) Nikki, I'll try for Saturday evening, don't make me give promises I might have to break. (*Listens. Chuckles.*) Don't be a hussy, I'll smack your bottom for you . . . Look, I have to get back. Yes. (*Warmer*) Yes. Yes, I miss you. Mmm. All right. Goodnight, Nikki. *A bientôt.* (*Receiver replaced.*) CARLION*'s point of view, through adjoining door.* PHILIP *sits on in* CARLION*'s chair for a moment longer, then rises, crosses in* CARLION*'s direction to the door, leaves.* CARLION *waits some moments longer, then eases the adjoining door to and locks it behind his back. He stands looking inwards on the room. From his point of view we see only darkness. The billiard light clocks on. We see* DOLLIE, *hand on light cord. They look at each other.*)

DOLLIE: Wa.

CARLION: (*Agreeing*) Mmm. (*Pause.*) It's like watching a man shit. (*He crosses to a leather wall bench, sits on it.*) Where were we?

DOLLIE: (*Chuckling*) I don't remember.

(*Pause.*)

CARLION: They're in my barn. It's wrong. It's wrong.

DOLLIE: (*Soothing*) Sh. Sh.
CARLION: What're you worth now, Doll?
DOLLIE: No idea.
CARLION: Where is it all, South Africa?
DOLLIE: Some of it.
CARLION: What's his name, your fourth?
DOLLIE: Van Der Biek. Bert. Why, are you short?
CARLION: You could do worse. (*Silence.*) Doll.
DOLLIE: Mmm?
CARLION: Give us a kiss, old love.

(DOLLIE *takes his outstretched hands. Bends to kiss him. The kiss is fat, quite lusty, tongues wetly in evidence, but with ultimately no build, a thing-in-itself. Finally he pulls her on to his knee and places his head on her bosom.*)

Should've married me, Doll.

DOLLIE: Ha. You were always lover material, Frederic, even all those years ago. Glad you married Daisy?

(*He says nothing.*)

CARLION: Do you think Daisy knows? About us, I mean.
CARLION: Chooses not to, I think.

(*Slight pause.*)

CARLION: Ever had opium, Doll?
DOLLIE: No. I never have.
CARLION: I had opium once. In India. Stuck it up my bum. A fingerful.

(*He shows her on his finger. That's all. She waits, but there's nothing.*)

DOLLIE: How was it?
CARLION: (*Thoughtful*) It was good.

(*Pause.*)

DOLLIE: Do you want me to do anything for you?
CARLION: Like what?
DOLLIE: I don't know. Picked something up in America, my third was mad on it.
CARLION: Oh yes? What was that?

DOLLIE: I don't know if I want to say it. Out loud, anyway.
(*He leans a helpful ear to her lips.* DOLL *whispers for some time. Pulls away eventually for* CARLION*'s reaction. His face is blank. He sits working it out for ever.*)

CARLION: (*Eventually*) I don't understand.

INT. SMALL DRAWING ROOM. NIGHT

Nineteen-year-old JAMES BLAIR, *standing with back to fire, drink in hand, speaking to* ROBERT *and* ANDREW OLIPHANT (JUN.). *Company depleted. Only* ALICE, OLIPHANT (SEN.), HARCOURT *and* WHELDON *remain, an informal group, away from the youths, talking casually. Trail top of speech over image of* CARLION. JAMES *already the brigadier he may become.*

JAMES: It's perfectly simple. It's *perfectly* simple. We attack Russia at once. Hit her hard and for keeps. That's the threat now. Either that, or we say goodbye to India and the whole caboodle . . .

ANDREW: But that's *exactly* what the Germans were saying.
(*There's a silence.*)

JAMES: Well, it doesn't make it any the less true . . .
(ROBERT *nods, baffled.*)

ROBERT: What, you mean to say India'll go communist?

JAMES: Not just India, the whole bloody shoot. Look at Greece, look at Italy, look at this place, for God's sake. Who do you think's behind these squatters, in London, here, if it isn't communists? People need leading. Always have.
(OLIPHANT (SEN.) *approaches.*)

OLIPHANT: I think you should go up now, Andrew.
(*He smiles at the other two. There's a tense moment before* ANDREW *takes his leave silently, hating it.* OLIPHANT *returns to his group, who are standing, ready to retire.*)

HARCOURT: . . . I can't say I think forcing issues is the way forward just now. No point ending up with jam on our snouts . . .
(WHELDON *nods agreement.* ALICE *darkening.*)

OLIPHANT: (*Casually*) I'll give my investment manager a call in the morning, see what he comes up with, Alice (*Pause.*) On the other thing . . . I think we should talk on tomorrow . . .

ALICE: (*Low voice, unconspiratorial*) Absolutely. But my position's clear. Robert, yes. An outsider, possible. Philip, out of the question.

WHELDON: (*Ambling towards stairs*) Robert's too young, Alice. But I know what you mean . . .

(*They move on and out.* HARCOURT *finishes drink, places glass on table.* FAITH *in, checking.*)

HARCOURT: Ah, Faith. Just the girl. Wanted a word.

(*She stands in door, indicating she has things to do. He crosses, follows her out towards stair area.*)

INT. STAIRWELL. NIGHT

HARCOURT: You interested in a job, Faith?

FAITH: I have a job.

HARCOURT: I'm looking for something big in the next government . . . I shall need someone I can trust as private secretary. Bear it in mind. (*Pause.*) Carlion won't live for ever, hmm?

(*He smiles, plods off upstairs. She waits for a moment, then goes into the hall, clicks out a light or two, as the house settles. Sees the desk light on through* CARLION*'s study door. Approaches. Clocks the room's empty.*)

INT. STUDY. NIGHT

FAITH *notices something. Picks up Philip's cigarette case, left by the telephone. Close up the case in her hands. A simple inscription: 'Nikki's'. Over this, a single abrupt cry – of pain, or joy, or wonderment – from a nearby part of the house. She stands, eyes on air, sensing the source.*

EXT. SEAL PARK. NIGHT

Night. The house. A few lights on in upper rooms. A single light on ground floor. Bring up BBC wireless coverage of the first election results.

INT. DAISY'S ROOM. NIGHT

Mute tight shot of DAISY, *sleeping, in moonlight, her teeth glinting in a glass by her bed. Trail a second Labour gain.*

INT. MARGARET'S ROOM. NIGHT

Pillow shot, mute, of MARGARET, *on her back in her sexy black silk nightdress, having her left breast massaged, very slowly, by* HARCOURT*'s right hand. The movement gets slower; stops.* MARGARET *opens her eyes. Her point of view reveals* HARCOURT *sleeps. Another Labour gain.*

INT. CORRIDOR. NIGHT

Corridor, dimly lit. Moving shot of hand holding gold cigarette case. Movement stops. We hear a gentle knock. Another labour gain.

INT. STABLES. NIGHT

Slow walking track (or equivalent) reveals sleeping families bedded for the night. The track stops every few paces; a light flashes; then on.

EXT. HOUSE. DAY

Still, fine, tranquil. A WOMAN *carrying a case approaches the front doors. Begin another sound trail.*

INT. DINING-ROOM. DAY

Wireless on dresser continues to spout. Slow track around half-empty table (no DAISY, CARLION, DOLLIE, SIR PIERS, NANNY); *shell-shocked faces already turning morose.* PHILIP *sitting apart from others, towards top of table, listening impassively. Clock establishes late morning. We hear Harold Macmillan has lost by nine thousand votes at Stockton-on-Tees, the first Cabinet Minister to go. The room whooshes with hurt and fear, as the steel goes in.* TEDDIE *and* WILLIAM *in, laughing and jossing.* GUY WHELDON *kisses his son quiet, with something approaching savagery. The room falls silent again.* OLIPHANT (SEN.) *wipes his lips on a napkin, stands up, leaves the room.*

OLIPHANT: Excuse me. I have some calls to make.

(*The commentary goes on.* PHILIP *studies the families, sizes them up, as they mutter, listen, gasp, shake their heads. A commentator makes the first reference to falling share-prices – industrials, trading, overseas, gilts. The Carlion pictures look down, confident, disinterested. A shot from within the room shows the* WOMAN *approaching the dining room, the battered case in her hands. She wears a belted mac, a black beret. She's thirty-seven, dark, sturdy. She stops, unobtrusive, some feet from the doorway. Looks in. Her point of view of the room. Fainter sounds of wireless ahead of her.* OLIPHANT*'s telephone call from under the stairs to her rear.* JAMES BLAIR *passes, says good morning very properly to the stranger,* en route *for breakfast.*)

INT. STAIRWELL. DAY

The WOMAN *turns away, back towards the staircase, silently taking in the house. She spots* OLIPHANT *in profile at the stair-desk. He's making tight-lipped notes. He asks for breweries, finance houses, home rail, coal, Rhodesian mining, South African diamonds. He says 'What?' in crescent disbelief to each quotation. The* WOMAN *walks on. Sees* NANNY *coming downstairs.* NANNY *sees her suddenly.*

NANNY: My, my. Miss Virginia. Where have you been? My dear girl.

(*She takes* VIRGINIA *in her arms, hugs her child to her little body.*)

VIRGINIA: Hello, Nanny Grump.

NANNY: Big girl now. You *have* grown. I'm going for breakfast. Have to keep my strength up. Everybody's here. Wait till I tell your mother . . .

VIRGINIA: Nanny, where's Daddy?

NANNY: Not seen him. Went to Spain, I think. Try the study.

(*She leaves smiling.* VIRGINIA *places her case down.* OLIPHANT *comes out of the recess, sees* VIRGINIA. *Long silence.*)

OLIPHANT: (*Disbelief, anger, fear, all finally mastered*) Hello, Virginia.

VIRGINIA: (*Levelly*) Hello, Andrew.

(*Pause. Wireless thinly relayed, at this distance.*)

OLIPHANT: Excuse me.

(*He moves off towards dining room.* VIRGINIA *watches him quietly.* OLIPHANT (JUN.) *in from tennis,* ELIZABETH *and the* TWO BOYS *in tow. Stops as he sees* VIRGINIA. *They look at each other in silence.*)

VIRGINIA: Hello, Andrew.

ANDREW: (*Dazed behind the mask*) Hello, Mother.

VIRGINIA: What does one say?

(ANDREW *waits a second.*)

ANDREW: Excuse me. I'm late for breakfast.

(*He passes her and on into dining room.* VIRGINIA *heads for rear of house.*)

INT. DINING ROOM. DAY

Young OLIPHANT *enters dining room. He sits by his father. The room's sepulchral.*

PHILIP: (*To* NANNY) Charlie Chaplin!

(NIGEL *and* TEDDIE *laugh into their napkins.*)

NANNY: (*Adamant*) No.

(FAITH *in. A few covert flicks pass between her and* PHILIP.)

OLIPHANT (SEN.): (*To* WHELDON) It's a disaster. Millions wiped off in an hour's trading. I'll have to get up there . . .

PHILIP: I give up, Nanny. Who did you just meet in the hall?

NANNY: (*Triumphant*) Your sister.

PHILIP: (*Snorting*) Oh Nanny.

NANNY: Virginia.

(*Shots of faces,* PHILIP*'s first, then* OLIPHANT'S, ALICE*'s,* MARGARET*'s, finally* PHILIP*'s again. A cluster of Tory defeats from the wireless.* NANNY*'s very much amused by her* coup *without really understanding it.*)

MARGARET: (*out of shot; eventually*) Don't be silly, Nanny.

OLIPHANT: (*Toneless; out of shot*) It's true. I saw her too.

(*In the background,* MATTHEW HARCOURT, *Under-Secretary at Treasury, loses his seat.*)

INT. HALL. DAY

VIRGINIA *stands outside Carlion's study door, studying the grain of the wood, remembering other times there. Sounds of wireless election coverage from within. She knocks.*

INT. STUDY. DAY

CARLION *stands at the window, looking down towards the barn. The wireless is on but no longer listened to. The knock again, which he hears and ignores. On the desk are an open box of cartridges, a shotgun, and a leather-bound volume, open.*

VIRGINIA: (*Very quietly*) Daddy.

CARLION: (*Slowly, not turning*) Virginia?

VIRGINIA: Happy Something.

(*He turns, very slowly, half expecting to find himself alone in the room. She smiles, gently.*)

Ghosts. That why you have the gun?

CARLION: The gun? (*Sees it.*) No, I have people in my barn, want 'em out . . .

VIRGINIA: (*Softly*) The people are everywhere now, Daddy.

CARLION: (*Sitting at desk*) Thought you might be dead, Gin. Frederic . . .

(*She looks at the room, remembering.*)
I've been looking at old whatsisname's diaries again . . .
(*He indicates portrait of second baronet over mantelpiece.*)

VIRGINIA: Philip.

CARLION: Remember? I used to read them to you . . . ?
(*She nods, facing him. He looks at her, looks down at book, almost shy now. The wireless works relentlessly on: Sir Walter Riddall out in Lincoln, causing low-key stir and speculation about projected size of socialist majority.* PHILIP *enters quietly behind* VIRGINIA *through open doorway, is neither heard nor seen.* VIRGINIA *becomes aware of him during the reading. Pleasure passes between them, and fear for their father's state.*)

CARLION: Eighteen forty-nine. Monday, February 27th. One entry. 'What does it profit a man if he have the whole world and cannot shit of a morning without bleeding?'

PHILIP: (*Easily*) Dad, got to let Ginnie go, Mother wants to see her . . . Hello, Froth.
(*They hug warmly, old friends and allies from the past.* CARLION *crosses to the window, turning his back on the embrace.*)
(*Close, warm but* sotto.) I've got a million things to ask you, I bags you after Daisy. You look . . . changed. And very very beautiful . . . Before lunch, mind . . .

VIRGINIA: (*Laughing*) All right, you're on. Where will I find Mother?
(*She moves to take her leave of her father.* PHILIP, *taking her arm, indicates best not.*)

PHILIP: The Little Room. He'll buck up later . . . You know Andrew's here? And your son?
(*She nods calmly, leaves.* PHILIP *dwells by the door. Watches his father. Sir Oliver Simmonds is beaten in Duddleston.*)

CARLION: She was my daughter. (*Pause. Casual*) Margaret's husband's out. Did you hear?

PHILIP: (*Carefully*) Yes. Bad show.

CARLION: What's happening?

PHILIP: I think it's what they call Letting the People Speak.

CARLION: No, no; in the *City*.

PHILIP: Carlion's down six and threepence in the first half-hour of trading. Want me to do anything?

(*Long pause.*)

CARLION: Everything. Passes.

PHILIP: (*Eventually*) It's possible.

(CARLION *turns, picks gun up from desk, hands it to* PHILIP. PHILIP *frowns, puzzles.* CARLION *sits at desk again, thin hands masking thin face.*)

What am I supposed to do with this, Dad?

CARLION: Whatever is necessary.

PHILIP: (*Distinct*) Father. Go and take a nap.

CARLION: (*Face in hands still*) Do something for me.

PHILIP: You're tired. (*Pause.*) What?

(CARLION *looks at* PHILIP *through his fingers. His eyes are red, exhausted. He says nothing.*)

EXT. SEAL PARK. SUNSET

Snapshots of stables from upper window at front of house. Still day. The shots develop, picking out several unattended horses cropping at will. Wireless sound trail recaps the state of the parties at noon.

INT. NURSERY. SUNSET

Shot of VIRGINIA, *camera poked through upper window. She finishes. Looks on, speaking to someone behind her in the room. A man's head looms over her shoulder in a crude and fierce Lord Kitchener mask. She turns, laughs. The nursery is now a general depository, its traditional infrastructure, rocking horse, swing, toys, desk, etc., buried beneath the accumulated junk of many disused years.*

PHILIP: (*From within mask*) Your country needs you.

(*He points dramatically at her. She laughs again, saddening. He removes the mask.*)

Remember?

VIRGINIA: Freddie made it. Scared Nanny Grump half to death with it in the middle of the night.

PHILIP: That's right. She thought it was old Kitchener himself come to do battle with her body . . .

(*They share the laugh, easier in the past tense, wary about the present.*)

(*Pointing out*) Same old Seal.

(*She looks. Says nothing.*)

See Mother?

VIRGINIA: Yes. (*Pause.*) What are *you* doing here anyway? Thought you'd washed your hands.

PHILIP: Yes. (*Long pause.*) Just couldn't find a towel.

(*He wanders around for a moment, as if seeking one. Sits finally, side-saddle on the headless horse, his feet among trunks and boxes.*)

Not you though, eh?

(*She smiles tightly, looks away out of the window.*)

Go on (*Recapping* VIRGINIA *into the account*) After Spain. I heard from Blair, I think, you were in Madrid in 'thirty-nine. The Foreign Office told father you'd almost certainly been taken by the fascists . . . And then the war covered you up completely.

VIRGINIA: I went to France. Had two remarkable months with a comrade I'd met in Alicante. Went underground.

(*She shrugs.*)

PHILIP: Busy girl. (*Pause.*) Mother thought you didn't write because you were living in sin with somebody else's husband . . .

(VIRGINIA *laughs.* PHILIP *laughs.*)

You tell her all this?

VIRGINIA: What sense could she make of it? (*Pause.*) I mentioned the underground, she thought I was talking about the Métro. . . . A girl's life is marrying, breeding, scheming, for Mother. For all of them. Perhaps even for you, Pip. (*Pause.*) You married or anything?

(*He shakes his head.*)

It was strange seeing my husband again. And the boy. They had

grown . . . unreal . . .
(*She taps a temple. Silence.*)

PHILIP: (*Almost quizzical*) Why, Gin?
(*She looks. Why what?*)
All of it. You left a child, a marriage . . . for what? A trench in Alicante? A cellar in Montmartre?

VIRGINIA: I was young. Very romantic. I felt I needed to . . . purge my guilt for all this, for all it stands for in my person. (*Pause.*) Mainly, though, I wanted to connect.
(*He questions her with his eyes.*)
With history. Which is millions of people living the only life they have but not the only life there is . . . (*She spreads her hand at the estate.*) This has to end, Pip. Not because I still feel guilty about it, but because it really does stand in the way – class, title, privilege, wealth, influence, connection. (*Pause.*) I came back to help.

PHILIP: You were always a bit . . . heroic, Froth. Passionate.

VIRGINIA: Modelled myself on you.
(*He laughs, disturbed, crosses to the swing, sets it in movement.*)

PHILIP: Believe it or not, I saw you from the top of a 37 bus not long ago.
(VIRGINIA *blinks, surprised, off guard.*)

VIRGINIA: Really? Where?

PHILIP: Shoe Lane. Corner of Fleet Street. You were coming out of some office building. You had my camera round your neck.
(*He indicates it.*) I wish you'd called me, Froth.
(*She moves down the room, passes him at the swing, stops to look out of the far wall window beyond.*)
So why are you here now?

VIRGINIA: (*Turning towards him*) Impulse. Self-indulgence. Perhaps a little love. I had some work down here and remembered it was Carlion week. (*Pause. Smile.*) Maybe a hint of masochism too.
(*She turns away, looks out of the window.* PHILIP *joins her there.*
(*That (their) point of view of the barn.*)

PHILIP: (*Out of shot over this*) You heard about the barn people.

(*Close up.*) Hop-pickers mostly. Working Carlion farms. (*Pause.*) Perhaps this is the millennium, do you think? Be nice to think we were . . . making history . . .

(*She looks at him carefully. He stares out of the window, face dry, lips tense. He looks like* CARLION.)

VIRGINIA: Would you object?

PHILIP: Object? Me? Why would I do that?

VIRGINIA: I don't know. I don't know what you believe any more.

PHILIP: (*Weighing it*) Believe. (*Pause.*) In the main I have come to believe that *belief* is not really my bag.

(*Silence. She goes on looking at him. He continues staring out of the window, fiddles a cigarette into his mouth.*)

My crazed father . . . my . . . pathetic father . . . wants me to take over. (*He glances at her suddenly.*) All I have to do is believe. (PHILIP *smiles.*) The old man's been this way since brother Frederic bought it . . . You know about . . .

(*She nods.*)

So.

(*She turns back into the room, dealing with it.* PHILIP *turns, watching her.*)

(*Light*) What work are you doing, Gin?

(*She turns to look at him.*)

Down here?

VIRGINIA: (*Carefully*) It's a piece I'm writing. On the country. (*Pause.*) No one can *make* you do *anything*, Pip. You're your own man.

PHILIP: I know.

VIRGINIA: You especially, Pip.

PHILIP: Absolutely. (*He looks out at the grounds.*) God, but I hate the country.

(VIRGINIA *moves to her original window. Stares out. They stand at separate windows, seeing different things, as it were, back-to-back. In* VIRGINIA*'s point of view we see a Carlion horse-drawn dray pulling up in the forecourt, a single keg of beer on the back, which the cart-driver begins to unload.*)

(*Out of shot.*) Remember Blackie?
VIRGINIA: Blackie Ashford the poacher?
PHILIP: (*Out of shot*) He's butler now.

EXT. SEAL PARK. DUSK

Long shot of house, mid-evening, quite dusky for July. The ballroom shines with light, people. Voices over this image, sotto, *placed inside growing ambient chat.*
PHILIP: (*Casually*) Are you sure you don't mind . . . wouldn't mind?
FAITH: (*Quite easy*) Not at all. Why should I?
PHILIP: Faith, you are *amazing* . . . What do you think *they* would say . . . ?

INT. BALLROOM. EVENING

Shot of table (in area of dining room), filled with flowers, letters, telegrams, presents laid out in glittering patterns. Sound of social chat, glasses and greetings.
FAITH: (*Voice over; simply*) Does it matter?
(*Close up.* PHILIP, *impressed by her cool. He watches her (his point of view) teasing some flowers into place on the display table.*)
PHILIP: Do we call it a deal, Tats?
FAITH: (*Matter of fact*) You're going to have to stop patronizing me, you know.
(*She smiles. He nods, serious. Aahs, exclamations, from the others up the room.* PHILIP *turns to look.* CARLION *and* DAISY *are arriving. They look splendid. Applause breaks out.* DAISY *smiles greetings;* CARLION *is grave but collected. The assembly moves towards the doors to greet the pair.* PHILIP *approaches the fringe. A clock is striking nine. Compliments flow.* DAISY *explains the delay –* MATTHEW HARCOURT *is in the house and is expected to join them soon.* PHILIP *catches* VIRGINIA*'s eye. Like* PHILIP, *she's fringing. Unlike the rest of the women, she wears no make-up, head-adornment or jewellery of any*

kind. FAITH *arrives at* PHILIP*'s shoulder, from behind.*)
(Sotto, *casual*) If we get through *tonight*, we can survive anything . . . (*She moves through the people.*) Lady Carlion, would you like to see the presents and things, I've laid them out by the dining room . . . ?

DAISY: Thank you, Faith. I would indeed. (DAISY *sees* PHILIP *busy fading into the protective background.*) Philip, give me your arm, there's a dear boy. (*To* OLIPHANT (SEN.)) Andrew, the brooch is *very* exotic, quite lovely, thank you . . .
(*The group has begun breaking up.* DAISY *wades on.* PHILIP *joins her. Take her in zoom focus* (*close up*) *from presentation table position.*)
(*To* PHILIP) Dear Ginnie, she looks so . . . meagre, divorce has ruined her, been in *France*, she says – you know, they *say* they served rats, stewed rats in the restaurants – I have never liked the French . . . Aah.
(*Cut to the presentation table.*)
How perfectly . . . (*She searches for the word*) . . . vulgar. (*She touches a few things, reads a few telegrams, casually.*) I had no idea you hated your father quite so much, Philip.

PHILIP: (*Looking around at people in their area*) Mother . . .
(*The part-time butler,* ASHFORD, *limps up.*)

ASHFORD: Would her ladyship care to say where I'm to put the young lads . . . ?

DAISY: Yes, yes, of course . . .
(*She beckons* PHILIP *to accompany her.*)

INT. DINING ROOM. EVENING

PHILIP *crosses to a sideboard, studies something we don't see under a cloth.* DAISY*'s deciding the seating.*

PHILIP: (*Replacing cloth carefully*) Put them next to Virginia. That's what the poor brats want.

DAISY: (*Deliberately, casual*) Well, we can't always have what we want, you know *that*, Philip . . . Thank you, Ashton.

ASHFORD: Ashford, madam.

DAISY: Thank you, Ashford. All looks splendid.

(ASHFORD *leaves. The candles blaze on the table, leaving room quite dark beyond. Silver screams. Twenty place settings.* DAISY *scans.*)

(*Checking a silver fork*) You were saying, Philip . . .

PHILIP: (*Suddenly, deciding something*) Mother, there are things you should know.

DAISY: (*Still busy; light*) Things?

PHILIP: About me. (*He takes out his gold case, lights a cigarette.*) There's someone I care for very much. In town. Someone I in a way live with, but can't marry.

DAISY: So, marry someone you can. That needn't be affected. I assume she's an understanding sort of person . . . ?

PHILIP: It's a man.

DAISY: What's a man? (*She looks at him. He's very straight, serious.*) Oh, I see. (*A sudden, extraordinary cackle.*) What, you mean you're a mashed potato?

PHILIP: Not exclusively. But yes.

DAISY: I see. So?

PHILIP: It's impossible . . .

DAISY: (*Finished; factually*) No, it isn't. (DAISY *moves round the table, passes* PHILIP, *heading for the door. Turns back in to look at him.*) When I was nineteen and just married, I watched the fourth baronet, your father's father, do it to a sheepdog in the Orangery. (*Deliberate pause.*) You are the only person I have ever told. (*Pause.*) You have only to state your terms.

(FAITH *appears in doorway.*)

FAITH: I don't want to alarm anyone, but half the men have disappeared and Sir Frederic was carrying his gun.

PHILIP: I'd better go . . .

(*He moves quickly, energized. Passes* VIRGINIA *in doorway. A look. He's gone.* FAITH *follows him out.* VIRGINIA *stands in doorway. Her mother looks at her.*)

DAISY: Won't you join me?

(VIRGINIA *enters the room.*)

Can you see cigarettes anywhere?

(DAISY *goes on checking things on the table.* VIRGINIA *looks for cigarettes, finds some by the covered object* PHILIP *has looked at. She lifts the cloth. We see a small metal cask with Carlion's, etc., printed on the top. She takes a cigarette and matches to her mother.*)

VIRGINIA: Here.

DAISY: Ah, good. (*She lights one.*) Have you spoken with Philip since you arrived?

VIRGINIA: Yes.

DAISY: How did he seem to you?

VIRGINIA: Changed.

DAISY: Yes. I think he's growing up.

(*They look at each other very frankly for a longish time. Raised voices from stables area. Some cheering, rowdiness.*)

VIRGINIA: (*Grave*) Father always said he'd make a man of him.

(*She turns to leave the room.*)

DAISY: How long do you propose staying?

VIRGINIA: (*In doorway*) I leave tomorrow.

DAISY: As you wish. Be good to your father, won't you. He understands . . . nothing of the last ten years . . . (*She gestures* VIRGINIA*'s last ten years.*) He doesn't realize you left for good.

(VIRGINIA *absorbs her mother's meanings, nods, leaves.* DAISY *sits down, the cost showing.* DOLL *comes in.*)

DOLL: What the hell's going on, Daisy?

EXT. STABLES. NIGHT

PHILIP, *arrived, hard of breath.*

ROBERT: (*Over*) We're shipping them out, Uncle Pip. Great fun eh?

(*Shot of the stables, alive, lit, rowdy, a small fire blazing inside. The men* – JAMES BLAIR, ANDREW, HUGH, OLIPHANT (SEN.), GUY WHELDON, EDWARD CARLION *and* SIR PIERS BLAIR – *stand watching the locked doors, ten or so yards behind* CARLION, *who welts the door with the butt of his gun. The men all have stout walking sticks. Behind the men, at some distance, the boys:* NIGEL, TEDDIE. *Over this last sequence of shots:*)

WHELDON: Minimum force, brother-in-law. It *is* trespass.

(PHILIP *senses the massed weight, the feeling, of the group. He's appalled, fascinated. Watches. The doors open. The stable teems with the squatters, men, women, kids. They're poor, quite ragged: itinerant workers and their families in the main, down from the East End for the hopping. A few chickens scrawn their way around. The barn stills a little, as the gun and the ring of men impinge within. Several men advance a few feet out, protectively.* PHILIP *pushes forward to join his* FATHER, *who has said something to the leading man.*)

MAN: (*Pushing forward, short, gnarled; showing his hands*) See these? (*They're destroyed, ripped away by years of hopping.*) Twenty-eight years I've been coming down here to harvest your hops, and every year we've asked for a pair o' bleeding gloves to do it in. We're through askin'. You know somethin'? This is the best place I've put my head down all year. You treat your horses better than you treat us . . .

CARLION: (*Bleakly*) My horses have names . . .

(*He levels the gun from the hip. The men stare at the gun. Women begin to gather children, drift backwards.* PHILIP *steps between his father and the barn.* CARLION *hands him the gun. Sounds from the barn entrance.*)

MAN'S VOICE: You wanta get that old bugger certified, he's a proper bloody loonie . . .

(PHILIP *stands, back to the stable, his eyes bright, the gun taut in his hands. Trail top of next speech over.*)

INT. DINING ROOM. NIGHT

Slow track round table of listening families.

PHILIP: (*Over*) It's tempting for less fortunate people to see only the tenth of our lives that is, if you like, privilege. What they do not see – and cannot know – is the submerged remainder that is duty. Though perhaps they'd learn something, as indeed I did, from a postscript from my father scrawled on a letter from my mother, sent me while I was still at school. It said: 'Three things to inspire you – God, Family and Country. Not necessarily in that order.'

(*Close up.*) ALICE, *chill smile;* CARLION, *glowing quietly;* DAISY, *brows raised, watchful.*)

(*Close up.*) Blairs, Oliphants, Wheldons, Lansings, Harcourts . . . Carlions . . . I am privileged to propose: the Family.

(*Everyone stands. The family. Some formal, not over-enthusiastic compliments on the puzzlingly fulsome, committed toast.* VIRGINIA *watches, does not join the toast, though she stands. They sit.* PHILIP *remains standing through the chat.*)

If one might be permitted a personal word, ladies and gentlemen . . .

(*Table quietens again.*)

When I came here at the weekend, I was greeted by my father – long noted for his plainness in these matters – with a short but withering list of my deficiencies, three items *in toto*: wife, clubs, clothes.

(*Some laughter.*)

Let it be known, therefore, that in a possible excess of filial piety, I have (1) had myself nominated for White's and the Carlton, (2) made an early appointment with a Tailor of Repute; (3) entered into certain negotiations with a lady – whose name I do not propose to divulge at present – who I trust will not keep me waiting longer than is decent or bearable . . . Thank you.

(*He sits. Surprise, comment.* FAITH *smiles calmly, all brain.*)

ALICE: (*Across the table from* PHILIP, *through speculative chatter.*) You won't overreach yourself, will you, brother-in-law, in this hectic post-war reconstruction . . .

PHILIP: (*Intimate, friendly*) It's difficult to please everyone, Alice. (*He smiles.*) As I think brother Frederic discovered . . .

ALICE: (*Stopped*) Frederic? What's . . .

PHILIP: (*Silk*) I have seen sworn affidavits from members of his company attesting to the manner of his death . . . (*Pause. He pours more wine, smiles charmingly, small-talking.*) I doubt the Palace would be favourably disposed to grant his widow's request for the baronetcy, when Father's gone, should they ever see the light of day . . .

(ROBERT *calls 'Fine speech, Uncle Pip' from down the table.* PHILIP *thanks him.*)

Two stories, remember?

(*Her face is stone. She looks at* FAITH, *on* PHILIP*'s left.* FAITH *looks calmly back at her.* CARLION *stands, at the head of the table. Silence grows. Children are shushed. He stands, head down, for some moments.*)

CARLION: (*Holding glass up*) Daisy.

(*A moment. People stand. 'Daisy'.* DAISY *sits on. Exchanges one look with* CARLION. *Applause. Sittage.* DAISY*'s on her feet.*)

DAISY: Thank you. I think this might prove an appropriate moment for ladies and children to withdraw . . .

(*Women and children stand noisily, the men too, chat welling.* ASHFORD *enters, carrying the port in a coaster, which he sets by* CARLION *at the head of the table.* DAISY *leans over to kiss* PHILIP*'s cheek.*)

(*Casual,* sotto) Wonderful piffle!

PHILIP: (*Kissing her*) Thank you, Mother.

(*She passes on, and out. When the dust settles, we see* VIRGINIA *has not moved. The men resume their seats uncomfortably, a little puzzled, flicking looks at each other.* PHILIP *lights a cigarette.* CARLION *taps the table with his thumbs.* OLIPHANT (SEN.) *coughs.* EDWARD CARLION *blows his nose.*)

VIRGINIA: Could I ask what happened at the barn?

PHILIP: (*After silence*) They were persuaded to move on.

(VIRGINIA *stands eventually, nods, walks slowly out, looking at no one, passing* ASHFORD, *shadowy by the door. They exchange a very brief look.* ASHFORD *looks back towards the table, where the disquiet has been palpable.* CARLION *passes the port round. The atmosphere thickens, darkens, the women gone.* ASHFORD, *outside the light, stares impassively. Sense of strain, tension, expectancy, generating mainly from the senior active males (*OLIPHANT, WHELDON, HARCOURT, EDWARD). *The young men* – JAMES BLAIR, ANDREW OLIPHANT, ROBERT CARLION – *are simply eager.* SIR PIERS *is well pissed, humming snatches of 'We'll meet again' disconcertingly.* PHILIP *looks up the table at* CARLION.)

CARLION: (*At last very rational, at huge cost*) I think it quite important to let you all know that I have asked Philip to take Frederic's place at Carlion's and that he has agreed to do so. Since the major stockholders are present at this table, I'd be interested to receive provisional ratification of the proposal now.

(*Silence.* SIR PIERS *utters 'Don't know where, don't know when' and falls silent. Silence.* PHILIP *broods, very contained.*)

SIR PIERS: Boy made a fine speech.

(*Silence again. Men look at their port.*)

HARCOURT: What, a permanent appointment, you mean?

(*No answer from* CARLION.)

EDWARD: (*Mild, placid*) I don't think anyone here would harbour any doubt about Philip's ability, would they?

OLIPHANT: (*At last*) Managing a major firm isn't just a matter of . . . ability, though, is it? It's a question of will. Desire, if you like. Frankly, I'm surprised Philip wants it . . .

(*He looks in* PHILIP*'s direction.* PHILIP *ignores him.*)

WHELDON: Maybe it's my legal training, but I'd be happier if we could agree what's being proposed here. Is it Philip as Managing Director or Philip as Chairman we're discussing, Frederic?

(CARLION *looks at* PHILIP. PHILIP *stares at his glass.*)

CARLION: (*Wavering*) Well, in the first instance, it may be . . .

PHILIP: Both.

(*The room clenches, draws breath.* PHILIP *looks at each in turn:* OLIPHANT, HARCOURT, WHELDON, EDWARD, *his father,* ROBERT (*who has not spoken*).)

What's the final state of the parties, Matthew?

HARCOURT: One or two still undeclared, but the socialists appear to have a majority approaching two hundred . . .

PHILIP: What's the state of the market, Andrew?

OLIPHANT: (*Reluctant*) Bad . . .

PHILIP: How have your home rail shares done today, Matthew? What about coal, Sir Piers?

(*They have no answer.*) (*Cool. Tough.*) I don't suppose it's entirely slipped your notice, gentlemen, that today, Thursday, 26th July, the people of this country declared war on us. This whole discussion may already be obsolete. Before the year's out, we may all be living in the West Indies on such capital as we've been able to muster from the expropriation of our possessions the socialists have been elected to effect. The ship's *sinking*, gentlemen. That's water around your ankles. (*Pause.*) Now, if I'm to enlist, I shall need safeguards. Crucially, I shall need to know I have sole authority to chart the course ahead. (*Long pause.*) Both. And now.

OLIPHANT: I'm not at all sure we're in a position . . .

HARCOURT: Philip makes sense. I have a copy of the socialists' Election programme in my room, if anyone would care to read it. Or as Winston would have it, the Thieves' Charter. Coal, railways, steel, utilities, medicine, Bank of England . . . and that's only what they say they'll take . . . With this sort of majority, who's to say where they'll stop? Confiscation of land could be on the cards, housing, property taxes, transport, insurance . . . It's not inconceivable they could close the public schools and get rid of the House of Lords altogether. . . . Philip makes sense. They will have to be fought. And the fight will have to be led.

(*Silence.*)

CARLION: (*Suddenly*) Robert?

ROBERT: (*Slowly*) Well, I can't speak for Mother, Grandfather, but . . . for myself, I'd have no difficulty in working with Uncle Pip . . .

EDWARD: Nor me. None at all.

(CARLION *carries on down the table.* HARCOURT *nods;* WHELDON; OLIPHANT *finally, tight-lipped.*)

SIR PIERS; Great pity young Pip didn't fight though, for all that . . .

CARLION: (*Measured*) He will, Peephole. Bank on it.

PHILIP: (*Curt*) Good. I hope you'll call an early meeting of the Board to have it confirmed. (*Pause.*) I shall, of course, expect my father's seat on all your respective boards.

(*Some blinks. No one demurs.*)

Let's drink to that, shall we? (*He crosses to the sideboard, unveils the metal cask we saw earlier, begins filling glasses from the tap.*) I had something special sent down from town. Might take a little getting used to, but in time I think you'll grow to like it . . . Something the Carlion lab boys've been working on . . .

(*He carries a tray of glasses round. The men study the contents, sniff it.*)

(*Back to chair.*) Let me give you: The Future.

(*They drink. No one likes it.* SIR PIERS *spits it out.*)

SIR PIERS: Good God Almighty, weasel piss!

PHILIP: (*Laughing*) Almost. Actually, re-carbonated beer. Half the price to make, travels, keeps for ever. All we have to do is make it taste a little less like weasel piss and we could be in clover . . . (*He holds the glass up.*) Our health.

(VIRGINIA *enters behind* CARLION. *She has changed, wears mac and beret, carries her suitcase. She stares at the surprised men for some moments.*)

Didn't realize you were off so soon. Do you need a car?

VIRGINIA: No.

PHILIP: Gin, this is not your business.

VIRGINIA: No. (*Pause.*) But I've never been able to resist a good funeral. One day – soon, I hope – there'll be a banging at your door. It will be the people. Because they'll be English, they'll probably give you a third-class rail ticket to Dover or Southampton, when they ask you to go. Personally, I would not object if they simply disembowelled you in front of your children and fed your bits to the chickens. Because I feel that, were there a

God, he would want you to suffer for the suffering you cause.
(*Silence of embarrassment. They're in the presence of spectacularly bad form. Finally*:)

YOUNG ANDREW: (*Calm contempt*) I thought the ladies had retired, Mother.
(*She looks at him for a moment, leaves the room without answering.* CARLION *is very white, strained, maybe damaged.* PHILIP *stands, excuses himself, follows* VIRGINIA *out.*)

EXT. HOUSE . NIGHT

VIRGINIA *leaving, bag in hand.* PHILIP *arrives in lit doorway.*

PHILIP: Ginnie, wait.
(*She stops, turns. He approaches her.*)
(*Gently*) Don't go like this, Gin.
(*She glistens whitely in the gloom, says nothing.*)
This is how we are, you know that. 'The rich are always with us'?

VIRGINIA: Oh yes. I know how you are. Thank you for the story.

PHILIP: (*Unfazed*) *Picture Post*, at a guess.

VIRGINIA: Perhaps.

PHILIP: Good copy. (*Pause.*) You won't be friends.

VIRGINIA: (*She turns, walks off.*) (*On move*) Not while there's a war on.
(PHILIP *watches her, gnomically self-contained.* FAITH *appears in the doorway behind. He joins her. They re-enter the house. Stand by the door in the hall, watch the men slowly rejoining the women by the fire. Beyond them, servants move back and forward to the dining room.*)

INT. DINING-ROOM. NIGHT

Philip's place at table. His cigarette case lies on the table. A tattooed hand opens it, extracts a Sobranie Russian; follow up to ASHFORD, *lighting it with candle. Maids up from the village urge each other on with their chores, anxious to finish and get home.* ASHFORD *crosses to the barrel, pours himself a glass, stands, mock elegant, glass in one hand, preposterous cigarette in the other. He raises his glass in toast to the table. There's a hard little smile on his face.*

EXT. SEAL PARK. DAY

Cars line the driveways, as the families leave. We see most of it in long shot, picking out only salient moments for closer attention, e.g. old NANNY *carrying the baby and being helped into Alice's car along with* ROBERT *and* LINDSEY. *Over this*:

ATTLEE'S VOICE: '. . . Here at home we have our own great tasks. We have to bind up the wounds of war. We have to reconstruct our ruined homes – a great task in itself . . . I believe that what we have done this week will give heart to all those all the world over who believe in freedom, democracy and social justice . . . Let us go forward as comrades in a great cause . . . through the difficult years, to the greatest era which is opening before us . . .'
(*We hear the all-clear siren sound.*)

ARCHIVE FILM

Mute film, slowed, of the Hiroshima A-bomb.

EXT. VILLAGE. NIGHT

Mute film. Night. We see PHILIP, *his hands resting on* CARLION*'s wheelchair, faces lit up by fire. Pull slowly out, through fire, to reveal scene. A V.J. bonfire on edge of village. Labourers and their wives dance. Men play mouth-organs, whistles, squeeze-boxes. Dancing, old and young. Drink flows. Happiness, energy. We see the* CARLIONS *in shadows, screened by trees and shrubs, strangers at the feast. A cheer goes up as someone drags up an effigy. Someone else straightens the battered topper, the mock-up Eton collar. A cheer as the effigy is lifted on its pole into the centre of the fire. Cut to* CARLION, *close up; from dark, puzzled reaches.*

CARLION: What is it? Is it a funeral?

PHILIP: (*Close up; deliberate*) I rather think it is, Father. (*Pause.*) They have not yet noticed that the grave is empty.

(*Singing: 'Roll Out the Barrel', lusty, vital. We see a stout wooden barrel being lifted on to a trestle table. A man taps it. Cheers. Steady zoom in, to end on the barrel's stamp: Carlion's Brewery, London EC4. Fade out.*)

Oi for England

Characters

SWELLS
FINN
GLORIA
LANDRY
NAPPER
THE MAN

Oi for England was first shown on Central Television in April 1982. The cast was as follows:

SWELLS	Ian Mercer
FINN	Adam Kotz
GLORIA	Lisa Lewis
LANDRY	Richard Platt
NAPPER	Neil Pearson
THE MAN	Gavin Richards

Director	Tony Smith
Producer	Sue Birtwhistle

Music by Andy Roberts

Oi for England was first performed at the Royal Court Theatre, London, as part of the Young People's Play Scheme, on 9 June 1982. The cast was as follows:

SWELLS	Peter Lovstrom
FINN	Paul McGann
GLORIA	Beverley Martin
LANDRY	Dorian Healy
NAPPER	Robin Hayter
THE MAN	Paul Moriarty

Director	Antonia Bird
Musical Director	Andy Roberts
Designer	Chris Townsend

Part One

The main cellar room, brick and plaster, in the basement of large Victorian house in Moss Side, Manchester. A door opens on to corridor and cramped wash and lavatory area. On the walls signs of fitful tenancy: pics, posters, badges, scrawls. The floor is cluttered with miscellaneous goods looted during riots. The names and logos of principal Manchester stores (Lewis's, Lillywhite's, Safeway's, etc.) are prominent on boxes, containers and carrier bags. Three young skinheads are playing instruments and singing: LANDRY *(nineteen) on drums,* SWELLS *(eighteen) and* FINN *(seventeen) on guitar. As they sing,* GLORIA *(fifteen), Manchester Jamaican in school uniform, can be seen at the half-open door, bobbing her head to the beat.*

In England's green and pleasant land
There's them as sit and them as stand,
There's some as eat and some as don't,
And some who will and a few that won't.

Oi, oi, join the few.
Oi, oi, it's me and you.
Oi, oi, what'll we do?
Oi, oi, turn the screw.

Sick of this, sick of all the shit,
Sick of them as stand while the other lot sit,
Sick of being treated like a useless tit,
Sick of being shoved, sick of being *hit*!

Oi, oi, me and you,
Oi, oi, coming through.
Oi, oi, what'll we do?
Oi, oi, turn the screw.

Keep the light on, you in charge,
You with the butter, us with the marge.
Take extra precautions before you retire –
This time a song, next time the *fire*!

Oi, oi, coming through,
Oi, oi, me and you,
Oi, oi, more than a few,
Oi, oi, turning the *screw*!

(*The song ends. An uneasy, frustrated silence, ruptured by the odd cough and twang.* LANDRY, SWELLS *and* FINN *stand or sit in separate silences.* LANDRY *tightens the skin on a side drum.* SWELLS *plucks at a little chord that he's far from having mastered.* FINN *watches* SWELLS*'s sullen efforts with distaste, anger and depression at work on the young face.* SWELLS *senses the unspoken criticism. He goes on practising. Ironic handclap from doorway.* SWELLS*'s eyes snap at* GLORIA.)

SWELLS: Piss off, chocolate drop. Black get.

(GLORIA *laughs and sticks her middle finger in the air.*)

FINN: We're practisin'.

GLORIA: Yeah?

(*She laughs again.* FINN *grins a little, seeing some of his own joke.*)

FINN: What d'ya want?

GLORIA: Me dad says . . . (*Rubs finger and thumb together*) . . . eight quid owin'.

(FINN *looks briefly, bleakly, at* SWELLS *and* LANDRY. SWELLS *shakes his head.* LANDRY *doesn't even look up, still tautening skin on drum.*)

FINN: Tomorrer.

GLORIA: Said that last week.

(*Silence.* GLORIA *studies the group:* FINN *and* SWELLS *study her.* LANDRY *drubs the side-drum with his fingers, sound growing, his ear close, attentive.*)

LANDRY: (*Cutting sound abruptly*) Tell 'im later tonight maybe.

(FINN *looks at* LANDRY, *who takes the look; looks at* SWELLS, *who looks at* GLORIA.)

SWELLS: (*Hard, sudden*) Right?

GLORIA: (*Slow, unfazed*) Who're you? Macho Man?

(SWELLS *swings his guitar off his shoulder, moving towards her.* GLORIA *shifts almost invisibly into a taut, armoured, martial-arts crouch.* SWELLS *stops.*)

LANDRY: Give it a rest, creambun.

(SWELLS *stares on at* GLORIA.)

Give it a *rest*.

(SWELLS *sniffs, spits very deliberately at* GLORIA*'s feet, turns to sit, legs spread, Martens rampant, in the old roundback that provides the room's seating.*)

SWELLS: A'm not 'anging around 'ere all night, right? Either we're doin' someat or we're not.

FINN: We're doin' someat. 'E'll be 'ere. (*To* GLORIA) All right?

GLORIA: 'E needs it. Thc cash.

FINN: 'E'll have it.

GLORIA: You're Kath Finney's brother, aren't yer?

FINN: Yeah.

(SWELLS *snorts.* FINN *stares at him.*)

GLORIA: Saw 'er at the Caribbean, Sat'day. UB40 were on.

FINN: Aye?

SWELLS: (*Contemptuous*) UB40. (*He spits.*)

GLORIA: What'll I tell 'im then?

(NAPPER *in behind her, a plastic bag in hand.*)

NAPPER: What'll you tell who, Topsy?

(GLORIA *looks at him carefully.* NAPPER *is big, larded, denim jacket over braces and skin, Manchester United scarf knotted round waist, blue neckchain tattooed on his right fist. He's high at something, pleased and nervy. Throws cans of Worthington E at the surprised three.)*

Friday. Rent Day. Right? Right.

(He casually removes a brown packet from his jacket pocket, fiddles several notes from it. GLORIA *counts. He waits.)*

GLORIA: Eight.

(NAPPER *counts out two more, gives them to her.)*

NAPPER: Bye, Topsy. Say hello to Kunte Kinte, won't you?

GLORIA: *(Levelly)* Eat dick.

(She turns. THE MAN *blocks the doorway. He stares at her, stone-eyed, then steps aside, giving* GLORIA *half the doorway. Her face passes close to* THE MAN*'s as she leaves. His nostrils flick.)*

NAPPER: Hi. Come in. S'er old man's basement. S'where we work out.

(THE MAN *walks into the room. He's tallish, slim, calm, chill, about forty. He wears a long, unbuttoned leather overcoat in dark brown, a black round-necked wool sweater.* FINN *and* LANDRY *stare at him. He looks them over.)*

THE MAN: *(Quiet, almost pleasant)* I've got half an hour. Impress me.

FINN: Why? Who're you?

(THE MAN *frowns, looks at* NAPPER.)

LANDRY: What's goin' on, Napper?

NAPPER: *(To* THE MAN) Eh, look, I'm sorry, 'aven't 'ad a chance t'ave a word . . .

SWELLS: Are we doin' out or what?

NAPPER: Shurrit, will yer!

LANDRY: *(Big, raw, hard)* Never mind 'shurrit'. What's goin' *on*? We said eight o'clock. You're a bleedin' hour late, Napper.

NAPPER: Right, right, I'm explainin', aren'ta?

FINN: Coulda fooled me, Napper.

THE MAN: *(Calmly, to* NAPPER) Sort it out, eh? I'll be in the van. Ten minutes?

(He leaves, almost weightlessly.)

NAPPER: *(Following him to doorway)* It'll be all right. Five minutes is plenty.

THE MAN: (*A shadow on stairway*) Good . . .

(*He's gone.* NAPPER *turns back into the room.*)

NAPPER: You've no piggin' idea, you lot, 'ave you?

FINN: We don't bring people here, Napper. S'what we said . . .

NAPPER; Oh, did we? An' who brought 'is soddin' sister here then?

LANDRY: Was different. Pigs were crackin' 'ead that night.

NAPPER; Landry, fer Christ's sake, give it a rest, will yer? I mean, this may be your scene bangin' away in a cellar. I'm after someat better, you know?

(*He's pacing. Reaches* SWELLS*'s outstretched Martens. Looks at them.* SWELLS *moves them, reluctantly.* NAPPER *walks another way, the dominance asserted, the ritual barely visible.*)

FINN: Like what?

NAPPER: Oh, like *playing*, you know? Like at a gig, you know? Fer money, with an audience, like. Ye've 'earda that, 'ave yer? People *do* do it . . . out *there*.

LANDRY: Stop wankin' off, Napper.

NAPPER: (*Fierce*) Look, Landry, when you can find eight green 'uns for this 'ole, you can call me a wanker, all right?

(*He smiles a bit, pulling it back.* LANDRY *smiles.*)

SWELLS: Yeah, where'dya gerrit?

(*Pause.*)

NAPPER: (*Sniffs*) Gorrit from 'im.

SWELLS: What, is 'e a puff?

(LANDRY *laughs.* FINN *smiles.* NAPPER *comes down.*)

NAPPER: You're a *nit*, you. Wharrayer?

SWELLS: (*Giggling*) I'm a nit.

(*He puts his hard, knuckled hands out in front of him.* NAPPER *places his own quite carefully against them. There's dried blood on* NAPPER*'s left hand.*)

'S that?

NAPPER: 'Ad a brush. Wi' one of our little brown brothers. Bugger bit me.

(*Shows him. They laugh, remove their hands, the ritual dissolved.*)

FINN: What is 'e then?

NAPPER: Oh, not much. 'E's just a feller lookin' for a skinband for a carnival he's puttin' on in Platt Fields, sixth o' next month. (*He sniffs, opens another Worthington E, studies his impact.*) London band's let 'im down . . .

SWELLS: Yer kiddin'.

NAPPER: Pillock.

LANDRY: What, fer money?

NAPPER: Thirty quid. (*Pause. Searches for clinching inspiration. Pats pocket.*) Ten up front.
(*He grins, clenches his fist, smacks the air with it, the ball in the back of the net.* SWELLS *stamps his Martens, happy.* LANDRY *looks at* FINN, *shrugs his shoulders to say 'Sounds good?'*
(Slinging his guitar) Ladies and gentlemen, bit of order for a new band from Moss Side, making a long overdue first public appearance today. Let's hear it for . . . *White Ammunition*! (*The crowd goes rapturous in the back of his throat. He belts out several chords.*) What do yer say? 'E's outside in 'is van. 'E wants to 'ear us play. I rest me case.
(*He winks at* SWELLS. SWELLS *pecks his nose with his thumb, happy.*)
Do I ask 'im or what?
(*He's a step to the door, unhooking his guitar.*)

FINN: Who is 'e?

NAPPER: Who is 'e? He's The Man.

FINN: 'S is name?

NAPPER; Landry, can you explain to Finney 'ere what's goin' on?

FINN: 'S is *name*?

NAPPER: (*Blowing*) I don't bloody *know* 'is name, prick. They call 'im The Man.

FINN: Kind of a name's that?

NAPPER: What kind of a name's *Napper*? 'S a name. Ask 'im.

FINN: Where'd yer meet 'im?

SWELLS: Oh, come on, Finn, soddin' nora, what's it matter where 'e fuckin' met 'im?

FINN: I wanna know who I'm dealin' with.

NAPPER: Listen, sunshine, you're not dealin' with anyone. 'E's dealin' with *us*.

SWELLS: Fuckin' A.

NAPPER: (*Suddenly*) Look, I'm fetchin' 'im down.

LANDRY: (*Up from drums and down the room*) 'Old it, Nap. 'E's not goin' anywhere.

(NAPPER *turns back again. Stands in doorway, tense, angry*.)

What's the rush?

NAPPER: (*Deliberate*) No rush, Landry. Let the bugger go. The offers *we've* had, we should worry. Let 'im join the queue.

LANDRY: (*Even*) Not sayin' that, Napper. Just give us the story. We bin waitin' over an hour, right? We were meant to be practisin'.

NAPPER: All right, all right, all right. I'm late. I'm sorry. Someat cropped up. Burra met this guy, right? An' 'e's serious.

FINN: Where?

NAPPER: What?

FINN: Where d'ya meet 'im?

NAPPER: Where'da meet 'im? Met 'im in a pub.

(*Silence. They eye each other. A police siren flirts to life a quarter of a mile away. A second joins in*.)

FINN: What pub?

NAPPER: Skin pub, off the Oldham Road.

FINN: What's it called?

NAPPER: Don't remember. Prince of someat.

FINN: Prince a Wales?

NAPPER: Coulda bin. Yeah.

(*The sirens die. The name hangs.* FINN *looks at* LANDRY. *Walks back down room. Squats against side wall, arms on knees*.)

SWELLS: Prince a Wales. Our Rit's husband used ta use it. 'S all right.

(LANDRY *looks at* NAPPER. *Shakes his head. Looks at* FINN, *who's withdrawn*.)

NAPPER: What the fuck's wrong *now*?

SWELLS: (*Shrugs.*) Search me.

FINN: I'm English. I don't wear a swastika for nobody.

(*Silence.*)

NAPPER: What's 'e on about? (*Down room*) What you on about, you?

FINN: (*Disengaged, deliberate*) Prince a Wales. 'Itler's bunker. NF, BM, the lot.

NAPPER: Oh, Christ, 'ere we go. (*Striding, puffing*) When're you gonna grow up, eh? T'man's offerin' *work*. 'Eard of it? That thing people used to do quite a lot of, once. Listen, you wanna spend t'rest of yer life knockin' corner shops off an' singin' tough in a cellar, that's your look-out. I wanna *do* someat. (*Pause. Indicates the room.*) I thought that's what this was about. (*Pause.*) I'll play in a long white frock if I 'ave ter.

SWELLS: You'd look nice in a frock, Nap.

(*Silence again.* FINN *sits tight-lipped, withdrawn.* SWELLS *looks at* LANDRY, *who's undecided and fulcral.* NAPPER*'s quite taut, unable to push further.*)

(*Up room, at* FINN) Anyway, you're not fuckin' English, you're fuckin' Irish.

FINN: (*Deliberate*) I'm English.

SWELLS: You're fuckin' Irish.

NAPPER: 'E's English. It's 'is grandad who's Irish. (*To* LANDRY, *conciliatory*) 'E's not one o' them nutters.

FINN: 'E's a nutter.

NAPPER: 'E'da said, wunne?

FINN: They don't *say*. You find out.

NAPPER: Finn, they put concerts on. MMI, they're called. I've seen tickets. *Bona fide*. On the level. Dead straight. (*To* LANDRY) What do you think, Lan?

LANDRY: I don't mind. (*To* FINN) What d'ya think?

(FINN *says nothing.*)

Do no 'arm t'play fer 'im, anyroad.

FINN: (*Sharp*) We're called *Ammunition*, Napper.

NAPPER: (*Sullen*) Yeah, whatever you say, Finney.

SWELLS: (*Slow*) What's wrong wi' callin' usselves white?

NAPPER: Ammunition's fine. All right.

(FINN *looks at* LANDRY, *then stands and gathers his guitar.*)

LANDRY: Best get your man.

(NAPPER *nods, elated. Legs it up the stairs.* SWELLS *gathers his guitar.* LANDRY *returns to his kit.*)

SWELLS: (*As if it had never stopped*) Your Kath reckons she's Irish.

FINN: She is.

LANDRY: What we gonna play?

SWELLS: Yeah, come on, Finn.

FINN: (*Casual*) I couldn't give a shit.

SWELLS: You're the music man.

FINN: Doesn't matter. The Man's not 'ere for music.

LANDRY: (*Hardening a touch*) You don't *know* that, Finn.

FINN: (*Bleak*) Yeah, well, I 'ope I'm wrong. I do. 'Cos I'm sicker doin' nowt. Drive yer daft. Eat, sleep, sit, stand.

LANDRY: (*A touch tougher*) Yeah, well, why don't we stop pullin' our plonkers an' get someat worked out, all right?

(*Pause.* FINN *nods eventually.*)

Right. Now it dunt matter what we play s'far as 'e's concerned (*Nods in* SWELLS*'s direction*), cos 'e can put 'is two chords anywhere. What d'ya reckon we do best, Finn? 'S down ter you, son.

(*He's distracted by two fire engines racing through streets close by.* NAPPER *in the doorway.*)

Wharappened?

NAPPER: No sign of 'im. Pissed off waitin', I suppose. (*He kicks a box, quite viciously.*) Sick o' this.

SWELLS: Did you look?

NAPPER: Course I fuckin' looked! You think I went up there and closed me fuckin' eyes? You henry.

(*Silence. He prods a carton with his boot.*)

SWELLS: (*Defending the question, surly*) Coulda bin parked in t'next street.

NAPPER: *'E dropped* me 'ere, 'im and 'is mate, pillock. I know where 'e was parked. 'E's gone. Scarpered. Whoosh. I'm sick as a pig. (*Silence.*)

FINN: So. We got ten quid for nowt. Easy money, eh, Napper?

(NAPPER *finds this not funny. A moment.*)

LANDRY: (*Beating air above drum skin with manic speed*) Let's *do* someat. (*He belts a cymbal, wild, energy rushing from him, anger cording arms, jaws. He stills the brass eventually, levels out slowly. Calm*) I don't wanna spend the night arguin' wi' me mates.

FINN: I say we practise.

(*He looks at* SWELLS. SWELLS *looks across to* NAPPER, *who's reached the grid window, below pavement level, behind the drum kit.* NAPPER *broods.* SWELLS *shrugs indifference, compliance.*)

What you say, Nap?

NAPPER: (*His back to the others, quiet*) I say fuck this, Finn. It's a waster time.

(*Silence.*)

FINN: (*As quiet*) No, it ain't.

(NAPPER *makes no answer.*)

We've bin arrit six months, less. Took us over a month to loot the gear. Two afternoons a week, you an' Swells from scratch. We'll get a gig when we're ready.

NAPPER: (*Turning*) We got a gig. You pissed on it. A job. (*Snapping slightly*) Who do you think you bloody *are*, anyway?

LANDRY: I'm askin' one more time . . .

NAPPER: (*Abrupt*) I say we go an' do a few shops. Could be another big 'un, by the sound of it. All right, Swells?

SWELLS: Yeah.

NAPPER: Lan?

(LANDRY *lays his sticks down. Shrugs, lifeless.*)

What you say? Get on the street? Bit o' fun. Kick some head. (*He runs at the room, delivers a terrifying box-kick in the air. Ends up with his back to doorway.*) Come on, Finn. Let's do it. I promised me Auntie Winnie I'd try and gerrera microwave.

(THE MAN *is in the doorway. He stands in silence.* NAPPER *has become*

aware of him through their stares.)
Thought you'd gone . . .

THE MAN: (*Quiet, simple*) I'm 'ere. Ready to impress me?
(*He scans them.*)

NAPPER: Er, yeah. Yeah, sure.
(NAPPER *looks at the others. Eyes move to* FINN. *He waits, then slings his guitar across his shoulder and begins the set-up. They join him.* THE MAN *sits on the roundback half way down the room. He's taken a walkie-talkie receiver from his coat pocket. He places it on his knee. They're about ready, up the room.*)

THE MAN: (*Reminding himself*) What you call yourselves?

FINN: Ammunition.

THE MAN: White Ammunition, right?
(FINN *looks at* NAPPER. THE MAN *watches* FINN*'s look.*)

LANDRY: (*Quiet*) 'S it gonna be, Finn?
(FINN *plays a sudden strong introductory sequence. The others get ready.*)

FINN: (*On brink of their entry*) . . . Sod the Lord – pass the ammunition . . .
(*And they're away.*)

There's gonna be a death,
Gonna be a killing.
Someone up there's gonna cop it one day,
God and weather willing.

Law and order, up your arse.
The orders are yours and the law's a farce.
Watch out for the crash, the course is collision.
Sod the Lord – pass the *ammunition*!

(*They play with verve. A colossal noise.* SWELLS *plays well above himself.* NAPPER *begins to relax.* LANDRY*'s hard and subtle Charlie Watts.* FINN *is the music, and good.*)

There's blood on the wall.
It's a quid to a shilling
Someone up there's gonna measure his length,
God and weather willing.

(THE MAN *is listening. The tranceiver's still on his knee. His fingers are on the volume control, adjusting it. The police radio frequency can be heard. Outside the action is building.*)

Law and order, up your arse.
The orders are yours and the law's a farce.
Watch out for the crash, the course is collision.
Sod the Lord – pass the *ammunition*!

Part Two

The action is continuous. The song deafens. Their involvement and passion are touchable: energy and spirit collect, cohere in performance.

There's gas on the streets;
It's not for a filling.
Someone up there nearly wasn't tonight,
God and weather willing.

Law and order, up your arse.
The orders are yours and the law's a farce.
Watch out for the crash, the course is collision.
Sod the Lord – pass the ammunition.

(*They repeat the chorus a last time; it's shouted, handclapped, terrace-chanted, driven on* LANDRY*'s drum.*)

Law and *order*, up your *arse*!
The orders are *yours* and the law's a *farce*!
Watch out for the *crash*, the course is *collision*.
Sod the *Lord* – pass the *ammunition*!

(*Chordflare, cymbals. Silence. They stand for moments, triumphantly dazed at having heard themselves and high on that energy,* THE MAN *down the room barely remembered. It's some while before they hear and react to the closer and more clamant sound of the clashes taking place in neighbouring streets, which the end of the music has uncovered.*)

SWELLS: (*Moving to grid windows*) Shaggin' nora, listen to that lot.

LANDRY: (*Head turned*) Close. C'be a big 'un.

(NAPPER, *still in the music, catches* FINN*'s eye.*)

NAPPER: (*Small grin, touching guitar*) Good, eh?

FINN: (*Smiling*) Fair.

(*In a sudden short lull in the street noise, their attention is pulled to the broken sound of* THE MAN*'s voice down the room. He stands with his back to them, foot up on chair seat, murmuring into the tranceiver. He is talking to Roy, a contact in a van parked outside. Roy is in touch by CB with other vans and bases in the south of the city. It's a simple but effective system for deploying and mobilizing active cadres, particularly on riot nights.* THE MAN *bleeds information on black and police movements from Roy, feeds back instructions.*)

THE MAN: Tell Willie sit still, we'll call him; tell Mac t'get down to the Barley Mow an' see if Watt's lot're about . . .

(*It's casual, quite practised, not self-dramatizing. Din rises from nearby streets again, surging, ebbing, but the four lads continue to watch* THE MAN. *They hear next to nothing of the exchange, but sense connection with the action on the streets. When they speak, it's* sotto, *among themselves.*)

SWELLS: 'S 'e up to?

LANDRY: Prob'ly ord'rin' curry 'n chips at t'Dakker.

NAPPER: 'Ushitup, 'e'll 'ear yer.

SWELLS: 'Ey, 'e's norra blueboy, is 'e? Looka this soddin' *stuff.*

(*Surveys the room's loot. Cupboards bulge.*)

NAPPER: Dickhead. Think I'd bring a bleedin' rozzer 'ere?

SWELLS: Yer fuckin' daft enough.

NAPPER: Hunh.

FINN: (*Deliberate*) 'E's no blueboy.

(NAPPER *looks at* FINN *sharply, expecting trouble.* FINN *stands by the grid-window, listening to the disturbance slip towards riot.*)

(*Bleak*) 'Eavy shit.

(*He looks at* LANDRY.)

LANDRY: Me mam's down t'Troc. Bingo.

NAPPER: (*Sharp* sotto) 'Ey up.

(THE MAN*'s almost with them, silently claiming the space. The open tranceiver bubbles and spurts on the chair he's left it on. The lads wait in silence:* NAPPER *and* SWELLS *expectant, alert;* LANDRY *quiet,* *impassive;* FINN *remote, at the window.* THE MAN *stops some paces from them, says nothing, lips pursed as if in thought.)*

THE MAN: Listen to it. Listen to England. Listen.

(*Some looks pass between* NAPPER, LANDRY *and* SWELLS. FINN *has resumed his retracted squat by the wall.*)

NAPPER: (*Uneasy*) What'dya think ter music?

THE MAN: (*Deadpan*) Was a riot.

(*Nothing.* THE MAN *is a heavy presence. Eating space, doing nothing. Feet shift.* FINN *watches through hooped hands.*)

NAPPER: (*Nervy*) Warrabout t'job?

THE MAN: It's possible. Do you want the job?

NAPPER: You kiddin'? Course we want the job.

(THE MAN *scans them. Questions* FINN *silently.* FINN *remains still.*)

LANDRY: (*Quietly*) What *is* the job?

(*A sputter down the room.* THE MAN *listens. It passes.*)

THE MAN: Free concert, Platt Fields, May the sixth. Skinfest. Truckin' a lotta people in. Fifteen, twenty thousand mebbe. Heavy. London band – Shed Brigade? – 've given back word.

SWELLS: Chelseaboys. Ffff.

(*Pause.*)

THE MAN: Might be a bit grown-up fer you lads.

(*A sudden thrash of police trucks at top of street as they charge a crowd. Screams, oaths, thuds, cries, running feet, the pop of shattering missiles, a gleam of petrol bombs. They listen.*)

SWELLS: KGB's busy. Bastards.

(*The noise recedes, their street not chosen.*)

NAPPER: (*Annoyed by the distraction*) What the *fuck's* goin' *on* out there?

(LANDRY *shrugs ignorance.* SWELLS *is definitely 'search me'.*)

THE MAN: (*Almost casual*) Know the Union Jack Club?

NAPPER: Raby Street? Just round t'corner.

THE MAN: Crowda kids trapped inside.

SWELLS: What, coppers got 'em, you mean?

THE MAN: (*Shakes head*) Blacks.

(*Silence.*)

Hundreds of 'em.

(*Silence.*)

Anderton's Puffballs're tryin' ter scatter 'em. No go.

(*Pause.*)

Those lads need help. They're gonna burn.

(NAPPER *looks around the room, gauging temperature.*)

NAPPER: Mebbe we'll go down there, eh? (*Waits.*) See what's goin' on.

SWELLS: (*Shrugs*) Sure.

LANDRY: (*Shrugs*) Why?

(FINN *stays still.* THE MAN *studies them.*)

THE MAN: Gonna tek a chance and book you. Don't let me down. Platt Fields, May the sixth. Get there for five. I'll want four numbers. It's thirty quid in green uns on the night, nothin' up front. That's the deal.

NAPPER: Great.

SWELLS: Great.

THE MAN: You *got* four numbers?

NAPPER: (*Fractional check*) . . . Sure. Yeah.

LANDRY: D'you say nothing up front?

THE MAN: (*Calm*) On the night. That's the deal.

(LANDRY *looks at* FINN. FINN *looks at* NAPPER. NAPPER *refuses contact.*)

SWELLS: (*Innocently*) Who do we ask fer? When we get there?

THE MAN: Just ask for The Man. They'll know. (*On his way*) Got any questions, ask 'em now. I'm due elsewhere.

(*He's down by the chair and indicating his movements to Roy in the van.* NAPPER*'s elated, jabs* SWELLS *on the biceps.* SWELLS *grins, picks out 'James Bond' theme on guitar, wafting it subtly towards* THE MAN *on the tranceiver.* LANDRY *watches* FINN *guardedly.* FINN *stands abruptly, one movement from hunkers to upright.* THE MAN *begins closing aerial, pocketing set. Two fire engines slither past the top of the street, brief instants down the night's long and slippery pole.* THE MAN *turns in the doorway.*)

OK?

FINN: (*Very simple*) I gotta question.

NAPPER: Man's on his way, Finn boy.

(NAPPER *and* THE MAN *exchange brief looks, a thin hint of obscure collusion somewhere, but a long way from the nose.*)

FINN: (*Moving forward a little*) S'about the songs.

THE MAN: Yeah?

NAPPER: Knock it off, Finn, *we* can sort that out.

THE MAN: Leave 'im be. (*To* FINN) What about the songs, son?

FINN: 'S just workin' out what sort o' stuff you'll be needin' in Platt Fields on local election night . . .

(*It lies a moment between them, not visibly remarked by either.*)

We've got all sortsa stuff . . .

THE MAN: Like what?

FINN: (*Simply, as if summoning them*) Oh . . . 'Black and white, unite unite', that's one. 'The Nazis are coming, they've been before', 'Adolf didn't do it, it's all a packer lies', 'There's a jackboot where my brain used to be'. All sorts.

THE MAN: (*Deadpan, undrawn*) Ahunh. Interesting titles.

FINN: It'd 'elp if you could tell us where you're comin' from, wi' this concert.

(*Nothing.*)

You know, the politics . . .

THE MAN: Politics? Why're you raisin' politics? 'S a concert.

FINN: Yeah, only it's a free un, innit? An' if there's no dough on t'door . . .

(*He leaves the meaning to complete itself.*)

THE MAN: (*Calm, unhelpful*) Yeah? What?

(FINN *looks at* LANDRY, *as if wondering how much more he can say.*)

FINN: OK, I'll be straight wi' yer, mister, I know yer wanna gerroff . . .

(*Looks at* NAPPER, *whose eyes are large with anxious anger.*)

. . . I made them song titles up. We don't sing that kinda *shit*, all right? We call ourselves Ammunition cos we're ready for firin', but not against our own. So if you're from that Anti-Nazi League or any o' them other black-'n'-white-unite freaks, it's no deal. We're not interested. You might as well sling yer 'ook. Right, you 'ave it.

(FINN *breathes deep, thrusts hands in pockets, looks briefly at the others, as if pleased with himself for having got it off their chests.* NAPPER*'s stony, powerless now to intervene;* SWELLS *strokes his scalp with the palm of his hand, trying to fathom it;* LANDRY*'s twigged, likes* FINN*'s style.*)

THE MAN: (*Eventually*) You'll be Finn, right?

(FINN *nods.*)

Napper mentioned you might be trouble.

(THE MAN *walks back into the room, undoes his coat, takes out his cigarettes, lights one, offers.* SWELLS *and* NAPPER *take.*)

So. You guys got me down fer a nigger's man, that right?

(*He scans them swiftly.* SWELLS *shakes his head with alacrity.*)

NAPPER: (*Miserable*) Not me, mister. Listen, you get off. *We* can sort this out.

THE MAN: Get off? Ha. (*The laugh is short, one chill sound.*)

Somebody's gotta put this boy *right.*

(*He says this with sudden energy.* LANDRY *gets up from the drums, eases towards the arena.*)

Hear this. On the night of May the sixth – local election night, as you point out – Moss Side will see its biggest concert ever. Half a dozen bands, twenty thousand kids from all over the area, bussed and trucked from Liverpool, Widnes, Runcorn, Preston, Chorley, Bolton, Bury, Rochdale, Oldham, Ashton, Stockport, Salford . . . Doleboys like yourselves, school over years back, job not yet begun. English. Working class. White. (Them, *his hand indicates*) Sicker bein' kicked around, ignored, shat on, pushed to the bottom of the midden, up to their necks in brown scum, the diarrhoea their rulers have seen fit to flood this England with.

(*He indicates the street outside. The din has receded but remains, even at a distance, intense, bitter.*)

Their England. Made on the backs, made by the sweat and bone of the white working class, generation after generation. This England, run *by* foreigners, *for* foreigners. Jews, Arabs, coons, Pakis, wogs from all corners of the earth. Chocolate England. (*Long pause.*) Now. Anyone plays black-'n'-white-unite-unite at *that* concert better have a pretty fat club book, cos they're liable to get their throats ripped out before they reach the first chorus. Here . . .

(*He's fiddled a block of tickets from his coat pocket, hands* FINN *one, then the others.*)

'MMI presents', see it?

SWELLS: (*Seeing it*) Oh, yeah.

THE MAN: Movement Music Inc. Movement. (*One hand.*) Music. (*The other.*) Incorporated. (*The hands join.*) Concerts, music: politics by other means. All clear?

(*He looks at* FINN.)

FINN: Yeah. As a bell. Thanks fer tekin' t'trouble.

THE MAN: No trouble. (*Smiles.*) I'm glad to say. See you on the night?

FINN: You bet.

THE MAN: (*Into tranceiver*) Comin' up, Roy. Out. (*To them*) Ammunition. All right.

(*He leaves, like air. They stand in silence, listening for the sound of the front door pulling to.*)

NAPPER: (*Toneless*) Great.

(*They break up, a bit aimless, deflated. Some strains of anger and tiredness in the air.*)

SWELLS: What's goin' on?

(*He's pretty well ignored.*)

I don't gerrit.

(*Nothing.*)

Bleedin' 'ell . . .

(FINN *squats against the wall.* LANDRY *lies flat on an old mattress.* NAPPER *cases his guitar, then hunches down on the chair, a copy of the*

Sun *between his feet, open at page 3. He stares at the picture expressionlessly.*)

You're a load o' wankers, you lot, do you know? Are we doin' it or what, Nap?

(NAPPER*'s eyes remain on the page.*)

Wharrabout it, Lan?

(LANDRY *stares at the ceiling.* SWELLS *switches to* FINN.)

You reckon the man's a nutter, do you?

FINN: What do *you* think?

SWELLS: (*Frowns, thinks*) I dunno. 'Ow d'yer tell? Seemed all right ter me.

FINN: 'E's a Nazi.

SWELLS: Yeah? 'Ow d'yer mean?

FINN: Gas chambers. Concentration camps. Dictators.

(SWELLS *copes with this.*)

SWELLS: Oh. (*Strokes head.*) 'E sounded all right to me. (*Looks round at others.*) So we're not doin' it?

(LANDRY *and* NAPPER *give him nothing, remote in their respective spaces.*)

Fuck.

(*He sits on Landry's drum stool, pissed off, miserable. Silence. Distant din from streets, rising, falling.* SWELLS *looks towards* NAPPER, *wants him to argue for playing the gig.* NAPPER *sucks his damaged hand, stares on at the pic.*)

Anyroad, the man thinks we're turnin' up. Somebody's gonna have ter give back word. Bloody ain't gonna be me, I'll tell yer. He looks a mean bleeder.

NAPPER: (*Without looking*) Finn'll tell 'im. Won't you, Finn?

FINN: You tell 'im, Napper. You know 'im better.

(NAPPER *looks up, takes* FINN*'s look. A loveless moment.*)

LANDRY: (*From nowhere, not moving*) Time you reckon it is?

(*They're all watchless.*)

FINN: Nine?

SWELLS: (*Eventually, worrying on*) Thing I don't get, if 'e said there were nowt up front, 'ow come 'e gives yer ten quid advance? Nap?

(NAPPER, *back to the* Sun, *looks up briefly*.)

NAPPER: 'E didn't.

SWELLS: Yer a lyin' bugger, aren't yer? (*Thinks*.) So where'd it come from?

NAPPER: (*Simply*) I thieved it.

SWELLS: Yeah? Where from?

(NAPPER *thinks for a moment, then stands up and crosses the room to enter their space*.)

NAPPER: Where from? From a feller. (*Pause*.) Wanna know 'is name?

SWELLS: What yer talkin' about?

NAPPER: 'Ang on. (*He searches in his top pocket, draws out a brown envelope. Several bank notes overlap its edge. Reads*:) Mr . . . Jarwah . . . lal . . . Chor . . . jewry.

SWELLS: 'S that?

NAPPER: 'S 'is wage packet.

SWELLS: (*Laughing*) Yer kiddin'.

NAPPER: Straight up.

SWELLS: 'Ow'd yer gerrit?

NAPPER: 'Owda gerrit? I battered the fucker 'an took it off 'im.

(*He stares at* FINN, *then* LANDRY, *then* FINN *again*.)

(*Vicious*) Paid the fuckin' *rent*, right?

FINN: 'Ard, aren't yer?

NAPPER: 'Ard enough.

LANDRY: (*Remote*) 'Ard as a bucketa tripe.

NAPPER: 'Ard enough.

FINN: Work 'im over, did yer?

NAPPER: 'Im and me. One on one.

FINN: Bet 'e was real big, right?

NAPPER: Big enough.

FINN: Yeah. Indians. Huge. (*Pause*.) What you do, jump 'im?

NAPPER: I asked 'im fer a light. I'd left me matches in the Prince o' Wales. I was waitin' for a 93 outside Pailin's Mill. This feller walks past. I asked 'im fer a light. He's countin' 'is fuckin' wages. 'E walks right past me, couldn't give a toss, little black bastard's countin' 'is wages. I'm eighteen an' I've never 'ad a job in me fuckin' life! So I blobbed 'im one an' took the lot. Fifty-eight quid. Serves the fucker right. (*Beat.*) I'll tell yer someat else, smartarse, while we're at it. I'm *white*. I'm proud of it. I think it's the best thing ter be. I agree with the man. I ain't tekin' second place to no niggers 'n' yids in me own country. If 'e's a Nazi, so am I. I just think I'm English. What're you? Fuckin' *mick*, that's what you are. What d'you fuckin' know? Listen to that lot!

(*The din has flared again. Windows implode; the dull plug of gas canisters hitting air four streets away.*)

It could be us lot down there tonight at the Union Jack. Gettin' our 'eads kicked.

SWELLS: Not me. S'a lousy pint.

NAPPER: (*Withering him*) I'm just *saying*. Twat. (*To* FINN) I just don't get you. I don't. I don't know where yer comin' from. I don't know what yer about.

FINN: (*Slowly, distinctly*) Yeah, well, that's maybe cos you're *thick*, Napper.

(*Silence.* NAPPER *seems to swell.* FINN *gets tighter, tauter.*)

NAPPER: Callin' me thick?

(FINN *stands slowly, takes a half-pace forward, to free himself of the wall.*)

FINN: Just acknowledgin' a fact, Napper.

(LANDRY *gets up, quite quick and lithe. Places himself easily between them.*)

LANDRY: Cool down.

NAPPER: Stay out, Landry.

LANDRY: Cool *down*. (*He stares at each in turn.*) Not tekin' sides. You wanter fight, do it on t'street. Chances are you won't even be noticed. (*Waves at window.*) Not down here. We need this place. The old bugger upstairs'll throw us out.

(NAPPER *stares on for several moments, then makes for a cupboard.*

Takes two packs of Players No. 3 from a carton and stuffs them in his pockets.)

NAPPER: *You* may need this place, Landry. Personally, I couldn't give a *shite*. Personally, I think it's about washed out. (*To* SWELLS) I'm gonna do a coupla shops, if there's any goin'. Whadderyer think?

SWELLS: (*Sniffs*) Yeah. I don't mind.

NAPPER: (*To* FINN) I'll see if I can pick yer someat up on me travels. Golliwog, mebbe.

(*He leaves,* SWELLS *in tow.* FINN *follows them to the doorway.* LANDRY *looks for his jacket.* FINN *comes back towards him.*)

LANDRY: Gotta go. See if I can see me mam. This lot'll scare 'er ter death.

FINN: You played good.

LANDRY: Enjoyed it.

FINN: Best.

LANDRY: Think 'e means it? Napper?

FINN: (*Nodding*) Good riddance.

LANDRY: Nap's all right. Bit nervous.

FINN: Thought I'd 'ave a word wi' Tomo'. 'E plays a bit.

LANDRY: Yeah? Any good?

FINN: (*Smiling*) Good as Napper.

(LANDRY *chuckles.* FINN *chuckles.*)

LANDRY: Why not? (*On move*) See yer t'morra?

FINN: Yeah.

(LANDRY *stops, turns.*)

LANDRY: Wanna come?

FINN: No, it's all right.

LANDRY: 'Ya gonna do?

FINN: Mooch. Nowt.

LANDRY: Story of our lives.

FINN: Yeah.

LANDRY: Tekin' yer word for it, Finn. (*Simple*) I'da played. I don't really give a shite. I just wanna play. I just wanna *do* someat, get outa the pighole. (*Stubs the floor with his boot, no speaker but needing to speak.*) Don't really understand the rest of it. Politics 'n' that. Never really bothered. Look after me own business. (*Thinks.*) Cos no bugger else will. (*Waits for something. Nothing.*) I tell yer *someat* better 'appen. I'm sicka this lot. I am.

(FINN *nods.* LANDRY *zips his jacket, one motion.*)

Anyroad . . . takin' your word for it, Michael. See yer on the ice.

(LANDRY *leaves.*)

FINN: (*To empty room*) Yeah. See yer on the ice.

(*A police truck thrashes into the street outside, screaks past the window in pursuit. Petrol bombs flare in its path.* FINN *crosses to watch the night. Shouts, screams, some pain and fear. The din moves on again. He listens, watches. Footsteps on the stairway beyond the door. He hears them, tenses slightly, doesn't turn. The lights are switched out. The footsteps recede, then approach again. He turns.* GLORIA *stands in doorway.*)

GLORIA: (*Hand to switch*) Sorry. Thought I heard you go.

FINN: Leave 'em. Just off.

(*They look at each other bleakly across the darkened room.* GLORIA *is in streetgear: jeans, bomber, basketball shoes, wool hat, a heavy metal torch hooked round her wrist. She's hard, energized.*)

GLORIA: Stay 'ere a bit. Do yourself a favour.

FINN: 'Ow d'yer mean?

GLORIA: Asians're on the rampage. Crackin' 'eads. *Skin*'eads mainly.

FINN: I got no quarrel.

GLORIA: How will they know?

(FINN *ponders it. Moves a few steps into the room. Sits at Landry's drums.*)

FINN: 'S it about?

GLORIA: Old Asian guy got 'is faced kicked. Your lot. (*She touches her head, signifying skins.*) They don't like it. They're gettin' it together. Gorra gang of 'em caught down t'Union Jack on Raby Street. (*Pauses and laughs oddly.*) They're burnin' it down, man. Asians. Gettin' angry! 'Ad enough. All right!

(*She eyes him, curious. He sits impassive, eyes on drumskin.*)

Me dad's bin jumpin' up 'n' down in fronter t'telly. 'E were gonna come down 'n throw y'all out. (*Laughs again.*) Voted Conservative at t'last election.

(FINN *laughs a little in the darkness, a sad sound.*)

Where's yer mates?

(*He shrugs.*)

'S 'e a mater yours?

(*He looks. She chills into The Man's posture. He shakes his head.*)

What 'd'e want?

FINN: Ammunition.

(*She waits.*)

Lookin' for a band. For a gig.

GLORIA: Yeah?

(*Pause.*)

'D 'e get one?

(FINN *doesn't answer at once. A rubbish skip burns in the street outside. Flamelight washes and tumbles across the room.* FINN *shakes his head eventually.*)

FINN: 'E offered.

GLORIA: You turn 'im down?

FINN: Yeah.

GLORIA: Gerraway. Why?

FINN: Di'n't like 'is style. Di'n't like the deal. Why d'y ask?

GLORIA: (*Sniffs*) Smelt 'im a mile off. Real white man.

FINN: (*Quiet*) I'm a white man.

(GLORIA *swings the torch in her hand, beams it on his face, scrutinizes it.*)

GLORIA: Yeah, I guess y'are.

(*Surge of noise in adjoining street. The repeated splat of windows being crumpled by pick-helves one after another.*)

I gorra go.

FINN: (*Standing*) Down there?

GLORIA: Might 'ave a look.

FINN: Wait.

(*He walks to a tall cupboard, opens it, waves her to join him. She comes, reluctant and curious. She cannot read his mood. He stands inspecting the cupboard's contents. It is bursting with lifted miscellanea: hardware, electrical goods, sports gear, canned food, cigarettes, toothbrushes, shampoo, Chinese slippers, seed packets, soap powder, spring water, writing pads, Mothercare items, cutlery, chocolate bars, books. All in enormous quantities, grabbed at random.*)

GLORIA: Bin busy.

FINN: Mmmm. (*He's sifting, searching, occasionally locating.*) You'll need some things. Night like this. Could catch yer death.

(*He looks at her. She hasn't understood, wants to understand. The stare is frank between them, grows almost intimate.*)

Here.

(*He hands her things to hold, items of sportswear, two of most things.*)

Tek 'old.

GLORIA: (*Muted*) Wharrathey?

FINN: I'll show yer.

(FINN *takes a boxer's training cap from the gear she holds, straps it on to his head, draws a black balaclava over his head, to hide it: nods to* GLORIA *to do the same. They begin to prepare themselves, as if ritually, yet with a faint sense of mockery at the conceit they're inventing. They smile occasionally, helping each other with occasional items – batsman's chest protectors, hidden under jackets, shin pads, thick elasticated elbow pads, a cricket box for* FINN. GLORIA*'s eyes are demurely held down. During their gladiatorial transformation they speak very occasionally, small familiar sounds in the shadowed silence.*)

Be. Prepared. They are.

GLORIA: 'S your first name?

FINN: Michael.

GLORIA: Michael Finney. That English?

FINN: (*Thinking a little*) Irish.

GLORIA: Mine's Gloria.

FINN: That English?

GLORIA: Yeah.

(*Pause.*)

Why'd yer see that feller off?

FINN: 'E was a Nazi.

GLORIA: 'S that to you?

FINN: Me grandad used ter tell us about 'em. He were in Germany in t'war. Showed us a picture 'e took, in a concentration camp. I lived with 'im when I were little. (*Pause.*) A lot o' bodies. A lot. Like celery. Sticks. (*Pause.*) Fuck *that*. (*Pause.*) Me grandad says: if you're not a human, what are yer?

GLORIA: A Nazi.

FINN: Right.

(*They smile, quite dry. They're about finished. Changed, odd, like children, overgrown.*)

GLORIA: Listen. Don't you come. No place for honkeys tonight, Moss Side.

FINN: I'll 'ave *you*, right? No sweat. Give us a coupla minutes. I've gorra few things.

GLORIA: I've gorra get Pearl from across t'road. See yer on t'corner. (*She sweeps the torch into her two hands like a baseball bat, poised for the pitch, grins.*) All right!

(*She leaves, high, lively.* FINN *takes a sharp radio cassette and some tapes from the cupboard, closes the doors, carries the radio to* LANDRY*'s drums, places it down there, selects and inserts a tape. He begins cleaning up, casing guitars, collecting cigarette butts, beer cans, papers . . . The music sneaks into the room, follows him round it: 'As I roved out'. The song slows him, snares him, little by little, until he stands, guitar in hand, to focus on its dense, sad, very Irish sound. Without warning, he swings the guitar, smashes the radio from the drum and on to the floor, where it lies dead. He returns to trance for a moment. Draws deep breaths. Smashes the drums with a colossal clatter and deadly force. Systematically, he destroys drums, guitars, speakers, chair, surface contents in a deadly, speechless fury. He stops eventually. Stands with a guitar stock in his hand. He lays it quietly down. Studies himself carefully in a wall mirror. His face is calm, young, neat. His hands* *approach the mouth, insert a boxer's gumshield. The boy leaves the face. What's left is hard, barely recognizable. Suddenly, music starts up again in the room.)*

And I wish the Queen would call home her army
From the West Indies, Americay and Spain,
And every man to his wedded woman,
In hopes that you and I would meet again.